ONE MORE DANCE

ONE MORE DANCE

X. Louis-McGhee

Copyright Page for Wings of Love

One More Dance

© X. Louis-Mcghee 2025

Paperback ISBN: 979-8-9927540-0-1

Hardcover ISBN: 979-8-9927540-1-8

eBook ISBN: 979-8-9927540-2-5

Cover Design by: [Designer Name]

Interior Formatting by: Amna J

First Edition: 2025

Table of Contents

Table of Contents

CHAPTER 1:

BEST FRIENDS & BIG DREAMS

July 1941 – Booker T. Washington High
School, Montgomery, Alabama

The sun hung high and mean over Booker T. Washington High School's baseball field, baking the dirt and making the grass look like it hadn't seen rain in weeks.

Two figures stood near the pitcher's mound, sweat trailing down their backs, shirts half unbuttoned, the thick Alabama heat wrapping around them like a second skin.

"Alright, Benji," Samson "Sam" Wells said, rolling his shoulders. "Let's see what you got."

Benji smirked, tightening his grip on the baseball. "You sure? Wouldn't wanna mess up that pretty stance of yours."

Sam laughed. "Boy, shut up and pitch."

Benji exhaled, set his stance, and sent the ball flying.

Sam swung hard. CRACK!

The bat met the ball clean, sending it sailing high toward center field.

Benji cursed under his breath, turning to watch it fly.

Sam grinned. "Told you."

Benji scoffed. "Man, that was luck."

"Luck?" Sam leaned on the bat, smirking. "Nah, that was skill."

Benji jogged to grab the ball from where it landed, dusting it off before walking back.

"You tryna run it back?" Sam asked, tapping his bat against his shoulder.

Benji smirked. "Hell yeah."

The two had spent years on this field. Back in high school, they were part of the team, playing every position at some point.

Sam was the slugger, strong as hell, while Benji was fast, sharp, and could throw a perfect curveball.

But baseball was just something to do.

Benji's real dream?

Wasn't on the ground.

It was up there.

Sam caught the flicker in his eyes, following his gaze to the sky. "You think about it even when you pitchin', don't you?"

Benji didn't have to ask what "it" was.

He smirked, rolling the baseball in his hand. "What you think?"

Sam chuckled. "Man, one of these days, you gon' get yourself caught dreamin' and lose a game."

Benji grinned. "That why I got you to carry the team?"

Sam laughed, stepping up to the plate again. "Damn right."

Benji exhaled, focused, then threw.

Sam swung—miss.

"Ha!" Benji grinned. "Still got it."

Sam shook his head, getting ready again. "That was a fluke."

"Uh-huh," Benji teased, winding up for another.

The ball soared toward home plate just as the school bell rang in the distance, a reminder that even on the field, the real world was waiting.

But for now, for just a little longer, they could play.

After their game, they sat on the edge of the field, the sun lower now but still hot as hell.

Sam stretched his legs, arms behind his head. "Damn, I'm gonna miss this."

Benji raised an eyebrow. "Miss what?"

Sam sighed. "This. Just… life bein' simple."

Benji was quiet. He knew what Sam meant.

Things had felt different lately.

Like something was shifting.

"You ever feel like… like we stuck?" Sam asked after a moment.

Benji glanced at him. "What you mean?"

Sam sighed. "I mean… what's next, man? We just supposed to work at the mill like Marcus? Spend our days sweatin' and barely makin' enough to get by?"

Benji didn't answer right away.

Because he had the same damn thoughts.

"Some of us ain't meant to stay, Sam," Benji finally said.

Sam turned to look at him. "You mean us?"

Benji's jaw tightened. "Yeah."

Sam studied him for a moment. "Then what the hell we waitin' for?"

Benji let out a slow breath, gripping the baseball in his hands.

"Guess we ain't waitin' no more."

Montgomery's streets were quiet, settled into the lull of late afternoon.

Benji and Sam walked down the familiar dirt path, the weight of the day heavy but not unwelcome.

"You know," Sam said, tossing the baseball between his hands, "you never did tell me what it feel like."

Benji raised an eyebrow. "What what feel like?"

Sam smirked. "That moment. When you first throw a ball and it just… sails. That feeling. What it feel like?"

Benji thought for a second, then shrugged.

"Like it was always meant to fly."

Sam nodded, like he understood something deeper in those words.

"You ever think about that, but with a plane?" he asked.

Benji's lips quirked. "All the time."

Sam chuckled. "Yeah. I figured."

They reached the crossroads, where Sam's street split off from Benji's.

Sam turned to him, expression more serious now. "You meant it, right?"

Benji frowned. "Meant what?"

Sam held his gaze. "That we ain't meant to stay."

Benji's throat tightened.

He could still hear the mill in the distance, the sound of metal grinding, of men who never got out.

"Yeah," Benji said, voice steady. "I meant it."

Sam smirked. "Good. 'Cause I ain't lettin' you back out now."

Benji chuckled. "Wouldn't dare."

Sam grinned, tossing the baseball toward him.

"Same time tomorrow?"

Benji caught it without looking.

"Always."

And just like that, they went their separate ways.

But something had shifted.

Something had already begun.

The sun had just begun to dip below the treetops as Benjamin Davis stepped onto the porch of his family's small house, the wooden boards creaking under his weight. The scent of cornbread and stewed greens drifted through the open window, wrapping around him like a familiar embrace.

The screen door let out a soft creak as he pushed it open.

Inside, his mother, Clara Davis, sat in her usual chair near the kitchen, her fingers expertly weaving his little sister Naomi's thick curls into braids.

"You home before dark for once," Clara said without looking up.

Benji smirked, leaning against the doorframe. "Figured I'd give you a break from worryin' about me."

Clara huffed, still focused on Naomi's hair. "Boy, please. You'd have to stay home a whole week for me to get that kind of break."

Naomi giggled, her small legs swinging back and forth. "Told ya Mama keep track of you, Benny."

Benji chuckled, walking over and ruffling her head before dodging the half-hearted swat from Clara.

"Don't mess up my work," Clara warned, her hands still braiding with practiced ease.

Benji held his hands up in surrender, grinning. "Yes, ma'am."

Clara glanced up then, taking a quick look at her son. "You eat?"

"Had a little somethin' after playin' ball."

"That ain't a meal."

Benji shrugged, moving toward the stove. "Well, guess I better fix that, huh?"

Clara shook her head. "Mm-hmm. Always hungry, just like your daddy."

At the mention of Elijah Davis, Benji glanced toward the back door, knowing his father was likely out in the yard, cleaning up after a long day.

Before he could go check, heavy footsteps echoed from the hallway.

Marcus Davis, his older brother, strolled into the kitchen, shirt still dusty from the mill, his expression already carrying a hint of disapproval.

"You been out all day," Marcus muttered, grabbing a cup of water.

Benji sighed, bracing for whatever was coming. "And?"

Marcus leaned against the counter. "And you ever thought about actually helpin' out instead of runnin' around playin' games?"

Benji scoffed. "It ain't a game."

Marcus gave him a look. "It ain't work either."

Clara sighed, but didn't intervene. She knew better than to get between her boys when they started in on each other.

"Not all of us wanna spend our days in that mill, Marcus," Benji said, keeping his voice even.

Marcus took a slow sip of water before answering. "Not all of us got a choice."

The words hung in the air between them.

Benji's jaw tightened, but before he could fire back, another voice cut in.

"Benjamin."

Benji turned to see his father standing in the doorway, wiping his hands on a rag.

Elijah was a tall man, broad-shouldered, his presence filling a room even when he didn't say much. His face was lined with years of hard work, but his eyes were still sharp, still carrying that same quiet strength Benji had always looked up to.

"Yes, sir?" Benji asked, immediately straightening.

Elijah studied him for a long moment. "You got a job to do in the mornin'."

Benji frowned. "A job?"

Elijah nodded. "Crop-dusting over the Walker fields. They called me today. Need it done before the heat kicks up."

Benji felt a flicker of excitement. "You want me to do it?"

Elijah raised an eyebrow. "Ain't that what I just said?"

Benji grinned. "Yes, sir."

Marcus scoffed. "Oh, so he gets to fly around while the rest of us break our backs for scraps?"

Elijah's gaze flicked toward Marcus. "He got his own kind of work to do."

Marcus muttered something under his breath but didn't push it. Even he knew better than to argue with their father.

Clara, always the peacekeeper, let out a soft sigh and patted Naomi's shoulder. "Alright, baby, go on and get ready for bed."

Naomi pouted. "But I wanna hear 'bout Benny flyin'!"

Benji chuckled, tapping her nose. "I'll tell you all about it tomorrow, alright?"

She sighed dramatically but hopped down from the chair anyway, giving him a quick hug before disappearing down the hall.

Marcus shook his head, grabbing his plate. "Don't know why y'all let him keep livin' in the clouds. Ain't nothin' waitin' for him up there."

Benji didn't even blink. "Guess I'll find out for myself."

Marcus just shook his head again, muttering as he walked away.

Silence settled over the kitchen once he was gone.

Clara turned to Elijah, arms crossed. "You really trust him to handle a full job alone?"

Elijah leaned against the wall, studying his son. "Boy's been flyin' since he could walk. I reckon he's ready."

Clara didn't look convinced. "Just don't want him gettin' reckless."

Benji smirked. "Mama, I got the best teacher in the world."

Elijah let out a quiet chuckle. "We'll see about that."

Benji grinned, but inside, he felt something stronger than just excitement.

This was more than just another flight.

This was his chance to prove himself.

To his father. To his family. To himself.

Later That Night

Benji lay on the small cot in his room, staring at the ceiling, hands resting behind his head.

Through the window, the sound of crickets filled the air, a steady hum of life in the Alabama night.

His mind wasn't here, though.

It was already up there.

Already in the sky.

The thought of waking up before dawn, climbing into the cockpit, and feeling that rush—it was enough to make it damn near impossible to sleep.

A soft knock on his door pulled him back.

"Yeah?"

The door creaked open, and Naomi's small figure peeked inside.

"Still up?" she whispered.

Benji chuckled. "What you doin' awake, sissy?"

She padded over, curling up at the edge of his cot. "Couldn't sleep."

Benji raised an eyebrow. "That so?"

She nodded. "Thinkin' 'bout you flyin'."

Benji smirked. "You worried 'bout me?"

Naomi hesitated, then whispered, "Just don't want you to go too high and forget how to come back."

Benji felt something tighten in his chest.

He sat up, nudging her gently. "Ain't nothin' in the world gonna make me forget to come back home, you hear me?"

Naomi bit her lip. "Promise?"

Benji nodded. "Promise."

She studied him for a second, then sighed dramatically. "Alright. But you better tell me everythin' tomorrow."

Benji chuckled. "Deal."

She hopped off the cot, yawning as she made her way back toward the door.

Right before she left, she turned.

"Night, Benny."

Benji smiled. "Night, sissy."

As the door clicked shut, Benji exhaled, staring back at the ceiling.

Tomorrow, he'd be in the sky again.

And soon, if he had his way…

He'd never come back down.

The sky was still dark when Benjamin Davis stepped onto the small airstrip behind his house. The air carried the crisp, dewy scent of early morning, a contrast to the thick heat that would roll in by midday.

There she was.

His father's Curtiss JN-4 "Jenny", a sturdy old crop-dusting plane, sat waiting for him like a loyal friend. The plane had seen years of hard work, but to Benji, it was more than a machine. It was his first love.

Elijah Davis stood nearby, arms crossed, his sharp eyes watching every move Benji made.

"Pre-flight check," his father said, voice steady.

Benji nodded, already running through the routine he'd practiced dozens of times under his father's watch.

✓ Fuel levels? Good.

✓ Flaps and rudder? Moving smooth.

✓ Dusting system? Operational.

Everything was ready.

Elijah finally gave a short nod of approval. "Walker's fields need coverin' before the sun gets too high. You think you got this?"

Benji looked up at the sky, then back at his father. "I know I do."

Elijah studied him for a long moment before stepping forward. He reached out, gripping Benji's shoulder—firm, steady, strong.

"Have fun and be safe."

Benji swallowed, feeling the weight of those words settle deep in his chest.

"Yes, sir," he said softly.

Then he climbed into the cockpit.

The engine roared to life, sending vibrations through his hands as he gripped the controls.

This was it.

His first solo job.

His first real step toward the sky.

And as the wheels lifted off the ground, Benji grinned so wide it hurt.

The world fell away beneath him.

No mill.

No segregation signs.

No people tellin' him what he couldn't be.

Just him and the sky.

The orange-pink glow of sunrise stretched across the horizon as he banked the plane gently, aligning himself over Walker's cotton fields.

He reached for the dusting switch—just like he practiced—and released the spray in smooth, even passes over the crops.

✓ Turn.

✓ Spray.

✓ Adjust altitude.

Every motion was second nature.

Everything felt right.

By the time he finished the last field, he was sweating, but damn, did it feel good.

And that's when he got a little bold.

"Just one little move," he muttered, smirking.

With careful precision, Benji pulled the plane up sharply, angling the nose toward the sky.

The Jenny climbed higher and higher, almost weightless—then, with a smooth roll, he flipped her upside down for just a second before leveling out again.

It wasn't reckless. It was controlled.

And it felt damn incredible.

What Benji didn't know was that someone had been watching.

As Benji brought the plane back down for landing, Mr. Walker, the farm owner, stood near the edge of the field, arms crossed, staring up at the sky.

He was a big, burly white man in his late fifties, with deep lines from years in the sun and a constant air of authority.

Benji's heart kicked up a little when he spotted him.

Walker wasn't a bad man—but white folks with power always made Benji wary.

By the time Benji hopped out of the cockpit, dust still clinging to his skin, Walker was already walking toward him.

"You Elijah's boy?" Walker asked.

Benji straightened. "Yes, sir."

Walker studied him a long moment, then glanced back toward the sky.

"That little stunt up there—intentional?"

Benji swallowed. "Yes, sir."

Walker nodded. "Damn good flyin'."

Benji blinked. He hadn't expected that.

Walker glanced toward where Elijah was approaching. "Boy's got a gift," he said, loud enough for his father to hear. "I'd say he's got more sky in him than dirt."

Elijah's eyes flickered with something almost like pride as he stepped beside Benji.

Benji kept quiet, letting his father respond.

Elijah finally nodded. "Always said he was born for it."

Walker snorted. "Yeah, well, might be more than just a crop duster in his future."

Benji's heart thumped hard in his chest.

Maybe Walker didn't fully understand what he was sayin'— but Benji sure as hell did.

This was just the beginning.

Later that afternoon, Benji met up with Sam near the bus stop.

Sam leaned against a post, tossing a baseball in the air. "So how'd it go?"

Benji smirked. "Let's just say... I made an impression."

Sam chuckled. "I bet. You always showin' off."

Benji shrugged. "Man's gotta be remembered somehow."

Sam's grin faded slightly, turning more serious. "You ready to make a real impression?"

Benji raised an eyebrow. "What you talkin' about?"

Sam pulled a folded-up newspaper clipping from his pocket and handed it over.

Benji opened it, scanning the words.

TUSKEGEE AIRMEN RECRUITMENT – APPLY NOW.

He felt his breath hitch.

"That's what I been tryin' to tell you," Sam said, voice low. "They recruitin' right now, Benny. We go down there, we could be in the air for real."

Benji exhaled slow, heart pounding.

Sam leaned in, smirking. "So what you say? We get on this bus and go find our future?"

Benji grinned, rolling the baseball in his hands. "Hell yeah."

As they waited for the bus, a young white woman and an older white lady stepped out of a nearby shop.

The girl's bag suddenly ripped, sending books and papers tumbling onto the sidewalk.

"Jessica, dear," the older woman sighed, exasperated. "Honestly, you must be more careful."

"I got it, Mama," the girl muttered, kneeling to gather her things.

Benji stepped forward without thinking. "Lemme help."

The girl looked up just as he crouched down beside her.

Their eyes met.

Benji felt something tighten in his chest.

She was beautiful.

Long wavy blonde hair, striking blue-green eyes, and the kind of presence that made the world slow down.

She blinked at him, lips parting slightly—like she recognized something in him too.

Then, just as quick, she shook herself and grabbed a book. "Thank you."

Her mother, standing stiff beside her, narrowed her eyes at Benji.

"You should hurry along now, boy," she said, voice coated in that fake, polite venom.

Benji's jaw tightened.

But Jessica shot him a small, almost apologetic smile.

"Thanks again," she whispered.

Benji nodded once.

Then, as quickly as it happened, it was over.

The bus pulled up.

Sam clapped him on the back. "You good?"

Benji exhaled, shaking off whatever that moment was.

"Yeah," he said, stepping onto the bus.

As they took their seats, heading toward their future, he couldn't help but glance out the window—

And see Jessica still standing there, watching them leave.

CHAPTER 2:
THE FIRST STEP

July 1941 – Montgomery, Alabama →
Tuskegee, Alabama

The bus rattled down the dusty road, kicking up heat as it carried them farther from Montgomery. Benji leaned against the window, watching the open fields blur past.

Tuskegee was still an hour away.

He glanced at Sam, who sat beside him, arms folded, looking straight ahead with an easy smirk on his face.

"You nervous?" Sam asked, his voice light.

Benji smirked back. "Why would I be nervous?"

Sam shrugged. "We 'bout to sign up for somethin' real, man. This ain't no schoolyard talk no more."

Benji considered that, rolling his shoulders. "Guess I just figured… we always knew this was gonna happen."

Sam nodded. "Yeah. But it's different now."

Benji looked back at the road. The weight of it was settling in, but it wasn't fear. It was something else.

Anticipation.

Excitement.

Something that told him this was where he was meant to be.

The bus jostled as it hit a rough patch of road, and Sam reached into his pocket, pulling out the now-crumpled recruitment flyer.

He flattened it out against his knee, reading it for what must have been the hundredth time.

"U.S. Army Air Corps – Tuskegee Airmen Recruitment."

Benji eyed the words before looking past Sam, out the window again.

His mind drifted—not to the sky, not to the future, but to the girl outside the shop.

Jessica.

He hadn't meant to look at her for that long, but something about the way her blue-green eyes met his had stuck with him.

It wasn't disgust.

It wasn't even surprise.

It was… something else.

Sam chuckled a big grin on his face, shaking his head. "You still thinkin' about that white girl?"

Benji blinked, his focus snapping back. "What?"

Sam tossed a peanut into his mouth from the bag he'd bought at the station. "The girl you helped pick up her books. Don't play dumb—I saw you."

Benji exhaled, shaking his head. "You talk too much."

Sam smirked. "Ain't nothin' wrong with lookin'. Just don't be stupid."

Benji didn't respond.

The bus lurched forward as it pulled into the small station in Tuskegee.

The town was quieter than Montgomery but carried a different kind of energy. One that hummed with purpose—men walking with confidence, heads held high despite the times.

Benji and Sam stepped off the bus, adjusting their shirts from the ride.

Ahead of them, a bold wooden sign stood near a large brick building, its words stretched in sharp white letters:

"U.S. Army Air Corps – Tuskegee Airmen Recruitment."

Benji felt his pulse quicken.

This was it.

Inside, the air smelled like paper, ink, and fresh sweat.

The recruitment office was packed with young Black men, all waiting, some filling out forms, others being called to the front. The tension was thick, but Determined.

A recruitment officer, a tall, lean man with a sharp gaze and a uniform that looked like it had never seen a wrinkle, stepped forward as Benji and Sam approached.

"You two here to sign up?" he asked, his voice clipped and professional.

Sam nodded first. "Yes, sir."

The officer eyed them both, then motioned to the table where stacks of enlistment forms sat.

"Fill those out. Full name, age, height, weight. Then, you'll take the preliminary assessment."

Benji picked up a form, his fingers tightening around the edges.

This was real.

They sat down on one of the long wooden benches, pens scratching against paper as they filled in the blanks.

Name: Benjamin Elijah Davis

Age: 17

Benji stared at the number for a second, feeling it settle on the page.

He knew he was underage.

He knew there was a chance they'd reject him on the spot.

He thought about lying, but he knew better. That would only make it worse.

He handed the form in.

The officer glanced at it, his expression neutral until his eyes landed on Benji's age.

His brows lifted slightly. "Seventeen?"

Benji nodded, shoulders squared. "Yes, sir."

The officer studied him for a long moment, then gave a short nod. "Wait here."

Benji didn't move as the officer walked away, taking his form with him.

Sam leaned in. "You think they gonna cut you for that?"

Benji exhaled, gaze steady. "Guess we'll find out."

Minutes passed.

The officer returned, holding both their forms. He handed Sam's back, nodding toward the next step.

Then he looked at Benji.

"You'll still take the assessment. But your age might be an issue. You'll be reviewed by command after this."

Benji nodded. "Understood, sir."

The officer studied him a second longer, then turned away.

Sam nudged Benji. "At least they ain't send you home."

Benji smirked. "Not yet."

The recruits were led outside for the physical assessment.

A sergeant with broad shoulders and a rough voice stood waiting, arms crossed.

"Listen up!" he barked. "You wanna fly? You better be more than just good with numbers. You need stamina, strength, and control. If you can't handle this, you damn sure ain't gonna handle combat."

Benji rolled his shoulders, ready.

Push-ups.

Sit-ups.

Timed runs.

Benji and Sam held their own, but some of the other recruits struggled.

One man, tall and wide-chested, stumbled halfway through the run, gasping for air.

The sergeant narrowed his eyes. "You quittin' already?"

The man bent over, hands on his knees. "J-Just need a second, sir."

The sergeant scoffed. "You need more than a second, boy. You need a whole damn miracle."

Benji didn't slow down.

He pushed harder, sweat clinging to his back.

After the endurance drills, they moved on to hand-eye coordination tests.

Benji excelled.

His reflexes were sharp. His movements were smooth.

Sam kept up, but some men didn't make it.

Recruits were pulled aside, some arguing, others just lowering their heads.

Then, finally, the results.

The recruitment officer from earlier stepped forward, scanning a clipboard.

"Alright, listen up!" he called. "If I call your name, step forward. You've passed the preliminary assessment and are moving on to official processing."

Benji exhaled sharply.

"Samson Wells."

Sam grinned, stepping forward.

"Benjamin Davis."

His heart slammed against his ribs.

He stepped forward, his body feeling light, like he was already flying.

The officer paused, glancing at him for a moment longer than the others.

"Your age is still under review," he said. "But for now—welcome to Tuskegee."

Benji nodded firmly.

Sam clapped him on the back. "We in this, man."

Benji smirked. "Yeah. We are."

As they were led into the next room, Benji stole one last glance outside.

The sky stretched wide, endless.

Waiting.

And for the first time in his life, he knew he was exactly where he was meant to be.

Benji wiped the sweat from his forehead as he and Sam followed the other recruits into the next testing room. The physical assessment had been grueling, but this? This was the part he had been waiting for.

The written exam sat in front of him, a thick packet of questions ranging from mechanical knowledge to navigation, weather patterns, and mathematics.

Benji picked up his pencil, rolling it between his fingers as he took a deep breath.

"We've got this," Sam whispered beside him.

Benji gave a short smile and a nod, then focused on the first question.

The recruitment office was tense as the last few recruits turned in their papers. Officers moved between the rows of desks, collecting the exams, speaking in low, authoritative voices.

Benji exhaled, stretching his fingers. He had never taken a test like this before, but he knew one thing—he had nailed it.

The recruits were lined up once more as the head recruitment officer stepped forward, his sharp gaze scanning the line.

"Physical assessments complete. Written exams complete. But passing the test don't mean you passed the program."

Benji straightened his spine, fists at his sides.

"We got more applicants than we got space," the officer continued. "Some of you will move on. Some of you won't."

Benji felt the weight of that statement.

The recruiter glanced at his clipboard before his gaze landed on Benji.

"Davis."

Benji stepped forward. "Sir."

The recruiter studied him for a long moment before sighing. "You did well on your tests, son. But you're seventeen. Too young to enlist without a waiver. And we don't make exceptions easy."

Benji's stomach dropped. He had been ready for this, but hearing it still hit like a punch to the gut.

"Sir, with all due respect, I passed everything," Benji said, keeping his voice steady.

The officer didn't look impressed. "Ain't about that, son. It's the rules. You want to be an airman? You need to be eighteen. That means I should be sending you home."

Benji kept his face blank, but inside, his heart pounded.

The recruiter sighed again. "But..." He glanced over Benji's file. "Your numbers are good. Real good. Too good to ignore. So before I send you home, there's someone you need to talk to."

Benji swallowed, but nodded. "Yes, sir."

"Follow me."

The door shut behind him with a soft click.

Benji stood at attention, his back straight, his nerves running hot under his skin.

Behind the desk sat Captain Desmond Wright.

He was a man with sharp, intelligent light blue eyes, a lean build, and a presence that carried weight. His uniform was crisp, his boots polished to a mirror shine.

Wright studied him for a long moment, silent.

Then, he leaned back in his chair, arms folded.

"You think you can fly it, Davis?"

Benji met his gaze without hesitation. "I know I can, sir."

Wright tilted his head slightly, intrigued. "That so?"

Benji took a breath. "I'll be the best pilot you got."

Silence stretched.

Then, Wright grinned.

"Alright, son," he said, standing up. "Let's see what you got."

The afternoon sun hung low in the sky as Benji followed Captain Wright outside.

A small crowd had gathered near the edge of the airstrip—recruits who had already been accepted, officers, and instructors.

Sam was among them. The second he spotted Benji, he cupped his hands around his mouth and shouted.

"That's my boy!"

Benji smirked, shaking his head.

Wright led him toward a yellow and blue aircraft parked on the runway.

A Stearman PT-17.

A trainer plane.

Benji's heart jumped.

He had seen these planes before, read about them, dreamed about flying one.

Wright stopped beside the aircraft, turning to him. "You say you can fly, huh?"

Benji met his gaze. "Yes, sir."

Wright nodded. "Then prove it."

Benji slid into the cockpit, hands moving on instinct.

Throttle. Rudder. Stick. Instruments.

Everything felt right.

Wright climbed into the rear cockpit, adjusting his headset. "I'll be watching. You mess up, I'll know."

Benji tightened his grip on the stick.

"Yes, sir."

The engine roared to life.

He felt the vibration of it in his bones.

Wright's voice came through the headset. "Take her up, Davis."

Benji didn't hesitate.

The plane rolled forward. The ground beneath him blurred as the wheels lifted off the dirt runway.

And then—

Freedom.

Benji exhaled sharply, his body melting into the machine like it was an extension of himself.

The wind whipped past the open cockpit, sunlight bouncing off the wings.

His father's voice echoed in his head.

"Feel the wind, son. Trust her, and she'll carry you home."

Benji adjusted the stick, tilting the plane into a perfect climb.

Then, Wright's voice crackled through the radio.

"Not bad, Davis. But let's see if you're really as good as you think."

Suddenly—

The plane jerked sideways.

Wright had grabbed his own controls, forcing the aircraft into a sharp bank.

Benji's stomach lurched.

"Recover it," Wright ordered.

Benji gritted his teeth and fought the controls, leveling the plane just in time.

Before he could breathe, Wright cut the engine.

The plane dropped.

Benji reacted instantly.

Throttle forward. Nose down. Wind catching the wings.

The engine sputtered—then roared back to life.

They leveled out just above the tree line.

Wright chuckled in his headset. "Alright, Davis. You got guts. Let's see if you got skill."

Benji's grip tightened.

"Hold on, sir."

And with that—he pulled the plane into a steep climb, pushing past the limits of a normal test flight.

The crowd below gasped.

Sam was on his feet, yelling.

"YEAH! THAT'S MY BOY!"

Benji flipped the plane into a flawless barrel roll, then smoothly righted it.

The second the wheels touched down, he knew.

He had just proven himself.

Benji landed smooth, the wheels kissing the dirt like he had done it a thousand times.

As he climbed out, a few officers exchanged glances.

Some were impressed. Some were skeptical.

Sam ran up first, grinning wide. "Man, you made that look easy!"

Benji smirked. "It was."

Wright approached, arms crossed.

"You got skill, Davis," he said, his tone unreadable.

Benji stood tall, waiting.

"But I can't make promises. You're still underage."

Benji's stomach tightened.

Wright held his gaze. "We'll be in touch."

And with that, he turned and walked away.

Benji slid out of the cockpit, his boots hitting the dirt as the engine of the Stearman PT-17 hummed to a stop behind him. His body still felt light, as if part of him was still up there, cutting through the sky.

The crowd around the airstrip had thinned, but a few recruits still lingered, murmuring to each other. Some were impressed. Others were skeptical.

Benji didn't care about any of them.

He cared about one thing.

Had he done enough?

Before he could dwell on it, two men approached.

The first was tall and built like a boulder, his dark skin gleaming under the Alabama sun. He looked like he had never lost a fight in his life.

The second had a lean, athletic build, his stride easy but confident. His skin was a warm brown, and the way he carried himself reminded Benji of a man who had seen his fair share of victories.

They both stopped in front of him.

The taller one, the boxer, crossed his arms. "That was pretty impressive... for a kid."

Benji smirked. "Ain't no kid up there in the sky."

The second man chuckled, shaking his head. "Alright, alright, he's got some fire in him." He extended a hand. "Clarence Whitaker. But folks call me Ace. From California. Played ball for Grambling State before all this."

Benji clasped his hand, feeling the strength in his grip. "Benji Davis. From Montgomery."

The big man stepped forward next, his handshake firm as iron. "James Callahan. But you can call me Tex. From Texas, obviously. I used to box."

Benji raised an eyebrow. "Heavyweight?"

Tex grinned. "Damn right."

Sam jogged up, slapping Benji on the back. "Man, I thought you were about to crash that damn plane!"

Benji huffed. "You ain't got no faith in me?"

Tex chuckled. "If you can fly half as good as you talk, you might just be worth a damn."

Ace nudged Sam. "So you two boys from Montgomery?"

Sam nodded. "Yeah. We played ball together in high school. We been talking about this since we were kids."

Ace whistled. "That's somethin'. Not everybody got the guts to actually go through with it."

Benji shifted, rolling his shoulders. "This is all I ever wanted."

Tex eyed him. "Yeah? And what happens if you don't get in?"

Benji met his gaze, unwavering. "Then I keep tryin' until I do."

Ace smirked. "I like this kid."

Before they could say anything else, a voice barked from across the field.

"All recruits dismissed for the day! If your name was not confirmed, expect further notice by mail or official communication."

Benji's chest tightened.

This was it. Now, he could do nothing but wait.

Tex clapped him on the back. "Guess we'll see you boys around."

Ace nodded. "Good luck, kid."

Sam threw an arm around Benji's shoulder as they walked back toward the bus station. "Man, I don't care what they say—you flew that plane like you already had your wings."

Benji smirked, but the weight in his chest remained. "Guess we'll see if it's enough."

The bus swayed gently as it rolled along the country road, the golden glow of sunset stretching across the fields outside.

Benji rested his elbow on the windowsill, watching the horizon, lost in thought.

Sam was beside him, stretching out his legs, looking as relaxed as ever.

"You ever think about what's next?" Benji asked.

Sam cracked an eye open. "Next?"

Benji nodded. "After all this. The war, the fightin'—what happens when it's all over?"

Sam exhaled, rubbing his chin. "Man… I don't know. Maybe I stay in. Maybe I come back and figure out what life looks like without all this uniform mess."

He looked over at Benji. "You?"

Benji hesitated, then shook his head. "All I know is flyin'. Ain't never thought past that."

Sam smirked. "Maybe you just gonna fly forever."

Benji chuckled softly. "Maybe."

The bus hit a bump, jolting them both slightly.

For a moment, neither spoke.

Then, Sam nudged Benji. "You really think they gonna send you home?"

Benji stared ahead. "I don't know."

"Man, after what you just pulled? They'd be dumb to let you go."

Benji sighed. "Ain't about skill, though, is it? It's about rules. And rules ain't ever been made to help folks like us."

Sam didn't argue.

Because they both knew it was true.

By the time Benji stepped off the bus in Montgomery, the sky had darkened into a deep indigo, speckled with the first hints of stars.

The air was thick with summer heat, but a cool breeze whispered through the streets.

Benji adjusted his bag on his shoulder as he and Sam parted ways with a handshake.

"Tomorrow," Sam said.

Benji nodded. "Tomorrow."

He walked the familiar dirt path toward home, the smell of cooking and fresh laundry in the air.

When he reached the porch, he could hear his mother's voice inside, soft and steady, humming a hymn.

He stepped through the doorway, the wooden floor creaking beneath his boots.

His father sat in his usual chair, reading the Bible, his fingers slowly tracing the words.

Naomi sat on the floor beside her mother, her hair half-braided, eyes lighting up when she saw him.

"Benny!" she scrambled to her feet and ran to him, wrapping her arms around his waist.

Benji chuckled, ruffling her hair. "You miss me already?"

She grinned. "Mama said you were off flyin' today!"

Clara looked up from Naomi's hair, her gaze soft, but searching. "Did you do well?"

Benji swallowed, nodding. "Yeah, Ma. I did."

Elijah set his Bible aside, watching him closely. "And?"

Benji exhaled. "They said I was too young. But they also said… they'd be in touch."

A beat of silence passed.

Then, Elijah nodded slowly. "Good."

Benji met his father's gaze, searching for disappointment—but he didn't find any.

Just quiet understanding.

Clara smoothed Naomi's braid, then stood. "You must be starving."

Benji smiled. "I won't say no to food."

She disappeared into the kitchen.

Naomi tugged at his hand. "Tell me 'bout the plane, Benny! Did you go high?"

Benji laughed. "Yeah, sis. I went real high."

Elijah stood, stretching. "Come help me close up the barn after you eat."

Benji nodded. "Yes, sir."

As he sat down at the dinner table, his stomach still knotted with uncertainty, he knew one thing for sure.

Tomorrow, he would wake up and wait.

Wait for a letter.

A call.

A chance to prove that the sky was where he belonged.

CHAPTER 3:

THE LETTER ARRIVES & A
LIFE-CHANGING DECISION

September 1941 – Montgomery, Alabama

The last notes of the closing hymn faded into the warm, wooden rafters of St. Mark's Baptist Church, the congregation rising in unison. The scent of aged hymnals, perfume, and a lingering trace of fresh cornbread from the fellowship hall filled the air.

Reverend Elijah Davis closed his Bible with careful hands, his voice deep and steady as he gave the final blessing.

"The Lord tells us that faith without works is dead. If you believe in somethin', you best be willing to work for it. Ain't nothin' worth havin' without a little fight."

A chorus of "Amen!" rippled through the congregation as people turned to shake hands, share small smiles, and exchange Sunday pleasantries.

Benji sat with his family near the front, his hands resting on his knees, the weight of his father's words pressing into his chest. Today, those words meant more than ever.

He'd already enlisted. Made his choice.

But his fate still wasn't his to decide.

The congregation began spilling out onto the dirt road outside, the warm September sun filtering through the trees, casting golden light over the small church.

Marcus, his older brother, walked beside him, his usual easygoing stride noticeably tense.

"You told 'em yet?" Marcus asked low enough that only Benji could hear.

Benji shook his head, glancing toward their father, who walked ahead, shaking hands with members of the church.

Marcus sighed through his nose. "Mama's gonna have a fit, you know."

Benji knew.

The whole family knew he'd enlisted—that part wasn't a secret. But what they didn't know was that his age was a problem.

That he needed their father's signature.

Marcus tilted his head toward Sam, who was a few steps ahead, grinning as he flirted with one of the choir girls. "Sam's got no problem, does he?"

"He's eighteen," Benji muttered. "Nobody's stoppin' him."

Marcus shot him a look. "But you ain't."

Benji stayed quiet.

They reached the car, the old Ford's engine still warm from the drive over. Elijah and Clara climbed in first, Naomi squeezing between them in the front seat. Marcus, Benji, and Sam piled into the back.

The ride home was quiet, the kind of silence that wasn't uncomfortable, but heavy with unspoken things.

Benji could feel his father's gaze in the rearview mirror. Could feel the words waiting on his tongue.

He braced for it.

"You sure about this?" Elijah asked finally.

Benji's fingers curled against his slacks. "Yes, sir."

Elijah hummed low in his throat but said nothing more.

The house looked the same as it always did—modest but strong, white paint peeling a little in places, the front porch shaded by the big oak tree that had stood guard for decades.

Benji had lived here his whole life.

And now, in just a few days, he'd be leaving it.

Naomi darted ahead first, tugging at the bow in her hair as she skipped up the steps.

Then Benji saw it.

The military vehicle parked outside the house.

A tall, lean figure leaning against the porch railing, hat tucked under his arm, piercing blue eyes scanning the yard like he was committing it to memory.

Captain Desmond Wright.

Benji's stomach tightened.

His father's steps slowed. Marcus let out a low whistle. "Well, ain't this somethin.'"

Elijah's expression didn't change. He simply climbed the porch steps with measured ease, his voice calm as ever.

"Captain Wright."

Desmond straightened, nodding respectfully. "Reverend Davis." His gaze flicked to Clara. "Mrs. Davis." Then toward Marcus and Naomi.

But when his eyes landed on Benji, they stayed there.

Benji swallowed hard.

Elijah stepped forward, his broad frame nearly blocking the doorway. "What brings you by, Captain?"

Desmond exhaled, shifting slightly. "Your son."

Clara's body stiffened. Marcus glanced at Benji but said nothing.

Desmond met Elijah's gaze, speaking clearly.

"He's one of the best young pilots I've seen. Natural talent. Passed his exams at the top of his class." His lips twitched slightly. "Ain't seen hands like his in a long time."

Benji's throat was dry.

Desmond let the weight of his words settle before continuing. "But he's seventeen. The military requires eighteen for enlistment." He reached into his jacket pocket and pulled out a folded piece of paper.

Benji knew exactly what it was.

Desmond unfolded it, glancing briefly at Elijah before saying the words that would decide everything.

"With parental consent, the military is willing to make an exception."

Silence.

The kind that suffocates.

Elijah's jaw tightened. Clara let out a slow breath, stepping closer to Naomi as if steadying herself.

Elijah turned fully toward Benji now.

"You already signed up, didn't you?"

Benji held his father's gaze. "Yes, sir."

Marcus muttered something under his breath, dragging a hand down his face.

Clara shook her head, her voice a sharp whisper. "Elijah—"

Elijah didn't look away from Benji. His eyes—deep, knowing, unwavering—searched his youngest son's face as if seeing straight through to his soul.

"This what you want?"

Benji felt like the world had slowed.

"Yes, sir."

A pause.

Then, without a word, Elijah took the pen from Desmond's hand.

Benji felt his heart hammer as the ink touched the paper.

The signature looked so small against the stark white page, but it changed everything.

Desmond took the papers back, nodding once.

"We'll be in touch, Davis. You'll receive your official orders soon."

With that, he turned, stepping off the porch, his boots crunching against the dirt.

The engine roared to life, and within seconds, the vehicle disappeared down the road.

The silence left behind was thick.

Elijah finally turned toward Benji, his expression unreadable.

"Don't you die out there, boy."

Benji's throat tightened.

"I won't."

Elijah held his gaze for another long moment before giving a single nod.

Then he walked inside.

Clara remained where she stood, her arms now folded across her chest, her eyes shining with something unreadable.

Marcus blew out a sharp breath. "Well, damn."

Naomi peeked out from behind Clara, her small face crumpling.

"You're really going?" she whispered.

Benji knelt, brushing a curl from her forehead.

"Yeah, sissy."

Tears welled in her big brown eyes. "Why?"

Benji smiled softly, voice quiet but sure.

"Because I got wings."

Clara let out a shaky breath and turned away.

Elijah was the first to step inside the house, his tall frame moving quietly through the doorway. He didn't say a word, didn't glance back.

Clara followed, her steps controlled, but her back was stiff, her hands clasped so tightly together that her knuckles turned white.

Benji stood on the porch for a long moment, the autumn air heavy around him.

Marcus shifted beside him, exhaling sharply. "Well, damn."

Benji turned his head slightly.

Marcus shook his head. "Ain't no goin' back now, huh?"

Benji didn't answer.

Naomi stood beside him, small fingers fisting the fabric of her dress. She wasn't crying, but her eyes were red, her little shoulders tense.

Benji crouched down, resting his hands gently on her arms. " Sis…"

"You're really goin'," she whispered.

Benji smiled softly. "Yeah, sissy. I am."

Her lip trembled, but she jutted her chin out like she was trying to be strong.

"You gonna write me?" she asked.

Benji held out his pinky. "Pinky swear."

Naomi hooked her little finger around his, gripping tight.

Then, without another word, she turned and hurried inside, head held high like she hadn't just been sniffling.

Benji let out a slow breath and stood back up, glancing toward Marcus.

His brother watched Naomi disappear into the house, then exhaled, rubbing a hand down his face. "I hope you know what you're doin', Benny."

Benji didn't answer.

Marcus let out another breath before shoving his hands into his pockets and heading inside, his shoulders tense.

Benji remained on the porch for a moment, staring out at the yard, at the dirt road that led down past the church, at the trees rustling gently in the warm afternoon breeze.

This was home.

And in a few days, he'd be leaving it behind.

Clara stood in the kitchen, her hands resting on the counter. The tension in her shoulders hadn't eased since she'd walked through the door.

Benji hesitated in the doorway, watching her.

She knew he was there.

She was just waiting.

"Mama," he said finally.

She didn't move. "Your daddy signed it."

Benji nodded. "Yes, ma'am."

Clara inhaled sharply, her fingers flexing against the countertop before she finally turned toward him.

Her dark brown eyes locked onto his, searching his face, memorizing him.

"You always wanted to fly," she murmured.

Benji nodded slowly.

Clara swallowed, then stepped forward, cupping his face in her hands.

"You listen to me, Benjamin Elijah Davis," she said, voice steady but thick with emotion.

Benji stood straighter.

"You fight," she said firmly. "You hold your head high. You don't let no man—no man—tell you you ain't good enough."

Benji nodded once. "Yes, ma'am."

Her fingers tightened slightly against his jaw.

"And you come back home," she whispered.

Benji's throat tightened.

"Yes, ma'am," he said softly.

Clara exhaled shakily, running her thumb over his cheek before pulling her hands away.

She didn't cry.

She wouldn't let herself.

Instead, she turned back to the counter and muttered, "I'm makin' peach cobbler tonight."

Benji blinked.

She adjusted her apron, tying it a little too tight. "Might as well celebrate while we can."

Benji let out a soft breath, a small, knowing smile tugging at the corner of his lips.

That was the closest thing to approval he was gonna get.

The front door swung open, and Sam stormed inside like a hurricane, his grin wide and bright.

"BENJI! We in, baby!"

Benji barely had time to react before Sam grabbed him by the shoulders and shook him excitedly.

"You shoulda seen the telegram I got!" Sam whooped. "We leavin' for Tuskegee in just a couple days! A COUPLE DAYS, BENJI! You believe that?!"

Benji grinned, excitement finally breaking through the tension in his chest.

Marcus smirked, leaning against the doorframe. "Y'all actin' like y'all just got drafted into the Yankees."

Sam ignored him, turning to Clara with the biggest smile. "Mrs. Davis, I promise I'll keep an eye on your boy."

Clara arched a brow. "You, Samson Wells?"

Sam straightened, placing a hand over his chest. "Yes, ma'am. Ain't nobody touchin' my boy while I'm 'round."

Marcus scoffed. "That's what I'm worried about."

Sam grinned. "Man, Marcus, why you always hatin'?"

Marcus rolled his eyes, shaking his head as he walked toward the kitchen. "Y'all gon' give Mama a heart attack."

Clara let out a long breath, glancing between them before sighing. "Well… we best make sure y'all get sent off right."

Sam lit up. "You mean—?"

Clara gave him a stern look. "Don't get excited, Samson. Ain't no wild party gonna happen in my house."

Sam winked at Benji. "I'll take what I can get."

Benji chuckled, shaking his head.

Clara sighed again before turning toward the oven. "Marcus, get the peach cobbler out the icebox."

Naomi perked up. "Peach cobbler?"

Clara smiled faintly. "Might as well celebrate while we can."

Sam whooped, clapping Benji on the back. "See? Even your mama knows we gotta do it big!"

Benji grinned. "Yeah, yeah."

For a moment, everything felt normal.

But beneath the laughter, beneath the clinking of dishes and the sound of Naomi humming in the background, Benji felt it.

The clock was ticking.

In just a couple of days, everything would change.

The house was quieter than usual.

Benji sat on the edge of his bed, the small duffel bag open beside him, its contents neatly folded inside. He ran his fingers along the smooth fabric of his uniform shirt, then let out a breath.

This was it.

In a few hours, he'd be leaving home—leaving everything behind.

His eyes drifted to the framed photo on his nightstand, the one with him, Naomi, and Marcus sitting on the porch when they were kids. Naomi had been no older than five, sitting in his lap, while Marcus had thrown an arm around both of them, grinning wide.

It felt like a lifetime ago.

A soft knock at the door made him turn his head.

His father stood in the doorway, arms crossed. "You ready?"

Benji nodded. "Yes, sir."

Elijah stepped inside, his boots thudding softly against the wooden floor. He stopped by the dresser, picking up a small, silver pocket watch, worn but still working.

"This was my daddy's," Elijah said, running his thumb over the engraved initials. "Been in our family a long time."

Benji sat up straighter as Elijah turned and held it out to him.

"I want you to have it," Elijah said.

Benji hesitated, his fingers brushing the cool metal before curling around it. "Pops..."

"You take care of it," Elijah said, his voice steady but thick with something deeper. "And you take care of yourself out there."

Benji swallowed, nodding once. "I will."

Elijah gave a firm nod, then clapped him on the shoulder. "Come on. Bus ain't gonna wait."

Benji stood, grabbing his bag.

He took one last look at his room before following his father downstairs.

The walk to the station was quiet.

Benji, Elijah, Clara, Marcus, and Naomi strolled down the familiar dirt road, the same road Benji had walked a thousand times before.

This time, it felt different.

Sam was waiting at the corner, leaning against a post with his own bag slung over his shoulder. "Took y'all long enough," he teased, but his grin wasn't as wide as usual.

The bus stop wasn't far from the church, a small bench under the shade of a towering oak tree. The sun was starting to dip lower in the sky, casting everything in a warm golden hue.

Marcus pulled a few bills from his pocket, holding them out.

"Here," he said. "Little somethin' for the road."

Benji eyed the money. "Marcus, I don't—"

"Just take it," Marcus interrupted, shoving it into his hand. "And don't spend it all on somethin' stupid."

Benji smirked. "No promises."

Marcus snorted, shaking his head. "Damn fool."

Then, to Benji's surprise, Marcus pulled him in for a rare hug.

Benji froze for a second, then returned it.

When Marcus pulled back, he muttered, "Be safe, Benny."

Benji nodded. "You too."

Naomi stepped forward, her little fingers clutching something tightly.

"I made this for you," she said, holding out a small braided bracelet. "It's got good luck on it."

Benji smiled softly as he took it, tying it around his wrist. "Then I'll wear it every day."

Naomi's face lit up, but then her expression turned serious again. "And you better write me."

Benji grinned. "I will, sissy."

Clara stepped forward last, her arms already reaching for him.

She pulled him into the tightest hug, her fingers pressing into his back, as if she could hold onto him forever.

"Don't you dare forget where you come from," she whispered against his ear.

Benji swallowed hard. "Never."

Clara held on for another few seconds before finally pulling back, cupping his face.

Then, with one last deep breath, she let go.

The bus rumbled down the road in the distance, its silhouette growing larger against the setting sun.

Benji looked at his family one last time.

Then he turned toward Sam.

"You ready?"

Sam grinned, though his voice wasn't as cocky as usual. "Hell yeah."

The bus slowed to a stop, its doors creaking open.

Benji stepped forward, taking one last look at home.

Then he climbed inside.

The doors shut behind him.

And just like that—

He was gone.

CHAPTER 4:

JESSICA'S WORLD

July 1941 – Montgomery, Alabama

The Shaw residence was the kind of house that made people stop and stare. A grand, white-columned mansion set back from the street, surrounded by pristine hedges and a wrought-iron gate. The kind of house that whispered money, power, and old Southern tradition.

Jessica had lived here her entire life, but it never really felt like home. Not in the way it should.

She sat on the wraparound porch, a book open in her lap, though she hadn't read a single word in the past fifteen minutes. The late afternoon heat clung to the air, making everything slow and heavy. Somewhere in the distance, the faint hum of cicadas filled the space between conversations.

Inside the house, her mother, Margaret Shaw, was hosting a luncheon for the wives of politicians and business tycoons. Jessica had endured it for the first hour—smiling, nodding, answering questions about which suitor she was entertaining, which parties she would be attending, how proud her father must be of her.

It was all suffocating.

She glanced over at Josephine, the housemaid who had practically raised her, as she swept the porch steps.

"You're wearin' that look again, baby girl," Josephine said without glancing up.

Jessica sighed. "What look?"

"The one that says you'd rather be anywhere but here."

Jessica gave a small laugh, closing her book. "You know me too well."

Josephine smirked. "Somebody's got to."

The sound of heels clicking against the wooden floor echoed behind them. Jessica turned as her mother stepped onto the porch, her perfectly tailored dress pristine, not a single strand of blonde hair out of place.

"Jessica, darling," Margaret said smoothly, offering a rehearsed smile. "Why are you out here when we have guests inside?"

Jessica kept her expression neutral. "Just getting some air."

Margaret's eyes flicked to Josephine, then back to Jessica. "You'll need to change before dinner. Your father has some guests coming. He wants you to look presentable."

Jessica swallowed her sigh. Presentable. As if she weren't always expected to be on display.

Margaret turned to Josephine. "That'll be all."

Josephine gave a small nod before gathering her broom and disappearing inside.

Jessica watched her go, then turned back to her mother. "Who's coming to dinner?"

"Senator Whitmore and his wife. And, of course, Richard and his family."

Jessica barely resisted the urge to groan. Of course. Richard.

Richard Wellington had been circling her for the past year, much to her father's approval. He was handsome, well-mannered, and came from the kind of old-money Southern family that made for a perfect match.

The problem was, Jessica didn't want to be matched with anyone.

Especially not someone she felt absolutely nothing for.

Her mother studied her carefully. "You'll be polite."

Jessica met her gaze. "Aren't I always?"

Margaret smiled, but it didn't reach her eyes. "Good girl."

And with that, she turned on her heel and walked back inside, leaving Jessica alone once more.

Jessica exhaled slowly, her fingers tightening around the book in her lap.

Dinner with Richard. Another night of pretending. Another night of being exactly who they wanted her to be.

She wasn't sure how much longer she could keep it up.

Dinner at the Shaw residence was always an affair of quiet precision. The long mahogany dining table, adorned with polished silverware and candlelight, stretched beneath the glow of an elaborate crystal chandelier. The atmosphere was orderly, conversations measured, and expectations unspoken but ever-present.

Jessica sat between her mother and Richard Wellington, the young man her parents had been nudging her toward for months. Across from her, her father, Senator William Shaw, dominated the head of the table, his presence casting an unshakable weight over the room.

Her mother, Margaret Shaw, spoke in gentle tones, offering pleasantries and engaging their guests—a pair of military officers who were discussing the war in Europe with her father.

"Roosevelt won't be able to stay out of this war forever," one of the officers remarked, cutting into his steak. "Germany is gaining ground faster than anyone anticipated."

Shaw nodded, taking a slow sip of bourbon. "The American people still have no stomach for war. But that will change soon enough."

Jessica barely heard them.

Her mind was elsewhere—still lingering outside Washington & Sons General Store, where, hours earlier, a young man had knelt to help her gather the spilled contents of her bag.

She didn't know why she was thinking about it.

Or him.

He had been polite, quiet, his dark eyes meeting hers for only a brief moment before he had handed her the last of her belongings. Strong hands, steady movements.

It had been nothing, and yet—

Jessica swallowed and picked up her glass of water, trying to push the memory away.

"Jessica."

Her father's deep voice brought her back into the present. She straightened, smoothing her napkin.

"Yes, Father?"

"You've hardly spoken," he observed, tapping a finger against the rim of his glass. "Are you feeling unwell?"

Jessica forced a small smile. "No, sir. I was just thinking about the fall term."

Her mother perked up slightly. "Oh, have you finally decided which courses you want to take?"

Jessica hesitated before she spoke.

"I want to study law," she said finally, keeping her voice steady.

For a brief moment, silence fell over the table.

Her father exhaled through his nose, setting his glass down. "Law?"

Jessica nodded. "Yes, sir."

Margaret smiled tightly, smoothing the napkin in her lap. "Darling, you know how difficult that would be."

Jessica lifted her chin slightly. "I do."

Her father leaned back, studying her. "Jessica, your future is already laid out. You come from a family with influence, with status. There's no reason for you to struggle in a field that—frankly—wasn't designed for women like you."

Jessica felt a sting of frustration, but she kept her tone measured. "It's a respectable profession, Father."

"Perhaps," he said, tilting his head slightly. "For the right kind of woman."

Jessica pressed her lips together, fingers curling around her fork.

Before she could reply, Richard—who had been silent until now—cleared his throat.

"I think it's admirable," he said, his voice calm but sure.

Jessica turned to him, surprised.

Richard glanced at her, offering a small smile before addressing her father. "Jessica has always been sharp, sir. If she wants to pursue law, I have no doubt she'd do well at it."

Her father studied him for a moment before nodding slightly. "You've always had good judgment, Richard."

Richard inclined his head respectfully. "Thank you, sir."

Jessica barely heard the rest of the conversation.

Her father had dismissed her ambitions just as she had expected—but Richard's quiet support had caught her off guard.

She had always assumed he was merely another extension of her father's world—polished, predictable, and perfectly agreeable. But tonight, she saw something different.

She wasn't sure how she felt about that.

Later that evening, Jessica sat in her bedroom, staring at the dim light of her bedside lamp.

Her hair was brushed out, cascading over her shoulders, and she wore a silk nightgown that shimmered softly in the low light.

She should have been asleep.

Instead, she lay awake, her thoughts drifting in a direction she couldn't seem to control.

Not toward law school.

Not toward Richard.

But toward him.

The boy from the general store.

She didn't even know his name.

And yet, she could still feel the brief brush of his fingers against hers as he handed her back her things.

It was such a small thing—so insignificant—and yet, something about it had stayed with her.

Jessica exhaled slowly, turning onto her side.

She told herself it was nothing.

She told herself she'd forget by morning.

But deep down, she already knew that she wouldn't.

Jessica sat in the parlor, curled up in one of the high-backed chairs, the fire flickering low in the hearth. Outside, the crickets sang their evening song, the humid Alabama air pressing against the windows.

The night had been long—her father entertaining a group of political guests, men who spoke in clipped, assured tones about the future of the South. Jessica had sat quietly through the dinner, pretending to listen as her mother had. But now, in the quiet of the house, her thoughts drifted.

She had been thinking more about school lately—about college, about what she wanted. Her father hadn't been shy in reminding her of her true purpose: to marry well, to support a powerful man, to raise the next generation of Shaws.

But that wasn't what she wanted.

She let out a slow breath, glancing toward the staircase. She should go to bed.

Then she heard it—her father's voice, low and sharp, carrying from his study.

Jessica stilled. He was speaking to someone—another politician, or perhaps one of his military connections. She knew better than to eavesdrop, but something in his tone made her pause.

"… Ridiculous," her father muttered. "You know as well as I do, this whole program is a waste of resources. Colored boys in the sky? Can you imagine? What fool in Washington thought that was a good idea?"

Jessica's breath caught.

He was talking about the Tuskegee Airmen.

"I heard one of them nearly outflew a seasoned pilot during training," the other man said, amusement laced in his tone. "Some of 'em have a natural talent, I suppose."

Her father scoffed. "Natural talent won't save them in war. They don't have the discipline. It's all just a show—let them play soldiers for a while, and when the real fight comes, they'll realize the sky belongs to real men."

Jessica's stomach twisted.

She clenched her fists, heat rising in her chest. She hated the way he spoke. The way he dismissed them like they weren't even human.

Something about it unsettled her—more than usual.

She turned away, moving quickly down the hall. She needed air.

The kitchen was dimly lit, the scent of fresh biscuits still lingering from earlier. Josephine stood by the counter, pouring herself a cup of coffee.

Jessica hesitated in the doorway.

"You up late, baby?" Josephine asked, not looking up. "Should be in bed. Big day comin' up."

Jessica lingered for a moment before stepping inside, pulling out one of the chairs. "Couldn't sleep."

Josephine finally glanced at her, studying her with knowing eyes. She was in her late fifties, her hair streaked with silver but still full, pulled into a neat bun at the nape of her neck. She had been in this house since before Jessica was born, a quiet presence who had seen and heard far more than most people realized.

Jessica traced a finger over the wooden table. "What do you think about the Airmen? The Tuskegee program?"

Josephine paused, her fingers tightening around the cup.

"That why you can't sleep?" she asked, setting the coffee down and taking a seat across from her.

Jessica didn't answer, but she knew Josephine could see the truth on her face.

The older woman sighed, shaking her head. "Well, it's 'bout time, is what I think."

Jessica blinked.

Josephine leaned back, her gaze sharp. "I seen plenty of young men who dream of flyin'. But the world don't let 'em. They're born with wings, but folks like your daddy? They keep 'em in cages."

Jessica swallowed. "You know someone in the program?"

Josephine nodded. "My nephew, Marlon. Grew up in Selma. Boy could take apart a plane engine blindfolded. Always had his head in the clouds, dreamin' of flyin'. They told him no over and over again. 'Not for you, boy. Stick to fixing cars.'"

Her eyes darkened.

"But he didn't listen. He signed up. Got into the Tuskegee program just last month."

Jessica felt something shift inside her.

These weren't just names in the newspaper. These were real people.

"I hope he makes it," she said softly.

Josephine met her gaze. "They'll have to let him. Sooner or later, the world gon' change."

Jessica sat with that for a long moment.

Would it? Could it?

She wanted to believe it.

But her father's voice echoed in her head. The sky belongs to real men.

Jessica looked down at her hands.

"What if…" She hesitated. "What if the world doesn't change?"

Josephine smiled, but there was something sad in her eyes. "Then you change it, baby."

Jessica felt her throat tighten.

She didn't respond.

Didn't know if she could.

Josephine took another sip of her coffee. "Go on and get some rest. You got a party comin' up, and Lord knows your mama gon' have you dressed like a Christmas doll."

Jessica let out a quiet laugh, the tension in her chest easing just slightly.

She stood up.

"Goodnight, Josephine."

"Night, baby."

Jessica made her way upstairs, her mind still racing.

She couldn't shake it.

The way her father spoke. The way Josephine spoke.

And the way, for the first time in her life, she felt stuck between two worlds—one she had always known and one she had never dared to see.

As she lay down in bed, staring up at the ceiling, she knew sleep wouldn't come easily.

Because something inside her had shifted.

And there was no turning back now.

CHAPTER 5:

DANGEROUS DANCE

November 1941 – Tuskegee Army Airfield,
Alabama

The roar of the P-40 Warhawk filled Benji's ears as he gripped the control stick, the vibration of the engine thrumming through his fingertips. He had spent the last two months training, pushing his body and mind to the limits, but nothing compared to the way he felt up here—weightless, free, untouchable.

The Alabama sun cast a golden hue over the airfield below, stretching the shadows of the barracks and hangars into long, dark streaks. A flicker of movement to his right caught his eye—Sam's plane keeping perfect formation.

Benji smirked, rolling his shoulders before keying the radio. "Two months and you still can't keep up, Wells."

Through the crackling comms, Sam's laughter rang out. "Ain't about keeping up, Flyboy. It's about knowing when to strike."

Benji chuckled, gripping the throttle as he banked sharply to the left. The P-40 responded smoothly, rolling effortlessly through the air before leveling out again.

The past few months had flown by—literally. Training was grueling, both physically and mentally. Between early-morning drills, endless ground courses, and the constant scrutiny of Captain Desmond Wright, every day felt like a battle. But up here? This was where he belonged.

He yanked the stick back, climbing fast. Sam followed, but Benji had already planned his next move. At the peak of his climb, he killed his speed, letting gravity take hold. The nose of his plane tipped forward, and he fell into a controlled dive.

Sam cursed through the radio. "Damn, Benji! Give a man a warning!"

Benji laughed, pulling up just before hitting the airfield, skimming so close to the ground he could see Tex and Ace standing outside the barracks, their faces tilted upward.

He grinned, pushing the throttle forward and looping back around toward the control tower.

"Davis, you showing off again?"

The radio crackled to life with the unmistakable voice of Captain Desmond Wright.

Benji smirked. "No, sir. Just keeping my reflexes sharp."

Desmond's voice was unimpressed. "That right? Let's see how sharp they are. Bring it in. Now."

Benji sighed, leveling his wings. "Yes, sir."

Tuskegee Army Airfield – Flight Line

The moment Benji climbed out of his cockpit, Desmond was already marching toward him.

Sam had barely gotten his boots on the ground before Tex and Ace rushed over, laughing.

"Damn, Davis! You trying to give the Captain a heart attack?" Tex clapped him on the back.

Ace grinned. "I'll give it to you, though. That dive? Smooth as hell."

Benji smirked but quickly straightened as Desmond reached them.

"Wanna tell me what the hell that was, Davis?"

Benji wiped his brow. "Just getting comfortable in my plane, sir."

Desmond exhaled sharply, his piercing blue eyes locking onto Benji's. "Listen to me, kid. I know you got talent. I know you got skill. But you keep pulling reckless stunts like that, and one day, it's not gonna be a trick—it's gonna be your last damn flight."

Benji swallowed hard. "Understood, sir."

Desmond studied him for a long moment before finally exhaling. "Get cleaned up. You got somewhere to be tonight."

The barracks buzzed with energy. Pilots moved around, buttoning their dress uniforms, the smell of aftershave thick in the air.

Benji stood in front of a small, cracked mirror, adjusting his collar. His hands were steady, but deep down, something stirred in his chest.

Tonight wasn't just a dance. It was a test.

The first time the Tuskegee Airmen would be stepping into a world that didn't want them.

Sam whistled from his bunk. "You nervous?"

Benji smirked, adjusting his sleeves. "Why would I be nervous?"

Tex walked by, already dressed, shaking his head. "Y'all about to be surrounded by white girls who ain't never seen some of the most gorgeous ass men like us before. You should be nervous."

Benji chuckled, but deep down, he knew Tex wasn't wrong.

Ace leaned against the wall, grinning. "Man, one thing's for sure—this night? Gonna be one for the books."

Benji flexed his fingers.

Something told him Ace was right.

The military transport truck rumbled over the dirt roads leading toward Montgomery, the vibrations humming through the metal floor beneath their boots. The night air was thick with the scent of pine and distant smoke from a nearby factory.

Benji sat with his back straight, fingers tapping lightly against his knee. The anticipation in the truck was palpable, a quiet undercurrent of nerves running through the men, even if none of them would ever admit it.

Sam, sitting beside him, adjusted his tie for the hundredth time, huffing under his breath.

"Damn thing's choking me," he muttered.

Tex, sitting across from them, smirked. "That's just your big-ass neck."

Ace chuckled. "Or maybe it's the fact that we ain't supposed to be here in the first place."

No one responded to that.

They all knew the truth. They weren't invited. They were tolerated.

Captain Desmond Wright sat at the front of the vehicle, his legs spread casually, his sharp blue eyes scanning the men under the dim glow of the overhead light.

"Listen up." His voice was calm but firm, cutting through the noise of the rattling truck. "Tonight, you're walking into a world that doesn't believe you belong. They'll smile to your face and spit on your boots when you turn around. You keep your heads high. You keep your composure. You let your presence do the talking."

The men nodded in unison.

Desmond's gaze landed on Benji. "Davis."

Benji met his eyes. "Sir?"

"You understand what I'm saying?"

Benji swallowed, then gave a firm nod. "Yes, sir."

Desmond studied him for a moment longer before exhaling through his nose. "Good." He turned back to the rest of the men. "You don't drink. You don't start trouble. You represent more than just yourselves tonight. You represent every man waiting behind you, hoping to take that first flight. Don't give them a reason to doubt us."

A chorus of "Yes, sir" echoed through the truck.

Tex muttered under his breath, "Damn, I was hoping for at least one drink."

Ace smirked. "Guess you'll have to charm some debutante into slipping you one."

The truck slowed, then came to a rolling stop.

The back doors creaked open, revealing the bright lights of the Governor's Mansion.

Benji inhaled deeply. This was it.

The men stepped out onto the gravel drive, the massive white columns of the mansion standing like marble sentries against the dark sky.

The crowd was already thick, elegant couples moving in and out of the entrance, laughter and music spilling from inside. Women in shimmering dresses clung to the arms of their military escorts, their gloved hands resting lightly against polished lapels.

As Benji and the other airmen stepped forward, the energy shifted.

Whispers.

Eyes flicking toward them.

Glasses pausing mid-sip.

A group of white officers near the entrance turned slowly, their expressions ranging from mild curiosity to quiet contempt. One of them—a captain with slicked-back blond hair—leaned toward his companion and muttered something under his breath.

The man beside him chuckled, shaking his head. "Didn't know they let the colored boys in."

Benji clenched his jaw, his fingers curling into a fist at his side.

Tex shifted beside him. "You hear that?"

"Let it go," Desmond's voice cut through the tension, barely above a whisper, but laced with warning.

Tex inhaled sharply, then exhaled through his nose, keeping his hands at his sides. "Ain't worth it."

Benji forced himself to relax. He had been warned about this. They all had.

They walked up the steps, past the stares, past the murmurs, past the world that would rather pretend they didn't exist.

Inside, the mansion was breathtaking.

Golden chandeliers cast a warm glow over the ballroom, the polished marble floors reflecting the soft candlelight. The scent of expensive cigars and aged bourbon filled the air. The band in the corner played a slow, easy jazz tune, the melody weaving effortlessly through the chatter of the guests.

Benji had never been surrounded by this much wealth before.

Sam let out a low whistle beside him. "Damn."

Tex scoffed. "Some folks got too much money."

Ace smirked. "And too little sense."

Benji barely heard them. His gaze had already locked onto her.

Across the ballroom, Jessica Shaw stood at the center of a circle of officers, their smiles easy, their postures relaxed.

She was laughing politely, though her eyes flickered with boredom. The kind of laugh that belonged to a woman used to playing a role.

Her dress was deep green, satin hugging her curves in a way that made Benji's chest tighten. Her golden hair cascaded over one shoulder, curls perfectly arranged.

She looked like she belonged here.

And then—her gaze lifted.

Benji felt the air shift.

For a moment, everything else faded.

The music, the laughter, the weight of the world around them—all of it disappeared.

Jessica's lips parted slightly, her gaze running over him in quiet surprise.

Recognition flickered in her eyes.

Benji saw the exact moment she remembered.

The street. The bag. Their hands brushing.

And then—she smiled.

It was small. Just the faintest curve of her lips.

But it was there.

Benji swallowed hard, suddenly aware of how tight his uniform felt against his chest.

What the hell was he doing?

Jessica's eyes lingered on him for a heartbeat longer before she turned her attention back to the man speaking beside her.

But something in her posture had changed.

She wasn't listening anymore.

Sam clapped a hand on Benji's shoulder, jolting him back to reality. "You see what I see?"

Benji blinked. "What?"

Sam grinned, nodding toward the center of the ballroom. "A whole lotta women who don't know what they're missin."

Tex chuckled. "Oh Lord, here we go."

Ace smirked. "This is about to be real entertaining."

Benji exhaled, shaking off the moment.

Jessica Shaw was off-limits.

He knew that.

And yet, as he stepped further into the ballroom, he could still feel the weight of her gaze on him.

Even when she wasn't looking.

Even when she was smiling at another man.

Even when he told himself he should forget her.

Somehow, he already knew—this was just the beginning.

The evening had settled into an easy rhythm—for everyone except Benji.

The band played smooth, sultry jazz, couples swayed across the dance floor, and clusters of officers mingled with politicians and their daughters. The air was thick with perfume, cigar smoke, and the undertone of something else—tension, quiet but present.

Benji stood near the edge of the room with Sam, Tex, and Ace, a glass of untouched punch in his hand. He could feel the weight of Captain Desmond's gaze drifting across the ballroom every so often, always watchful, always assessing.

Tex leaned in. "Man, these folks don't even try to hide it. We're damn near a sideshow act."

Sam let out a low chuckle. "You surprised?"

Benji wasn't. But that didn't mean it didn't get under his skin.

He tried to push the discomfort aside, focusing instead on the music, the low hum of conversation, the crystal chandeliers gleaming overhead. His gaze skimmed the room—and landed on her.

Jessica.

She stood near the dance floor, her back straight, a polite smile on her lips as she listened to some lieutenant ramble on. But her eyes... they weren't really there.

Benji could tell she wasn't interested.

And yet, the lieutenant—a tall, square-jawed soldier with the arrogance of a man who never heard "no" a day in his life—didn't seem to care.

Benji watched as the man leaned in, saying something low, something meant only for Jessica.

She shifted, offering another forced smile, taking a half-step back. The lieutenant's hand shot out, curling around her wrist.

Benji moved before he could think.

His body just... reacted.

He cut across the ballroom, the confidence in his stride making it seem like he belonged, like he was just another officer going to claim his dance.

The lieutenant barely had time to register his presence before Benji reached out and grasped Jessica's free hand.

"Excuse me, but I believe the lady promised me a dance."

Jessica's eyes widened slightly.

For a second, just a second, the world stilled.

Benji felt the heat of her skin against his palm, the slight tremble in her fingers. But when he looked up, there was something else in her eyes—relief.

She didn't resist.

She let him lead her onto the dance floor.

The lieutenant scowled, his grip tightening for half a second before he let go, stepping back with a muttered curse.

Benji didn't look back.

The moment they reached the center of the floor, the band shifted into a slow, swaying melody.

Benji turned to her, one hand settling gently on the curve of her waist, the other still holding her hand.

Jessica hesitated for the briefest moment. Then—she stepped closer.

Her other hand found his shoulder, her touch featherlight but grounding.

Benji inhaled.

She smelled like lavender and something sweeter, something uniquely her.

His pulse hammered in his ears, but his body moved instinctively. They swayed, turning with the rhythm, feet brushing lightly against the polished marble.

He felt eyes on them. Hundreds of them.

Whispers. Gasps. Stares that burned.

But Jessica? She wasn't looking at anyone else.

She was looking at him.

"That was bold," she murmured, her voice barely above the music.

Benji smirked. "I figured you could use the save."

Her lips parted, her grip on his shoulder tightening just slightly. "I didn't need saving."

Benji raised an eyebrow. "No?"

Jessica exhaled softly, her gaze dropping to his chest. "No."

But she didn't pull away.

He felt the warmth of her through the fabric of his uniform, the delicate but firm pressure of her fingers in his.

It was reckless.

It was dangerous.

It was the most natural thing in the world.

Benji's voice dropped lower. "Tell me to stop, and I will."

Jessica's breath caught.

Her eyes lifted to his.

She didn't say a word.

From the sidelines, the reaction was immediate.

Women whispered behind gloved hands.

Men frowned, their jaws tightening.

A few officers chuckled in disbelief. The audacity.

Tex muttered under his breath. "That boy's got a death wish."

Sam, however, grinned.

"That's my boy."

Ace shook his head, a smirk tugging at his lips. "They're gonna have to drag him outta here."

And near the entrance, standing stiff and silent, Senator Shaw watched.

His fingers curled around the glass of bourbon in his hand, the ice shifting as he clenched his jaw.

His expression didn't change, but his eyes darkened.

He turned slightly, locking eyes with Captain Desmond, who had been watching the scene unfold with unreadable intensity.

Desmond's jaw ticked. He exhaled slowly, then began making his way across the room.

Benji didn't see him.

Didn't see anything except Jessica.

The Breaking Point

The song began to slow.

Benji loosened his hold just slightly, his fingers brushing against the silk of her dress.

Jessica was breathing unevenly, her lips slightly parted.

Neither of them spoke.

Neither of them moved away.

Then—the moment shattered.

A sharp voice cut through the air.

"Jessica."

She flinched.

Benji turned his head just as Senator Shaw stepped forward, his expression perfectly composed, his lips pulled into the ghost of a smile.

But his eyes were cold.

The music died.

The whispers grew louder.

Jessica took a small, deliberate step back, her fingers slipping from Benji's.

The loss of contact felt immediate.

Shaw glanced around the ballroom, his gaze sweeping over the stunned crowd before settling back on his daughter.

"My dear, you have such a generous spirit." His voice was smooth, calculated. "Always eager to show support for the less fortunate."

Benji's blood boiled.

Jessica's face paled.

But she didn't say a word.

Desmond finally reached them, stepping in subtly, his presence heavy.

His voice was even. "Davis."

Benji knew.

The moment was over.

The damage was done.

He took a step back, his chest rising and falling with controlled breaths.

Jessica looked at him—really looked at him.

For one fleeting moment, he saw something in her eyes.

Something that made his heart pound.

Something like regret.

Then, just as quickly, she turned away.

Senator Shaw extended his arm, and Jessica—**hesitating just slightly—**took it.

She let him lead her away.

The whispers grew into murmurs. The tension thickened.

Benji exhaled slowly, his hands clenching into fists.

He should leave.

He should walk away.

He should forget her.

But as he watched her disappear into the crowd, he already knew—he never would.

CHAPTER 6:

THE NOTE & A MIDNIGHT MEETING

November 1941 – Tuskegee, Alabama

"What the hell were you thinking, Davis?"

Captain Desmond Wright's voice cut through the low murmur of the barracks, sharp and filled with barely restrained anger. The dim overhead light flickered, casting long shadows over the bunks, but the weight of the captain's glare was what truly bore down on Benji.

Benji stood at attention, jaw tight, his body still buzzing from the events of the evening.

Desmond took a step closer, lowering his voice but not the intensity behind it. "You represent every single man in this program. And you think it's smart to put your hands on the senator's daughter? In a room full of men who'd love nothing more than to see you fail or worse?" His voice was tight, sharp as steel.

Benji held his ground. He wasn't foolish enough to argue, but he wasn't about to apologize for what felt like the most natural thing in the world.

Desmond let out a slow breath, shaking his head. "You've got a gift, Davis. You're one of the best pilots I've ever seen. But one more stunt like that, and you're out. Do you understand me?"

Benji nodded. "Yes, sir."

Desmond studied him a moment longer before exhaling sharply. "Get inside. Lay low." He stepped back, eyes still stormy. "And stay the hell out of trouble."

Benji turned and walked into the barracks, where a dozen pairs of eyes flicked toward him, some amused, others wary.

Sam, stretched across his bunk with his arms behind his head, let out a low whistle. "Damn, Flyboy. You sure know how to make an impression."

Tex chuckled, shaking his head. "That was some real cowboy shit you pulled, Davis."

Ace smirked. "Gotta admit, it was entertaining. Didn't think you had it in you."

Benji ignored them, shrugging off his jacket. As he did, something crinkled in the pocket. He frowned, reaching in, and pulled out a neatly folded note. His heartbeat quickened as he smoothed out the delicate script.

They say some places hold secrets. Let's make one of our own.

Midnight. The old church in Tuskegee.

His breath caught.

Jessica.

Benji exhaled slowly, staring at the words, his fingers running over the ink as if he could feel the weight of her decision, of what this meant.

This was reckless.

This was dangerous.

But he already knew—he was going.

The base was quiet when Benji slipped out, the chill of the November night settling over his skin. His steps were careful, deliberate, keeping to the edges of the airfield where the shadows stretched long beneath the moonlight.

He knew this was foolish. Knew that meeting her again, especially after what had already happened, was inviting trouble.

And yet, his feet kept moving.

The walk to the church was long enough for the weight of what he was about to do to settle in his chest. The air smelled of damp earth and cooling pine, the town of Tuskegee resting in silence beyond the hills.

Then, as he crested the final bend in the dirt road, he stopped short.

A car was parked just outside the church.

Benji's breath hitched.

It was sleek and polished, gleaming under the faint moonlight—a deep emerald-green 1941 Cadillac Series 62, its chrome reflecting the faint glow of the stars.

It didn't belong here.

His pulse quickened.

A car like that? Parked outside an abandoned church in the middle of the night? This wasn't just reckless—it was a risk.

For a split second, his instincts screamed at him to turn around.

Then, just as his pulse began to spike, something familiar drifted through the air—a soft, warm scent.

Lavender and vanilla.

Benji's heart slowed.

The fear didn't vanish, but it shifted—morphed into something else entirely.

Jessica.

He took a breath, steadying himself before stepping forward.

The church door creaked softly as he pushed it open, the warm scent of aged wood and dust filling his lungs. The space was dark except for a single candle near the altar, flickering against the stone walls.

And there she was.

Jessica stood near the front, her fingers trailing lightly over the worn edge of a pew.

She turned at the sound of the door closing behind him, her expression unreadable.

For a long moment, neither of them spoke.

"You came," she finally murmured.

Benji exhaled, stepping forward. "You asked."

Jessica's lips curved slightly, but there was something else there, something hesitant, like she wasn't sure if she should be relieved or afraid.

She took a breath. "What happened after I left?"

Benji ran a hand over his jaw. "My Captain nearly lost his damn mind."

Jessica frowned. "Because of me?"

"Because of my actions," Benji corrected.

She lowered her gaze, pressing her lips together. "I didn't think a dance would cause this much trouble."

Benji let out a short, humorless chuckle. "Neither did I."

The silence that followed was heavy, filled with all the things neither of them knew how to say.

Then, quietly, Jessica murmured, "I should thank you."

Benji tilted his head. "For what?"

"For stepping in." She looked at him, really looked at him. "You didn't have to."

Benji studied her, his voice even when he finally spoke. "And yet, here I am."

Jessica let out a small, breathy laugh, shaking her head. "You always this stubborn?"

Benji smirked. "Depends."

"On?"

"On whether or not it's worth it."

Jessica held his gaze, her eyes searching his. "And was it?"

Benji swallowed.

This was dangerous.

The way she was looking at him, the way the candlelight played against her skin, casting her in gold—it was dangerous.

But there was only one answer.

"Yeah," he said, his voice low. "It was."

Jessica inhaled softly, as if she hadn't expected him to say it out loud.

She took a step closer.

Benji didn't move.

The air between them was thick, charged with something unspoken but impossible to ignore.

Jessica swallowed. "This is reckless."

Benji's lips quirked. "So is sneaking notes into my pocket."

She shook her head, but her smile was there, barely visible, lingering at the corners of her lips.

"I don't know what I'm doing," she admitted.

Benji exhaled. "Me neither."

They stood there, in the quiet of the church, caught in something bigger than either of them.

Jessica looked up at him.

And for the first time—she didn't look away.

Jessica ran her fingers along the smooth wooden pew, tracing the faint carvings left behind by hands long before hers. The air inside the church was thick with stillness, dust lingering in the candlelight, untouched by time.

Benji sat across from her, elbows resting on his knees, fingers laced together. He wasn't sure why he came. Maybe it was curiosity. Maybe it was something else—something he wasn't ready to name.

Jessica tilted her head slightly, studying him like he was something rare. "You're quiet."

Benji exhaled through his nose. "Ain't much to say."

Jessica gave a small, knowing smile. "I don't believe that."

Benji arched a brow. "You don't know me."

Jessica shrugged. "Not yet."

Silence stretched between them. Not awkward. Just… there.

Benji shifted slightly, glancing around the abandoned church. The candle flickered between them, its warm glow casting long shadows against the stone walls.

"How'd you know this church was here?" he finally asked.

Jessica hesitated, her fingers stilling against the wood. "Josephine."

Benji frowned slightly. "Your housemaid?"

Jessica nodded. "She brought me here once when I was younger. Said it used to be a place of refuge, a shelter when people had nowhere else to go."

Benji let that settle. "Still feels like that."

Jessica studied him. "Did you grow up in a church?"

Benji gave a small smirk. "More than I wanted to."

Jessica's lips curved. "Let me guess—your father's a preacher?"

Benji chuckled. "Something like that." He exhaled. "Elijah Davis. Reverend and a crop duster. Always said faith and flying weren't that different."

Jessica's brows lifted slightly. "How so?"

Benji glanced at the candlelight, voice thoughtful. "You gotta trust in something bigger than yourself. Whether it's God or the wind beneath your wings."

Jessica absorbed that, rolling his words over in her mind. "I think I'd like your father."

Benji smirked. "He'd take some convincing."

Jessica grinned. "I can be convincing."

Benji leaned back slightly, watching her. She wasn't like other girls he'd met—not in the way she carried herself, but in the way she listened. Really listened.

"What about your family?" he asked.

Jessica exhaled slowly, fingers playing with the delicate pearl bracelet on her wrist. "My mother expects me to be perfect."

Benji smirked. "Seems like you already are."

Jessica scoffed, shaking her head. "Not in the way she wants."

Benji tilted his head. "What does she want?"

Jessica hesitated, then answered carefully. "To marry well. To be the kind of woman who hosts luncheons and knows how to smile without saying too much."

Benji's smirk faded. "And what do you want?"

Jessica's fingers curled slightly against the pew. "I want to be a lawyer."

Benji blinked, caught off guard. "A lawyer?"

Jessica's lips twitched. "What? You don't think I can do it?"

Benji shook his head. "Nah, just didn't expect it."

Jessica arched an eyebrow. "Because I wear pearls and go to tea parties?"

Benji chuckled. "Something like that."

Jessica's smirk softened into something more thoughtful. "I see how things are, Benji. And I know they won't change unless someone makes them." She hesitated, then admitted, "I want to be that someone."

Benji studied her, the firelight flickering in her blue eyes.

"You'd make a fine lawyer," he said, voice steady.

Jessica's breath caught slightly.

"You're the second person to tell me that," she murmured.

Benji lifted a brow. "Who was the first?"

Jessica hesitated. "Richard."

Benji exhaled sharply, nodding. "That the fella your folks want you with?"

Jessica's expression flickered. "Something like that."

Benji sat back slightly, watching her. He had spent his life fighting against what the world told him he could and couldn't do. It had never occurred to him that Jessica Shaw might be fighting her own war.

Jessica sighed, voice softer. "I envy you."

Benji frowned. "Why?"

"Because you know what you want," she said simply. "You don't let anyone tell you different."

Benji let out a short, humorless laugh. "Ain't that simple."

Jessica tilted her head. "Isn't it?"

Benji exhaled, running a hand over his jaw. "Maybe."

Jessica's gaze held his. "Do you love flying?"

Benji nodded. "Yeah."

Jessica studied him. "You should be proud of that."

Benji arched an eyebrow. "Of what?"

Jessica tilted her head slightly. "Of knowing what you want. Of being free."

Benji was quiet for a moment. "Ain't free, Jessica."

Jessica's lips parted slightly.

Benji exhaled. "Sky don't care about color. But the world does." He looked at her, voice low. "Men like me, we don't get to fly forever."

Jessica's throat tightened. "That's not fair."

Benji's jaw clenched. "It ain't about fair."

Jessica hesitated, then softly asked, "So why do it?"

Benji was quiet for a long moment. Then, finally, he said, "Because I'd rather fly for a little while than never at all."

Jessica swallowed, something aching in her chest.

Benji shook his head, giving a small smirk. "Didn't mean to go getting all heavy on you."

Jessica smiled. "I don't mind."

Benji watched her. She wasn't just talking. She meant it.

Jessica exhaled, then carefully asked, "Can I ask you something?"

Benji lifted an eyebrow. "Didn't stop you before."

Jessica grinned. "What's it like? Flying?"

Benji leaned back slightly, tilting his head in thought.

"It's like—" He exhaled, shaking his head. "It's like nothing else."

Jessica smirked. "That's a terrible description."

Benji chuckled. "Ain't something you can explain. It's... freedom. It's weightless. Like the world can't touch you."

Jessica's expression softened. "I'd like to see that."

Benji studied her. "Maybe you will."

Jessica tilted her head, curious. "Will you teach me?"

Benji blinked, caught off guard.

Jessica smirked. "If I'm going to be a lawyer, I should probably learn to fly first. It might be easier."

Benji laughed, shaking his head. "You're something else."

Jessica grinned. "So I've been told."

She exhaled, then stood slowly. "Will you meet me here again tomorrow?"

Benji hesitated for a moment before nodding once.

Jessica smiled, stepping toward him. "Good."

She reached into her pocket, pulling out a small folded piece of paper.

She slid it into his palm, her fingers brushing against his.

Benji frowned slightly. "What's this?"

Jessica smirked. "Something to remember me by."

With that, she turned and walked out, leaving the scent of her perfume behind.

Benji exhaled, looking down at the note.

Unfolding it, his eyes scanned the words written in elegant, looping script.

"Some things in life are worth the risk. I think you might be one of them."

Benji swallowed, chest tightening.

He folded the note carefully, slipping it into his pocket.

He should walk away.

But as he stared at the empty doorway where Jessica had been—

He already knew he wouldn't.

The morning sun burned hot against the Alabama sky, casting long, sharp shadows across the airfield. The weight of exhaustion pulled at Benji's limbs as he shoveled gravel onto the dusty road leading up to the barracks, his muscles aching from the relentless labor he'd been assigned. Sweat dripped from his brow, mixing with the dust that clung to his skin.

He should have been up in the air, feeling the wind push against his plane, the adrenaline of flight coursing through his veins. But instead, he was here, doing grunt work like a common recruit.

All because he couldn't resist dancing with Jessica.

Captain Desmond had been furious that morning, his face a mask of restrained anger as he had delivered Benji's punishment in front of the entire unit.

"You think you can act like a damn fool in front of Montgomery's elite and not face consequences? You've just made yourself a target, Davis. A target for people who don't want you flying. A target for people who would love to see you fail."

Benji had swallowed hard, taking the reprimand without argument. There was no point. He knew Desmond was right.

So now he was grounded from flying for the rest of the week and assigned extra duties—manual labor around the base, cleaning the barracks, and running errands like a low-ranked recruit. It was humiliating, but he had no choice but to take it.

As he heaved another pile of gravel onto the road, he heard footsteps approaching.

"Davis!"

Benji turned to see one of the lieutenants standing a few feet away, arms crossed. "Captain Wright wants to see you in his office. Now."

Benji dropped the shovel, wiping the sweat from his brow, and nodded. He didn't need to be told twice.

When Benji stepped into Captain Desmond Wright's office, the door clicked shut behind him, sealing them off from the noise outside. Desmond stood by the window, staring out at the airfield, arms folded tightly against his chest. His piercing blue eyes flickered toward Benji, unreadable.

For a long moment, the only sound in the room was the faint hum of the overhead fan.

Then Desmond spoke.

"Sit."

Benji obeyed, lowering himself into the wooden chair across from Desmond's desk, his posture stiff.

Desmond let out a slow breath and finally turned to face him fully. "You've got some explaining to do."

Benji clenched his jaw. "I wasn't trying to cause trouble, sir."

Desmond scoffed. "Then you have a funny way of showing it." He leaned forward, resting his hands on the desk. "Dancing with a white girl at the Governor's Mansion? In front of military officers and politicians? You don't think that was trouble?"

Benji met his gaze. "I wasn't thinking about all that."

"No, you weren't," Desmond said sharply. "You were thinking with your damn heart. And while that might serve you well in the air, it'll get you killed down here on the ground."

Benji's hands balled into fists on his lap. "I know the risks."

Desmond's expression hardened. "Do you? Because from where I'm standing, you just made a mistake that could cost you your career. Maybe even your life." He exhaled sharply, shaking his head. "Damn it, Davis. You grew up here. You know the rules. You know how this world works."

Benji felt a sharp pang of frustration rise in his chest. "That's the problem, Captain. I know the rules, but I don't want to live by them."

Desmond studied him for a long moment before sighing. He turned back toward the window, rubbing his jaw. "I get it."

Benji blinked, surprised.

Desmond let out a dry chuckle. "You think I don't understand? That I don't know what it feels like to be looked at like you don't belong?" He shook his head. "My mother was a Black woman from Harlem. My father was a white banker from New York. I was never white enough to fit in with his world and never Black enough to be fully accepted in hers. I spent my whole damn life feeling like I had to prove I was worth a damn."

Benji sat up straighter, absorbing Desmond's words.

Desmond turned back to him, his blue eyes sharp. "But I'll tell you what my father told me when I was young. He said, 'Son, you fight your battles where they count.'" He pointed toward the window. "Up there? That's your battlefield. That's where you make your name. Not in some damn ballroom, dancing with a girl you can't have."

Benji's stomach twisted. He didn't like hearing it, but deep down, he knew Desmond wasn't wrong.

Desmond sighed, rubbing a hand over his face. "Look, Davis. You're one of the best young pilots I've seen. Hell, you might just be the best the one day. But you need to be smarter. The world is already waiting for you to slip up. Don't give them a reason to clip your wings before you even take off."

Benji swallowed hard and nodded. "I understand, sir."

Desmond studied him a moment longer, then nodded. "Good. Now get out of my office. And keep your damn head down."

Benji stood, offering a sharp salute before turning to leave.

Just before he stepped out the door, Desmond's voice stopped him.

"And Davis?"

Benji turned back.

Desmond's expression softened just slightly. "Be careful."

Benji met his gaze, then nodded. "Yes, sir."

With that, he stepped out into the scorching Alabama sun, the weight of his choices settling heavy on his shoulders.

And deep down, despite Desmond's warning, he knew this wasn't over.

Not by a long shot.

CHAPTER 7:
THE DAY THE WORLD CHANGED

December 7, 1941 – Montgomery, Alabama

Two Weeks of Secret Meetings – Falling in Deeper

Jessica sat at her vanity, brushing her hair in long, slow strokes, the candlelight flickering against the delicate frame of her mirror. Her mother had already gone to bed, her father locked in his study, absorbed in some political discussion with his colleagues. The house was quiet, but inside Jessica's mind, there was nothing but noise.

Noise in the form of him.

For the past two weeks, she had been meeting Benji at the abandoned church in Tuskegee, slipping away under the guise of charity work. It had started with hesitant conversations—questions about their lives, their dreams, their fears. But somewhere along the way, it had become so much more.

He made her laugh. He made her think. He made her feel alive.

She never thought she would care for someone like him, let alone fall so fast, but every night they spent together made it harder to pretend that this wasn't real. That this wasn't dangerous.

And yet, she couldn't stop herself.

Her fingers traced the edges of the most recent letter he had slipped into her coat pocket the night before. She unfolded it carefully, her eyes scanning the words she had already memorized.

"Jessica,

I used to think nothing could compare to flying, but now I know what it's like to fall.

I think about you more than I should. More than I'm allowed to. I don't know what's happening between us, but I don't want it to stop. Do you?"

Her breath caught in her throat as she reread the last line.

Do you?

Jessica swallowed, staring at the words.

She already knew the answer.

The next morning, Jessica sat in the kitchen, absently stirring her tea as Josephine moved about, preparing breakfast. The familiar scent of biscuits and coffee filled the space, but Jessica wasn't paying attention.

Josephine noticed. She always did.

"You look troubled, baby girl," she said, setting down a plate of eggs and bacon in front of Jessica.

Jessica hesitated, then bit her lip. "Josephine... have you ever been in love?"

Josephine arched an eyebrow, pausing as she wiped her hands on her apron. "Now that's a loaded question," she said, tilting her head. "Why you askin'?"

Jessica hesitated, staring down at her teacup. "I... I think I might be."

Josephine's expression softened, but there was an unmistakable wariness behind her eyes. "And does this love have a name?"

Jessica swallowed hard. She had never outright told Josephine about Benji, but she wasn't a fool. Josephine had always been able to read her better than anyone.

"It doesn't matter," Jessica said quickly, shaking her head. "I just... I don't know what to do."

Josephine exhaled, setting a hand on her hip. "Love ain't easy. Especially not your kind of love."

Jessica flinched. "What do you mean, my kind?"

Josephine gave her a knowing look. "Jessica, you ain't blind. You know what happens in this town when folks step out of line."

Jessica clenched her hands in her lap. "I don't care what people think."

Josephine sighed, sitting down across from her. "Maybe you don't. But the world still does."

Jessica met her gaze, something stubborn in her expression. "I can't stop thinking about him," she admitted in a whisper.

Josephine's eyes softened. "Then you best be careful, baby girl. Because once you start down this road, there ain't no turnin' back."

Jessica nodded, pressing her lips together. She already knew that.

She just didn't realize how soon that truth would come crashing down.

That afternoon, Jessica had just settled into her father's study, flipping through one of his law books when she heard the shouting.

At first, she thought it was just another one of her father's heated discussions. But then she heard the urgency—the panic.

She rushed to the sitting room, where the radio was on full volume.

"We interrupt this broadcast with breaking news—The United States naval base at Pearl Harbor has been attacked by Japanese forces. Multiple battleships have been destroyed. Casualties are unknown, but reports indicate severe losses. President Roosevelt is expected to address the nation…"

Jessica's stomach dropped.

Her mother stood frozen, a hand to her chest, while her father clenched his jaw, pacing back and forth.

"That bastard Roosevelt knew this was coming," Senator Shaw growled, running a hand through his graying hair. "We're going to war."

War.

The word sent a chill through Jessica's spine.

Her heart lurched. Benji.

He had been training to be a fighter pilot for the Army Air Corps. Would he be sent overseas now? Would he be in danger?

She turned away from her father and rushed to her room, slamming the door behind her. Her hands trembled as she reached for her writing desk, grabbing her diary.

She flipped to an empty page, her breath uneven as she began to write.

Jessica's Diary Entry

December 7, 1941

Today, everything changed.

The world as I know it isn't the same anymore. America is at war. And Benji—

I don't even know if he's heard yet. But he will. And then what?

What happens to us?

I keep telling myself I'm not afraid. That I won't let the world dictate how I live, who I love. But right now, sitting here, all I feel is fear.

I think about the way he looks at me, like I'm something to be treasured. Like I matter beyond my last name, beyond my father's ambitions.

I think about the way I feel when I'm with him. Light. Free. Alive.

But is this foolish? Is it selfish? To keep meeting him in secret, to pretend like time isn't slipping away from us?

I don't want to say goodbye. Not yet. Not ever.

But war doesn't care about what I want.

Jessica's hand trembled as she closed the diary, her chest tightening.

She had planned to meet him tonight. She needed to see him, to hear his voice, to know that this wasn't over.

Tucking the diary away in her drawer, she stood, smoothing out her dress.

She had to get to Tuskegee.

She had to see Benji.

December 7, 1941 – Tuskegee Army Airfield, Alabama

The mess hall was unusually loud for a Sunday. Pilots and cadets were eating, talking, and joking, the tension of training briefly forgotten over trays of food.

Benji sat beside Sam, half-listening to Tex and Ace argue about some girl Tex had met in town.

"She was lookin' at me the whole time," Tex was saying, stabbing his fork into his cornbread.

Ace scoffed. "Man, she was probably wondering if you were gonna eat her whole damn plate, not just yours."

Laughter erupted from around the table. Tex muttered something under his breath, shaking his head as he took another bite of food. Benji smirked, about to make a comment himself, when—

The doors slammed open.

The sound of boots echoed as Major Spencer strode inside.

Instant silence.

"All pilots, to the hangar. Now."

That was all he said before turning on his heel and marching out.

Benji felt something tighten in his chest. He glanced at Sam, who was already pushing his tray away, his face serious. Across the table, Tex and Ace exchanged looks but wasted no time following orders.

The air outside felt different—charged. The men moved toward the hangar in tense silence, their boots crunching against the dirt.

By the time they arrived, dozens of airmen were already gathered, their faces tight with unease. The massive steel doors had been pulled open, sunlight flooding the space, illuminating the sleek, lined rows of aircraft.

Benji took his place beside Sam, standing at attention.

Then, Major Spencer stepped forward. And he spoke.

"This morning, at 7:55 a.m. Hawaiian time, the Japanese launched a surprise attack on Pearl Harbor."

A sharp inhale rippled through the crowd.

Benji's stomach dropped.

"Thousands of American servicemen are dead," Spencer continued. "Our battleships, our airfields—they hit everything. We are now at war."

The words rang out, settling deep into the bones of every man standing there.

War.

It was no longer just training. No longer just preparation. This was real.

Spencer's gaze swept over the assembled men, pausing briefly on the Tuskegee pilots.

"Some of you will be deployed. Some of you won't. We'll see what happens."

Benji saw the flicker of disdain in his eyes. We'll see.

"We are waiting on further orders from Washington," Spencer continued. "Until then, you will remain in training and follow every protocol to the letter. Dismissed."

Benji let out a slow breath. Sam exhaled beside him, his expression unreadable.

Then—

"Davis!"

Benji stiffened.

"Captain's office. Now."

The men around him shifted, murmuring among themselves. Sam shot him a sharp look, but Benji didn't respond. He squared his shoulders and walked toward the captain's quarters.

The air inside the office felt thick.

Benji stood at attention in front of Captain Desmond's desk.

Major Spencer leaned against the bookshelf, arms crossed. His smirk was sharp, cutting.

"You know why you're here, Davis?"

Benji clenched his jaw. "Yes, sir."

Spencer scoffed. "I bet you do."

Desmond exhaled slowly, rubbing his temple before fixing Benji with a hard stare. "Sit down."

Benji hesitated, then lowered himself into the chair across from Desmond's desk.

Desmond leaned forward, folding his hands together. "We received a call this morning. Your friend's father isn't too happy about what happened at the governor's mansion last month."

Benji didn't flinch, but his stomach twisted. Shaw.

Desmond's jaw tightened. "Senator Shaw called a contact in the military. He wants you out. Permanently."

Spencer let out a sharp laugh. "I'd say I'm surprised, but I'm not."

Benji swallowed hard, forcing himself to stay still.

Desmond tapped a folder on his desk. "I fought to keep you here, Davis. Again. But I need you to understand something—my hands are tied. If you so much as blink in the wrong direction, they'll have you gone."

Benji exhaled slowly. "Yes, sir."

Spencer shook his head. "I don't think you get it. You're hanging by a damn thread, boy."

Desmond's eyes flickered with warning, but he didn't correct him.

Benji met Spencer's gaze. "With all due respect, sir, I won't waste this opportunity."

Spencer let out a sharp, humorless chuckle. "We'll see about that."

Desmond leaned back in his chair. "You're grounded for another week. No flight time. Extra duties. You'll work in the hangar and assist maintenance crews."

Benji swallowed his frustration and nodded. "Yes, sir."

Desmond exhaled sharply. "Dismissed."

Benji stood, turned on his heel, and walked out of the office.

The cold December air hit him like a slap.

He stared out at the base, his heart hammering in his chest.

One more mistake, and he'd lose everything.

Benji's fists ached. His knuckles were raw from hours of scrubbing grease off engine parts, and his body was exhausted from extra duty. Every muscle in his frame protested as he walked across the base toward the exit gate, pulling his jacket tighter against the cold night air.

Grounded. Again.

The weight of it sat heavy on his chest. His flight training had been delayed for a week, but it might as well have been an eternity. War had officially begun, and if they were deploying soon, he needed every minute in the air. But thanks to Senator Shaw, he was stuck doing grunt work while his squad mates advanced.

He needed to clear his head.

There was a little Black-owned convenience store just off base, one he and Sam had been to a few times. It was nothing fancy—just a single-room store run by an older man named Mr. Carter, who always had a soft spot for the young airmen.

Benji figured he'd grab a soda, maybe some peanuts, and walk back. Anything to cool off before returning to the barracks.

He adjusted his collar and stepped through the door.

The little bell above the entrance jingled, and the scent of wood polish and tobacco filled the air.

Mr. Carter looked up from behind the counter. His face, weathered with age, broke into a knowing smile.

"Benjamin Davis," he greeted. "Ain't seen you in a while, son."

Benji nodded, shoving his hands into his pockets. "Been busy, Mr. Carter."

"I'll bet," Carter mused, wiping his hands on a rag. "Y'all heading to war now, huh?"

Benji hesitated, then nodded. "Not sure."

Carter sighed, rubbing his jaw. "Ain't right. Ain't fair." He leaned in slightly. "But you? You one of the best pilots I done heard of. You make sure them bastards don't forget that."

Benji managed a small smile.

He walked toward the back, grabbed a cold soda from the icebox, and brought it to the counter. He fished a few coins from his pocket and set them down.

Carter pushed them back.

"This one's on me," he said. "For luck."

Benji hesitated. "Appreciate it, sir."

Carter nodded. "You be careful out there, boy."

Benji turned, pushing the door open—

And stopped.

A truck was parked across the street.

Three white men stood beside it, smoking cigarettes, their eyes locked onto him the second he stepped outside.

His stomach tightened.

He knew that look.

They had been waiting for him.

Benji's grip tightened around the glass bottle in his hand as he stepped onto the dirt road.

"Hey, boy!"

The voice came from one of the men—broad-shouldered, thick-necked, a smirk curling his lips.

"Thought you was special, huh?"

Benji kept walking.

Boots scuffed against gravel.

He had almost reached the main road when—

A hand snatched his collar.

Benji whipped around, his fist slamming into the man's jaw.

The man staggered, cursing.

The second man lunged.

Benji ducked, his instincts sharp, years of backyard scraps with Marcus kicking in. He drove his shoulder into the man's ribs, sending him back, but the third came from the side—

A punch cracked against his temple.

Benji stumbled, vision blurring, but didn't fall.

He turned, swinging, his knuckles colliding with another man's face. Blood spurted from the man's nose as he cursed and reeled backward.

Then a boot connected with Benji's stomach.

The air rushed out of his lungs.

He dropped to a knee, gasping, but forced himself up just in time for another hit to his ribs.

His world spun.

The first man grabbed him by the jacket, pulling him forward—

"You think you can just dance with our women?" he spat. "Like you belong?"

Another fist crashed into his jaw.

Blood filled Benji's mouth.

But he fought.

He swung wild, connecting with one of their ribs. He twisted, shoving another back, using every bit of strength left in his body.

But there were too many of them.

A fist to his gut. A knee to his chest. More boots.

He hit the ground.

A voice—mocking, sharp—spoke above him.

"Let's see if you can still fly, nigger."

A boot slammed into his side.

Pain exploded through his ribs.

Another hit. Another.

His ears rang. His vision swam.

Then—

"HEY! GET THE HELL OFF HIM!"

The sound of a shotgun cocking cut through the night.

The men froze.

Through swollen eyes, Benji barely made out the shape of Mr. Carter, standing on the store's porch, shotgun raised.

"You best get before I start dropping bodies," Carter said, his voice like iron.

The men hesitated.

Then—they backed away.

One of them spat toward Benji, muttering, "Ain't over, boy."

Then they climbed into their truck, engine roaring to life, dust kicking up as they disappeared into the darkness.

Benji tried to push himself up, but his body wouldn't cooperate.

Pain radiated from his ribs, his face, his stomach.

Mr. Carter was suddenly there, crouching beside him.

"Gotcha, son," he murmured, slipping an arm under him.

Benji barely registered being dragged into the store.

The last thing he saw before darkness took him was the concerned face of the man who had just saved his life.

CHAPTER 8:

THE AFTERMATH

December 8, 1941 – Tuskegee Army Air
Field, Alabama

Benji's body ached like hell.

His ribs screamed with every breath, his jaw was tight with swelling, and one of his eyes refused to open. His knuckles were raw, torn open from the fight, and his head throbbed with a dull, punishing rhythm.

But despite the pain, despite the bruises and dried blood, his pride remained intact.

They hadn't broken him.

The infirmary smelled like antiseptic, and the dim overhead light buzzed faintly. The room was quiet, save for the occasional cough from another soldier a few beds down. Benji shifted, wincing as pain flared up his side.

"Don't move too much," a voice said.

Benji turned his head slightly, wincing as Captain Desmond Wright stood at the foot of the bed, arms crossed. His usually sharp uniform was slightly wrinkled, as if he had been sitting for too long. His face was unreadable, but his blue eyes burned with something fierce.

Concern. Anger.

Benji exhaled through his nose. "How bad do I look?"

Desmond arched a brow. "Like you went ten rounds and lost."

Benji smirked, though it hurt like hell. "Ain't lose. Just got outnumbered."

Desmond's jaw tightened. "Who?"

Benji hesitated. He could lie. He could tell Desmond it was just a random bar fight or some drunks looking for trouble. But looking at him now, Benji knew Desmond already knew.

"They were waiting for me outside Carter's store," Benji admitted. "Three of 'em."

Desmond exhaled, rubbing his fingers along his jaw. His silence was more telling than words.

"Did you fight back?"

Benji scoffed. "What do you think?"

Desmond's lips twitched, but there was no amusement in it. "And yet, you ended up here."

Benji clenched his teeth. "I put two of them down before the third cracked me over the head with something." His fingers curled into the sheets. "Cowards."

Desmond was quiet for a long moment.

"You should've expected this," he finally said.

Benji turned his bruised face toward him. "That why you had me scrubbing engines for a week?" His voice was hoarse, but there was no bitterness in it.

Desmond held his gaze. "No. I did that because I needed you to understand the weight of your actions. But this?" He gestured at Benji's beaten body. "This is why I told you to be careful."

Benji exhaled sharply through his nose. "So what? I just let them do this?"

Desmond's eyes darkened. "No," he said, his voice dropping low. "You rise above it."

Benji's pulse thumped in his ears.

"You're not some kid from Montgomery anymore, Davis. You're a soldier. A damn good one. And you need to act like it." Desmond's gaze bored into him. "You think they win if you fight back in the streets? No. They win if they take this from you. If they strip you of your future."

Benji swallowed hard, gripping the thin blanket covering him.

Desmond's voice softened just a fraction. "I know what this feels like."

Benji blinked, caught off guard.

Desmond exhaled, stepping closer, his expression unreadable. "You think I don't know what it's like to be hated for what I am? To be told I don't belong? My father was white, my mother Black. You know what that made me?" He leaned in slightly. "An outcast in both worlds."

Benji stared at him. He had never heard Desmond talk about himself. Not like this.

"I was never white enough for one side. Never Black enough for the other. Too light-skinned for some, too dark for others." Desmond's lips curled slightly, but it wasn't a smile. "You think I don't know what it's like to walk into a room and know damn well half the people in there don't respect you? That they're just waiting for you to fail?"

Benji swallowed.

Desmond straightened. "You think you're the only one who's had to prove himself?"

Silence stretched between them.

Finally, Benji shook his head. "No, sir."

Desmond nodded, satisfied. "Good." He stepped back. "Because you're gonna have to keep proving yourself. Every single day."

Benji exhaled. He already knew that.

Desmond's tone hardened. "Now listen to me, Davis. You're gonna get out of this bed, you're gonna get back to training, and you're gonna be better than every single man out there. Because that's the only way you win."

Benji's jaw tightened. "Yes, sir."

Desmond's gaze lingered for a moment before he gave a small nod.

"Good. Now rest up."

He turned, striding toward the door. But before he stepped out, he paused.

"Oh, and Davis?"

Benji glanced up.

Desmond smirked slightly. "I don't care how bruised up you are—you're still on latrine duty for a week."

Benji groaned, letting his head fall back against the pillow. "Damn, Captain."

Desmond chuckled under his breath. "Welcome to the Army."

And with that, he walked out.

Outside the Infirmary – The Others React

Desmond stepped into the hallway, his face unreadable.

Standing nearby were Sam, Tex, and Ace.

Sam's fists were clenched at his sides. "How bad is he?"

Desmond sighed. "He's alive."

Tex crossed his arms. "Who did it?"

Desmond didn't answer. He didn't have to.

Ace cursed under his breath. "Damn bastards."

"No," Desmond said. "They're cowards." He exhaled. "And Davis handled himself. Put two of them down before they got him."

Sam swallowed, his hands trembling slightly. "I should've been there."

Desmond's expression softened slightly. "No, you shouldn't have."

Sam looked up sharply.

Desmond continued. "Because if you were, they would've killed both of you."

Sam flinched.

Tex exhaled through his nose, his large frame rigid. "What now?"

Desmond's jaw tightened. "Now?" His voice was low. Controlled. Dangerous. "Now we make sure they don't win."

Sam's throat worked as he swallowed again. He nodded slowly, forcing the anger down.

Desmond looked over at them. "He'll be back to training in a couple of days."

Tex let out a long breath, shaking his head. "They don't stop, do they?"

"No," Desmond said. "They don't."

Ace muttered under his breath, shaking his head. "Damn shame. Boy just wants to fly."

Desmond's expression hardened. "Then we make sure he does."

Benji sat on the edge of his cot, rolling his sore shoulder. The bruises were still deep, still a constant reminder of what had happened outside that store. He shifted slightly, the dull ache in his ribs flaring up.

It wasn't the worst beating he'd ever taken.

But it was the one that mattered the most.

Sam sat across from him, still tossing that damn baseball in the air, catching it effortlessly before tossing it again. His expression was tight, eyes sharp.

"You gonna tell me what the hell is goin' on with you?" he finally asked.

Benji exhaled, rubbing the back of his neck. "Ain't nothin' goin' on with me, Sam."

Sam scoffed. "Right. And I got accepted into Harvard."

Benji didn't respond.

Because what was there to say? That he had been reckless? That he had stepped out of line? That he had gotten too close to something he knew damn well he shouldn't?

"Man, you don't have to tell me everything," Sam said, voice lowering. "But you gotta tell me somethin'. You been different. Off."

Benji finally looked at him.

Sam shook his head. "I see it, Benji. And don't even try to tell me it's just the war. It's somethin' else. Someone else?"

Benji clenched his jaw.

Before he could answer, the barracks door swung open, and Ace strolled in, holding a handful of letters.

"Mail call!" he announced, tossing envelopes onto bunks as he walked by.

Benji barely looked up. He wasn't expecting anything.

Then Ace stopped in front of him, holding up a letter between two fingers with a smirk.

"Well, well, well," he drawled, eyes full of mischief. "Our little pilot is growin' up so fast."

Tex leaned over from his bunk, grinning. "What we got, Ace?"

Ace held the letter up dramatically. "Gentlemen, this here is no ordinary letter. See the delicate cursive? The soft scent of perfume? This ain't from home."

Benji snatched it before Ace could say another word.

Sam raised an eyebrow. "Damn, Davis. You got a girl already?"

Benji shot him a look before turning the letter over in his hands.

It was a light blue envelope, her handwriting unmistakable.

Jessica.

His stomach tightened.

Tex chuckled, nudging Ace. "Think we lost him, man."

"Yep," Ace nodded solemnly. "Boy's already gone."

Benji ignored them, carefully tearing the envelope open.

Tex clapped him on the shoulder before heading out, Ace following. "Don't do nothin' stupid, kid."

Once they were gone, the teasing faded into silence.

And Sam was watching him again.

"That letter got anything to do with why you been actin' different?"

Benji hesitated.

Sam shook his head, voice quieter now. "Look, man. I don't care what it is. I just... I need you to let me in."

Benji didn't answer right away.

Then, he looked down at the letter, his chest tightening.

"I ain't sure how," he admitted.

Sam nodded slowly. "Then let's figure it out together."

Benji swallowed, fingers curling around the paper.

Then, finally, he read it.

Jessica's Letter – December 10, 1941

Benji,

I wasn't sure if I should write this.

I've started and stopped this letter three times already. Every time I tell myself I'm overthinking it, that I shouldn't let my mind wander, but...

You haven't been at our spot.

And I don't know why.

Maybe I'm imagining things, but I can't help but wonder if I said something wrong. If I overstepped. If I made you uncomfortable.

I wouldn't blame you if you changed your mind. Maybe I was foolish to think this was something we could do—to think this was something we should do.

But if it's not that… if something happened… I need to know.

I won't press. I won't ask questions you don't want to answer. But if you're alright—if you still want this—I'll be waiting.

Tonight. Midnight.

– Jessica

Benji stared at the letter, his pulse pounding.

She thought he had changed his mind.

She thought he didn't want this.

She was second-guessing everything.

And he hated that.

Benji exhaled sharply, folding the letter and pressing it to his chest.

He had spent the last few nights forcing himself to stay away, telling himself it was for the best.

But none of that mattered now.

She was waiting.

And he was going.

Later That Night – Slipping Out

Benji waited until the barracks settled.

The sound of steady breathing and the occasional rustle of blankets filled the room as the other airmen drifted into sleep.

Moving quietly, he reached for his boots, slipping them on before grabbing his jacket.

As he moved toward the door, Sam's voice came low from his bunk.

"You really goin'?"

Benji didn't stop. "Yeah."

Sam sighed. "You get caught, don't expect me to bail you out."

Benji smirked, adjusting his cap. "Ain't askin' you to."

With that, he slipped out into the night.

The Night Ride to Jessica

The cold air hit his face as he made his way down the darkened path.

He knew the base patrol shifts by heart now. Knew exactly when to move, when to cut through the hangars and avoid the eyes of the MPs.

By the time he reached the main road into town, his pulse was steady, but his heart was racing for another reason.

Jessica.

She thought he had changed his mind.

She thought this—whatever this was—was over before it even really started.

She was wrong.

His pace quickened, hands clenched in his jacket pockets.

The weight of the past few days melted away with every step.

Because in a few minutes, he'd be standing in front of her again.

And nothing else mattered.

The cold night air clung to Benji's skin as he neared the church, his breath curling in the moonlight. His boots crunched softly against the dirt path, the old wooden structure standing like a ghost in the darkness.

He slowed his steps when he saw it—the faint glow of headlights parked a little ways off, the sleek, familiar shape of the Cadillac tucked beneath the shadows.

His pulse quickened.

She was here.

Jessica.

He approached the side entrance, where the heavy wooden door was cracked just enough for a sliver of golden light to spill onto the ground. He hesitated for only a moment before stepping inside.

Jessica was waiting near the front, perched on the edge of one of the old pews, her hands folded neatly in her lap. The lantern beside her flickered, casting warm light over her pale blue dress, the soft curls pinned at the nape of her neck.

At the sound of his footsteps, she turned, her hazel eyes locking onto him instantly—and then they widened.

"Oh my God."

Benji barely had time to react before she was in front of him, reaching out, but not quite touching.

"What happened to you?" she whispered, her voice sharp with worry.

Benji shifted slightly, jaw tightening. He hadn't forgotten about the bruises, but he hadn't thought they were bad enough to warrant that reaction.

"Just a misunderstanding," he muttered.

Jessica wasn't having it.

She lifted her hand, hesitated, then finally let her fingers graze the edge of his jaw, where a dark bruise had settled beneath his skin.

Benji tensed under her touch. She was so soft. So gentle.

Jessica inhaled sharply. "Who did this to you?"

Benji shook his head, forcing a smirk. "Can't go around tellin' all my secrets."

Her lips pressed together, eyes narrowing. "This isn't funny, Benjamin."

He swallowed. She had used his full name, and something about the way it rolled off her tongue made him feel completely seen in a way he wasn't sure he was ready for.

"I'm fine," he said. "I can handle myself."

Jessica's gaze swept over him, unconvinced. She saw more than he wanted her to see.

"You're lying," she said softly.

Benji exhaled, his shoulders dropping slightly. "It ain't nothin' new."

Jessica stepped back, folding her arms across her chest. "Because of me?"

Benji's head snapped up.

Jessica looked away, her expression conflicted. "Tell me the truth. Is this because of what happened at the dance?"

Benji hesitated.

She already knew the answer.

His silence said enough.

Jessica's eyes shimmered, frustration and guilt warring inside her.

Benji hated seeing that look.

"Listen to me." His voice was steady, firm, cutting through her spiraling thoughts.

Jessica glanced up.

Benji took a slow step forward, closing the space between them.

"This ain't your fault," he said, voice low, certain. "Not even a little."

Her lips parted, like she wanted to argue, but Benji didn't let her.

"They would've come for me eventually," he continued. "For any of us." He let out a small, humorless chuckle. "Hell, I've been getting in fights since I was old enough to throw a punch."

Jessica frowned. "That's not a good thing."

Benji smirked slightly. "Didn't say it was."

Jessica let out a breath, shaking her head. She still didn't look convinced.

Benji sighed, then reached out—slowly—tucking his fingers beneath her chin, tilting her face toward him.

Her eyes widened slightly, but she didn't pull away.

"Jessica," he said, his voice softer now. Lower.

She swallowed.

"You are the most beautiful woman I've ever seen," he admitted, his thumb grazing the curve of her jaw.

Jessica's breath hitched.

"I can't get you out of my mind," Benji continued. "Even when I try."

Her lips parted slightly. Her lashes fluttered.

For the first time in his life, Benji wasn't sure who was in control of the moment.

Jessica exhaled, eyes flickering between his. Searching. Questioning.

Benji stayed still.

Then, slowly, she reached up and traced her fingers down the side of his face.

Benji's heart slammed against his ribs.

Jessica's gaze dropped to his lips.

Then, before he could process what was happening—

She kissed him.

It was soft, uncertain at first, like she was testing the waters. But then, Benji responded.

And everything else ceased to exist.

His hand slid from her jaw to the back of her neck, holding her there, like he was afraid she'd vanish.

Jessica let out a soft sound against his lips, pressing herself closer, and Benji's entire body ignited.

The scent of her—Lavender and vanilla—filled his lungs, drowning him.

He deepened the kiss, just slightly, tilting his head as he brought his other hand to her waist.

Jessica didn't pull away.

If anything, she leaned in more.

The whole world blurred.

The old church. The war looming ahead. The damn bruises on his ribs.

None of it mattered.

Not in this moment.

Not with her.

When they finally broke apart, Jessica didn't move right away.

Neither did he.

Her forehead rested against his, her breath mingling with his own.

They were both shaking.

Jessica let out a soft, nervous laugh.

Benji smiled.

"Well," he murmured. "Didn't see that comin'."

Jessica grinned, eyes still closed. "Neither did I."

Benji chuckled, running his thumb over the curve of her hip.

Then, reality slowly settled back in.

Jessica pulled back slightly, her expression shifting.

Benji immediately saw it.

The uncertainty. The fear.

She stepped back fully, clearing her throat, smoothing out the front of her dress.

Benji let her go, though he hated the loss of warmth.

Jessica inhaled deeply. "I should go."

Benji nodded, rubbing a hand over the back of his neck. "Yeah… yeah, probably."

Jessica glanced toward the door, hesitating for half a second.

Then, she turned back to him.

"Meet me here again?" she asked softly.

Benji didn't even have to think about it.

"Yeah," he said. "I'll be here."

Jessica smiled. A real smile.

Then, without another word, she turned and walked out.

Benji stood there, watching her go, his fingers still tingling from where they had touched her skin.

His chest still aching from the way she had kissed him.

And for the first time since everything had started—

He didn't feel like he was drowning anymore.

He felt like he could breathe.

Even if it was only for tonight.

CHAPTER 9:

A DANGEROUS LINE

December 10, 1941 – Montgomery,
Alabama

The road stretched before her, long and dark, the headlights of the Cadillac slicing through the cold Alabama night. Jessica's fingers tightened around the steering wheel, her heart still hammering from the kiss.

Her lips tingled—a phantom reminder of what she had just done.

She had kissed Benjamin Davis.

And she had wanted to.

Desperately.

Her pulse quickened at the thought, her hands trembling slightly against the wheel.

What have I done?

She exhaled, forcing herself to focus on the road.

She knew what this was.

Danger.

A kind of danger she had never touched before, never even considered.

And yet, the second she had pressed her lips to his, it hadn't felt wrong.

It had felt inevitable.

Jessica bit her lower lip, her thoughts running wild.

If anyone ever found out…

She shook her head, pushing the thought away.

She had enough to worry about.

And yet, she couldn't stop replaying it.

The way his hands had felt on her waist. The quiet, almost reverent way he had whispered her name.

The way he had kissed her back, as if he had been waiting for her just as much as she had been waiting for him.

Jessica swallowed, heat rising to her cheeks.

She shouldn't be smiling. She shouldn't be excited.

But she was.

She was.

Her foot pressed a little heavier on the gas, eager to put distance between herself and the church before she did something even more reckless.

That's when she saw them.

The flashing red and blue lights in her rearview mirror.

Jessica's breath caught in her throat.

Her stomach twisted violently as the siren wailed to life.

No. No, no, no.

She eased her foot off the gas, her hands tightening on the wheel as she slowly pulled the car to the side of the road.

The lights swirled behind her, illuminating the long stretch of empty road.

Jessica's pulse pounded.

This wasn't just any traffic stop.

Not here.

Not in Alabama.

And definitely not after she had just left him.

Her mind raced, trying to think.

What had she done wrong?

She hadn't been speeding. She had barely seen another car on the road.

So why was she being pulled over?

She swallowed hard, taking a shaky breath, forcing herself to stay calm.

You've done nothing wrong.

She repeated it in her head, over and over, as she reached for her father's registration papers in the glove compartment.

But even as she told herself that, she knew it wasn't true.

Because it didn't matter.

Not here.

Not when the wrong person decided she had.

Jessica pressed her lips together as the sound of boots crunching against the gravel grew closer.

Then, the shadow of a man filled the side mirror.

And she knew.

She knew before she even saw his face.

This wasn't just about a traffic stop.

This was something else.

Something worse.

There was a firm rap against the window.

Jessica inhaled sharply before slowly rolling it down.

A cold gust of air swept into the car, but it wasn't the wind that made her shiver.

It was the man standing on the other side.

Tall. Broad. A sheriff's deputy, wearing a dark uniform, his badge gleaming under the headlights.

But it was his eyes that sent a chill down her spine.

Sharp. Calculated.

And too damn curious.

"Evenin'," he drawled.

Jessica forced a small, polite smile. "Good evening, Officer."

He didn't smile back.

His gaze flickered over her face, lingering a second too long.

Then, he peered past her, into the car.

"You out a little late, ain't ya?"

Jessica gripped the steering wheel tighter. "I was on my way home."

His lip twitched.

"Is that so?"

Jessica swallowed, nodding.

The officer shifted, resting one hand on the roof of the car while the other sat casually near his holster.

A silent reminder.

Jessica's breath felt trapped in her lungs.

"You alone?" he asked.

Her stomach flipped.

"Yes, sir."

He studied her for a moment, and she knew what he was thinking.

A young woman, alone, driving this expensive of a car.

She could almost hear the assumptions.

"I assume this is your daddy's car," he said, his tone easy, but laced with something else.

Jessica nodded once. "Yes, sir."

There was no point in lying.

His gaze flicked toward the passenger seat, then the back.

Jessica didn't move.

Didn't breathe.

"Where you coming from?"

Her pulse thundered in her ears.

Think, Jessica.

Lie.

Make something up.

Don't let him see the truth on your face.

But before she could answer—

He beat her to it.

"Y'know," he said slowly, dragging his knuckles against the roof of the car, "there ain't much out this way 'cept the old colored church."

Jessica's stomach dropped.

Her fingers dug into the leather of the steering wheel, nails pressing deep.

The officer watched her closely.

He was waiting.

For her to react.

For her to slip.

Jessica forced herself to stay still.

To not blink. To not swallow. To not give him the satisfaction.

"I was at a charity event," she said smoothly. "A Christmas drive for the children's home."

His eyes narrowed just slightly.

Jessica held her breath.

Then, after what felt like an eternity—

The officer gave a slow, easy nod.

"Well," he drawled, pushing back off the car. "Ain't that just the sweetest thing."

Jessica exhaled.

Too soon.

Because just as she thought she was in the clear, the officer leaned forward again.

His gaze dipped lower.

And Jessica knew.

Knew the exact moment he saw it.

The faintest smudge on the corner of her lips.

A whisper of something that hadn't been there before.

Something left behind.

Jessica's veins turned to ice.

The officer tilted his head, his mouth curving just slightly.

Then, without another word, he took a slow step back.

"Drive safe, Miss Shaw."

Jessica didn't move.

Didn't breathe.

He tapped the roof of the car once.

Then turned and walked away.

Jessica forced her fingers to work, forcing them to roll up the window, forcing her foot onto the gas pedal.

The second she pulled away, her hands started shaking violently.

She pressed her lips together, her entire body trembling.

That had been too close.

Way too close.

Jessica's pulse pounded.

Her father could never know.

If word got back to him—

Jessica didn't even want to imagine what would happen next.

By the time Jessica pulled into the long driveway of her family's estate, her heart still hadn't settled.

She sat in the car for a moment, her fingers gripping the wheel, her breath uneven.

She had been reckless.

And yet…

She closed her eyes, Benji's voice whispering through her mind.

"You are the most beautiful woman I've ever seen."

Her lips parted, the warmth from earlier fighting against the terror from moments ago.

Jessica pressed her fingers to her mouth.

She should walk away.

She should never see him again.

But she already knew.

She wouldn't stop.

She couldn't.

Because for the first time in her life—

She had felt alive.

The moment Jessica stepped into the grand foyer of her family's estate, the warmth inside barely touched the ice spreading through her veins.

She wasn't cold.

She was burning.

Her breath was still unsteady, the heat of Benji's kiss lingering on her lips, the imprint of his touch seared into her skin.

God help her.

She could still feel the way his hands had cupped her face—firm, reverent, wanting.

The way he had looked at her, as if she was the only thing in the world.

Jessica sucked in a breath, pushing the thought away as she stepped deeper into the house. She had to compose herself, had to pretend like nothing had changed.

Because if her father even suspected where she had been—**what she had done—**it would be over.

The deep murmur of voices floated from the sitting room, her father's rich baritone unmistakable. She hesitated just outside the doorway.

"…the program is nothing but a political stunt," William Shaw was saying, his tone sharp with disdain. "They'll never see real combat, but Washington thinks handing them planes will pacify them."

Jessica's stomach clenched.

She knew what he was talking about.

The Tuskegee Airmen.

Her pulse quickened, but she forced herself to step forward, masking every emotion.

Inside, her father sat in his usual leather chair, his fingers curled around a tumbler of bourbon. His expression was unreadable, but Jessica knew that look well—it was the one he wore when he was deciding the fate of men.

Her mother, Margaret, sat beside him, hands folded in her lap, her own face a careful mask of quiet obedience.

Jessica stepped into the firelight, keeping her voice steady. "Father."

William Shaw's sharp blue eyes cut to her, assessing. "Jessica. You're home later than expected."

She nodded, forcing a small smile. "The charity event ran longer than I anticipated."

"Hm," he hummed, taking a slow sip of his bourbon. "And I assume it was successful?"

Jessica swallowed. "Yes."

Margaret's gaze flickered over her, eyes sharp, too knowing. "You look flushed."

Jessica's heart stopped.

She forced a light laugh, tucking a stray curl behind her ear. "The car was warm."

Her mother studied her for a beat too long before finally nodding.

Jessica exhaled, relieved—too soon.

Her father smirked, swirling his glass. "Jessica, tell me something."

She stiffened. "Yes, Father?"

His gaze pierced through her. "What do you think of the Negro pilots?"

Jessica did not flinch.

She could not flinch.

If he saw even a flicker of hesitation, he would tear her apart.

She chose her words carefully. "If they've been selected, they must have some level of skill."

Her father scoffed. "Skill?" He laughed, but it was cold, sharp. "You think they'll actually see combat? That they have what it takes to fight?"

Jessica clenched her fingers into her palm.

"I think time will tell," she said evenly.

He studied her.

Jessica did not blink.

Then, slowly, he chuckled, shaking his head. "Soft-hearted. Always have been."

Margaret sighed, her delicate features pinching in quiet discomfort. "William, that's enough."

Jessica wasn't soft-hearted.

She was on fire.

She turned sharply on her heel and left.

Because if she stayed in that room any longer, she would break.

Jessica sat at her vanity, the candlelight casting golden shadows across her reflection.

Her diary lay open before her, the ink barely dry from her breathless confession.

December 10, 1941

I kissed him.

And I can't stop thinking about it.

I don't know what this means.

I should feel ashamed.

I should feel terrified.

But all I feel is want.

Wanting to see him again.

Wanting to feel his hands on me again.

Wanting things I shouldn't want.

I can't want him.

But I do.

God help me, I do.

Jessica stared at the words, her breathing uneven.

She shouldn't have written them.

She shouldn't have felt them.

But she did.

She ached.

She felt restless, burning, desperate.

Benji had barely touched her.

And yet, her body craved more.

She pushed back from the desk, heart hammering, pulse thrumming between her thighs.

She needed relief.

She stood, pacing toward the bed, her silk nightgown brushing against her overheated skin.

The memory of his lips, the way he had looked at her as if she was the only thing in the world—it consumed her.

Jessica sank onto the mattress, her legs parting just slightly as she exhaled sharply.

Her fingers drifted down, skimming over the soft fabric of her nightgown, barely teasing herself.

She bit her lip.

It was wrong.

But so was kissing him.

And yet, she had.

And she wanted to again.

Her fingers slid higher, pushing aside the silk, dipping into the heat of her body.

Her back arched.

Her breath came in shallow gasps as she imagined his hands instead of her own.

She imagined his fingers tracing her thighs, his mouth pressing hot, open kisses along her skin.

A soft moan escaped her.

Her touch grew more urgent, more reckless, her fingers circling in slow, deliberate strokes.

She imagined him between her legs, his mouth there, his tongue making her fall apart.

She ached.

Her hips rolled, chasing the pleasure, her body growing tighter, hotter—

Benji's voice—**husky, raw—**whispering her name in her mind.

Her fingers worked faster.

She was so close.

Her body tightened, her breath catching—

And then she shattered.

Her legs trembled, her lips parting in a breathless cry as pleasure crashed over her, hot and blinding.

She collapsed against the mattress, chest heaving, her fingers still slick with evidence of her sin.

She swallowed hard, her pulse still erratic, her skin flushed and damp.

What had she done?

What had she become?

Jessica turned her head, staring at the diary on her nightstand, the ink gleaming beneath the candlelight.

I can't want him.

And yet—she did.

She reached for pillow, gripping it tightly as she tried to steady her breathing.

This was dangerous.

This was forbidden.

But as she closed her eyes, the pleasure still thrumming through her body—

She knew.

She was already too far gone.

Jessica lay still, the sheets tangled around her legs, her body still humming from the release she had just given herself.

Her heart pounded in her chest as she stared at the ceiling, the flickering candlelight casting shifting patterns across the smooth plaster.

What have I done?

The air still felt heavy, thick with the remnants of her pleasure and the weight of her thoughts.

She shouldn't have done that.

She shouldn't have let herself think of him.

But she had.

And God help her, she wanted more.

Jessica turned onto her side, pressing a hand to her flushed cheek, trying to calm the raging storm inside her.

This was madness.

This was forbidden.

And yet...

She licked her lips, still swollen from their kiss.

She could still feel the way his hands had cupped her face, his thumbs brushing against her skin like she was precious.

She wasn't supposed to crave him like this.

But her body had already betrayed her.

A knock at her door made her jolt upright, her breath snagging in her throat.

"Jessica?"

Her mother's voice.

Jessica's stomach dropped.

She scrambled to smooth out the sheets, trying to erase any sign of her sinful indulgence.

"Yes, Mother?" she called, keeping her voice even.

The door cracked open, and Margaret Shaw peered inside, her delicate features poised but unreadable.

Jessica forced a smile. Did she know? Could she tell?

Margaret's sharp blue eyes swept over her. "It's late."

"I was just writing in my diary."

Margaret glanced at the flickering candle on Jessica's nightstand, then nodded.

"Get some rest," her mother said quietly. Then, after a pause, "Your father expects you at the governor's luncheon tomorrow. Don't embarrass us."

Jessica swallowed hard, her pulse still erratic.

"I won't."

Margaret lingered for a moment longer before stepping back and closing the door.

Jessica exhaled, her shoulders sagging as she pressed a hand to her racing heart.

That was too close.

She turned her head, staring at the locket around her neck.

Her fingers curled around it.

She should feel ashamed.

She should feel guilt.

But she didn't.

Instead, she felt alive.

Sleep did not come easily.

Jessica lay in bed, her mind racing, her body still betraying her with its lingering heat.

She wanted to see him.

Needed to see him.

Tomorrow night.

The thought sent a thrill through her, her stomach twisting in anticipation.

She couldn't stop this.

She didn't want to stop this.

Jessica pressed her face into her pillow, smiling into the dark.

For the first time in her life—

She was choosing herself.

The next day, Jessica sat primly beside her mother at the Governor's Mansion, surrounded by Montgomery's most powerful and wealthy.

The room was gilded in elegance, filled with murmured conversations, clinking glasses, and the scent of expensive cigars.

Her father sat beside the governor, discussing politics, war, and the future of Alabama.

Jessica barely heard a word.

Because all she could think about was Benji.

His dark eyes.

His rough hands.

The way he had whispered her name just before she kissed him.

"Jessica?"

She jolted, blinking as her father's deep voice cut through her thoughts.

Every pair of eyes at the table turned toward her.

She froze.

"Yes, Father?" she said smoothly, keeping her posture straight.

William Shaw gave her an expectant look. "Richard asked you a question."

Jessica's stomach clenched.

She turned her head, finally noticing Richard sitting beside her, his blue eyes gentle but questioning.

He smiled slightly. "I was just asking how your charity work has been going."

Jessica forced a smile.

"It's been… enlightening," she said, choosing her words carefully.

Richard chuckled, taking a sip of his whiskey. "You always were the charitable type."

Margaret gave a pleased nod. "Jessica has a giving heart."

Jessica clenched her fists under the table.

She wasn't charitable.

She was restless.

And she was done pretending.

That night, Jessica slipped out of the house, her pulse thrumming with anticipation.

She knew the risks.

She knew what would happen if she was caught.

But none of it mattered.

She needed to see him.

The road stretched before her, the moon silvering the pavement.

Her hands gripped the steering wheel, heart pounding.

She thought of the way he had looked at her last night—like she was the only woman in the world.

She pressed her foot harder against the gas pedal, driven by something she couldn't name.

And when she finally arrived at the church, stepping out into the quiet night, her breath caught.

Because he was already there.

Waiting for her.

CHAPTER 10:

A RISK WORTH TAKING

December 11, 1941 – Tuskegee, Alabama

The old church sat in the quiet moonlight, weathered by time and neglect. The once-pristine white paint had faded to a muted gray, the wooden steps slightly warped from years of storms. But to Jessica, it was something else entirely—a sanctuary. A secret. A world separate from the one waiting for her back home.

She pulled up in her father's 1941 Cadillac Series 62, the purr of the engine smoothing out as she shifted into park. The drive had been quiet, save for the sound of her own heartbeat drumming in her ears. Her nerves should have settled by now; after all, this wasn't the first time. But something about tonight felt different.

Jessica stepped out, the night air crisp against her skin. She adjusted the fur-trimmed coat around her shoulders before shutting the car door softly behind her.

Benji was already there.

Leaning against the side of the church, arms crossed, jacket unzipped just enough to reveal the dark wool sweater underneath. The candlelight from inside flickered through the cracked window, casting long shadows against the dirt road.

His eyes met hers immediately, his lips twitching into something between amusement and frustration.

"You're late," he murmured.

Jessica smirked, tilting her head as she approached. "Well, you're here early. That just means you were too eager to see me."

Benji chuckled, shaking his head. "You always gotta have the last word, huh?"

Jessica stopped just in front of him, looking up through her lashes. "You're just figuring that out?"

Benji sighed, rubbing the back of his neck, but there was a ghost of a smile there. "One of these days, Jess."

Jessica grinned, stepping in closer, close enough that she could see the faint hint of stubble lining his jaw. "Not today, Benji."

Benji exhaled, shaking his head before motioning toward the entrance. "Come on. It's getting cold."

She followed him inside.

The wooden doors creaked as they shut behind them, sealing them into their hidden world. The air smelled like old wood and candle wax, with a faint chill seeping through the cracks in the walls.

Jessica stepped out of her coat, draping it over a pew before turning to face him. Benji had already gone to the small ledge where they kept the candles, striking a match. The soft glow illuminated the sharp lines of his face, the flickering light making the shadows dance over his cheekbones.

Jessica leaned against the pew, watching him. "You light them the same way every time."

Benji arched a brow as he touched the flame to the wick. "What?"

"You hold the match between your fingers for a second longer than you need to before lighting it. Like you're thinking about something."

Benji chuckled, shaking his head as he blew out the match. "You notice everything, don't you?"

Jessica smirked. "Maybe."

Benji turned to face her, arms crossing again. "Alright then, what else you got? What's the next thing I do that you got all figured out?"

Jessica tapped a finger against her chin, pretending to think. "Let's see… You rub the back of your neck when you're trying to hide the fact that you're thinking too hard. You roll your shoulders when you're tense—usually after flight drills. Oh, and my personal favorite?"

Benji narrowed his eyes. "Go on."

Jessica stepped in close enough that she could smell the faint scent of aviation fuel clinging to his jacket. "When you're watching me, and you think I don't notice, you do this thing where your jaw tenses—just a little. Like you're trying to convince yourself that you don't care as much as you do."

Benji blinked.

Jessica smirked.

Benji exhaled, shaking his head as he turned slightly away. "You sure do like to talk, don't you?"

Jessica chuckled, settling onto the pew beside him. "You like it."

Benji sat beside her, stretching his legs out slightly. "I like quiet."

Jessica nudged his knee with hers. "That's a lie."

Benji tilted his head toward her, giving her a pointed look. "That so?"

Jessica nodded. "You love the sound of an engine roaring to life. The way the wind rushes past when you take off. The way the world gets quiet up there."

Benji studied her for a moment, something shifting in his expression.

"You talk like you've been in a cockpit before," he murmured.

Jessica shrugged. "Not yet."

Benji smirked. "Yet?"

Jessica grinned. "Someday."

Benji leaned back against the pew, letting out a low chuckle. "You surprise me, Shaw."

Jessica's smile softened. "You're not what I expected either, Davis."

Benji exhaled, glancing at her hands. "Your father know you're out here with the likes of me?"

Jessica's smirk faded. "No."

Benji nodded slowly. "Didn't think so."

Jessica looked down at her hands, the weight of reality settling between them. "You think this is stupid, don't you?"

Benji was quiet for a moment before he sighed. "I think it's dangerous."

Jessica looked up at him, eyes searching. "And yet, here we are."

Benji held her gaze. "Yeah," he murmured. "Here we are."

The silence between them was heavy, but not uncomfortable. Jessica felt the warmth of his presence beside her, the steady sound of his breathing, the way his fingers flexed against his knee as if he were holding something back.

She didn't know what made her reach for his hand, but she did.

Benji stiffened slightly before exhaling, letting her fingers slip between his. His hands were rough, calloused from years of working, flying, fighting for something bigger than himself.

Jessica traced her thumb over his knuckles, feeling the heat of his skin against hers.

"You ever think about just leaving?" she asked softly.

Benji's jaw tightened. "Every day."

Jessica swallowed. "And what stops you?"

Benji looked at her then, really looked at her.

"You."

Jessica inhaled sharply, her fingers tightening around his.

And suddenly, she was leaning in.

Benji's breath hitched, his free hand lifting to cup the side of her face, his fingers brushing against her cheek.

Jessica's lips parted slightly, her heart pounding.

And then—

She kissed him.

It was slow, hesitant at first, but then Benji pulled her closer, his hand slipping behind her neck, deepening it.

Jessica sighed into his mouth, her fingers twisting into the fabric of his jacket.

Benji shifted, pulling her onto his lap, his hands sliding to her waist, pressing her against him.

The warmth of him was intoxicating, the way he tasted—like smoke and something untamed.

His lips left hers, trailing down her jaw, to her neck—

Jessica gasped, her head tilting back—

And then—

Benji stopped.

Breathing hard, his forehead pressed against hers.

Jessica blinked, dazed, lips swollen. "Why'd you stop?"

Benji exhaled sharply, his hands tightening around her waist. "Because if I don't stop now, I won't stop at all."

Jessica bit her lip, her pulse still racing.

She didn't move off his lap, not yet.

"Will you meet me again tomorrow?" she whispered.

Benji closed his eyes for a moment before nodding. "Yeah, Shaw. I'll be here."

Jessica smiled softly. "Good."

She climbed off his lap, smoothing out her dress before grabbing her coat.

Benji watched her go, exhaling hard as the door shut behind her.

This was a risk.

But damn it—he was already too far gone.

The old church had never seen a Christmas quite like this.

A single candle flickered in the quiet sanctuary, casting a soft glow over the wooden pews and the dust-speckled air. Outside, the cold Alabama night wrapped around the abandoned building, the wind whispering through the cracks in the wooden walls.

Jessica tightened her coat around her shoulders as she stepped inside, her breath visible in the chill. Her heart pounded—not from fear, but from the anticipation that had built over the past few weeks.

It had been nearly a month since that first kiss. A month of stolen nights, hushed laughter, fingertips brushing in the dark. A month of something neither of them dared to name out loud.

And tonight, it was Christmas.

Benji was already waiting.

He sat on the edge of a pew, elbows on his knees, rubbing his hands together to warm them. He looked up when she entered, and despite the dim light, she could see the warmth in his eyes.

"Thought maybe you weren't coming," he murmured.

Jessica smiled, pulling off her gloves and tucking them into the pocket of her coat. "I couldn't stay away even if I tried."

Benji smirked, shaking his head. "You always know the right thing to say, don't you?"

Jessica stepped closer, slipping onto the pew beside him. "Only when it's true."

For a moment, they just sat there, listening to the wind whistle through the broken windowpane. The silence between them was easy, familiar, the kind of quiet that didn't need to be filled.

Jessica turned to look at him, studying his profile. The strong jaw, the curve of his nose, the way his lips parted slightly when he was deep in thought.

"What?" Benji asked without looking at her.

Jessica shook her head. "Nothing. Just… you ever think about what you'd be doing if things were different?"

Benji exhaled through his nose. "All the time."

Jessica waited.

Benji tilted his head back, looking up at the ceiling as if he could see straight through to the sky. "If things were different... I'd still be flying, I think. Not in the military, though. Just... free. My own plane, maybe. Flying wherever I wanted, whenever I wanted."

Jessica smiled softly. "That sounds nice."

Benji turned to her. "What about you?"

Jessica hesitated, folding her hands in her lap. "I'd be in school. Studying law."

Benji's lips twitched. "I can see that."

Jessica arched a brow. "Oh?"

Benji nodded. "You like to argue."

Jessica gasped, swatting his arm playfully. "I do not!"

Benji chuckled, catching her wrist before she could pull away. His thumb traced absent circles over her skin. "I like it, though," he murmured. "I like that you know what you want. Ain't a lot of people like that."

Jessica swallowed, her heart thudding against her ribs. "You know what you want too."

Benji held her gaze, his fingers still wrapped around her wrist. "Yeah," he said quietly. "I do."

The air between them thickened. Jessica wasn't sure who moved first, but suddenly, she was closer, his warmth chasing away the winter chill. His hand slid up her arm, to the side of her face, his thumb brushing over her cheek.

Jessica closed her eyes, leaning into him.

Then, just as their lips were about to meet, Benji pulled back slightly.

Jessica blinked in confusion as he reached into his pocket, pulling out something small, wrapped in brown paper.

"Merry Christmas, Shaw," he said, pressing it into her hand.

Jessica frowned, looking down at the package. "You got me a present?"

Benji smirked. "It's Christmas, ain't it?"

Jessica hesitated, guilt washing over her. "I… I didn't get you anything."

Benji shrugged. "You're all the gift I need."

Jessica's breath hitched, her fingers tightening around the package.

Slowly, she peeled back the wrapping, revealing a small silver locket. The delicate chain glinted in the candlelight, and when she flipped it over, she saw the tiny initials etched into the metal.

B. & J.

Jessica's throat tightened.

"Benji…"

"It ain't much," he said, rubbing the back of his neck. "But I figured… if we can't be seen together, at least you'd have something. A piece of me."

Jessica swallowed past the lump in her throat. She had never owned anything so personal, so precious.

She looked up at him, eyes shining. "It's perfect."

Benji let out a breath, relief flickering across his face. "Yeah?"

Jessica nodded. "Yeah."

She unclasped the chain, lifting it to her neck. Benji reached forward, his fingers brushing against her skin as he fastened it for her. The touch sent shivers down her spine.

When he finished, she pressed her palm over the locket, feeling the cool metal against her skin.

Then, unable to stop herself, she leaned in and kissed him.

This time, there was no hesitation, no second-guessing.

Her hands found his jaw, his neck, fingers curling into his hair as she deepened the kiss.

Benji groaned softly, his hands gripping her waist, pulling her closer.

She didn't care that the church pew was hard beneath her. She didn't care that the candlelight flickered dangerously as the wind howled through the broken windows.

All she cared about was the way he kissed her—like he had been waiting his whole life for this moment.

When they finally pulled apart, Jessica was breathless.

Benji rested his forehead against hers, his hands still cradling her waist. "Merry Christmas, Jess."

Jessica smiled, her fingers tracing the collar of his jacket. "Merry Christmas, Benji."

Outside, the wind howled. But inside, wrapped in the warmth of each other, the world felt quiet.

Safe.

Whole.

Even if just for a little while.

Jessica didn't want to leave.

The warmth of Benji's body next to hers, the way his fingers idly traced circles against the fabric of her coat, the gentle weight of the locket resting against her skin—it all made the cold outside seem a world away.

She tilted her head back against the pew, watching as Benji exhaled, his breath visible in the chilly air. He looked so at peace in the dim candlelight, the flickering glow casting soft shadows over his face.

"This night's gonna end too fast, isn't it?" she murmured.

Benji sighed, nodding. "They always do."

Jessica bit her lip. "Wish we could stay here forever."

Benji turned to her, a lazy grin pulling at his lips. "You'd get cold. And hungry."

Jessica smirked. "You'd figure out a way to keep me warm."

Benji chuckled, shaking his head. "You keep talkin' like that, and I'll have to find out."

Heat curled low in her stomach at the teasing note in his voice, but she didn't push it—not yet.

Instead, she let the silence stretch, let herself soak in the moment, let herself pretend that outside this old church, the world wasn't waiting to pull them apart.

The candle had nearly burned down by the time Jessica sighed and stood.

"I should go," she murmured, though she didn't make a move toward the door.

Benji stretched his legs out, nodding slowly. "Yeah."

Jessica hesitated, then reached out, running her fingers through his curls. "I'll see you tomorrow?"

Benji leaned into her touch, his eyes slipping shut for a brief moment before opening again.

"I'll be here," he promised.

Jessica smiled, then turned to leave, wrapping her coat tighter around herself as she stepped into the night.

The cold hit her instantly, but she barely felt it. Her heart was too full, her body too warm from the lingering press of Benji's lips against hers.

She reached her car and slid into the driver's seat, gripping the locket around her neck.

She had never felt like this before.

Not with any of the boys her father had introduced her to. Not with Richard, despite his charm and easy smile.

Benji made her feel alive.

And that terrified her.

As she turned the key in the ignition, she whispered a silent prayer that whatever this was—whatever they were becoming—wouldn't be ripped away before it had a chance to bloom.

Benji sat there long after Jessica left, staring at the closed doors of the church.

His fingers traced the spot where she had been sitting, the warmth of her still lingering in the wood.

He had never been one to believe in fate, but damn if it didn't feel like the universe had pushed Jessica Shaw straight into his path.

With a sigh, he stood, blowing out the candle before stepping into the cold night. His boots crunched against the frozen ground as he made his way back to base, his mind still full of her.

By the time he reached his bunk, the world outside had shifted.

The base was quiet, but not in the usual way.

It was the kind of quiet that came before a storm.

Benji felt it in his bones.

Something was coming.

Something big.

He just didn't know what yet.

As he lay down, the locket she had given him warmed against his chest.

Whatever happened next, he knew one thing for certain.

He wasn't letting go of Jessica Shaw.

Not for anything.

Not for anyone.

CHAPTER 11:

THEIR LAST NIGHT

April 1, 1943 – Tuskegee, Alabama

The world had changed in two years. The war raged on. The headlines screamed of battles fought and lost. The Tuskegee Airmen had trained, bled, and proved themselves in the skies. And now—now it was time.

Deployment orders had come that morning.

Tomorrow, they would leave.

Benji sat on the steps of the old church, the same place where everything had begun for them. The same place where they had whispered their dreams, shared stolen kisses, and let themselves believe—if only for a few fleeting moments—that the world outside didn't exist.

Now, the weight of reality pressed down on his shoulders.

Tomorrow, he would be gone.

His fingers fidgeted with the pocket watch his father had given him, flipping it open and closed, listening to the soft click of the latch. A habit. A distraction.

A car pulled up, its headlights cutting through the darkness.

Jessica.

She was driving her father's Cadillac—same as always. The same car she had driven the first night she had met him here, back when things had been new and uncertain. Back before they knew just how deep they would fall.

The engine cut off, and a moment later, she stepped out.

Benji stood as she approached, taking her in.

She was breathtaking.

She always had been.

But tonight, there was something different. Something raw in the way she looked at him, like she was trying to memorize every detail.

She stopped just in front of him, close enough that he could smell her perfume, the familiar scent that had become a part of his world.

Neither of them spoke.

Jessica lifted a hand, pressing her palm to his cheek.

He closed his eyes for a moment, leaning into her touch, savoring it.

Then he opened them, and the look on her face nearly undid him.

"I hate this," she whispered.

Benji swallowed hard. "Me too."

She exhaled sharply, dropping her hand. "I knew this day would come. I knew from the beginning."

Benji nodded. "So did I."

Jessica took a shaky breath. "Doesn't make it any easier."

"No," he agreed. "It doesn't."

Silence stretched between them.

Then Jessica reached for his hand, lacing her fingers through his.

"Come inside with me," she said softly.

Benji didn't hesitate.

He followed her into the church, the door creaking as it swung shut behind them.

The candlelight flickered, casting long shadows along the worn wooden pews. The space had become theirs over the years—more than just a meeting place. It had become their sanctuary.

Tonight, it would become something more.

Jessica turned to him, her fingers tightening around his.

"I don't want to say goodbye out there," she said. "Not in front of everyone. Not where I have to pretend like it doesn't break me to watch you leave."

Benji reached up, brushing a strand of hair behind her ear. "Then we won't say it."

Jessica let out a small, shaky laugh. "That's not how it works, Benji."

Benji smiled faintly. "Maybe not. But I don't care."

She studied him for a long moment.

Then, slowly, she lifted onto her toes and kissed him.

It wasn't like the other kisses they had shared over the years.

It was deeper. Heavier. Full of desperation and unspoken words.

Benji wrapped his arms around her, pulling her against him, drinking her in like she was the only thing keeping him grounded.

She was.

His hands slid into her hair, cradling the back of her head as he deepened the kiss, pouring everything he couldn't say into it.

Tomorrow, he would be gone.

Tonight, she was his.

And he was hers.

Benji's hands were on her waist, warm and firm, grounding her even as her world tilted. The way he kissed her—slow and deep, like he was memorizing the shape of her lips—made her heart pound so hard she swore he could hear it.

Jessica's back pressed against the wooden pew as Benji leaned over her, their breaths mingling in the flickering candlelight. Every nerve in her body was on fire, anticipation coiling low in her stomach.

She had wanted this—had thought about it more times than she cared to admit. But now, with his hands moving up her sides, his fingers trailing the curve of her waist, she felt something deeper than just desire.

This was a moment she would never forget.

Benji pulled back just enough to look at her, his dark eyes searching hers. "You sure?"

Jessica answered by grabbing his shirt and pulling him back down into a kiss.

He groaned softly against her lips, his hands tightening on her hips before sliding up to cup her face, his thumbs brushing over her cheekbones with a gentleness that sent shivers down her spine.

She reached for the buttons of his uniform jacket, fumbling slightly, her hands shaking with nerves and excitement. Benji chuckled against her lips, helping her push the heavy material off his shoulders.

The sight of him like this, stripped down to just his undershirt, his muscles taut under his dark skin, stole her breath.

"You're beautiful," she whispered, running her hands over his chest, feeling the steady thrum of his heartbeat beneath her fingertips.

Benji huffed out a laugh, dipping his head to press his lips to her throat. "You're the one who's beautiful."

His hands skimmed down her arms, over the soft fabric of her dress, before slipping under the hem, his fingers grazing along her thigh.

Jessica gasped, tilting her head back as he traced slow, teasing circles on her bare skin.

"Benji," she breathed, her fingers tangling in his short curls, pulling him closer.

He lifted her effortlessly, her legs wrapping around his waist as he carried her deeper into the church, away from the open pews.

The old wooden floor creaked beneath their weight as he set her down gently near the altar, his lips never leaving hers.

His hands roamed her body with purpose now, sliding up her back, finding the zipper of her dress.

Jessica swallowed hard as the fabric loosened, pooling around her shoulders.

Benji pulled back just enough to watch as she let the dress fall, leaving her standing in nothing but her slip and lace undergarments.

His gaze darkened, his breathing uneven.

"Damn," he murmured, his fingers skimming down her arms before gripping her waist. "You're perfect."

Heat rushed to her cheeks, but before she could respond, Benji dipped his head, kissing the delicate skin of her collarbone, trailing his lips lower, lower—

She let out a soft moan, arching into him, her fingers digging into his shoulders.

Benji lifted her again, pressing her against the cool stone wall of the church, his body flush against hers. She could feel every inch of him—his strength, his warmth, the hard press of his desire against her thigh.

Her body trembled with need, aching for more.

"Tell me what you want," he whispered, his lips brushing against her ear.

"You," she gasped. "I just want you."

Benji growled low in his throat before capturing her mouth again, his hands gripping her thighs, holding her steady as he pressed against her, rolling his hips in a slow, deliberate grind that made her whimper.

"Jessica," he rasped, his forehead resting against hers. "I don't—I've never—"

She cupped his face, understanding instantly.

"Then let me show you," she whispered.

Benji swallowed hard, his eyes searching hers.

Then he nodded.

Jessica guided his hands to her body, showing him what she liked, what made her gasp, what made her sigh his name like a prayer.

He caught on quickly, his movements growing more confident, more demanding.

Her slip joined the rest of their clothes on the floor, leaving her bare beneath him.

Benji paused, just looking at her, his hands tracing slow, reverent patterns along her skin.

"You're the most beautiful thing I've ever seen," he murmured, his voice thick with emotion.

Jessica reached for him, pulling him down to her, their bodies pressed together in the candlelit darkness.

She guided him, whispered against his lips, showed him how to move, how to take her apart and put her back together.

And when he finally sank into her, a shuddering breath escaping his lips, Jessica knew—this wasn't just a night of passion.

This was something deeper.

This was love.

And it would change everything.

Benji shuddered as Jessica's hands traced fire over his skin, her touch electric and knowing. He had never done this before—not like this, not with anyone—but the way she guided him, the way her body responded to him, it was like she had been made just for him.

He pressed her back against the cool stone of the church wall, his lips tracing the curve of her neck, sucking gently, then harder, leaving a mark. A brand. Proof that she was his, even if only for tonight.

Jessica gasped, tilting her head to give him more, her fingers digging into his bare back, nails scratching just enough to make him groan.

"You feel so good," he murmured against her skin, voice thick with want.

She arched into him, pressing her hips forward, rolling them against his in slow, sinful friction that sent a sharp bolt of pleasure through them both.

"More," she whispered, her breath hot against his ear.

Benji's control snapped.

He grabbed her thighs, lifting her off the ground with ease, and she wrapped her legs around his waist, locking him in place.

Their bodies fit together perfectly, like they were made to be this way.

"Jessica," he groaned, pressing her harder against the wall, grinding against her, feeling the heat of her through the last scrap of lace between them.

She moaned, gripping his shoulders, rocking into him with desperate need.

"Take it off," she pleaded, tugging at his undershorts.

Benji hesitated for half a second, nerves flickering, but when she reached down, her fingers brushing over him, his restraint vanished.

Clothes hit the floor.

Skin met skin.

He pressed against her entrance, the heat of her making his breath catch. Jessica's fingers curled into his hair, pulling him down into a slow, deep kiss as she guided him in.

Benji groaned as he sank into her, his head dropping to her shoulder, the feeling overwhelming.

"Fuck," he whispered, voice wrecked.

Jessica gasped, her grip on him tightening. "Benji…"

He held still for a moment, his body shaking, giving her time to adjust, but she didn't want slow. She didn't want careful.

She wanted him.

"Move," she commanded, rolling her hips.

Benji's control snapped.

He pulled back, then drove into her, his rhythm deep and slow at first, savoring every inch of her, every gasp that left her lips.

Jessica moaned, nails raking down his back. "Harder," she demanded.

Benji obeyed.

He thrust into her with deep, punishing strokes, pressing her back against the wall, his grip on her thighs firm enough to bruise.

Jessica cried out, her body arching, her head falling back against the stone, lost in the pleasure.

"God, Benji—"

"Say my name again," he growled, his teeth grazing the sensitive skin of her throat.

She gasped. "Benji."

He groaned, his hips snapping forward harder, deeper.

Jessica's body clenched around him, drawing him in, holding him tight. She was fire and silk, heat and desperation, taking everything he gave and begging for more.

"Fuck, you feel so good," he groaned against her mouth, swallowing her moans as he kissed her hard, their bodies moving in perfect sync.

Her fingers clawed at his back, gripping him like she never wanted to let go.

"Benji—I'm close," she gasped, her body trembling.

He reached down, pressing his fingers against the bundle of nerves between her legs, rubbing slow, firm circles as he thrust into her harder, faster.

Jessica shattered.

Her body clenched around him, her nails raking down his back as she came apart with a cry of his name.

Benji cursed, his rhythm stuttering as she milked him, drawing him to the edge.

"Jessica—"

He groaned, his body tensing, his thrusts becoming erratic before he buried himself deep inside her, pleasure crashing over him like a tidal wave.

He pressed his forehead against hers, both of them panting, their bodies trembling from the intensity of it all.

For a long moment, they just stayed like that—connected, catching their breath, wrapped in each other.

Benji finally pulled back just enough to cup her face, brushing a damp curl from her cheek.

"You okay?" he murmured.

Jessica smiled, breathless. "More than okay."

He kissed her, slow and deep, memorizing the way she tasted, the way she felt.

Because by tomorrow, he'd be gone.

And neither of them knew if he'd ever come back.

CHAPTER 12:

DEPLOYMENT DAY

April 2, 1943 – Tuskegee Army Air Field,
Alabama

The Alabama morning was crisp, the sky painted in soft hues of orange and pink as the first light stretched over the horizon. The air smelled of damp earth and magnolias, carrying a weight of both promise and farewell.

Benji stood by the porch, his duffel slung over his shoulder, the gravity of the moment pressing down on him.

His father, Elijah, adjusted his hat, studying him with the quiet intensity only a father could. "You fly smart, son. Don't take chances that don't need taking."

Benji nodded. "Yes, sir."

Elijah sighed, stepping forward. His hand landed firm on Benji's shoulder, giving it a reassuring squeeze. "And don't you let no man tell you that you ain't got a right to be up in that sky."

Benji swallowed against the lump forming in his throat. "I won't, Pop."

Clara wiped at her eyes before thrusting a cloth-wrapped bundle into his hands. "I packed you some biscuits for the train. You best not be skipping meals out there."

Benji smirked. "Yes, ma'am."

Naomi stepped forward, looking up at him with those big, wide eyes that had always made him weak. "I already gave you something," she said, motioning toward the bracelet tied securely around his wrist. "So you can't lose."

He crouched down to her level, tapping her chin lightly. "That's right, sissy. I ain't gonna lose."

Marcus stood beside Sam, arms crossed, jaw tight. "Try not to get yourself killed," he muttered, his way of saying he cared.

Benji gave him a smirk, offering his hand. Marcus hesitated, then gripped it firmly, pulling him into a rare embrace.

Sam clapped a hand on Benji's back. "You ready, Flyboy?"

Benji exhaled, looking around at the only home he'd ever known. "Yeah," he said. "I'm ready."

The sound of an approaching truck signaled the moment was over. He turned away from his family and climbed up into the vehicle, the engine rumbling beneath him.

As they pulled away, he kept his eyes forward, heart steady but heavy.

No looking back now.

The train station was packed, a mix of uniforms and civilians, the air filled with the sounds of hurried goodbyes and last-minute reassurances. The

Tuskegee Airmen stood together, their crisp uniforms standing out in the sea of movement.

Benji scanned the crowd, his heart quickening when he spotted her.

Jessica stood near the far end of the platform, away from the masses. She was dressed in a navy-blue dress, her curls pinned neatly beneath a small hat. She looked elegant, untouchable—yet her eyes softened when they met his.

She couldn't come to him.

She couldn't even acknowledge him.

Instead, Josephine stepped forward, her expression unreadable. Without a word, she held out a neatly folded scarf and an envelope.

Benji took them carefully.

"She wanted you to have these," Josephine murmured, her voice barely above a whisper.

His fingers curled around the delicate fabric—a sky-blue scarf. He lifted it slightly, inhaling. It smelled just like her.

"Thank you," he said, voice low, eyes flicking to Jessica once more.

Josephine hesitated, then leaned in. "Come back to her," she whispered.

Benji exhaled slowly. "I will."

Jessica's gaze never wavered.

The final boarding call rang out, slicing through the station like a blade.

Benji clenched the scarf and letter tightly before stepping onto the train.

As the train pulled away, his eyes remained locked on her until the station disappeared from view.

His grip on the scarf tightened.

He would come back.

He had to.

The Journey to War

The rhythmic clatter of train wheels against the tracks filled the cabin as the men settled in. Outside, the Alabama landscape faded, giving way to unfamiliar terrain.

Tex stretched, letting out a long whistle. "Well, boys, this is it."

Ace smirked. "Getting nervous, Callahan?"

Tex shrugged. "Hell yeah. Anyone who ain't is lying out their ass."

Sam leaned back, arms crossed. "We trained for this. Time to prove we belong up there."

Benji remained quiet, turning the envelope over in his hands before carefully unfolding the letter.

Jessica's handwriting was delicate but sure.

Benji,

I don't know how to say goodbye to you, so I won't.

I'll just say this—come back to me.

And when you do, I want to hear all about the sky.

Until then, I'll be waiting.

– Jessica

He exhaled slowly, his heart aching at the simplicity of it.

Ace nudged him. "Our young Benjamin is growing up so fast."

Benji rolled his eyes, stuffing the letter back into his pocket. "Shut up, Ace."

Ace grinned. "I'm just saying, if that's from a certain senator's daughter, you got more than just war waiting on you when we get back."

Tex chuckled. "Yeah, Benji. Maybe she'll be at the station with open arms."

Benji smirked, shaking his head, but deep down, he knew—Jessica would be waiting.

April 4, 1943 – Newport News, Virginia

Two days later, they arrived in Newport News, stepping onto the bustling docks where a massive military transport ship loomed before them.

Tex let out a low whistle. "Damn. Guess this is home for the next few weeks."

Ace grinned. "Better than swimming across."

The men lined up, their duffel bags slung over their shoulders as they boarded the ship.

Benji stood at the rail, watching as the shoreline of America grew smaller.

He reached into his pocket, fingers brushing against the photo tucked inside.

And he whispered the promise to himself once more.

"I'll come back to you."

April 24, 1943 – Casablanca, Morocco

The Atlantic crossing was grueling—weeks spent avoiding German U-boats, the constant sway of the ship, the looming reality of war.

But at last, land.

Casablanca rose before them like a mirage—dusty streets bustling with movement, the scent of spice and salt thick in the air. The sounds of foreign tongues, the distant hum of war still present in every direction.

Tex clapped Benji on the back. "We're really here."

Benji nodded, adjusting his duffel. "Yeah."

His fingers curled around the scarf still wrapped around his writst.

He wasn't leaving this place without making it back to her.

Casablanca, Morocco – 99th Fighter Squadron Training Grounds

The North African sun was relentless, bearing down on the field where the men of the 99th Fighter Squadron drilled from dawn until dusk. Sweat clung to their skin, dust caking in their boots, but nobody dared to slow their pace. This wasn't just training anymore—it was preparation for survival.

"Move like your damn life depends on it—'cause soon enough, it will!" Captain Wright's voice rang through the open field as they pushed through another grueling drill.

Benji wiped the sweat from his brow, his muscles burning from the long hours under the sun. His lungs ached, but he refused to be the first to slow down.

"Come on, Flyboy, that all you got?" Sam grinned beside him, keeping pace.

Benji smirked, shaking his head. "Ain't nothing slow about me, Wells. I'm just letting you feel fast for once."

Tex let out a booming laugh as he jogged past. "Damn, Davis, I didn't know you was runnin' charity races now."

Benji chuckled, shaking his head as they finally came to a stop, breathing heavy. A moment later, Captain Wright strolled toward them, his piercing blue eyes scanning their faces.

"Mail just arrived from the States," he said, holding up a stack of envelopes.

Immediately, the energy shifted. A murmur went through the group as the men straightened up, waiting to hear their names.

Benji's heart thudded in his chest when he saw an envelope in Wright's hands, the handwriting unmistakable.

Jessica.

"Benjamin Davis," Wright called, tossing the letter to him.

Benji caught it with steady hands, his pulse quickening. He turned away from the group, stepping toward a shaded spot by the barracks as he unfolded the letter with careful fingers.

Montgomery, Alabama – The Shaw Residence

Jessica sat at her writing desk, the dim candlelight casting flickering shadows against the walls. She pressed the pen to paper, exhaling as she tried to gather her thoughts.

She had been writing to Benji since the moment he left, and each time she received a letter in return, it felt like breathing again.

Tonight, her emotions were heavier. She wasn't sure how to put them into words.

Benji,

I hope this letter reaches you quickly. I don't know how much mail gets through, but I've been writing almost every day.

I wish I could say things are easier now that I've gotten used to you being gone, but I can't. I miss you. It's as simple as that.

Montgomery feels empty without you. I still go to our church, but it's different. Everything is.

I don't know what it's like over there for you, but I pray you're safe. That you're still smiling that cocky little smirk of yours.

You better come back to me, Benji. I don't think I could bear it if you didn't.

Until I see you in the skies,

Jessica

Jessica sighed, folding the letter carefully and pressing it to her chest for a brief moment before sealing it.

She turned toward Josephine, who was standing near the doorway, her expression gentle.

"You want this sent out first thing?" Josephine asked.

Jessica nodded. "Please."

Josephine smiled knowingly. "That boy's holdin' your heart, ain't he?"

Jessica hesitated, then let out a soft breath. "He always has."

Casablanca – Benji's Response

Benji read her words twice before folding the letter carefully and tucking it into his jacket. His heart was pounding—not from nerves, but from something deeper.

Sam plopped down next to him, tilting his head. "That from your girl?"

Benji nodded, unable to stop the small smile creeping onto his lips.

Sam smirked. "She say she miss you?"

Benji scoffed. "What you think?"

Tex let out a laugh as he and Ace strolled over. "Damn, Davis. She got you grinnin' like a lovesick fool. You over there sighin' like a schoolboy."

Benji rolled his eyes. "Y'all some haters, that's all."

Ace chuckled, shaking his head. "Nah, man, I respect it. I just didn't expect you to be the one goin' soft on us."

Benji smirked. "Ain't nothin' soft about me."

Ace shot him a look. "You sure? 'Cause that letter got you lookin' real sentimental right now."

Tex grinned, nudging Benji's shoulder. "Man, let the boy be in love. You jealous, Ace?"

"Hell nah," Tex cut in before Ace could answer. "I love my Black queens too much."

"Hell yeah, we do," the other men chimed in, laughing.

Benji shook his head, chuckling as he pulled out a piece of paper and began to write his response.

Jessica,

Seeing your letter today was the best thing that's happened to me in weeks. I swear, just seeing your handwriting makes the war feel a little further away.

I miss you too, Jess. More than I can say.

The heat here is brutal, the training's even worse, but I don't mind. Every time I'm up in the air, I feel like I'm one step closer to home. One step closer to you.

You gave me that scarf the day I left, and I've had it wrapped around my control stick ever since. Every time I fly, it's like you're right there with me.

Keep writing to me, Jess. I don't know how long this war is gonna last, but as long as I have your letters, I know I can get through it.

Keep your wings steady, Flyboy

Benji folded the letter carefully, slipping it into an envelope before standing up.

"Here," he said, handing it off to one of the men organizing the mail shipment back to the States.

Tex slung an arm around Benji's shoulders, grinning. "Just make sure you don't get shot down before you make it back to her."

Benji smirked, but those words settled deep.

Because Jessica was waiting.

And no matter what, he was going to survive this war for her.

June 1943 – Tunisia, North Africa

99th Fighter Squadron Airfield – The First Mission

The sun hung high over the Tunisian airfield, turning the sand into shimmering waves of heat. Sweat clung to Benji's skin beneath his flight suit, but he ignored it, rolling his shoulders as he stood alongside the rest of the men of the 99th Fighter Squadron.

Captain Desmond Wright stood at the front of the formation, his piercing blue eyes scanning them all, assessing, measuring. He had been harder on them than any instructor before, but Benji understood why now.

They were about to go up for the first time in a real fight.

"The 99th is being put to the test today," Wright said, his voice sharp, commanding. "Escort mission. We're protecting a formation of B-25 bombers heading into enemy-occupied territory. Our job is to make sure they make it in and out alive."

Benji stood straight, gripping his helmet. He'd been waiting for this moment.

"Stick to your wingman," Wright continued. "Eyes up. And remember—this ain't training anymore. You slip up, you die."

The air felt heavy, the weight of reality sinking in.

"Get to your planes," Wright ordered. "Time to show 'em what we can do."

Benji turned on his heel and jogged toward his P-40 Warhawk, running a gloved hand over its metallic surface before climbing into the cockpit. The red tail gleamed in the sunlight, a symbol of what they represented.

Strapping in, he reached down, adjusting the sky-blue scarf wrapped around his control stick. Jessica's scent had long since faded, but the memory of her hands tying it there remained.

He took a breath, fingers gripping the controls.

Over the radio, Wright's voice crackled through.

"Start your engines."

The Sky Over Italy – The Test of War

They had been flying for nearly an hour when the warning came through.

"Enemy fighters, five o'clock high!"

Benji snapped his gaze upward.

Messerschmitt Bf 109s.

They moved fast, sleek and deadly as they cut through the sky toward them.

"Stay in formation!" Wright barked.

The German fighters broke apart, splitting into two groups—one going for the bombers, the other coming straight for the 99th.

And just like that, chaos erupted.

Machine gun fire streaked through the sky, planes twisting and diving as the battle unfolded.

Benji gritted his teeth, rolling his P-40 hard to the right, lining up a shot on a Messerschmitt bearing down on a bomber.

He squeezed the trigger.

RAT-TAT-TAT-TAT-TAT!

Bullets ripped through the enemy fuselage, sending smoke trailing from the engine. The pilot bailed out just before the plane spiraled toward the sea below.

Benji barely had time to register the kill before another fighter locked onto him.

He jerked the stick left, rolling into a tight spiral.

"Davis, break left!" Wright ordered.

Benji did, feeling the rush of wind as tracers whizzed past his wing. The Messerschmitt stayed locked on.

A voice cut through his radio—Sam.

"I got him, Benji, keep flying straight!"

Benji did. He trusted Sam with his life.

Seconds later—gunfire erupted behind him.

The German fighter burst into flames, spiraling down toward the ocean.

"Hell yeah!" Sam whooped.

Benji let out a breath. "Appreciate it, brother."

Sam's voice was still buzzing with adrenaline. "That's one each, let's keep going."

But Benji wasn't done.

His eyes locked onto a Messerschmitt diving toward one of their bombers.

He didn't think—he moved.

Pushing the throttle, he closed the distance, bullets streaking past his canopy. The bomber was nearly in range of the enemy fire.

Benji barreled down from above, his sights locked.

"Come on…" he muttered.

He fired.

The bullets ripped through the Messerschmitt's cockpit, and the plane exploded in midair.

Benji pulled up hard, barely avoiding the debris.

"Damn, Davis!" Ace's voice crackled through. "Where the hell you learn that?"

Benji smirked, breathing heavy. "My pops."

Before anyone could respond, Wright's voice came through.

"Regroup—escort the bombers home. Mission complete."

Benji exhaled. His hands were still trembling.

But they had done it.

Returning to Base

As they landed back at base, the weight of what had just happened settled over them. Mechanics rushed in, checking over their aircraft, but none of them spoke right away.

Benji climbed down, pulling off his helmet, running a hand through his sweat-damp hair.

Sam was the first to walk up. "Damn, Flyboy. You were on fire up there."

Benji smirked, but before he could respond, Tex slung an arm over his shoulder. "Yeah, yeah, but let's be real. I had the cleanest shot out there."

Ace scoffed. "Man, shut your ass up. We all know Davis was putting on a damn air show."

Tex grinned. "I still say he's showing off for someone."

Benji rolled his eyes. "I don't know what y'all talkin' about."

Ace smirked. "Oh, so you just happen to be writing letters every night?"

Tex chuckled. "Our little hotshot got a lady waiting back home?"

Benji hesitated just a second too long.

Tex's grin widened. "Oh, now I gotta know."

Benji shook his head. "Y'all need to mind your own damn business."

Tex laughed. "That's a yes."

Sam was quieter than the others. Benji could feel his eyes on him.

Benji gave him a look. Not now.

Sam nodded once but didn't say a word.

The Letter to Jessica

That night, under the dim glow of the barracks, Benji pulled out his pen and paper.

> ➤ Jessica,

I don't know where to start. Today, I saw death up close. I took another man's life for the first time. I keep telling myself it was him or me, but it don't make it any easier.

But I made it, Jess. I'm still here. And I'll keep making it. Because I promised you I would.

I wish I could hear your voice right now. Just for a second. I keep thinking about that last night together. About how I almost didn't leave because of you.

I'm counting down the days until I can come back to you. Until I can see you smile again.

Until I see you in the skies,

Benji

He folded the letter carefully, tucking it into the outgoing mail.

As he leaned back against the wall, exhaustion finally settling in, he let out a breath.

The first mission was done.

But there were more coming.

And he had to survive them all.

For Jessica.

For himself.

For the men who stood beside him in the skies.

Because this was war.

CHAPTER 13:

THE SICILY ESCORT MISSION

July 1943 – Over the Mediterranean, Near Sicily

The sky stretched endless and blue over the Mediterranean, but Benji knew better than to take comfort in it. War had a way of corrupting beauty.

The 99th Fighter Squadron soared in formation, their P-40 Warhawks slicing through the air as they escorted a fleet of B-17 Flying Fortresses toward enemy-occupied Sicily. The mission was clear—keep the bombers safe while they rained hell down on German and Italian strongholds below.

Benji adjusted his grip on the controls, his eyes scanning the vast sky. His instincts were sharp now, battle-hardened. This wasn't like their first mission— he knew what to expect, knew the feeling of an enemy fighter creeping into his blind spot.

The radio crackled. Captain Desmond Wright's voice cut through the static.

"Stay tight, eyes open. We'll be hitting enemy airspace soon."

Benji flexed his gloved fingers, exhaling slowly.

"Y'all ready for this?" Ace's voice came through, cool as ever.

"Hell yeah," Tex drawled. "Ain't nobody touchin' our bombers."

Sam's voice was quieter. "Just keep your heads on straight."

Benji smirked. "You sound nervous, Sammy."

"I just don't like flying through death traps, is all," Sam muttered.

Benji shook his head. They all knew what was coming.

Sicily's coast loomed ahead, the island stretching beneath them, its rolling hills and fortified towns painted with the scars of war. Somewhere down there, German and Italian anti-aircraft guns were waiting.

Benji could already see the black puffs of flak bursting in the distance.

He swallowed, forcing his body to relax.

Enemy Contact – The Ambush

The silence didn't last.

"Enemy fighters inbound! Eleven o'clock high!"

The call came from one of the bomber pilots, and suddenly, the sky was alive with chaos.

Messerschmitt Bf 109s, sleek and deadly, dove from above, their machine guns lighting up the sky with streaks of fire.

Benji's heart slammed against his ribs.

"Break formation! Engage!" Captain Wright ordered.

Benji rolled his P-40 hard to the right, breaking away from the bombers and diving into the fight.

His eyes locked onto an enemy fighter barreling toward a B-17, machine guns blazing.

"Not today," Benji muttered, shoving the throttle forward.

He lined up the shot, feeling the familiar rush of adrenaline.

RAT-TAT-TAT-TAT!

His bullets tore through the Messerschmitt's tail, sending it spiraling toward the sea.

"Scratch one," he muttered, banking left.

But the fight was just beginning.

Dogfight Over Sicily

Tex's voice rang through the radio. "I got one on my ass!"

Benji snapped his head to the right. A Messerschmitt was glued to Tex's tail, guns blazing.

"Hang tight, I'm coming," Benji said, yanking his stick back and looping behind them.

Tex's plane weaved through the sky, dodging tracers by inches, but the German pilot stayed locked on.

Benji pushed the throttle, lining up his sights.

RAT-TAT-TAT!

His bullets shredded the enemy plane's right wing, sending it plunging toward the ocean below.

Tex let out a breath. "Damn, Davis. Owe you one."

Benji barely had time to respond before another fighter came for him.

He saw it too late.

Gunfire ripped past his cockpit.

Benji cursed, yanking the stick hard and rolling into a steep dive. The Messerschmitt followed, staying locked onto him like a wolf on prey.

The world spun as Benji twisted and turned, trying to shake him.

"Shit—he's on me!"

Sam's voice cut through. "Bring him left!"

Benji did.

Sam came out of nowhere, firing a clean burst.

The Messerschmitt exploded into flames.

Benji exhaled, glancing to his right where Sam's plane hovered beside him.

"Saved your ass again," Sam teased.

Benji smirked. "Don't get used to it."

Above them, bombs rained down on Sicily, plumes of smoke and fire rising from the enemy strongholds.

The B-17s had done their job.

"Regroup!" Wright's voice ordered. "Mission accomplished."

Benji exhaled.

They had made it.

This time.

The sky was eerily calm now, the chaos of battle fading into the hum of engines and the distant, receding smoke from the bombing run over Sicily. Benji flexed his fingers on the stick, the adrenaline still pulsing in his veins. His heart was slowing, but the weight of the fight lingered.

"That was a hell of a mission," Tex muttered over the radio.

Ace let out a breath. "Could've been worse."

"Could've been better," Sam countered.

Benji frowned at the tone in his best friend's voice. It was sharp, clipped, not the usual mix of relief and adrenaline that came after a mission.

"Alright, boys, bring it home," Captain Wright ordered.

They banked left, heading back toward their airstrip in Tunisia.

Benji settled into formation beside Sam's plane, glancing over at his friend. Sam flew steady, his grip sure, but Benji could feel the distance—something that hadn't been there before.

The airfield came into view, a long stretch of dust and steel glinting in the North African sun. One by one, the squadron touched down, their tires kicking up clouds of dirt as they rolled to a stop.

Benji climbed out of his P-40 Warhawk, pulling off his helmet and running a hand through his damp curls. He glanced toward Sam, who was already unstrapping himself from his cockpit, his expression unreadable.

Something was off.

Tex and Ace were already joking about how many kills they claimed, but Benji barely heard them. He caught up to Sam as he made his way toward the barracks.

"Hey."

Sam kept walking.

Benji grabbed his arm. "Sam."

Finally, Sam turned. His face was tense, his jaw tight.

Benji had known him too long not to recognize that look.

"What's going on with you?" Benji asked, lowering his voice.

Sam exhaled sharply, rubbing the back of his neck. "You really wanna know?"

Benji folded his arms. "Yeah. I do."

For a moment, Sam just stared at him. Then, with a frustrated shake of his head, he muttered, "Not here. Walk with me."

Benji followed him toward the edge of the airfield, where the distant hum of engines faded into the desert wind.

They stopped near a row of grounded aircraft, the sun dipping lower in the sky.

Sam turned to him, his expression unreadable. "You been different, man. Distracted."

Benji frowned. "Distracted? I just saved your ass up there."

Sam let out a humorless chuckle. "Yeah, and I saved yours. But I ain't talking about flying, Benji." He sighed, running a hand down his face. "You know how long we been best friends?"

Benji raised an eyebrow. "Since forever."

"Then why the hell do I feel like I don't know you no more?"

Benji's stomach twisted. He knew exactly where this was going.

Sam shook his head. "I ain't stupid. I see it in your eyes, man. When you read them letters. The way you disappear at night, the way you keep lookin' off like your mind's somewhere else." His voice lowered. "It's a girl, ain't it?"

Benji didn't say anything at first. He had spent weeks avoiding this conversation, pretending like Sam wouldn't notice. But Sam always noticed.

Benji exhaled, glancing away. "…Yeah."

Sam let out a breath like he already knew but had needed to hear it from Benji's mouth. "Who is she?"

Benji hesitated.

Sam's eyes narrowed. "Benji—"

"It's Jessica Shaw," Benji admitted, cutting him off.

The name hit like a bullet.

Sam took a step back. "You're lyin'."

Benji shook his head. "I ain't."

Sam blinked, his face a mixture of disbelief and something deeper—something closer to fear.

"You mean to tell me," Sam said slowly, "that the girl you been sneakin' around with… is the senator's daughter?"

Benji didn't answer. He didn't need to.

"Jesus Christ, Benji," Sam muttered, raking a hand through his hair. "You lost your damn mind?"

Benji's jaw tightened. "It ain't like that."

"Then what's it like?!" Sam snapped. "You think her daddy's just gonna let this slide? You think the world's gonna be fine with this?"

Benji's voice was steady. "I don't care what the world thinks."

Sam let out a bitter laugh. "Well, you should. 'Cause it's gonna kill you, Benji. And it might kill her, too."

Benji felt his fists clench at his sides. He knew Sam wasn't saying it to be cruel. He was saying it because he cared. But it still burned.

"I love her," Benji admitted, his voice raw.

Sam stared at him, something shifting in his expression.

For a moment, neither of them spoke.

Then Sam exhaled, rubbing his face. "Damn it, man."

Benji looked away, his throat tight.

"Does she love you?" Sam asked quietly.

Benji swallowed. "Yeah. She does."

Sam closed his eyes for a long moment. When he opened them, some of the sharp edges in his gaze had softened.

"You really all in on this, huh?"

Benji nodded. "Yeah, I am."

Sam sighed heavily. "Then I guess I gotta have your back. Like always."

Benji let out a breath, something between relief and gratitude settling in his chest.

Sam shook his head. "This is gonna be a damn mess, Benji."

Benji smirked. "Ain't it always?"

Sam chuckled, the tension finally breaking. "Yeah. Guess it is."

The sun dipped lower, casting long shadows over the airfield.

And for the first time since they had deployed, Benji felt lighter.

The officers' club pulsed with energy by the time Benji, Sam, Tex, and Ace stepped through the doors. The air was thick with cigar smoke, whiskey, and the distant melody of jazz spilling from a gramophone in the corner. This was one of the few nights they could pretend they weren't at war.

Tex cracked his neck. "Ain't nothin' better than a drink after a good mission."

Benji smirked, still feeling the weight of today's escort mission in his shoulders. Sicily had been rough. The flak had been heavier than expected, and the bombers had barely made it out.

Sam nudged him. "First round's on you."

Benji raised a brow. "Oh, so now I'm just a free wallet?"

Ace clapped him on the back. "Damn right."

They pushed toward the bar. The bartender barely glanced at them as he poured their drinks—his usual indifference was better than open hostility, which they'd gotten plenty of before.

Benji lifted his glass. "To keepin' those bombers safe and bringing our asses home in one piece."

The others raised theirs in agreement.

They had barely taken a sip before the trouble started.

A group of white officers occupied a table in the corner, their voices carrying just a little too loudly now that the squadron had walked in.

Benji felt their stares before he even turned his head.

Tex let out a long sigh. "Here we go."

"Relax," Ace muttered. "Ain't no reason to start somethin' tonight."

But then, one of them stood.

A tall lieutenant with sharp blue eyes and a jaw that looked like it had been carved from stone. Benji knew him.

He'd seen him at the Governor's mansion two years ago. The same bastard who had tried to drag Jessica onto the dance floor.

Benji's grip tightened on his glass.

The lieutenant smirked as he stepped closer. "Well, well. If it ain't the little Negro with the fast feet."

The room went still.

Sam stiffened beside him. Tex rolled his shoulders. Ace just exhaled through his nose, looking ready to break something.

Benji didn't move. Didn't react. He wasn't about to give this man the satisfaction.

The lieutenant leaned against the bar, eyes narrowing. "Didn't think I'd see you again after that little stunt. Dancing with a girl who wasn't yours to touch."

Benji kept his voice even. "Ain't no law against dancing."

The lieutenant's smirk widened. "Maybe not in the North. But you should've learned your lesson back home."

The words were a warning. A reminder of what had happened after that dance—the bruises, the humiliation.

Benji kept his face blank, but inside, the anger simmered.

The lieutenant's grin turned cruel. "Or maybe you like steppin' outta line. Maybe you like pretending you belong." His voice lowered to a sharp edge. "Or maybe you just like white pussy."

The glass in Benji's hand shattered.

Before anyone could react, his fist connected with the lieutenant's jaw.

The man went down hard.

Then all hell broke loose.

Tex swung first, sending another officer crashing into a table.

Sam barely ducked in time before one of the men came at him, catching the bastard in the stomach with a solid right hook.

Ace, quick as always, sidestepped a punch and drove his fist into a man's ribs.

Benji didn't even hesitate—he was on the lieutenant before the man could get back up.

They crashed into the bar, knocking over bottles, fists flying.

The lieutenant got a good shot in, catching Benji across the jaw, but it barely slowed him down.

Benji slammed his elbow into the man's ribs, then drove his knee into his gut.

The lieutenant gasped, stumbling.

Benji grabbed him by the collar, dragging him close. "You wanna run your mouth now?"

The lieutenant spit blood, sneering. "Still just a boy pretending to be a man."

Benji didn't think. He slammed the bastard's face into the bar counter.

The crunch of bone and cartilage filled the air.

The lieutenant crumpled to the ground, out cold.

The fight wasn't over—Tex was still tossing punches like he was back in the ring, and Sam had his arms locked around another officer, wrestling him down.

Ace knocked one last guy off balance before turning, breathing hard. "We done?"

Benji looked around. The bar was wrecked. Tables overturned, chairs broken, and white officers groaning on the floor.

Tex wiped his mouth, grinning. "Damn. That was fun."

Sam wasn't grinning. He was breathing hard, looking at Benji like he'd just done something real stupid. "We gotta go. Now."

Before they could move, the doors burst open.

Military police stormed in.

"STAND DOWN!"

Benji exhaled, heart still pounding.

Tex muttered, "Shit."

Ace raised his hands in surrender.

Sam whispered, "This ain't good."

Benji looked down at the unconscious lieutenant at his feet.

No.

This was about to be real bad.

CHAPTER 14:

SILENCE IN THE LETTERS

September 1943 – Montgomery, Alabama

J essica sat by the window of her bedroom, fingers tracing the edge of a blank sheet of paper. The ink bottle beside her sat untouched. For the first time in months, she had nothing to write.

Because Benji wasn't writing back.

Her eyes flickered to the stack of old letters, neatly tied with a ribbon on her nightstand. The last one was dated April 1943, right before he had deployed. Since then—nothing.

At first, she told herself it was just the war. Maybe letters took longer from overseas. Maybe he was too busy flying missions, dodging bullets in the skies over Europe.

But months had passed.

Other wives and sweethearts whispered about letters arriving from their men overseas. Even Richard had mentioned receiving news from his friends stationed abroad.

Benji's silence was deafening.

Jessica swallowed hard, fighting the ache in her chest.

Had something happened to him? Was he injured? Was he—

She forced the thought away before it could take root. No. He was alive. He had to be.

Still, doubt gnawed at her.

Did he forget about her?

No. That wasn't possible.

Not after everything. Not after the way he had held her the night before he left, kissing her like he was afraid he'd never get another chance.

Not after the way he had looked at her.

Like she was his entire world.

Jessica clenched her jaw, hands gripping the letter she had intended to write. It had been sitting there for weeks, waiting.

Waiting for what?

For a reply that would never come?

For a sign that she hadn't been foolish to believe in the promises he whispered against her skin?

The frustration and hurt twisted in her gut, a storm she had no power to calm.

A sharp knock on the door startled her.

"Jessica," her mother's voice rang out. "Come downstairs. You're needed."

Jessica took a steadying breath before standing, smoothing out her dress. She had grown tired of being needed—at the charity events, at the luncheons, at her father's carefully arranged political gatherings.

It had been like this since May, when her father had discovered her letters.

Flashback – May 1943

She had been in the study, scribbling another letter to Benji when the heavy oak door swung open.

Her father, Senator Shaw, stood in the doorway.

Jessica's heart stopped.

She hadn't even had time to hide the letter before he was in front of her, his sharp eyes scanning the page, the ink still fresh.

His expression darkened. He didn't even have to read it all. He already knew.

Jessica braced herself, expecting him to yell. To demand answers.

But instead—he smiled.

And somehow, that was worse.

"So this is how you've been spending your time."

Her hands trembled as she tried to grab the letter, but he plucked it away effortlessly, scanning the words.

Then, with deliberate care, he tore it in half.

Jessica gasped, reaching for it, but he held up a hand.

"Enough." His voice was smooth, calculated. "You are not to write him again. Do you understand me?"

She felt rage rising in her throat, but before she could respond, he leaned in, voice dropping to a near whisper.

"You've already embarrassed this family once, Jessica. I will not allow you to do it again."

That was the last time she had written to Benji.

The next day, her mother had taken her shopping. New dresses, new hats, new appearances to uphold.

The following week, Richard began escorting her to luncheons, smiling as though nothing had changed.

By June, she had fully stepped into the life her father had mapped out for her.

By July, she was suffocating.

By August, she had started to believe that maybe Benji had forgotten her, too.

Present – September 1943

Jessica walked downstairs, her hands folded neatly in front of her.

Her mother, Margaret, sat in the drawing room, pouring tea, ever the image of control.

Senator Shaw stood near the fireplace, his gaze cool and unreadable.

Richard was there, too. He always was, lately.

Jessica sat, schooling her expression. She had become very good at wearing masks.

Her father set his bourbon glass down, studying her with mild curiosity. "You've been quiet, Jessica. Your mother says you spend too much time in your room."

Jessica gave a small smile. "I didn't realize solitude was a crime."

Richard chuckled, shaking his head. "No one's saying that. I think your father just means we miss your company."

Jessica glanced at him. Richard was kind. Polite. Well-mannered. He wasn't cruel like her father.

But he wasn't Benji.

He never would be.

Senator Shaw took a slow sip of his drink. "Perhaps it's time you stopped dwelling on the past and focused on your future."

Jessica stiffened.

"We're having dinner at the Governor's estate next week," her mother said, setting her teacup down. "It would do you well to be in good spirits."

Jessica nodded once, but she was already drowning them out.

The walls felt too tight.

Their voices, their expectations, their plans—it was a cage, and she was suffocating inside of it.

That night, she slipped into the kitchen where Josephine was finishing the dishes.

The older woman didn't turn.

"Your father's still watching your mail," she murmured, voice low.

Jessica swallowed hard, sinking into a chair. "I know."

Josephine wiped her hands on a cloth before finally facing her. "Ain't no letter, baby girl. I checked."

Jessica let out a slow breath. She had expected that.

She looked up, voice barely a whisper. "You think he forgot about me?"

Josephine sighed, pulling out a chair beside her.

"You know what I think?"

Jessica shook her head.

Josephine leaned in. "I think your daddy's been hiding your letters."

Jessica's heart stopped.

Slowly, the pieces started to fit together.

The missing letters. The silence. The sudden shift in her father's control over her life.

Had Benji written her back?

Had he been reaching for her all this time, just for her father to steal his words from her?

The realization hit like a freight train.

Jessica clenched her fists, breathing hard.

Josephine reached over, squeezing her hand gently. "You ain't gotta sit here and let them shape you into what they want. The Jessica I know? She's got fire."

Jessica stared down at their joined hands.

For months, she had let herself be pushed, shaped, molded into something she wasn't.

All because she thought Benji had given up on her.

But if Josephine was right…

If he had still been writing…

Jessica's chest tightened.

She had to find out the truth.

And if she found those letters?

God help whoever tried to stand in her way.

Jessica barely slept that night.

Josephine's words echoed in her mind.

"I think your daddy's been hiding your letters."

She lay in bed, staring at the ceiling, her body tense with frustration and heartache. She wanted to believe it wasn't true—that her father wouldn't do something like that.

But she knew better.

She had spent her whole life watching Senator Shaw control everything, shaping reality to fit his narrative.

Jessica had been a fool to think he would allow her to love a man like Benji without interference.

Her pulse pounded as she sat up, swinging her legs over the edge of the bed. The night was quiet, the house settled into its usual stillness.

Maybe she could find the letters.

Maybe—just maybe—her father had kept them somewhere in his study.

Jessica hesitated only a moment before rising to her feet, slipping into her robe. She cracked her door open, peeking into the dim hallway.

The house was still.

She moved silently, making her way toward her father's study.

The heavy oak door was locked. Of course it was.

Her stomach twisted.

She knew where he kept his keys.

For a long moment, she stood frozen, debating whether she was truly willing to take this risk.

Then, she thought of Benji.

Of the months of silence.

Of all the nights she had lain awake, wondering if he had ever even thought of her.

If he had written to her.

She had to know.

She turned and crept toward her parents' bedroom, her breath shallow.

The small table near the door held exactly what she was looking for—her father's pocket watch, a half-empty glass of bourbon, and his keyring.

Her fingers barely brushed the metal before a voice cut through the dark.

"What are you doing?"

Jessica gasped, whirling around.

Her mother stood in the doorway, her nightgown flowing like a ghost in the dim light.

Jessica swallowed hard, steadying herself. "I—I was just getting water."

Margaret Shaw's gaze flickered to the keys, her expression unreadable.

Jessica expected her to demand an explanation, to call for her father.

But instead, she sighed, stepping closer.

"You're looking for his letters, aren't you?"

Jessica's breath caught in her throat.

Her mother studied her, then slowly reached for the glass of bourbon on the table.

"He burned them."

Jessica felt like the floor had vanished beneath her.

"No." Her voice was barely a whisper.

Her mother took a slow sip of bourbon before setting the glass down with a soft clink. "You knew he would never allow it, Jessica. You should have expected this."

Jessica's hands curled into fists.

"So that's it?" she choked out. "You're just going to stand by while he takes everything from me?"

Margaret's lips pressed into a thin line. "I've learned, my dear, that fighting your father is a losing battle."

Jessica's heart pounded, rage burning beneath her skin.

But she saw something in her mother's eyes—something weary. Resigned.

Jessica realized then that Margaret Shaw had spent her entire life doing what was expected of her.

And she would never fight back.

But Jessica would.

She turned on her heel and walked away, ignoring her mother's voice calling after her.

She didn't need to find the letters to know the truth.

Her father had stolen them.

And she would never forgive him for it.

The Plan to Leave

Jessica didn't sleep.

By morning, she had made up her mind.

She needed to leave Montgomery.

If she stayed, she would suffocate. Her father would keep controlling her, keep shaping her into something she wasn't.

And she couldn't spend another second waiting for a letter that would never come.

She needed to start over.

Somewhere far from here.

And she knew exactly where.

That afternoon, she waited until her father left for his office before entering the study—not to look for the letters, but for something else.

His checkbook.

Jessica had learned long ago that the best way to get something past her father was to make it look like his idea.

He donated to charities constantly—his way of maintaining an untouchable public image.

She pulled out a blank check, her hand steady as she wrote a generous sum. Enough to get her to Chicago. Enough to secure her place in law school.

She made it out to herself, writing in the memo line: Shaw Family Charitable Fund.

It was a gamble. But she knew her father barely glanced at the donations he made. As long as it looked like another act of generosity, he wouldn't question it.

Jessica slipped the check into her purse and smoothed out her dress.

Step one was complete.

Now, she just needed to tell Josephine.

Late That Night – Confiding in Josephine

Jessica sat at the small wooden table in the servants' quarters, hands wrapped around a steaming cup of tea.

Josephine sat across from her, arms folded, studying her carefully.

"You sure about this, baby girl?"

Jessica nodded. "I can't stay here, Jo. I need to go."

Josephine sighed, shaking her head. "Your daddy ain't gonna like it."

Jessica's jaw tightened. "He doesn't have to."

Silence stretched between them.

Finally, Josephine exhaled and leaned forward, taking Jessica's hands in hers. "Alright. Tell me what you need."

Relief flooded Jessica's chest.

"I need your help getting out of here. I can't let them know until I'm already gone."

Josephine nodded, determination setting in her eyes.

Jessica bit her lip. "And… if you find anything—anything from Benji… will you send it to me?"

Josephine's gaze softened.

"You already know I will."

Jessica swallowed hard, squeezing her hands.

She was leaving.

She was taking her future back.

And she was going to find out the truth about Benji—even if it took her all the way to Chicago.

Jessica adjusted the hat on her head, pulling it low enough to shadow her features as she stepped onto the cracked sidewalk of a quieter part of Montgomery. The air was thick with late summer heat, making the fabric of her dress stick uncomfortably to her skin, but she barely noticed.

Every step she took felt heavier, more final.

This was it.

Her heart pounded as she reached the small shop tucked between two buildings, its wooden sign slightly faded but still legible: Lewis & Sons Pawn & Trade.

A Black-owned business. One her father would never dare step foot in.

Jessica exhaled through her nose, steadied herself, and pushed open the door.

A bell jingled overhead, the scent of aged leather and old wood filling her nose. The shop was cluttered with all sorts of items—watches, instruments, radios, and jewelry displayed behind a thick glass case.

A tall man in his sixties stood behind the counter, wiping down a silver pocket watch. His graying beard framed his strong features, his dark eyes flicking up at her presence.

For a second, he seemed surprised to see a woman like her in here, dressed in wealth and privilege.

"Afternoon, Miss," he greeted cautiously, setting the watch down. "What can I do for you?"

Jessica swallowed, then reached into her purse and pulled out a small velvet pouch, placing it on the counter with a trembling hand.

"I need to sell these."

The shopkeeper studied her for a moment before slowly untying the pouch and spilling the contents onto the counter.

Diamonds. Pearls. Gold. The kind of jewelry that came from money—the kind that didn't usually end up in a pawn shop.

Jessica's throat tightened. Each piece had a memory attached to it. Her mother's gifted earrings. A necklace given on her sixteenth birthday. A diamond bracelet from her father after her first society gala.

She was giving it all up.

The man picked up one of the pieces—a sapphire ring—and inspected it under the light.

"These are worth a lot," he murmured. "You sure about this?"

Jessica nodded. "I just need enough to get out of here."

He looked at her then. Really looked.

His eyes softened in understanding.

Without another word, he set the ring down and pulled a small scale from beneath the counter. He weighed the pieces carefully, occasionally glancing up at her as if expecting her to change her mind.

After a few minutes, he set his pencil down and exhaled.

"I can give you three hundred dollars."

Jessica's stomach twisted.

That was nothing compared to what the jewelry was actually worth. Some of those pieces alone were valued at thousands.

But she didn't have time to negotiate.

"That's fine."

The man studied her again, then nodded. He stepped into the back and returned with a stack of bills. He counted them out carefully, placed them in an envelope, and slid it toward her.

Jessica took it without hesitation.

She was almost free.

As she turned to leave, his voice stopped her.

"Miss," he said, leaning slightly forward, his tone gentler now. "Whatever you're runnin' from… I hope you find what you're lookin' for."

Jessica hesitated for half a second.

Then she met his gaze and nodded.

"Me too."

She stepped out of the shop, the weight of her decision settling into her bones.

This was real.

She clutched the envelope tight, her feet moving swiftly down the street.

Tomorrow, she would cash her check from her father's "charity" and have enough to start over.

Tomorrow, she would leave Montgomery for good.

Tomorrow, she would be one step closer to freedom.

And one step further from Benji.

Because she still didn't know.

Did he love her?

Did he still love her?

Or had she been a fool for believing he ever would?

Jessica swallowed hard and kept walking.

There was no turning back now.

CHAPTER 15:

THE CONSEQUENCES OF A FIGHTER'S TEMPER

July 1943 – Over the Mediterranean, Near Sicily

Flashback – The Holding Cell

The air inside the makeshift holding cell was thick with stale sweat and the metallic tang of dried blood. The bruises on Benji's ribs throbbed with each breath, but he wasn't about to let it show. Across from him, Tex was slouched against the wall, arms crossed over his chest like he was settling in for a nap. Ace sat on the bench, knuckles still raw, a smirk tugging at the corner of his lips.

Sam, however, wasn't smiling.

Benji could feel his best friend's glare burning a hole through him, but he refused to look his way. He knew exactly what Sam wanted to say. He also knew

Sam was holding back because Major Spencer and Captain Desmond had just entered the room.

Spencer, a stocky white man with cold eyes, paced in front of them, hands folded behind his back. The way he looked at them wasn't new—it was the same way most of the white officers looked at the 99th: like they were an experiment that had gone on too long.

Desmond stood a few feet behind him, arms crossed, his expression unreadable.

"You boys sure know how to make a name for yourselves," Spencer said, his voice laced with disdain. "I should've had every one of you discharged, but I'm not in the mood for the paperwork."

Benji clenched his jaw.

"You think this is funny, Davis?" Spencer continued, eyes narrowing in on him. "Breaking a superior officer's nose? Brawling in an officers' club? You were already on thin ice, and now you just handed me every reason to send you packing."

Benji kept his mouth shut.

Spencer turned his glare to Tex and Ace. "And you two? You were supposed to be officers, not damn street fighters."

Tex smirked. "Didn't know defending ourselves was against regulations, sir."

Spencer's face reddened. "Defending yourselves? You Negroes threw the first punch!"

Benji felt his fists clench. "With all due respect, sir, that ain't true."

Spencer scoffed. "I don't care. You think any of this matters?" He let out a sharp laugh. "This squadron is already hanging by a thread, and you lot just made it a hell of a lot easier for them to scrap the whole damn program. The next time I hear about one of you so much as sneezing the wrong way, you're gone. Understood?"

None of them responded.

Spencer exhaled sharply, rubbing his temples like he was exhausted by the sight of them. "Effective immediately: Davis, you are demoted to Second Lieutenant. You will be assigned extra duties for the remainder of your time here. Cleaning, loading equipment—whatever needs to be done when you're not flying. You will not be leading a damn thing anymore. If you so much as look at another officer the wrong way, I will have you shipped back stateside."

Benji felt his stomach drop, but he didn't let it show.

Spencer turned to Tex and Ace. "Consider yourselves lucky you're not getting the same. Get the hell out of my sight."

The guards stepped forward to unlock the cell.

As the others filed out, Desmond lingered, looking at Benji.

"Davis," he said, voice lower, calmer. "Walk with me."

Outside the Holding Cell – Desmond's Warning

Benji followed Desmond out into the cool night air. The base was quiet, save for the distant hum of aircraft engines being prepped for tomorrow's mission.

Desmond stopped near a row of jeeps, crossing his arms. "I told you to keep your head down."

Benji exhaled, rolling his shoulders. "I wasn't about to let that bastard run his mouth."

Desmond narrowed his eyes. "That bastard just cost you your rank. And almost cost you your wings."

Benji looked away, staring at the dirt beneath his boots.

Desmond sighed, shaking his head. "I know what that was really about. You saw him—the same officer from that dance back in Alabama, didn't you?"

Benji stiffened but didn't deny it.

Desmond rubbed his temples. "Look, I get it. But you can't do this, Davis. Not here. Not now. You think these white officers are waiting for you to prove yourself? No—they're waiting for you to fail. And you just gave them exactly what they wanted."

Benji let out a sharp breath. "What was I supposed to do? Let him say what he said?"

"Yes," Desmond said firmly. "Because you're bigger than this. Because you're better than this. Because if you let your emotions run you, they win."

Benji stayed silent, his jaw tight.

Desmond exhaled. "You still got your wings, Davis. Don't make me regret saving your ass."

Benji finally nodded. "I won't."

Desmond studied him for a long moment, then nodded back. "Get some rest. We've got a mission at dawn."

Present Day – Pre-Mission Briefing

The next morning, the 99th Fighter Squadron gathered for their mission briefing. The P-40 Warhawks were still lined up on the airstrip, but word had already spread that they'd soon be transitioning to P-51 Mustangs. The Luftwaffe had been getting more aggressive, and the bombers needed faster, better protection.

Sam took charge of the briefing now that he was leading the section.

"We're flying cover for B-25 Mitchells hitting enemy positions near the Gustav Line. Expect heavy flak and enemy fighters. We go in, protect the bombers, and get out clean. Stick to formation, keep your heads on a swivel, and don't play hero. Got it?"

A round of "Yes, sir" echoed.

Benji sat quietly, listening. It was strange, not being the one leading. The demotion stung worse than any bruises from the fight. But he had brought this on himself.

Sam glanced at him briefly, a silent message in his eyes. Don't do anything stupid today.

Benji gave a slight nod.

Desmond stepped forward. "Launch at 0600. Gear up and be ready to fly."

As the squadron began filing out, Tex nudged Benji. "Ain't it weird, not hearin' them call your name to lead?"

Benji exhaled through his nose. "Feels like I got my damn wings clipped."

Tex grinned. "Well, you still get to fly. And you still get to shoot some Krauts out the sky. So could be worse."

Benji smirked, shaking his head. "Could always be worse."

As they walked toward the airstrip, Benji felt the familiar weight of Jessica's sky-blue scarf wrapped around his control stick. He still hadn't heard from her. Still hadn't received a single letter.

But she was still with him.

Somewhere out there, she was waiting.

And he wasn't about to let a demotion, a bar fight, or a war keep him from making it back to her.

The morning air was crisp with the lingering chill of the Italian countryside as Benji tightened the straps of his flight suit. The eastern horizon burned orange with the approaching dawn, casting long shadows over the airfield.

The P-40 Warhawks stood lined up in a perfect row, their noses pointed toward the battlefield that awaited them. Though word had spread about their eventual upgrade to the P-51 Mustangs, today, they still had to make do with the rugged fighters that had carried them this far.

Benji slid on his leather gloves, exhaling a steady breath. His mind was clear—focused. The tension from the bar fight still clung to him, but there was no room for distraction now. Today, they were heading straight into enemy fire.

Sam walked up beside him, adjusting his parachute straps. "Feeling good?"

Benji smirked. "Always."

Sam snorted. "That's a damn lie."

Benji chuckled. "Yeah, well… it's a good one."

Tex and Ace joined them, helmets tucked under their arms. Tex stretched his broad shoulders, rolling his neck. "They say we might be gettin' some new toys soon," he mused. "You think those Mustangs fly as smooth as they say?"

Ace shrugged. "Wouldn't know. But I sure as hell wouldn't mind finding out."

Sam shifted, looking over the squadron as the ground crew bustled around, fueling the planes and making last-minute checks. His expression grew serious. "Alright, listen up. We're flying top cover for B-25 Mitchell bombers. Enemy flak's expected to be heavy, and there's been chatter about increased Luftwaffe activity near the Gustav Line."

Benji nodded, rolling his shoulders. The Germans were digging in hard as the Allies pushed deeper into Italy. The Luftwaffe had been more aggressive lately, defending every stretch of land with everything they had.

Sam continued, "Stick to formation. Stay sharp. We get those bombers in and out, we go home. No hero shit, got it?"

Tex smirked. "What if the hero shit gets us medals?"

"Then you better hope I ain't the one writing the damn report," Sam shot back.

Ace chuckled. "You heard him. Keep it tight, keep it clean."

Benji checked his cockpit one last time. His hands brushed over Jessica's sky-blue scarf, still tied neatly around the control stick. It had been months since he'd heard from her. Months of wondering, of sending letters into silence.

He clenched his jaw, willing the thoughts away.

Focus.

The ground crew signaled them—it was time.

The squadron climbed into their cockpits, securing their helmets and fastening their harnesses. Engines roared to life, propellers slicing through the morning air.

Benji's radio crackled as Captain Desmond's steady voice came through.

"Red Section, this is Lead. Wheels up in thirty seconds."

Benji adjusted his grip on the throttle. He could feel his pulse, steady and sure.

The mission was clear.

Get the bombers to target. Protect them at all costs. Bring everyone home.

Tex's voice came through the radio. "Well, boys. Let's get this shit done."

The Sky Turns to Fire

Fifteen minutes after takeoff, they spotted the bombers—dozens of B-25 Mitchells flying in tight formation, their silver bodies gleaming under the morning sun.

Benji's P-40 moved into position, flanking one of the bomber groups. The pilots inside gave a small wave of acknowledgment. The bomber crews respected the 99th Fighter Squadron—they had seen what the Tuskegee Airmen could do, and they trusted them to keep them alive.

Everything was smooth at first. Clear skies, steady altitude.

Then—

"Bandits! Two o'clock high!"

The call came through like lightning.

Benji's head snapped up. A formation of Messerschmitt Bf 109s was descending fast, their sleek frames cutting through the sky like daggers.

Luftwaffe fighters.

Benji tightened his grip on the stick. This was it.

"Alright, boys," Sam's voice came over the radio, calm but sharp. "Break formation. Engage."

Engines roared as the 99th split off, climbing to intercept.

Benji's heart pounded. He spotted one—no, two—enemy fighters coming in hot.

He pushed the throttle forward, the P-40 shaking as he surged ahead. His eyes locked onto one of the Messerschmitts, its gun ports flashing as it opened fire.

Benji rolled hard left, the tracer rounds barely missing his wing.

He gritted his teeth. "Not today, you son of a—"

He pulled back on the stick, looping up and around, cutting behind the German fighter. The enemy pilot tried to bank right, but Benji was already there, lining up his sights.

Rat-tat-tat-tat!

His .50 caliber machine guns roared. The rounds ripped through the Messerschmitt's fuselage, smoke spilling from the engine.

The enemy plane spiraled, then exploded in a fiery burst.

Benji exhaled sharply. One down.

But there was no time to celebrate.

A second Bf 109 dove straight for him.

Benji jerked hard to the right, avoiding the burst of bullets that zipped past his canopy.

"Davis, watch your six!" Sam's voice rang through the radio.

Benji gritted his teeth. The Luftwaffe pilot was good—sticking to him like glue.

Tex's voice crackled in. "I got you, kid—break left!"

Benji didn't hesitate. He yanked the stick left, rolling his P-40 into a hard turn. The enemy fighter followed—right into Tex's crosshairs.

"Tex, now!"

Tex's guns lit up the sky. The Bf 109 exploded in midair.

Benji let out a breath. "Damn. Good shooting."

Tex chuckled. "Don't mention it."

But the fight wasn't over.

Ahead, the B-25 bombers were now taking heavy flak from the ground. Explosions erupted around them, shrapnel tearing through the air.

More enemy fighters were still incoming.

Benji's radio crackled. "Stay on the bombers! We lose them, we lose everything!"

Sam's voice was tight, commanding.

Benji re-centered himself. This was their job. Protect the bombers. Keep them in the sky.

He surged forward, eyes locked on an enemy fighter closing in on one of their bombers.

Not on his watch.

Benji dived, lined up his shot, and pulled the trigger.

The Aftermath

By the time they made it back to base, the sun was already beginning to set.

The mission had been a success—the bombers had delivered their payload, and despite the Luftwaffe's relentless attack, most of them had made it home.

But not all of them.

Tex sat on the wing of his P-40, helmet in his lap, staring off toward the horizon. Ace stood nearby, silent.

Benji wiped the sweat from his brow, glancing toward the empty spaces on the airstrip.

Two of their men hadn't come back.

Two empty bunks. Two fewer pilots at the mess hall.

He exhaled, jaw tight.

Sam walked up beside him.

"They knew what they signed up for," Sam murmured, but his voice was heavy.

Benji nodded. He knew. But it didn't make it any easier.

His hands unconsciously brushed over Jessica's scarf, still wrapped around his control stick.

He had survived today.

But he wasn't sure how many more tomorrows they had left.

Benji sat on the edge of his cot, staring down at the stack of letters in his hands. The envelope on top was from his mother, the familiar slant of her handwriting immediately easing some of the tension in his chest. He had received three letters today—one from his mother, one from Naomi, and one from Marcus.

He thumbed through them slowly, savoring each one. But none of them were from Jessica.

It had been months now since he last heard from her. Every letter he sent had been met with silence. At first, he told himself it was just the war. That maybe her letters were getting lost. That maybe she was busy.

But the doubt was creeping in.

Had she moved on?

Had she finally realized that it was easier to live the life her father wanted than to fight for something that felt impossible?

Benji exhaled sharply, running a hand over his face. He didn't want to believe it. He couldn't believe it.

But the silence—it was deafening.

Across the barracks, Tex and Ace were playing a game of cards, their laughter low and tired. The mood was always different after missions. A little more subdued. A little more aware of how quickly things could change.

Benji let the letters rest on his lap as he carefully untied the sky-blue scarf from his control stick, bringing it to his nose. It still smelled like her, faint but undeniable. The scent unlocked memories—Jessica's fingers brushing against his, the warmth of her lips on his, the way she had looked at him the night before he left.

He closed his eyes for a moment, wishing he could hear her voice.

"Benji."

He blinked, looking up.

Sam stood in front of him, hands on his hips, his expression unreadable.

Benji cleared his throat. "What's up?"

Sam tilted his head toward the letters. "Another batch come in?"

Benji nodded, tapping the pile beside him. "Yeah. Ma says Naomi is causing hell at school, talkin' about how she's smarter than her teacher."

Sam chuckled. "Sounds about right."

Benji smirked, but it faded fast. He turned the unopened letters over in his hand before setting them down.

Sam didn't miss the hesitation.

"Still nothing from her?" he asked.

Benji shook his head. "Nope."

Sam sat down on the cot across from him, sighing. "Damn."

Benji didn't say anything.

Sam leaned forward, resting his elbows on his knees. "Alright, tell me straight—what are you thinkin'?"

Benji exhaled, staring at the floor. "I dunno, man. Maybe… maybe she don't feel the same way no more."

Sam frowned. "Nah. That don't sound right."

Benji scoffed. "Then what does? I been writin' her since I left. Every week, every mission, every damn chance I get. And I ain't heard a word."

Sam was quiet for a long moment.

Then, he shrugged. "You ever think maybe it ain't her?"

Benji frowned. "What the hell does that mean?"

"I mean, you know who her daddy is. Shaw ain't the type to just sit back and let his daughter write love letters to a Negro fightin' overseas. You really think that man ain't pullin' some strings?"

Benji's jaw tightened. "You think he's takin' 'em?"

Sam lifted a brow. "Wouldn't be surprised. Man's got power, Benji. If he don't want you hearin' from her, he's gonna make damn sure you don't."

The thought hit hard, because it made too much sense.

Benji rubbed his temple. "Damn."

Sam clapped a hand on his shoulder. "Listen, I dunno what's happenin' with Jessica. But I do know one thing—you ain't the type to give up easy."

Benji let out a tired chuckle. "Yeah, well, maybe I should be."

Sam smirked. "Not your style, man."

They sat in silence for a few moments, the weight of everything settling between them. Outside, the engines of distant planes hummed low, a constant reminder of the war they were still fighting.

Sam leaned back against the cot, stretching his legs out. "Y'know, it's kinda crazy."

Benji looked over at him. "What is?"

Sam exhaled, shaking his head. "We been dreamin' about flyin' since we were kids. And now? We're here. We're actually doin' it. Fightin' the war, just like we said we would."

Benji's gaze drifted to the ceiling, a small smile pulling at the corner of his lips. "Yeah. We are."

Sam grinned. "And you? You're the best damn pilot I've ever seen, Benji. You belong up there."

Benji huffed a laugh. "Took you long enough to admit it."

Sam chuckled, tossing a pillow at him. "Yeah, yeah. Don't get cocky."

Benji dodged it, grinning. "Too late."

They fell into a comfortable silence, the kind that only came from years of knowing someone better than you knew yourself.

Sam ran a hand over his head, his expression softening. "I know this war's got us all feelin' some kinda way. But whatever happens? You ain't alone, man."

Benji looked over at him, something settling in his chest.

He nodded. "I know."

Sam smirked. "Damn right, you do."

Benji exhaled, grabbing the scarf again, fingers tightening around the fabric.

He didn't know if Jessica's silence was because of her father, because of the war, or because she had decided to let him go.

But he knew one thing.

He wasn't giving up.

Not yet.

CHAPTER 16:

THE BATTLE OF ANZIO

January 1944 – Over the Skies of Italy

A couple days later suns gone down the airfield was quiet, but the weight of war still clung to the night like fog. The last few weeks had been relentless mission after mission, loss after loss. Most of the boys had given up on sleeping in the barracks, instead catching rest wherever they could.

For Benji, that meant his plane.

He was slumped in the cockpit of his P-40 Warhawk, his flight jacket pulled tight around him, Jessica's worn photograph still clutched between his fingers. Even in sleep, he held on to her.

A firm nudge shook his shoulder.

"Wake up, Flyboy."

Benji stirred, groggy, before blinking against the dim glow of the airstrip lights.

Sam was standing beside the plane, arms crossed, smirking. "Damn, man, you really out here sleeping like this?"

Benji sat up, rubbing his face. "What time is it?"

"Late." Sam leaned against the wing, peering up at him. "Figured I'd check on you before I turn in. You missed dinner, by the way."

Benji let out a long breath. "Not hungry."

Sam's gaze flicked to the photo in Benji's hand. "You dreaming about her again?"

Benji glanced down at the picture—Jessica's soft eyes, the smile that always felt like home. His thumb brushed over the worn edges.

"Something like that."

Sam chuckled. "Damn, man. That girl's got you bad."

Benji smirked. "I know."

Sam tapped the metal frame of the plane. "What's she gonna say when she finds out you've been sleeping in this tin can instead of a bed?"

Benji sighed. "Not much choice. Missions keep coming in. Feels like I just landed, and they're already briefing us for the next one."

Sam nodded. "Yeah, it's been rough. Hell, even the new guys are already looking like old men." He exhaled, the humor fading from his voice. "Ain't how I thought this would be, you know? When we first signed up?"

Benji didn't answer right away. He knew what Sam meant.

They had dreamed of flying, of proving themselves, of making it home heroes. But war had a way of taking dreams and turning them into survival.

"You thinking about home?" Benji finally asked.

Sam nodded slowly. "Yeah. Thinking about Janie. Thinking about how much time I've spent out here instead of with her."

Benji studied his best friend. "You planning on marrying her when this is over?"

Sam scoffed. "Man, if I make it out of here, I'll marry her that same damn day."

Benji smirked. "That eager, huh?"

"Look," Sam said, more serious now. "You and I both know nothing's promised out here. I ain't waiting around for a tomorrow that might not come. If I get the chance, I'm grabbing it with both hands."

Benji nodded. He understood that better than most.

They sat in silence for a moment, just the distant sound of the wind rolling over the airstrip.

"You ever think about what comes after this?" Sam asked.

Benji exhaled. "Yeah. I wanna fly, but not for the war. I wanna teach. Help kids like us take to the skies."

Sam grinned. "Now that I can see. Lieutenant Davis, the fearless instructor."

Benji smirked. "Something like that."

Sam tilted his head toward the photo. "And what about her?"

Benji ran his fingers over Jessica's face. "I'm gonna find her. No matter how long it takes."

Sam smiled, but there was something unreadable in his eyes. "Yeah, Flyboy. I bet you will."

There was a beat of silence, just the distant hum of the airfield filling the space between them.

Sam exhaled, rubbing a hand over his jaw. Then, almost casually, he said, "You know, I never cared about flying the way you do."

Benji frowned, turning to look at him. "Then why'd you join?"

Sam shrugged, smirking. "Because you did. Somebody had to keep your stubborn ass in check."

Benji stared at him, reading between the lines. The weight of what Sam wasn't saying pressed in.

Sam chuckled, giving the side of the plane a small pat. "Ain't saying I regret it. Just saying… if you weren't here, neither would I be."

Benji felt something tighten in his chest. "Sam—"

"Don't start, Flyboy," Sam interrupted, grinning. "Just make sure all this crazy flying of yours means something."

He slapped the side of the plane. "Alright, man, I'll let you get back to dreaming about your girl. Try not to freeze out here."

Benji chuckled. "I'll manage."

Sam turned to go, but then hesitated. He looked back, his smirk fading.

"Hey, Benji?"

"Yeah?"

Sam held his gaze for a long moment, something unsaid hanging in the air.

"When you do marry that girl, make sure I get an invite."

Benji grinned. "Wouldn't dream of having it without you."

Sam nodded, satisfied. Then he gave a small salute, turned, and disappeared into the night.

Benji sat there a moment longer, staring at the empty space where his best friend had stood.

The sun was just beginning to break over the Italian coastline, casting streaks of soft gold against the frozen horizon. At 20,000 feet, the air was thin, crisp, and quiet—too quiet.

Benji flexed his gloved fingers around the stick, feeling the familiar hum of his P-40 Warhawk vibrating through his bones. The cockpit was his second skin, a place where he could forget about everything but the mission.

But today, something felt off.

The 99th Fighter Squadron was running escort duty for a squadron of B-24 Liberators, protecting them from enemy fighters as they bombed German defenses near Anzio. They had done this countless times before, but this time, there was an unease settling in Benji's gut.

"Stay tight," Captain Desmond's voice crackled over the radio. "Flak's gonna be heavier than hell."

Benji glanced to his right, catching a glimpse of Sam's plane, Call Sign 'Steel', keeping steady formation. His best friend tipped his wings in a small, cocky wave.

"Just another day at the office, huh, Flyboy?" Sam's voice came through the radio, light-hearted but steady.

Benji smirked. "Let's get these boys home in one piece."

Tex and Ace flew a little ahead, scanning for enemy activity, while Benji and Sam covered the tail end of the formation. The bombers were slow, cumbersome, and vulnerable—prime targets for enemy Luftwaffe fighters.

And then, the silence shattered.

"Bandits! Eleven o'clock high! Messerschmitts, inbound fast!"

The radio exploded with chatter as a swarm of German Bf 109s came diving in from above, their machine guns lighting up the sky.

Benji cursed and yanked the stick hard to the left, pushing his Warhawk into an evasive maneuver. Tracers ripped through the sky as the enemy fighters closed in on the bombers.

"Break, break!" Captain Desmond ordered.

Benji opened fire, his .50 caliber machine guns roaring as he caught a Messerschmitt in his sights. The rounds shredded through the enemy fighter's fuselage, sending it spiraling down in a plume of smoke.

Sam whooped. "That's one for the Ghost!"

Benji barely had time to celebrate before two more German fighters came barreling toward him.

"Shit, I'm on it!" Sam called, banking hard to intercept.

Benji rolled, dodging the first volley of gunfire, his heart pounding against his ribs. He could hear the engines roaring around him, the chaos of battle swallowing them whole.

The bombers were still pressing forward, trying to reach their target, but they were sitting ducks without fighter cover.

"Stay on the bombers!" Desmond barked. "Do not break formation!"

Sam's voice cut in. "Negative, I got a bogey lining up on one of the bombers—he's gonna take it out!"

Benji's stomach twisted.

"Sam, fall back! We'll handle it!"

But Sam was already moving.

Through the blur of battle, Benji caught sight of his best friend breaking formation, gunning his Warhawk straight toward an incoming Messerschmitt that was lining up its cannons on a B-24 bomber.

Benji's blood ran cold.

"Sam, don't—"

But Sam never hesitated.

His Warhawk dove in at full speed, guns blazing. He tore through the German fighter, bullets ripping into its fuselage. The Messerschmitt exploded into a fireball.

The bomber was safe.

But Sam was wide open.

Benji saw it a second too late.

A second Messerschmitt appeared out of nowhere, its guns locked onto Sam's plane.

Benji slammed his throttle forward, pushing his Warhawk to the limit.

"Sam, break left! BREAK LEFT!"

Sam tried. But he wasn't fast enough.

The enemy fighter opened fire.

Bullets ripped through Sam's cockpit, through his fuselage, tearing his plane apart.

"No!" Benji roared.

Sam's Warhawk burst into flames, the nose dipping as smoke poured from the engine.

"Sam! Can you hear me? Pull up!"

Silence.

Benji watched in horror as his best friend's plane spiraled downward.

He could barely make out Sam's voice through the static. It was weak.

"Tell my mama I love her."

The Warhawk hit the earth below and exploded on impact.

A scream ripped from Benji's throat, but it never made a sound.

Sam was gone.

Just like that.

Everything inside Benji shattered.

And then, the devil arrived.

A silver-nosed Messerschmitt Bf 109 streaked across the sky, its wings glinting in the morning light. It moved with unnatural precision, like it had been born for the hunt.

Benji's breathing hitched.

This pilot was different.

This wasn't just another German fighter.

This was him.

The White Wolf.

Benji's hands tightened around the stick. His pulse pounded in his ears. He could barely hear the frantic radio chatter, the calls for retreat, the orders from Captain Desmond.

None of it mattered.

The White Wolf's plane dipped low, circling the wreckage of Sam's burning aircraft like a predator admiring its kill.

Rage unlike anything Benji had ever felt burned through his veins.

He threw his plane into full throttle.

"I got him," Benji growled into the radio.

Ace's voice was sharp. "Benji, fall back! You hear me? Fall back!"

But Benji was already locked in.

This bastard wasn't walking away.

He rolled his Warhawk into a tight loop, lining up with the Messerschmitt's tail.

The German pilot didn't run.

Instead—he smiled.

Benji could see it, even through the distance between their cockpits.

A slow, knowing smile.

Like he had been waiting for this moment.

Benji's hands shook on the trigger.

He pulled back.

And the White Wolf disappeared.

One second he was there.

The next—he was gone.

Benji's eyes darted frantically, scanning the skies. Where the hell did he—

Gunfire erupted behind him.

The Messerschmitt came out of nowhere, cutting through the clouds, bullets tearing past Benji's wings.

The bastard had outmaneuvered him.

Benji yanked the stick, his plane twisting violently through the air. His Warhawk wasn't built for this kind of chase. The Messerschmitt was faster, lighter, deadlier.

And the White Wolf knew it.

He toyed with Benji, circling him, chasing him down.

Tex's voice roared through the radio. "Benji, get the hell outta there!"

But Benji barely heard him.

His best friend was gone.

And he was alone in the sky with a ghost.

The sky was a graveyard.

Benji's P-40 Warhawk tore through the battlefield, the metal vibrating beneath his hands as his engine howled. Smoke. Fire. Blood. The screams of dying men crackled through the radio, mixing with the staccato rhythm of gunfire.

Sam was gone.

Benji couldn't breathe. Couldn't think.

His heart pounded against his ribs as he yanked the stick hard, pulling his Warhawk into a breakneck turn. The Messerschmitt clung to him like a shadow. The silver-nosed fighter was fast, too fast, too sharp.

This was no ordinary German pilot.

This was Werner Galland. The White Wolf.

Benji had heard the name whispered among their ranks—a ruthless Luftwaffe ace with an undefeated record. He toyed with his kills, baited them, hunted them, and then ended them.

And now, he had set his sights on Benji.

Benji's fingers clenched around the stick, his knuckles white.

"You were too slow, little Black Bird," Galland's voice crackled through the comms, thick with an arrogant German accent.

Rage burned through Benji's veins, his stomach twisting.

Sam was dead.

Because of him.

And now this son of a bitch was taunting him.

Benji slammed the throttle forward, the Warhawk groaning under the strain. The G-forces crushed him into his seat, his vision tunneling as he spiraled through the sky.

He needed an opening. A moment. A breath.

But Galland stayed right on him.

It was like flying against his own reflection—every move, every instinct, countered with precision.

Benji's hands were slick with sweat.

Damn it.

He had to make a choice.

Chase revenge and risk getting himself killed?

Or turn back and protect the bombers that were barely holding their own against the swarm of German fighters?

He sucked in a breath.

He knew what Sam would've done.

"Next time," Benji growled, breaking off the chase.

Galland didn't pursue.

Instead, he hovered for a fraction of a second, watching, like a predator letting its prey run.

And then, he vanished into the clouds.

Benji pulled his plane back into formation, jaw clenched so tight it hurt. This wasn't over.

Not by a long shot.

The Aftermath – Returning to Base

Benji's Warhawk touched down on the runway, the wheels screeching as he brought the bird to a shaky stop. His hands felt like stone against the controls.

As soon as he popped the canopy and unfastened his harness, his body revolted.

The second his boots hit the ground, his stomach heaved.

Benji lurched forward, gripping the edge of the plane as vomit spewed onto the dirt. His whole body trembled—from exhaustion, from grief, from the unbearable weight of what had just happened.

The airfield around him blurred.

Voices shouted in the distance, the smell of burnt fuel and metal thick in the air. Footsteps pounded toward him.

"Benji!"

Strong hands gripped his shoulders.

Tex.

Benji couldn't move. Could barely breathe.

His chest shuddered with each ragged inhale, his entire body drenched in sweat despite the winter air. Tears burned his eyes.

Sam was dead.

And he hadn't been able to save him.

Tex crouched in front of him, his usually carefree expression grim.

"Come on, brother," Tex murmured, gripping the back of his neck. "You gotta breathe. Just breathe."

Benji squeezed his eyes shut. But all he saw was Sam's plane going down.

The fire. The smoke. The silence.

Tex shook him, voice steady. "Look at me, man."

Benji did.

Tex nodded. "We're gonna get through this."

Ace appeared behind them, rubbing the back of his neck. His jaw was tight, his eyes dark with loss.

He didn't say anything. He didn't have to.

Benji finally forced himself to stand, his knees weak, his hands shaking.

Captain Desmond was already striding toward them, his expression unreadable.

"The bombers made it," Desmond reported, his voice clipped. "But we lost Sam. Two other men injured."

Benji swallowed hard. He already knew that. But hearing it felt like a blade being driven deeper into his ribs.

"You good, Davis?" Desmond asked, studying him.

Benji nodded once. "Yeah."

Lie.

Desmond's eyes flickered to Tex, who gave a slight shake of his head.

Desmond exhaled sharply through his nose. "Get cleaned up. Debrief in one hour."

Benji barely heard him. The moment Desmond walked off, he turned on his heel and headed straight for his tent.

He couldn't be around them right now.

He couldn't breathe.

The candle on the wooden crate flickered as Benji sat on his cot, staring at the folded piece of paper in his hands.

Sam's letter.

His last letter.

The ink was slightly smudged from sweat, his own hands still trembling as he unfolded it.

Benji—

If you're reading this, guess I finally met my match, huh?

First off, don't be mad at yourself. You always take things too hard. I made my own choices, and you damn well know that.

Second, don't let this war take more from you than it already has.

You still got flyin' to do, Benji.

And you still got her.

Don't waste what you got left.

—Sam

Benji's breath hitched.

His hands curled around the paper. His chest burned.

He should've saved him.

He should've done more.

But he hadn't.

And now Sam was just another name on a list of men who weren't coming home.

The Sky Calls Again

The next morning, Benji stood by his plane, his gaze locked on the sky-blue scarf tied around his control stick.

Jessica's scarf.

It still smelled like her.

He hadn't heard from her in months. Not a single letter since April. But he still wrote to her.

He still told her about the war.

About his dreams.

About how much he missed her.

And he still waited for a letter that might never come.

Ace came up beside him, arms crossed.

"You ready?"

Benji inhaled sharply, nodding once.

"Yeah."

Tex clapped him on the shoulder. "Let's go show these Germans they ain't got shit on the 99th."

Benji climbed into the cockpit, adjusting his helmet.

As the engine roared to life, his grip tightened on the stick.

The war had taken his best friend.

It had taken his peace.

But it wasn't gonna take him.

Not yet.

Benji glanced at Sam's empty spot in the formation.

Then, staring out at the open sky ahead, he whispered:

"I'll see you in the skies, brother."

And then he took off.

February 1944 – Chicago, Illinois

Jessica sat near the window of the small coffee shop, her hands curled around a cup of tea that had long gone cold. The world outside was coated in fresh snow, the streets bustling with bundled-up figures moving through the icy wind, but she barely noticed. The hum of conversation and the faint crackle of jazz playing on the record player in the corner of the café drifted around her, background noise to the thoughts that had been plaguing her for weeks.

Her fingertips tapped against the porcelain rim of her cup as she stared at the newspaper folded neatly in front of her. The ink smelled fresh, the pages crisp, but she hesitated to open it.

She wasn't sure when this ritual had started. Maybe from the moment Benji left for war, or perhaps from the first time she realized her father had been intercepting their letters. But every time a new edition of the paper arrived, she flipped straight to the war section.

Not for news on battle strategies, not for updates on the front lines—just for the names.

The lists of the fallen.

Every time she ran her fingers down the columns, her heart pounded like a war drum, bracing for the moment when she might see his name.

She exhaled sharply, then forced herself to move, turning the pages with careful precision, scanning each name like a lifeline.

Don't be there. Don't be there. Don't be there.

Each letter she had sent had been met with silence. No response. No confirmation that he was even still alive. She had told herself it was just the war, that his letters were lost in transit, but a quiet, gnawing fear whispered otherwise.

What if he had moved on?

What if he stopped writing because he wanted to?

What if he was—

Her stomach twisted, and she shook the thought away before it could root itself too deeply.

Jessica dragged her finger down the page, her breath hitching every time she passed a "D."

Then—she froze.

Her heart lurched into her throat, the letters blurring in front of her eyes.

A name she knew.

A name that wasn't Benji's, but one that felt like a punch straight to the ribs.

Samson Wells – KIA, Italy.

Jessica's vision wavered, her breath strangling in her chest.

Sam.

She knew that name.

Benji had spoken of him in letters, in the soft moments between kisses, in the way his smile reached his eyes whenever he mentioned his best friend.

His brother in everything but blood.

And now, he was gone.

Jessica pressed a hand to her mouth, her fingers trembling against her lips. The small paragraph beneath his name gave so few details. Killed in action during a mission over Italy. No mention of how, no way to know if it had been quick, if he had suffered, if Benji had been there—if Benji had seen it happen.

She inhaled sharply, but the breath didn't come easy.

If Sam was gone, what did that mean for Benji?

Was he okay?

Was he—?

Jessica's hands clenched the paper so tightly it crumpled beneath her grip.

She couldn't sit still.

Tossing a few coins onto the table, she rushed out into the cold, barely feeling the icy bite of the wind as it cut through her coat. The city swirled around her in a blur of movement—people brushing past, streetcars rattling, the world moving on like nothing had changed.

But everything had changed.

Her boots clicked against the pavement as she walked, not caring where she was going, just needing to move.

The moment she had left Montgomery behind, she had thought she had freed herself—had thought she was finally in control of her own life. But this? This was worse than anything she had ever felt.

Not knowing.

She needed to do something.

She needed to know.

She turned down the first street she saw with a Western Union sign in the window. Pushing inside, she barely noticed the warmth as she approached the desk.

The young man behind the counter looked up, giving her a polite but wary smile.

"Good afternoon, miss. How can I help you?"

Jessica swallowed hard, pulling her gloves off with shaking fingers. "I'd like to send a telegram overseas," she said, her voice tighter than she expected.

"Military?"

She nodded.

The clerk grabbed a form and slid it across the counter. "Fill this out, and we'll get it sent out as soon as we can."

Jessica reached for the pen, hesitating.

Who would even receive it? Did Benji's squadron still have the same base? What if he wasn't there anymore?

Her hands shook as she started writing.

TO: LT. BENJAMIN DAVIS, 99TH FIGHTER SQUADRON.

She took a breath and continued.

HAVE NOT HEARD FROM YOU IN MONTHS. ARE YOU SAFE? THINKING OF YOU. PLEASE RESPOND. – JESSICA.

She stared at the words for a long moment. They felt inadequate. They didn't say I miss you. They didn't say I need to know if you're still breathing.

But it was all she could manage.

She slid the form back to the clerk. He scanned it, then nodded. "We'll get this sent out. Response time varies, but hopefully, you'll hear something soon."

Jessica forced a tight smile, mumbling a thank-you as she turned away.

She wouldn't hold her breath.

That night, Jessica sat on the floor of her small apartment, knees pulled to her chest, the only light coming from the soft glow of the lamp beside her. The newspaper lay crumpled on the table, the name Samson Wells still screaming at her in black ink.

She thought of Benji.

Of his smile.

Of the way he had held her that night in the church, like she was the only thing anchoring him to the earth.

She wrapped her arms tighter around herself.

For months, she had been trying to focus on law school, trying to carve out a life for herself in this city, but tonight, she felt like she was back in Montgomery. Back in that house where her father had ripped her letters apart.

For the first time in a long time, she felt completely helpless.

Josephine had written to her just last week, promising that she was still keeping an eye out for Benji's letters. That if she found anything, she would send them to her.

But what if there were no letters?

What if Benji had given up?

What if he had stopped writing—because he wasn't alive to write anymore?

Tears burned behind her eyes, but she refused to let them fall.

She reached for her diary, flipping it open to a blank page.

Then, with a deep breath, she dipped her pen into ink.

February 1944.

I saw Sam's name today.

I don't know if Benji is still alive.

I sent him a telegram, but I don't expect a response. I don't even know if it will reach him.

I have to believe he's still out there. I have to.

Her grip on the pen tightened.

But what if he's not?

Her hand trembled as she pressed the pen to the page.

And for the first time in months, she wrote his name.

Benji.

The ink smudged from the tear that fell.

CHAPTER 17:

THE REMATCH

---

*May 1944 – 332nd Fighter Group (Red
Tails) Deploys to Italy*

The air above Italy stretched out endlessly, a deceivingly beautiful expanse of blue masking the violence that lurked within it. The roar of Benji's P-51 Mustang's engine filled his ears, blending with the radio chatter of his squadmates. His grip on the control stick was firm, but beneath his leather gloves, his fingers twitched. It had been months since Sam's death, but the pain hadn't faded. It lived inside him, settling deep in his bones, a reminder of what this war had stolen.

And still—no word from Jessica.

Benji had written, but no letters came in return. Maybe she had moved on. Maybe she had never really been his to begin with. The thought tightened his chest, but he forced it aside. This was war.

"Stay sharp, boys," Captain Desmond Wright's voice crackled through the radio. "Enemy territory ahead. No mistakes."

"Copy that, Cap," Benji replied, scanning the sky.

A formation of silver P-51 Mustangs with their signature red tails cut through the clouds beside him. Just months ago, they had been the 99th Fighter Squadron, proving themselves time and again in a military that doubted them. Now, with the merger into the 332nd Fighter Group, they were bigger, stronger—but also under tighter scrutiny.

Some pilots welcomed it, seeing it as a chance to solidify their legacy. Others, like Benji, saw it for what it was—another way the brass tried to control them. They had spent years being underestimated, shuffled around, given outdated equipment. Now that they were too damn good to ignore, the higher-ups wanted them contained.

None of it mattered when you were in the sky.

Tex's voice cut through the radio, as cocky as ever. "Think these Krauts will give us a real fight, or are they gonna run scared today?"

Benji smirked. "You sound disappointed, Tex."

"Damn right, I am. I'm itching to put these Mustangs to work."

Desmond interrupted. "Heads on a swivel. Luftwaffe could be anywhere."

Benji exhaled, his pulse steady. Something felt wrong. He had learned to trust his instincts, and right now, they were screaming.

Then, the radio crackled again—but this time, it wasn't one of theirs.

"Little black bird," a smooth, heavily accented voice slithered through the frequency.

Benji's heart slammed against his ribs. He hadn't heard that voice since Sicily.

White Wolf.

His fingers curled tighter around the stick as his eyes darted across the sky, searching. The sky was clear, but he knew better.

"I thought you died with your friend," White Wolf continued, his German accent curling around every word like a snake. "Shame. But today, you join him."

Benji's jaw locked. Sam.

"Son of a—"

"Stay focused, Davis," Desmond warned. "He's baiting you."

Benji exhaled through his nose. He knew Desmond was right. He knew White Wolf wanted him to react. But logic didn't matter when rage burned through his veins.

Then, out of nowhere—a silver streak came out of the sun.

"Break! Break!" Desmond yelled.

Benji yanked the stick hard left as a hail of bullets ripped through the air where he had just been. His Mustang shook from the shockwave. His stomach lurched, but his hands were steady.

"Shit, they're all over us!" Tex cursed.

Benji whipped his plane around, scanning—there. White Wolf's Messerschmitt BF-109 cut through their formation like a blade, moving with deadly precision.

Benji punched the throttle, pulling into an aggressive climb, pushing his Mustang to its limits.

"You can't run, little black bird," White Wolf taunted, his voice maddeningly calm. "You're mine."

Benji's lips curled in a snarl. "Try me."

He twisted into a corkscrew, barely evading another burst of gunfire. White Wolf was toying with him—and that pissed him off more than anything.

"Ace, Tex, you got eyes on him?" Benji barked.

"I'm on your six, Davis!" Ace's voice rang through. "Coming in—"

Static.

Benji's breath caught. He snapped his head back just in time to see Ace's plane take a direct hit.

"NO!"

Ace's Mustang erupted in flames, spinning out of control toward the earth.

"Punch out! Ace, get out!" Tex screamed.

Benji watched, helpless, as Ace's canopy slid back—he was trying. But then, his plane vanished into the thick clouds below.

Gone.

Silence.

Benji's blood roared in his ears. His vision blurred at the edges, rage twisting in his gut. Sam. Now Ace.

"Tex, get the hell out of here!" Desmond ordered. "Davis, pull back!"

Benji didn't move.

No. Not again. He wouldn't run this time.

His hands tightened, muscles coiled, heart pounding. He wasn't thinking anymore. He was feeling. He was fury.

Benji rolled his Mustang over and prepared to dive straight at White Wolf, guns blazing.

"Benji, MOVE!" Desmond's voice snapped through his headset, yanking him out of the haze.

Instinct took over. He yanked back on the stick, rolling into an inverted dive just as White Wolf's cannons shredded the air where he had been.

Desmond cut across the sky, forcing White Wolf into evasive maneuvers. Tex laid down covering fire. It gave Benji just enough time to break away.

"Next time, little black bird," White Wolf's voice was smug. "You won't escape."

And just like that, he vanished into the clouds.

Benji's breathing was ragged. His hands trembled over the controls. This wasn't a fight. This was a warning.

Ace was dead. And Benji had been powerless to stop it.

"We're heading back," Desmond said, voice grim. "Now."

Benji didn't argue.

As they turned back toward base, the weight of another lost brother settled deep in his bones.

He had survived—but at what cost?

The base was unusually quiet when they landed, though Benji knew it wasn't silence—it was mourning.

The moment his wheels touched down, he exhaled a breath he hadn't realized he was holding. The rumble of his Mustang's engine, the familiar resistance of the stick in his hands, the solid ground beneath him—it was all real. He was alive.

Ace wasn't.

Benji pulled off his helmet, resting his forehead against the cool metal for a second before climbing out of the cockpit. His boots hit the tarmac harder than usual, his legs stiff from tension.

A group of ground crewmen watched him, their faces tight with the same grim expression. They had seen the sky burn today. They had seen one of their own go down.

Tex had landed just before him. He stood next to his plane, head down, shoulders hunched, helmet still clutched in his hands. His breathing was ragged, and from where Benji stood, he could see Tex's knuckles were white from gripping his helmet too tight.

Benji swallowed hard and walked over.

Tex didn't move when Benji stopped beside him.

For a long moment, neither of them spoke.

Tex finally broke the silence, his voice raw. "I—I should have had his back, man." His shoulders shook, but he didn't look up. "I should've—damn it."

Benji clenched his jaw. "It ain't on you."

Tex let out a humorless chuckle, shaking his head. "Yeah? Tell that to Ace." He exhaled shakily, eyes finally lifting toward Benji. His pupils were dark, hollowed out by grief. "One second he was there. Next..." Tex's voice cracked.

Benji felt it too. That sharp, aching void in his chest.

Sam. Now Ace.

His brothers were disappearing one by one.

Tex rubbed his face hard, as if trying to erase the guilt from his skin. "I keep thinking—I should have been faster, should've seen him coming. But I didn't. I just—" His voice faltered. He turned, bracing his hands on the wing of his plane, his back heaving with controlled breaths.

Benji didn't push him. He knew what it felt like to lose someone like this, to carry a weight that no words could lift.

Instead, he did the only thing that made sense.

He reached into his flight jacket and pulled out his flask. He held it out toward Tex.

Tex hesitated before finally grabbing it. He unscrewed the cap and took a long swig, his throat bobbing as the burn hit. He let out a slow breath, staring at the ground.

"Thanks," he muttered, handing it back.

Benji took a sip too, feeling the whiskey burn its way down his chest, warming a place inside him that had gone cold.

For a long time, they just stood there, staring at the airstrip, listening to the distant hum of engines and the low murmur of men unloading their planes.

Tex finally spoke, voice low. "You ever think… maybe we ain't making it out of this?"

Benji's throat tightened.

Of course, he had thought about it.

But he didn't say it out loud.

Instead, he forced a smirk. "You trying to psych me out, Tex?"

Tex snorted, shaking his head. "Nah, man. Just… just thinking."

Benji sighed, leaning against Tex's plane. He tilted his head back, staring at the sky. The same sky where Ace had just vanished.

"He went out fighting," Benji finally said.

Tex exhaled sharply. "Damn right, he did."

A pause.

Then Tex turned to him. "You gonna write his family?"

Benji's stomach twisted. That was the thing about war. Somebody had to write the letter.

He thought about Ace's mother, about the way Ace had always talked about home, about his sister and how he was going to teach her to drive when he got back. All the things that would never happen now.

Benji inhaled slowly. "Yeah."

Tex nodded, but neither of them moved.

The reality was settling in—Ace wasn't coming back.

Benji looked down at his hands. They weren't shaking anymore, but the weight in his chest had only gotten heavier.

Tex shifted beside him. "We gonna get that son of a bitch, right?"

Benji didn't hesitate. "Yeah. We are."

White Wolf had made one mistake.

He left Benji alive.

And that was going to cost him.

Benji didn't know how long he and Tex stood by the plane, staring at nothing. The weight in his chest wasn't leaving, but he had learned to carry it. That's what war was—you kept moving, even when the dead stayed behind.

A voice cut through the haze.

"Davis."

Benji turned to see Captain Desmond Wright standing a few feet away, his expression unreadable. The rest of the squadron was busy—some heading to debrief, others silently walking toward their barracks, all carrying the same hollow weight in their eyes.

"Walk with me," Desmond said.

Benji exchanged a look with Tex, who gave a small nod before heading off. With a sigh, Benji wiped his hands on his flight suit and fell into step beside his captain.

The two men walked toward the edge of the airfield, away from the noise of engines and murmured conversations. The sun had started to set, casting long shadows over the tarmac. The smell of fuel and sweat clung to the air.

Desmond was quiet for a long moment, then he finally spoke.

"How are you holding up, Davis?"

Benji let out a short, humorless laugh. "I'm breathing."

Desmond didn't smile. "That ain't what I asked."

Benji exhaled, dragging a hand down his face. His body was exhausted, but his mind wouldn't stop running. Images of Sam, of Ace, of fire and falling metal—they wouldn't leave him alone.

"Feels like every time I blink, someone else is gone," Benji admitted. His voice was rough, edged with something raw.

Desmond nodded. "War does that. Makes you feel like the world is getting smaller. Like there's only so many of us left, and the clock is ticking."

Benji swallowed hard. "Sam. Now Ace." He shook his head. "Hell, Cap… I don't know if I can keep watching my brothers drop outta the sky like that."

Desmond's gaze didn't waver. "I know. And I know you, Davis. You keep holding onto that weight, it's gonna break you."

Benji clenched his jaw. He didn't know how to let go of it.

They stopped walking, standing near a row of sandbags stacked against the base perimeter. Desmond crossed his arms, looking up at the sky.

"Loss is a hell of a thing," he said. "And grief—grief is heavier than any plane you'll ever fly. But you can't let it sink you. 'Cause this fight ain't done.

And the moment we start flying for revenge instead of the mission?" His eyes flickered to Benji's. "That's when we don't come back."

Benji looked away, staring at the ground. His boots were covered in dust, like everything else out here. Nothing ever stayed clean.

Desmond sighed. "Sam would've told you the same thing."

Benji flinched at that. He knew Desmond was right, but it still hurt. Sam had always been the one keeping him steady, cracking jokes when things got too dark. And Ace—Ace had been the kind of guy who made it feel like they'd all make it home.

Now they were both gone.

Benji took a slow breath. "I don't know how to stop feeling like this, Cap."

Desmond was quiet for a long moment. Then, he simply said, "Find something to hold onto, Davis. Something that makes this worth it."

Benji let out a short, bitter chuckle. "Yeah? And what the hell is that supposed to be?"

Desmond gave him a look. "You tell me."

Benji started to say he didn't know—but that wasn't the truth.

Because the answer had always been there.

Jessica.

Her name hit him like a punch to the gut. He hadn't let himself think about her, not really, not since Sam died. It hurt too much. The letters he had sent—no response. Maybe she had moved on. Maybe she had never cared as much as he did.

But if she was gone, then why did he still hold onto her picture every night before he slept?

Why did he still hear her voice in the back of his mind when the sky went quiet?

"Davis." Desmond's voice pulled him back. "You got something?"

Benji's fingers curled into fists. "Maybe."

Desmond studied him, then gave a small nod. "Good. Hold onto it."

The captain clapped a hand on Benji's shoulder before walking off, leaving him standing there, staring at the sky.

The stars had started to come out.

And for the first time in a long time, Benji let himself think about her.

CHAPTER 18:

THE FALL OF THE LITTLE

BLACK BIRD

Summer 1944 – Ploesti Oil Raid

The air over Ploesti burned.#

From this high up, the oil fields below looked like a sea of fire, thick black smoke rising in towering columns, stretching toward the sky like the hands of the damned. Flak exploded all around them, bursting like hellfire, shaking the sky itself.

Benji's P-51 Mustang roared through the chaos, weaving between the bombers they were protecting. The Red Tails had one job: escort the heavies and make sure they got out alive. But the Luftwaffe wasn't making it easy.

His eyes scanned the sky, every muscle taut with the kind of focus that came only from survival.

Tex's voice crackled through the radio. "Tally two o'clock high! They're diving in hard!"

Benji snapped his head to the right. A squadron of Messerschmitts had just broken formation, swooping down like vultures.

"Break off! Break off!" Captain Desmond's voice cut through the static.

Benji pushed his throttle to the max, feeling the familiar pull of G-force as he banked hard. His heart pounded, the Mustang vibrating beneath him, eager to chase, eager to kill.

Then—he saw it.

A lone fighter, slicing through the sky like a silver blade.

Not like the others.

Faster. Sharper.

White Wolf.

Benji's breath turned ice cold.

That voice slithered into the radio again.

"Ah… little black bird. There you are."

Benji's fingers clenched around the stick. The rage that had been simmering inside him since Sicily, since Sam, since Ace, surged up like a storm.

"I've been waiting for this," Benji snarled, banking hard to meet him head-on.

White Wolf didn't hesitate.

Neither did he.

The sky became a battlefield of two.

Benji cut left, rolling into a climb, baiting him. White Wolf followed, but Benji anticipated it—snapping the Mustang into a sharp dive, rolling inverted, pulling his nose back up at the last second to gain the advantage.

For a moment, he had him.

He pressed the trigger—bullets ripped through the air—

White Wolf rolled at the last second.

Benji cursed, correcting, pushing his Mustang to its absolute limits. The plane screamed with effort.

The world spun into chaos.

The bombers. The smoke. The gunfire. The dance of death between two aces.

Then—Tex's voice in his ear.

"BENJI! HE'S TRYING TO BAIT YOU—"

Too late.

The moment Benji pulled up, White Wolf was already waiting.

The first shot shredded his left wing.

The second tore through the fuselage.

And the third—

A sharp, searing pain exploded through his side.

Benji's breath hitched. The world blurred. His fingers weakened.

Blood. So much blood.

His vision swam, the cockpit spinning around him.

Alarms blared. Smoke poured from the controls. His Mustang was going down.

No. No, not like this.

His breath was ragged, each one harder than the last. His vision tunneled, but his hand—his hand reached, gripping onto something soft, something warm.

Jessica's scarf.

It was still wrapped around the control stick. Now drenched in his blood.

God, he could smell her.

For a moment—just a second—he wasn't in the war.

He was back home. Back in the darkened church where they had first held each other. Where she had traced her fingers along his jaw and whispered, "Come back to me, Flyboy."

He exhaled sharply, his grip loosening.

He wasn't coming back.

"BENJI, YOU GOTTA EJECT!"

Desmond's voice yanked him back.

He could barely hear him anymore, everything muffled, distant.

His fingers fumbled for the ejection handle.

He was slipping.

He was dying.

Tex was shouting something, but he couldn't make it out.

They had to finish the mission.

They had to protect the bombers.

He wasn't making it out.

But they would.

Benji gritted his teeth. Not yet. Not yet.

He yanked the ejection handle.

The canopy blew open.

Wind ripped at him.

And then—

Darkness.

Silence.

For a long time, Benji felt nothing. No pain. No war. No falling. Just an endless void, stretching out in every direction. Weightless. Empty.

Then—a voice.

Soft at first, but growing clearer, familiar.

"Damn, Davis. Took you long enough to get here."

Benji's eyes fluttered open.

He was standing—on solid ground. But not just anywhere. Montgomery. The fields behind his father's old church stretched before him, golden in the afternoon sun.

And standing a few feet away, grinning like a fool—

Sam.

Benji's breath caught. His heart twisted. Sam looked just like he did before the war. No uniform. No bruises. No blood. Just his best friend, standing there with his arms crossed, shaking his head.

"You got yourself in a real mess, Flyboy."

Benji opened his mouth, but nothing came out. He couldn't breathe. Couldn't move.

This wasn't real.

Sam chuckled, stepping forward, clapping a hand on his shoulder. "Damn, you're worse than I thought. You look like you just seen a ghost."

Benji tried to speak, but his throat felt raw. His head was heavy, the world around him warping at the edges.

"You—" He swallowed hard. "You're dead."

Sam's grin faltered, something softer settling in his eyes. "Yeah. I know."

A gust of wind blew through the field, and suddenly, they weren't alone.

Another figure stood behind Sam. Ace.

Benji's stomach lurched.

Ace was leaning against an old fence post, arms folded, a smirk playing at his lips. But there was something in his eyes. Something unreadable.

"Damn, kid," Ace said, shaking his head. "We told you to watch your six."

Benji's chest felt tight.

This wasn't real. It couldn't be.

"I—" His voice cracked. "I tried."

Sam exhaled, giving him a sad smile. "Yeah, man. We know."

Benji's vision blurred. He didn't want this. He didn't want to be standing here, in this place, in this limbo, talking to the men he had failed to save.

"You're not supposed to be here yet," Sam added.

Benji's breath hitched. Yet.

His body tensed. Somewhere deep in his chest, something called him back.

No.

He wasn't supposed to be here.

Not yet.

Sam's smile faded. Ace straightened.

And then—they were gone.

The golden fields vanished, replaced by something softer. Warmer.

Jessica.

Benji blinked, his chest aching.

She was there.

She was real.

She stood in front of him in the dim glow of a lantern, wearing that soft blue dress he loved, the one that brought out her eyes.

His throat tightened.

She smiled, tilting her head, just like she always did.

"You came back," she whispered, her fingers reaching for his.

Benji grabbed her, pulling her in tight.

His breath hitched. She was warm. She smelled like lavender and vanilla. She was real.

"I thought I lost you," he murmured against her hair.

Jessica pulled back just enough to look at him, her eyes shining.

"You did," she whispered.

Benji's heart stopped.

Then—her fingers pressed against his chest.

Firm. Urgent.

"Wake up, Benji."

Benji's body jerked.

Jessica's face started to fade, her warmth slipping away.

"No," he gasped, gripping her tighter. "No, don't go—"

Her voice echoed.

"Come back to me, Benji."

Then—

Pain.

Blinding, sharp, searing pain.

Reality. Pain. The War.

Benji's eyes snapped open.

The world blurred and swayed. Shadows moved above him, voices echoing in rapid Italian.

Pain crashed over him like a tidal wave.

His side was on fire. His chest felt like it had been cracked open.

He tried to move.

A soft but firm hand pressed him down.

"Sta fermo! Lay still."

A woman's voice.

His vision focused. A face appeared above him—dark eyes, a white headscarf, a nurse's uniform.

"You are safe, but you must not move."

Benji tried to speak, but his throat was raw. His body was heavy. Weak.

Another voice, male this time, speaking hurried Italian.

More movement. More voices.

His head swam.

He wasn't dead.

But he sure as hell wasn't safe.

His vision flickered.

Then—darkness again.

The next time Benji woke, everything hurt.

His side throbbed, every shallow breath sending a sharp, white-hot pain through his ribs. His head was heavy, the world tilting and swaying as he struggled to open his eyes.

The room was dim, the air thick with the scent of damp earth and something medicinal. A basement? No—a bunker. The walls were rough stone, shelves lined with scavenged supplies stacked haphazardly.

He wasn't in a hospital.

He wasn't in Allied hands.

Something moved beside him. A shadow. Then—that voice again.

"Piano, piano." Soft, measured, but firm. Stay still.

Benji blinked hard, trying to focus. A woman hovered over him, her face lined with exhaustion but her eyes sharp and watchful.

The nurse.

She was young—maybe his age, maybe older—but war had a way of making people look ancient. Her white headscarf was smudged with dirt and blood, her sleeves rolled up to her elbows.

"Where…" Benji's voice cracked. He barely recognized it. "Where am I?"

The nurse glanced at the doorway before leaning in. "Safe. But not for long." Her accent was thick, her English careful.

Safe? No. Not safe. Just… not dead.

His fingers twitched, weakly searching for something—Jessica's scarf.

It was gone.

His throat tightened.

Not just the scarf. Everything. His Mustang. His cockpit. His picture of Jessica.

Burned. Lost. Gone.

Something cold settled in his gut.

A voice—a man this time. Italian, hurried, clipped. Another figure stepped into the room, carrying a rifle slung over his shoulder.

Benji's instincts flared.

His hand jerked toward his hip—no sidearm.

The man gave a small, amused scoff. "Americano."

Benji's teeth clenched.

The nurse sighed, placing a firm hand on Benji's chest, pushing him back against the cot. "Do not move. You will rip your stitches."

Benji exhaled sharply, frustration twisting with the pain in his ribs. "Who the hell are you?"

The man in the doorway raised an eyebrow, adjusting his rifle. "The people who pulled you out of that field before the Nazis did."

Benji's vision blurred at the edges. His body was too weak, too heavy, too broken.

The nurse dipped a rag into a small bowl, pressing it to his forehead. "Your plane crashed north. We found you bleeding in the fields."

Benji's heart pounded. "How long?"

The nurse hesitated. "Three days."

Three days.

He'd been missing for three days.

His squadron thought he was dead.

Jessica thought he was dead.

Hell, he almost was.

A wave of exhaustion crashed over him, his body sinking into the cot.

The male partisan stepped forward, crossing his arms. "We cannot keep him here. If the Germans come—"

"They will come," the nurse interrupted.

A beat of silence.

Benji's mind was still fogged, but the reality was clear.

He was trapped. Behind enemy lines. Wounded. A ghost.

His breath shook.

The war had taken everything from him.

And now, he had to find a way to take something back.

To survive.

CHAPTER 19:

THE BREAKING POINT

Summer 1944 – Chicago, Illinois

The office smelled of ink, paper, and determination.

Jessica sat at a desk covered in newspapers, pamphlets, and legal documents, her fingers idly tracing the edges of a petition for fair housing rights. The hum of typewriters and hushed conversations filled the room as activists worked tirelessly to combat discrimination in the city.

She had been volunteering with the Congress of Racial Equality (CORE) for months now, helping organize sit-ins, drafting legal paperwork, and connecting Black veterans with resources. The war might have taken Benji across the ocean, but she had chosen to fight her own battle here in Chicago.

Still, she wasn't really listening. She hadn't been for weeks.

Not since Benji stopped writing.

Not since the silence replaced his letters.

A soft thud landed in front of her, breaking her trance.

"Jess, are you even hearing me?" Anna, one of the organizers, leaned on the desk, eyebrows raised. "I just said we're planning a direct action at the Wabash Avenue department store next week. We need law students like you to help draft defense strategies if people get arrested."

Jessica forced a nod. "Of course. Send me the case details."

Anna studied her. "You check the newspaper every day, don't you?"

Jessica stiffened, her pulse spiking.

Anna sighed and pushed a folded copy of the Chicago Defender toward her.

Jessica hesitated, her fingers hovering over the page before she finally unfolded it.

Her eyes flicked past the headlines—"Black Workers Demand Fair Wages," "NAACP Legal Victories Continue,"—until she reached the military section.

Her heart pounded.

Her stomach twisted as she reached the MIA list.

And then—her world stopped.

DAVIS, LT. BENJAMIN – MIA

Jessica couldn't breathe.

The edges of the paper blurred.

No. No, no, no.

Her throat closed.

"Jessica?" Anna's voice softened. "What is it?"

Jessica couldn't answer. She couldn't speak.

Her vision swam, the letters twisting together, the ink smearing in her mind.

Missing in action.

Not dead. But not alive, either.

Benji was gone.

The petition beneath her hands crumpled as her fingers clenched.

Her chair scraped loudly against the wooden floor as she shoved back.

"Jess, wait—"

"I have to go," she choked out, grabbing her bag, breath shallow, uneven.

She barely registered the voices calling after her as she rushed out the door, her heels striking the pavement, the city blurring around her.

He can't be gone.

He can't be.

The streets of Chicago closed in around her, but she barely noticed the cars honking, the conversations, the jazz music spilling from a record shop.

Somewhere in her haze, she reached her apartment, her hands trembling so badly she nearly dropped the key as she fumbled with the lock.

When she finally pushed the door open, she stumbled inside, slamming it shut behind her.

And then she saw it.

A package.

Sitting on her small table by the door.

Her chest seized.

It was from Josephine.

Jessica's hand shook as she reached for it. The weight of it sent a chill down her spine.

With a strangled breath, she tore the package open—

Letters spilled out.

Jessica's hand shook as she reached for it. The weight of it sent a chill down her spine.

With a strangled breath, she tore the package open—

Letters spilled out.

Dozens of them. Some aged, the paper slightly yellowed, others newer, the ink still dark.

Benji's handwriting.

Jessica gasped.

Her knees buckled.

She dropped onto the floor, surrounded by years of his love, his words, his longing.

Her fingers trembled as she picked up the first one, her breath catching on a sob before she even unfolded it.

Dear Jessica,

The ink blurred as tears slipped down her face.

She reached for another—then another.

His words cut through her, slicing her open, flooding her with every moment she had missed, every heartbreak she had never known.

He never stopped writing.

She let out a broken sob, clutching a letter to her chest as she collapsed completely, curling into herself on the floor.

She had lost him.

And now, it was too late.

Jessica couldn't stop shaking.

Her hands clutched at the letters, Benji's words bleeding into her fingers, his love pressing against her chest like a weight she couldn't bear. Her vision blurred with tears spilling freely, hot and unrelenting, soaking into the delicate paper.

How?

How had this happened?

She tried to breathe, but her throat constricted, her sobs breaking into uneven gasps.

He had written to her.

Over and over again.

Her hands fumbled with the pages, desperately unfolding one, then another.

Her breath hitched as she forced herself to read.

March 1943

My love,

I don't know if this letter will reach you, but I have to try. Every time I close my eyes, I see you. Every time I hear the wind rush past my cockpit, I think about that night in the church when you asked me to stay, and God, Jessica, I wish I could have.

Sam keeps saying I talk about you too much, but I don't care. I carry you with me everywhere, Flygirl. If I ever stop writing to you, it'll be because I can't anymore.

Until I see you in the skies,

Benji

A strangled sound tore from her throat.

She pressed the letter to her chest, her body trembling as if trying to hold him in, as if trying to stop him from slipping away.

Her fingers reached for another letter, her movements frantic, almost desperate.

She unfolded the paper with shaking hands.

July 1943

Jessica,

They sent us on another mission today. I lost count of how many now. I can still feel the shake of the plane, the smell of fuel, the burn of the sun through the canopy. But you—you're still here. In my mind. In my hands, even when they're gripping the stick.

You told me to come back to you. I don't know if I can, Jess. I don't know if I'll make it. But if I don't—if I don't get to kiss you again, I need you to know something.

I was yours. Always. Even when I tried not to be.

If I could touch you right now, I'd memorize every inch of you, so I'd have something to hold onto in the dark.

Until I see you in the skies,

Benji

A cry ripped from her lips.

She covered her mouth with her hand, as if it could contain the pain, but it kept breaking out of her, spilling over, wrecking her.

How could this have happened?

How could she have been waiting for him, believing he had given up on her—while he had been out there, writing, hoping, loving her from thousands of miles away?

She was suffocating.

Her hands dug into her chest, fingers clutching at the fabric of her blouse, nails pressing into her skin as if trying to tear out the grief that had rooted itself inside her.

She reached for another letter, but this time—her fingers hesitated.

Because she knew.

She knew where this was going.

She could barely see through her tears, but she forced herself to look at the date.

April 1944.

Just months ago.

Her fingers tightened around the page, her pulse pounding as she unfolded it.

April 1944

Jessica,

I don't know if you're getting these, but I can't stop writing. It's the only thing that feels real anymore.

Sam is gone.

I can still hear him laughing, still see him giving me that stupid grin before every mission. I keep expecting to turn my head and see him in the next plane over. But he's not there. He's never going to be there again.

Jess, I don't know how to do this without him.

I don't know how to do this without you.

I keep holding onto the picture you gave me, but it's fading. The edges are worn, the ink is starting to smudge. I'm afraid if I lose it, I'll lose you too.

I don't want to forget your face. I don't want to forget the way you looked at me that night when I gave you the locket. You told me I'd find my way back to you.

I don't know if I believe that anymore.

But I'll keep flying.

And if I don't make it—if this war takes me like it took Sam, I just need you to know—I love you. I've always loved you.

Until I see you in the skies,

Benji

Jessica screamed.

The letter slipped from her hands as she collapsed forward, sobbing uncontrollably.

Her body shook, the sound of her cries filling the small apartment, but no one was there to hear her.

She was alone.

Alone with his words.

Alone with the love he had sent across the ocean, only for her to never read them.

She curled into herself, clutching at her locket, the one she had worn every day, the one he had given her for Christmas.

The one that still held his picture.

Her fingers tightened around it, pressing it against her chest.

He was gone.

But she still had this.

She still had him.

And she would never, ever let go again.

Somewhere in Northern Italy – Two Weeks After the Crash

The pain had become a companion.

At first, it was sharp—every breath a dagger between his ribs, every movement a punishment. Now, it was dull, constant, a reminder that he was still alive.

Benji lay on a thin mattress tucked into a corner of the underground shelter. The walls were rough stone, the air damp, thick with the scent of earth, smoke, and dried blood. A resistance hideout.

Two weeks.

Two weeks since he had been pulled from the wreckage of his crash, barely breathing, barely conscious. Two weeks since he had been wiped from existence.

The world thought he was dead.

Hell, part of him felt dead.

He shifted slightly, biting back a grimace. His side still burned, the gunshot wound knitting together far too slowly. The Italian nurse—Lucia, he'd learned—had done what she could. Cleaned it, stitched it, fought off infection. But he had lost too much blood. His body was weak.

He hated feeling weak.

A voice broke through the quiet.

"Americano, sei sveglio?"

Benji cracked one eye open as Matteo, one of the partisans, crouched beside him, studying him like he wasn't sure whether he was alive or a ghost.

"Yeah," Benji muttered, his voice hoarse. "Unfortunately."

Matteo smirked, tossing him a piece of bread wrapped in cloth. "You should eat. You need strength."

Benji caught it with slow, careful fingers. His hands still shook sometimes. "Not sure stale bread is gonna bring me back to life."

"Better than starving," Matteo said, standing up.

Benji huffed a small laugh and took a bite anyway. It was dry, but he didn't care. His stomach had been empty for too long.

Matteo leaned against the wall, adjusting the rifle slung over his shoulder. "Germans are looking for you."

Benji's jaw tensed.

"Word spread," Matteo continued. "They know an American pilot survived the crash. They think the resistance is hiding you." His dark eyes flicked toward Benji's bandaged side. "If they find you, they will kill you."

Benji nodded slowly. "That supposed to scare me?"

Matteo smirked. "No. It means we have to move soon."

Benji let out a slow breath, tilting his head back against the wall. He already knew that. He had heard the murmured conversations, the restless tension in the hideout.

Staying here much longer would put everyone at risk.

Still, his body felt like lead. The wound wasn't fully healed, but war didn't wait for recovery.

"Where to?" Benji asked.

Matteo hesitated. "There is a route. Dangerous, but possible. We move at night, avoid patrols. If we reach the safe house in the next town, we may find someone who can get you closer to Allied lines."

Benji exhaled through his nose.

Enemy territory. Weak body. No weapons. No air support.

And yet—he wasn't dead.

He wasn't done yet.

Benji's hand instinctively reached toward his cockpit—only to find nothing.

The scarf was gone.

The picture was gone.

His fingers curled into a fist.

He had lost everything.

Except his will to fight.

He pushed himself up, wincing, ignoring the pain screaming through him. He had no choice.

"Alright," Benji said, eyes hard, jaw set. "When do we leave?"

Matteo grinned. "Tomorrow night."

Benji gave a slow nod.

One way or another—he was getting out of here.

And if he did—he was going home.

CHAPTER 20:

THE GHOST OF WAR

Northern Italy – Two Weeks on the Run

The night swallowed them whole.

Benji moved silently through the dense trees, every step precise, every muscle taut. The cold bit into his skin, even through the tattered jacket Matteo had given him. His boots—stolen from a dead German soldier—were stiff, uncomfortable, but they kept him moving. Kept him alive.

He was two weeks deep into enemy territory, still a fugitive, still fighting to stay ahead of the patrols.

Matteo led the way, crouched low, his rifle slung over his shoulder. Behind them, two other partisans—Luca and Nico—moved in formation, watching their backs.

They had been traveling at night, resting in abandoned farmhouses, hiding in cellars, eating whatever they could scavenge. The farther they moved from his crash site, the safer it became—but only by inches.

Every night was the same. Walking. Hiding. Surviving.

And every night, Benji fought to stay on his feet. The wound in his side still burned, healing too slowly. He had stopped bleeding days ago, but every movement still sent fire through his ribs.

It didn't matter.

Pain meant he was alive.

And being alive meant he had a chance.

Matteo raised a fist—a silent signal. Stop.

Benji froze, hand tightening around the small knife he carried.

Luca slinked ahead, peering through the trees toward the distant road. The faint glow of lanterns flickered—a Nazi checkpoint.

Benji's jaw locked.

Matteo turned to him, speaking barely above a whisper. "Too dangerous to go straight. We take the long way."

Benji nodded, exhaling through his nose. He had learned quickly—no unnecessary risks. One wrong step and they'd all be dead.

They diverted, moving parallel to the road but keeping hidden beneath the trees.

As they walked, Benji caught the distant sound of laughter. German soldiers talking, drinking, playing cards around a fire.

It made his stomach turn.

How many times had he seen his own men do the same thing? Laughing, joking—until the next mission took them away.

Sam had laughed like that.

Ace, too.

Benji swallowed the knot in his throat and kept moving.

The Safehouse

By dawn, they reached an abandoned mill.

Luca scouted first, ensuring it was clear before waving them in. The air inside was stale, thick with dust. Broken wooden beams stretched across the ceiling, holes letting in thin slivers of morning light.

Matteo motioned for Benji to sit.

"You're pushing too hard," he muttered.

Benji huffed but lowered himself against the cold stone wall. His legs screamed in protest.

Matteo sat across from him, pulling something from his coat—a folded newspaper.

"Picked this up in the last town," he murmured. "Thought you might want to see it."

Benji frowned as Matteo tossed it toward him. The pages were smudged, worn from use.

Benji hesitated before unfolding it.

At first, nothing stood out. War reports. Propaganda. Casualty lists.

And then—

His heart stopped.

Right there. Printed in black ink.

DAVIS, LT. BENJAMIN – MIA

Benji's throat tightened.

He stared at his own name, his hands going still.

Missing in action.

Not captured. Not found.

Just… gone.

His chest felt hollow. The world around him faded, the noise muffled beneath the roar in his ears.

How many people had seen this?

How many people thought he was dead?

His squadron. Tex and Captain Wright.

His family.

Jessica.

Benji exhaled shakily, his fingers gripping the paper until it crumpled.

Matteo watched him carefully. "You alright?"

Benji forced himself to nod, swallowing hard. "Yeah."

A lie.

Because for the first time since the crash, he truly felt like a ghost.

Week 5 Behind Enemy Lines – Finding an Escape Route

The longer Benji survived, the stronger he became.

His body still ached, but the pain had dulled into something he could live with. The fever that had gripped him for days had finally broken, and though his ribs still screamed whenever he moved too fast, he could move.

That meant he could fight.

That meant he could get home.

But first, they had to get out of enemy territory.

The Plan

Matteo crouched beside him in the dimly lit barn they were using as shelter for the night, his face shadowed, his voice low.

"There's a network," he murmured. "Partisans and Allied spies. If we get to the next town, we can find them."

Benji rubbed his fingers against his temple, thinking. "How far?"

"A day's travel. Maybe two, if we're careful."

"And then?"

Matteo exhaled. "Then, if you're lucky, they smuggle you out."

Benji didn't like if.

But he had no choice.

He had to take it.

The Journey Continues

The next night, they moved.

Benji had learned to walk like a shadow. Stay low. Stay quiet. Stay alive.

The path ahead was dangerous—German patrols, informants, traps. If they were caught, there would be no trial, no prison.

Just a bullet.

They traveled mostly at night, keeping off the roads, taking the long way around small villages.

Benji hated the waiting, the sneaking, the constant feeling that someone was watching him.

He belonged in the sky.

Up there, the fight was clear. No hiding. No crawling through the dirt like a hunted animal.

But now?

Now, he was prey.

A Close Call

They had just passed the outskirts of a village when Luca suddenly raised a fist.

Benji froze.

The sound of boots on gravel.

A German patrol.

Benji barely had time to react before Matteo grabbed his sleeve, yanking him into the shadows of an old stone wall.

He held his breath.

Six soldiers. Rifles slung over their shoulders. Laughing, talking—oblivious.

But if they turned...

Benji's fingers twitched. No gun. No real weapon. Just a knife. It wouldn't be enough.

The soldiers stopped.

One of them lit a cigarette, taking a long drag. His boots scraped the dirt, his eyes scanning the road—

Benji's grip tightened.

Matteo barely breathed.

Then—one of the soldiers said something, and they moved on.

Benji didn't exhale until the boots had faded into the night.

Matteo let go of his sleeve. "That was close."

Benji wiped sweat from his brow. "Too close."

Reaching the Safe House

By dawn, they found it—an old vineyard, mostly abandoned.

A partisan safe house.

The woman who greeted them was older, her face lined with age, but her eyes were sharp.

"Americano?" she asked, studying Benji.

Matteo nodded.

She clicked her tongue, motioning them inside.

Benji stepped over the threshold, one step closer to getting home.

One step closer to Jessica.

Week 8 – Crossing the Line

The road was long, winding through hills and burned-out villages, but at the end of it—freedom.

Benji had dreamed about this moment for weeks. The thought of finally reaching his own men, stepping onto Allied ground, hearing English that didn't come with a German accent or the weight of war.

But now, as he moved toward the U.S. outpost, his body was heavy.

Eight weeks of running, hiding, bleeding.

Eight weeks of being a ghost.

Matteo and the other partisans had led him as far as they could, but the rest… the rest, he had done on his own.

Now, the checkpoint loomed ahead—barbed wire, sandbags, and the familiar sight of American uniforms.

Benji's pulse quickened.

Two soldiers with rifles stepped forward as he approached.

"Halt!"

Benji stopped.

One of the soldiers squinted at him. "Who the hell are you?"

Benji took a breath, willed his voice to work.

"Lieutenant Benjamin Davis. U.S. Army Air Corps."

Silence.

The soldiers exchanged looks.

Then one of them took a cautious step forward. "Say that again?"

Benji straightened. His uniform was dirty, torn, barely recognizable. But his voice? His voice was strong.

"Lieutenant Benjamin Davis. Tuskegee Airmen."

One of the men cursed under his breath. "Jesus Christ."

The other soldier's eyes widened. "Wait… Davis? Davis from the 332nd?"

Benji nodded once.

"Holy hell." The soldier turned and bolted toward the nearest tent.

Back From the Dead

The outpost erupted in a flurry of movement.

Benji barely had time to register the commotion before he heard a voice—a voice that hit him like a punch to the gut.

"Benji?"

Tex.

Benji turned, and there he was—Tex, standing in the middle of the damn outpost, eyes wide, face pale as if he were staring at a ghost.

"Son of a—"

Tex didn't finish. He was already moving, closing the distance, grabbing Benji by the shoulders.

"Damn it, Davis!" His voice shook. "We thought you were dead!"

Benji tried to smirk, but his throat was too tight.

"Yeah, well," he rasped, his body finally giving in to exhaustion. "Takes more than a Nazi bastard to kill me."

Tex let out a choked laugh, but his grip was solid, steady.

Then—another voice.

Deep. Steady.

"Davis."

Benji turned and saw Captain Wright.

The man was standing stock still, his expression unreadable, but his blue eyes—his eyes said everything.

Benji held his gaze.

"Captain."

Desmond exhaled sharply, stepping forward. For a moment, he didn't speak.

Then, finally—he clapped a firm hand on Benji's shoulder.

"Damn good to have you back, Lieutenant."

Benji let out a slow breath.

It was over.

He had made it.

But somewhere, beneath the relief, beneath the exhaustion…

His mind drifted to Jessica.

CHAPTER 21:

THE COST OF SURVIVAL

January 1945 – U.S. Military Base, Italy

B enji had been back for less than twelve hours when the full weight of military protocol came crashing down on him.

After weeks of fighting to survive in enemy territory, the Army wasn't about to take his return at face value. Missing soldiers didn't just come back. Not without questions. Not without suspicion.

So, instead of rest, instead of relief, he was stuck in an infirmary, strapped to a bed, poked, prodded, and questioned.

Medical Evaluation

The room was sterile, cold, unforgiving.

A doctor hovered over him, muttering instructions while a nurse checked his vitals. His body ached, the bandages on his side still fresh, his skin still thin from weeks of malnourishment.

He barely listened as the doctor rattled off his condition.

"Bullet wound—through and through. No infection, but you lost too much blood. You're underweight. Bruised ribs. Dehydration. You need rest."

Benji huffed. "Rest is a luxury, Doc."

The doctor shot him a look, clearly unimpressed. "Well, Lieutenant, it's a luxury you're taking whether you like it or not."

Benji smirked, but his exhaustion won out. His body sank into the thin mattress, his limbs heavy.

As much as he hated being here, it was the first real bed he had slept in for two months.

The First Letter

Benji's hands were shaky as he pulled a sheet of paper toward him.

They had let him write one letter home.

His mother. Naomi. Marcus. They all thought he was dead.

How many nights had they sat awake, grieving him?

His fingers hovered over the paper, his chest tight.

Then, slowly, he wrote.

Dear Mama,

I don't even know where to start.

I know you must have thought you lost me, but I need you to know—I fought my way back. I never stopped fighting.

I know it's been months. I know it must've been hell. But I need you to tell Naomi, Marcus, and Pop that I made it.

I ain't the same, Mama. This war has taken too much. But I swear to you, I'm still standing.

Tell Naomi I still owe her a dance.

Tell Marcus he better not have touched my records.

Tell Pop I still remember every word he ever told me.

And tell them all that I love them.

I'll be home soon.

—Benji

He exhaled, rubbing his face before folding the letter and sealing it.

Then, before he could second-guess himself, he grabbed another page.

This one wasn't for his family.

It was for Jessica.

He stared at the blank sheet for a long moment, his heartbeat uneven.

Would she even read it?

Would she even care?

He didn't know.

But he still wrote.

Dear Jess,

I don't know if you'll get this. I don't know if you even care anymore. But if there's even a chance you're still waiting for me—I need you to know I'm alive.

I was shot down over enemy territory. I spent months trying to get back. It damn near killed me.

But I couldn't stop.

Not without knowing if you were still waiting on the other side.

I don't know why you stopped writing me. Maybe you moved on. Maybe this war changed things. Maybe you just don't love me anymore.

But I still love you.

I still dream about the last time I saw you. The last time I held you.

I don't know what's waiting for me when this is over.

But if you're still there—I'll find my way back to you.

Until I see you in the skies,

Benji

His hands clenched as he folded the letter. He didn't let himself hesitate.

He just sealed it.

And sent it.

Debriefing & Interrogation

The next day, two men in clean-pressed uniforms walked into his hospital room.

Benji didn't need an introduction.

Military Intelligence.

They weren't here to welcome him back.

One of them—a lean, pale officer with sharp eyes—sat down in the chair beside his bed, crossing one leg over the other.

The other—a stockier man with a scar across his cheek—stood with his arms folded.

Neither of them looked pleased.

"Lieutenant Davis," the first man said, flipping open a thin file. "You've been missing in action for nearly two months. Do you understand why that raises concerns?"

Benji didn't blink. "I understand war's hell, sir."

The officer's lips thinned. "Where were you?"

"Hiding. Running. Trying not to die."

Silence.

The standing officer finally spoke, his voice hard. "You were found deep in enemy territory, Lieutenant. Alone. That doesn't look good."

Benji's blood turned cold.

He knew where this was going.

They thought he was compromised.

Or worse—a traitor.

Benji leaned forward despite the protest of his aching ribs. "I got shot down over Ploesti. Spent two months trying to get back. There's nothing else to it."

The sitting officer gave a small, unimpressed nod. "We'll see."

Benji's fingers curled into fists.

They weren't going to believe him.

It didn't matter that he had bled for this country. That he had fought, survived, lost everything just to come back.

They still didn't trust him.

The standing officer stepped closer. "Until we finish our assessment, you are to remain here under watch. Understood?"

Benji's jaw tightened.

"Understood."

The men nodded and left without another word.

Benji exhaled slowly.

He wasn't free yet.

A Choice to Make

That night, Captain Desmond walked in.

Benji glanced up, watching as the older man studied him carefully.

Then, finally—Desmond sighed.

"You're gonna be given a choice."

Benji sat up slightly, ignoring the pull in his ribs. "What choice?"

Desmond's eyes were unreadable. "You've been through hell, Davis. You've done your time. They're gonna offer you the chance to go home."

Benji stilled.

Home.

He could see it—his mother's face, Naomi's laughter, the warm streets of Montgomery.

He could go home. Leave all this behind.

But then—he thought about Sam. Acc. Every man who didn't get that choice.

And he thought about White Wolf.

He thought about how this wasn't over.

His jaw set.

"No."

Desmond's brow lifted slightly. "No?"

"I'm not going anywhere," Benji said, voice solid. "Not until I see this through."

Desmond studied him for a long moment.

Then, he gave a small, knowing nod.

"Good," he murmured. "Then get ready."

Because the next battle was coming.

And Benji would be there to finish the war.

Benji had been back for two weeks.

Two weeks of medical checkups, psych evaluations, and endless questioning from intelligence officers who still weren't convinced he was the same man who had been shot down.

He had passed every damn test, every interrogation.

Yet, he could still feel eyes on him.

Even now, as he laced up his boots in the barracks, he could hear the hushed voices of the other pilots nearby.

They weren't sure what to make of him.

To them, he was a man who had come back from the dead.

A man who had survived something most didn't.

And maybe—that made him dangerous.

Benji ignored them, rolling his shoulders, testing his strength. His body wasn't at a hundred percent yet, but it was getting there.

He wasn't the same man who had crawled out of a wreckage in enemy territory.

He was a soldier again.

A pilot.

And today—he was getting back in the air.

The First Flight Back

Captain Desmond was waiting for him on the airstrip.

The sky was clear, crisp. The January cold bit at the edges of his flight suit, but Benji hardly noticed.

Desmond stood near a P-51 Mustang, arms crossed, eyes unreadable.

"You sure about this, Davis?" Desmond asked.

Benji's grip tightened on his helmet. "I need to fly."

Desmond studied him for a moment before giving a small nod.

"All right," he said. "Then let's see if you still remember how."

Benji climbed into the cockpit, his fingers wrapping around the controls.

For the first time in months, he felt at home.

The engine roared to life, the vibrations thrumming through his body.

He took a slow breath.

Then, with a steady hand—he took off.

The moment his wheels left the ground, everything else fell away.

The doubts. The whispers. The weight of everything he had been through.

Up here, it didn't matter.

Up here, he was free.

Building Back Confidence

Benji spent the next several days training.

At first, his movements were stiff, his reflexes dulled from months of survival rather than combat.

But Desmond was there.

Watching. Evaluating. Pushing him.

"Faster, Davis!"

Benji gritted his teeth, pushing the Mustang harder, feeling the pull of G-force.

Desmond's plane swooped in behind him, testing him, forcing him to react under pressure.

It was brutal.

It was exhausting.

It was exactly what he needed.

By the end of the week, Benji had regained his edge.

His body was stronger. His mind was sharper.

And when he landed after his final practice run, Desmond was there— smirking.

"You're ready."

Benji exhaled, pulling off his helmet.

His hands were steady.

He nodded.

"Yeah. I am."

January 1945 – Chicago, Illinois

Jessica sat at the small wooden table in her apartment, a cup of coffee long since gone cold beside her.

The Chicago winter rattled against the window, the wind howling through the streets, but she barely noticed.

Her world had shrunk down to the newspaper in her hands.

She unfolded it carefully, like she always did.

Like she had done every morning since the war took him away.

She told herself it was habit. That it was just routine.

But the truth?

The truth was, she still looked for his name.

Even after all this time.

Even after she had seen those three haunting letters beside it—MIA.

Missing.

Like he had just disappeared, like the earth had swallowed him whole.

She had told herself she had accepted it.

She had tried to believe he was gone.

But somewhere deep inside her, she had never stopped searching.

Her fingers tightened around the edges of the paper as she scanned the latest reports, her pulse steady—until suddenly, it wasn't.

Her eyes landed on a single line of text buried in the war updates.

Her heart stopped.

DAVIS, LT. BENJAMIN – RETURNED TO ACTIVE DUTY, 332ND FIGHTER GROUP

Jessica couldn't breathe.

Her fingers curled against the paper, the ink smudging beneath the sudden tremor in her hands.

Her chest tightened, her vision blurring as she read it again.

And again.

And again.

Her breath came out uneven, shaky, her body frozen in place.

He's alive.

The words barely formed in her mind before a choked sob tore from her lips.

She slapped a hand over her mouth, her whole body quaking as relief and disbelief crashed over her at once.

Her mind raced.

Where had he been?

Had he been hurt?

Why hadn't he written?

Did he even know she was still waiting?

Her hands moved on their own, shoving the newspaper aside as she reached for the writing desk tucked against the wall.

She grabbed a telegraph form, her breath shallow, uneven.

Her fingers trembled as she pressed the pen to the paper.

She didn't know what to say.

Didn't know how to capture everything that was tearing through her chest.

She didn't even know if he would read it.

But she had to try.

She had to let him know.

TO: LT. BENJAMIN DAVIS – 332ND FIGHTER GROUP, U.S. MILITARY BASE, ITALY

My heart stopped when I saw your name.

I thought I lost you.

Please write back.

     – Jess

She stared at the message, her heartbeat pounding in her ears.

Too much.

Not enough.

It didn't matter.

She shoved the paper into the envelope, sealing it with shaking hands.

She didn't even grab her coat before rushing out the door, her boots clicking hard against the apartment steps as she hurried into the cold.

By the time she reached the telegraph office, her face was flushed, her breath clouding in the icy air.

She slammed the form onto the counter.

"Send this," she whispered, barely able to get the words out.

The telegraph operator gave her a brief glance before taking it. "Destination?"

"Italy," she breathed. "U.S. military base."

He nodded, stamping the form. "It'll go out within the hour."

Jessica let out a shaky breath, her hands still trembling at her sides.

She turned, stepping back out into the Chicago cold.

She had done all she could.

Now all she could do—

Was wait.

CHAPTER 22:

THE TELEGRAM BEFORE WAR

March 23, 1945 – U.S. Military Base, Italy

The barracks were quiet.

Not because the men were asleep—no one slept before a mission like this.

They all knew what was coming.

March 24, 1945—the longest bomber escort mission of the war.

They had been briefed earlier that evening. This was it.

The war was reaching its final stretch, but that didn't mean it was getting easier. If anything, it was getting worse.

More desperate.

The enemy had nothing left to lose.

Neither did Benji.

He sat at the small wooden desk in his quarters, staring at the map laid out in front of him. The plan was clear:

Escort the bombers. Defend at all costs.

Fly into the heart of Germany.

Straight into the lion's den.

And if the reports were right—they'd be waiting.

The Luftwaffe was still deadly, still relentless.

This was going to be hell.

Benji exhaled slowly, rubbing a hand down his face. His ribs still ached faintly, a reminder of how close he had come to dying.

A reminder of why he was still here.

Sam. Ace. Every man they had lost.

They would have given anything to be here, to keep fighting.

Benji wasn't about to let them down.

A knock on the door pulled him from his thoughts.

Tex stuck his head in.

"You gonna sit there and brood all night?" he asked.

Benji huffed, pushing the map aside. "Just making sure I know what we're flying into."

Tex stepped in, leaning against the bunk. "We're flying into a damn death trap, that's what."

Benji didn't argue. They both knew the risks.

Instead, Tex tossed something onto the desk.

"You got a telegram."

Benji's breath caught.

His fingers twitched before he even reached for it. No one had sent him a telegram since he'd been back.

He unfolded the small slip of paper, eyes scanning the message.

Then—his world stopped.

TO: LT. BENJAMIN DAVIS – 332^(ND) FIGHTER GROUP, U.S. MILITARY BASE, ITALY

My heart stopped when I saw your name.

I thought I lost you.

Please write back.

Jess

Benji's lungs locked.

He had to read it twice.

Three times.

His fingers clenched around the paper, his pulse hammering in his ears.

Tex noticed his reaction, frowning. "What is it?"

Benji swallowed hard, his throat dry.

Jessica.

She knew.

She knew he was alive.

After all this time.

His hands tightened into fists. God, he had written to her. Over and over. And now—now she was reaching out?

He didn't know what to feel. Relief. Anger. Hope.

Tex leaned over, reading the telegram before letting out a low whistle.

"Well, damn."

Benji didn't respond. His heart was still racing.

Tex clapped a hand on his shoulder. "You gonna write her back?"

Benji exhaled sharply.

"Not yet."

Tex raised a brow. "Not yet?"

Benji set the telegram down, his jaw tightening.

Tomorrow, he was flying into hell.

If he didn't make it back, what was the point of writing?

Tex studied him for a moment before nodding slowly.

"I get it," he murmured.

Silence settled between them.

Then—Tex patted the desk. "Well, don't get shot down again. You're running out of second chances."

Benji huffed a small laugh, but it didn't reach his eyes.

Tex left, shutting the door behind him.

Benji sat there for a long time, staring at Jessica's words.

He traced his fingers over the ink, memorizing every letter.

Then, slowly, he folded the telegram, tucking it into the pocket of his flight suit.

If he made it back—

If he survived tomorrow—

He'd write her back.

But first, he had a war to finish.

Benji sat alone in his barracks, the dim overhead light casting long shadows across the wooden floor. The telegram lay open in his hands, the thin paper slightly creased from how many times he had unfolded and refolded it.

His fingers traced the words.

My heart stopped when I saw your name.

I thought I lost you.

Please write back.

    – Jess

His throat felt tight.

He had waited so long to hear from her.

For months, he had written letter after letter, hoping, praying that one would reach her—that one would be returned.

But nothing had come.

Until now.

She had thought he was gone.

And now? Now she was asking him to write back.

He wanted to. God, he wanted to.

But not yet.

Because tomorrow, he was flying into the most dangerous mission of the war.

And if he didn't come back—

Benji exhaled sharply, folding the telegram with careful precision before tucking it into his flight suit.

He would carry her words with him.

And if he made it back, he'd write her the letter she deserved.

Mission Briefing: A Flight Into Hell

March 24, 1945 – 0330 Hours

The briefing room was packed. Every pilot, every leader of the 332nd Fighter Group was here.

Captain Desmond stood at the front, his face grim, the weight of what was coming etched into every hard line.

Benji sat beside Tex, his back straight, his hands folded in his lap. He knew what was coming. They all did.

Desmond's voice was steady, commanding. "Gentlemen, tomorrow we fly the longest bomber escort mission in history. 1,600 miles, round trip, straight into the heart of the Reich."

A murmur rippled through the room.

Tex let out a low whistle. "Jesus."

Desmond continued, unfazed. "We'll be protecting B-17 Flying Fortresses bombing a Daimler-Benz aircraft factory in Berlin. We expect heavy resistance."

Benji's jaw tightened. Of course they did.

The Luftwaffe was crumbling, but that made them even more dangerous.

Desmond gestured to the map behind him, where the route was marked in red ink.

"Standard enemy engagement," Desmond said. "Initial contact—Messerschmitt Bf 109s and Focke-Wulf 190s. Those will be your first wave."

Benji nodded to himself. They had seen those before. They could handle them.

But then—Desmond's voice dropped lower.

"And we expect Me 262 jet fighters."

Silence.

Benji felt the shift in the room—a ripple of tension.

Tex muttered under his breath, "You gotta be kidding me."

The Me 262s. The first jet-powered fighters. Faster, deadlier than anything they had faced before.

Desmond's eyes swept the room.

"These jets are faster than us," he said plainly. "You will not outfly them. But they can't turn like we can. They're heavier in a dogfight. Use that against them."

Benji's fingers curled into a fist.

They had spent this war fighting for respect. Fighting to prove themselves.

And now?

Now they would fly into hell itself.

Desmond's voice was unwavering.

"We protect the bombers. We bring them home. This is our moment, gentlemen."

He locked eyes with Benji.

"You ready for this, Davis?"

Benji met his gaze, unflinching.

"Yes, sir."

Takeoff: The Red Tails Take Flight

The runway hummed with energy.

Engines rumbled, men moved with quiet efficiency, checking planes, strapping in.

Benji climbed into the cockpit of his P-51 Mustang, the red tail gleaming under the pale morning light.

He took a slow breath, feeling the telegram pressed against his chest.

Her words. Her voice. Her love.

He wasn't just flying for the mission.

He was flying for everything.

He flipped the switches, the Mustang roaring to life beneath him.

"Tower, this is Red Leader. Requesting clearance for takeoff."

A pause, then the response crackled over the radio.

"Red Leader, you are cleared for takeoff. Bring them home."

Benji pushed the throttle forward.

The Mustang lurched, speeding down the runway.

Then—he was airborne.

His fingers curled tighter around the stick.

Ahead of them lay Berlin.

And waiting for them?

The Luftwaffe's last stand.

First Wave: The Swarm of Messerschmitts

An hour into enemy territory, the call came.

"Bandits! Eleven o'clock high!"

Benji's pulse spiked.

He turned his head and saw them—a dark cloud of Messerschmitt Bf 109s tearing through the sky.

"Here we go," Tex muttered over the radio.

Captain Desmond's voice was sharp. "Stay in formation! Defend the bombers!"

Benji locked in.

The 109s dove down fast, cannons blazing.

The first explosion ripped through the air as one of the B-17s took a direct hit.

Tex cursed. "They're coming in hot!"

Benji gritted his teeth. He pulled back on the stick, climbing high, looping behind one of the Messerschmitts.

The German pilot never saw him coming.

Benji's finger squeezed the trigger.

The .50-caliber guns erupted.

Bullets tore through the fuselage, shredding metal and fuel lines.

The Messerschmitt went up in flames, spiraling toward the ground.

"Splash one," Benji murmured.

Tex whooped. "That's my boy!"

But there were too many of them.

Another 109 latched onto Benji's tail, guns screaming.

He banked hard, rolling left, feeling the bullets whip past him.

Tex's voice was tight. "Davis, you got one on you—"

Before he could react, another Mustang swooped in, cannons blazing.

Benji caught the red markings—Desmond.

The Messerschmitt erupted in a fireball.

Desmond's voice crackled through the radio. "Keep your head on a swivel, Davis."

Benji exhaled sharply, hands steady on the stick.

"Yes, sir."

But as he scanned the battlefield, his gut tightened.

Because something was coming.

Something faster. Deadlier.

A streak of silver cut across the sky.

Benji's heart slammed into his ribs.

The Me 262s had arrived.

And the real fight was about to begin.

The sky was chaos.

Benji had no time to think—only react.

The Me 262 jets cut through the battle like streaks of lightning, faster than anything they'd ever seen.

But speed wasn't everything.

And Benji knew it.

He rolled hard, pressing into the seat as the G-force pulled at his bones. His Mustang screamed through the turn, his vision narrowing to a tunnel as he swung behind one of the German jets.

It tried to pull away—but Benji was already there.

His fingers squeezed the trigger.

The .50-caliber guns roared.

Bullets ripped into the jet's engine.

Flames exploded from the fuselage.

The Me 262 broke apart midair, spiraling toward the earth.

One.

Tex's voice crackled through the radio, hyped as hell. "That's one, Davis! You're on fire!"

Benji didn't answer. He was already tracking the next target.

Another 262 cut across the bombers, tearing into a B-17 with explosive cannon fire.

Benji angled sharply, pushing his Mustang to its limits.

The German pilot didn't see him coming—until it was too late.

Benji fired in short, brutal bursts, watching as the jet's left wing shredded into pieces.

The pilot bailed out, his parachute deploying seconds before the wreckage vanished into the clouds.

Two.

"Davis, you're a damn machine!" Tex barked. "Stay with me—we still got bogeys everywhere!"

Benji clenched his jaw. He spotted a third Me 262 barreling straight for a bomber, its nose lined up for a kill shot.

Not today.

Benji pushed the throttle past redline.

The Mustang shook violently, its engine screaming as he surged forward.

The jet pilot must have realized too late.

Benji fired.

The jet erupted into a fireball.

Three.

Tex's Mustang tore through another fighter, his voice wild. "Hell yeah, that's three down! This is our sky, baby!"

Benji barely had time to register the words.

Because at that moment—he felt it.

A presence.

A shadow behind him.

Him.

The radio crackled.

"Ah, my little black bird. You are harder to kill than I expected."

Benji's blood turned to ice.

White Wolf.

Benji didn't hesitate.

He pulled hard left, banking into a brutal roll. The enemy jet followed, moving like a phantom, perfectly mirroring his every move.

Benji's pulse hammered.

This was it.

The rematch.

The bastard who had shot him down over Romania—the man who had haunted him ever since.

Benji leveled his breath, hands steady on the stick.

This time, he wasn't the hunted.

This time, he was the hunter.

The Final Duel

The White Wolf didn't wait.

The Me 262 screamed forward, cannons firing.

Benji dove instantly, pushing his Mustang past safe limits.

The sky twisted around him.

The force threatened to tear him apart.

But he didn't let go.

His plane groaned under the pressure, but he kept control, rolling out just as the jet overshot him.

Now.

Benji yanked the stick, snapping into an impossible climb, putting himself right behind White Wolf.

The German pilot realized the trap too late.

Benji fired.

The bullets grazed the jet's left wing.

Not enough to take him down. But enough to make him bleed.

White Wolf pulled into a spiraling dive, trying to shake him.

Benji followed.

Captain Wright voice came through the radio, frantic. "Davis, you're pushing too hard—pull back—"

No.

Not this time.

Not after everything.

Benji's Mustang shuddered under the stress, his wings rattling.

But he kept going.

Faster. Harder. Deeper into the dive.

White Wolf was trying to lose him in the clouds—but Benji wasn't letting him go.

The Mustang cut through the sky like a blade.

Benji lined up the shot.

White Wolf's voice crackled through the radio, calm.

"You are good, little black bird. But not good enough."

Benji gritted his teeth.

"We'll see about that."

He fired.

The bullets ripped through the jet's fuselage, hitting the right engine.

Fire exploded from the Me 262.

Benji kept firing, making damn sure this was over.

The jet detonated midair.

White Wolf was gone.

Five.

Benji finally let out a breath.

His hands were still steady.

His Mustang was damaged, his fuel low.

But he was alive.

And this time, he wasn't the one falling from the sky.

Aftermath: The Flight Home

The battle was over.

The bombers were still flying.

The mission was a success.

Benji's Mustang limped back to base, low on everything.

As he broke through the clouds, the setting sun bathed the sky in gold.

His fingers brushed against his flight suit.

The telegram.

Jessica's words.

He had made it.

Tomorrow, he'd write her back.

But tonight?

Tonight, he let himself fly.

Not just as a soldier.

Not just as a survivor.

But as a legend.

CHAPTER 23:

THE WAR ENDS – A NEW
MISSION BEGINS

May 8, 1945 – U.S. Military Base, Italy

The war was over.

The radio announcement had come early in the morning, the crackling voice of a BBC correspondent declaring it to the world.

"Germany has unconditionally surrendered to the Allied Forces. The war in Europe is over. This is Victory in Europe Day."

For a moment, there had been silence.

Benji stood outside the barracks, the Italian morning sun just beginning to stretch across the airfield. The usual hum of Mustang engines warming up was absent. There were no briefings, no missions, no rush to the flight line.

For the first time since he had stepped foot in Italy, there was nothing to fight.

Tex stood beside him, a cigarette hanging loosely from his lips, staring off into the distance.

"So that's it?" Tex muttered, voice flat. "Just like that?"

Benji exhaled, rubbing a hand over the back of his neck.

"Just like that."

Tex took a long drag, shaking his head. "Damn. Feels... strange."

Benji didn't answer.

Because Tex was right. It did feel strange.

For months, their world had been dogfights, survival, death. They had woken up every day not knowing if it would be their last.

Now?

Now there was nothing but silence.

The war was over.

But for some reason, Benji didn't feel relieved.

He felt... adrift.

The Celebration That Didn't Feel Like One

The base was alive with celebration.

Pilots and ground crews poured whiskey into tin cups, slapped each other on the back, shouted and sang in the fading sunlight.

But Benji?

Benji just sat on the wing of his Mustang, staring at the horizon.

Tex nudged his shoulder. "You ain't gonna drink?"

Benji huffed a short laugh. "You ever see me turn down whiskey?"

Tex smirked. "Never."

Benji took the flask Tex offered him, but he didn't drink right away.

Instead, he glanced over at the other men, the ones who were still here.

And the ones who weren't.

Sam. Ace.

This was for them, too.

Tex patted his knee. "Hell of a ride, huh?"

Benji nodded slowly, lifting the flask in a silent toast.

"To the ones who made it," he murmured.

Tex clinked his cup against it. "And the ones who didn't."

They both drank.

The whiskey burned down his throat, but it didn't warm him the way it should have.

Because deep down, he knew—his war wasn't over yet.

A New Path Forward

Later that evening, after most of the celebration had died down, Benji found himself in Captain Desmond Wright's office.

The older man leaned against his desk, his flight jacket unzipped, eyes sharp but thoughtful.

Tex sat beside Benji, both of them waiting.

Desmond studied them for a long moment before exhaling through his nose. "You boys ever think about what comes next?"

Tex let out a short laugh. "Haven't had time."

Desmond nodded. "Well, time's here."

Benji stayed quiet.

Because that was the question that had been gnawing at him all day.

What now?

What did a man like him do when there were no more planes to chase, no more battles to win?

Desmond reached into his desk, pulling out a folder.

"There's a program starting up in Chicago. Aviation training for young men—especially Black kids who want to fly. They need instructors."

Benji's heart stilled.

Desmond slid the papers toward them.

"You two got combat experience," Desmond continued. "Real leadership. They could use pilots like you."

Tex lifted a brow. "You saying we should be teachers?"

Desmond smirked. "I'm saying you should give kids a chance to fly before they gotta go to war to do it."

Benji stared at the paperwork, his fingers brushing over the edges.

It was so different from what he had pictured.

He had imagined going home, maybe picking up where he left off. But this?

This was a chance to build something.

To make sure the next generation of Black pilots didn't have to fight so damn hard just to get into the sky.

Benji took a slow breath.

He could do this.

He wanted to do this.

Tex exhaled beside him, rubbing his jaw. "I don't know, man. I was kinda hoping to just sit on a beach somewhere for a few months."

Desmond chuckled. "That an official 'no'?"

Tex sighed dramatically, then turned to Benji. "You in?"

Benji met his gaze, then looked back at Desmond.

His hand curled into a fist.

"I'm in."

Desmond nodded approvingly. "Good. We leave in two months."

Tex groaned. "Guess I better enjoy my beach while I can."

Benji chuckled softly.

For the first time in weeks, he knew where he was going.

He had spent the war fighting for his place in the sky.

Now?

Now he was going to make sure others got their chance, too.

July 1945 – Montgomery, Alabama

The train pulled into Montgomery Station under the scorching Alabama sun.

Benji sat by the window, his duffel bag at his feet, his uniform neatly pressed but worn in ways only war could do.

The steam from the locomotive hissed into the humid air as passengers began to shuffle off. Benji didn't move right away.

He just sat there, staring at the town he had once called home.

Everything looked the same.

But he wasn't the same.

He was older now. Wiser. Hardened.

And more than anything—he was missing a part of himself.

Sam.

Benji exhaled slowly, adjusting the brim of his cap before grabbing his bag. His boots hit the wooden planks of the platform, and he took his first steps back into a world that had moved on without him.

Montgomery was still Montgomery.

The familiar streets, the chatter of folks at the corner stores, the scent of fresh bread from Lizzy's Bakery down the street—it was all still here.

But Benji felt like a ghost walking through it.

The war had aged him in ways time never could.

He passed by a group of young men, boys barely out of high school, laughing and carefree.

That had been him and Sam, once.

Before the war.

Before the world had ripped them apart.

His footsteps slowed as he reached a modest white house with a wraparound porch.

Sam's house.

He clenched his jaw, his fingers tightening around his bag.

This was something he had to do.

Sam's mother answered the door, her hands wiping flour from her apron.

For a moment, she just stared.

Then her eyes welled up with tears.

"Oh, my Lord."

She pulled him into a hug before he could say anything, holding on tight. As if he was the last piece of Sam she had left.

Benji's throat tightened.

"I'm sorry, Mrs. Wells," he murmured.

She pulled back, shaking her head. "No, baby. You came home." Her voice cracked. "I prayed every night that at least one of you would come home."

Benji looked past her, spotting Sam's father sitting in his chair on the porch, staring out at the trees.

Mr. Wells had always been a strong man—a quiet strength, never rattled.

But now?

Now his face was lined deeper, his shoulders a little heavier.

Benji stepped forward. "Sir."

Mr. Wells didn't look at him right away.

"You see him go?" he asked, his voice rough.

Benji swallowed hard.

"Yes, sir."

Mr. Wells finally turned to face him. His eyes were tired.

But beneath that—Benji saw the same thing he had been carrying all these months.

Grief.

Regret.

And something else.

Something like understanding.

"He fought, didn't he?" Mr. Wells asked.

Benji nodded firmly. "He fought like a hero."

Mr. Wells studied him for a long moment before nodding.

"He was always gonna follow you into the fire." A small breath. "Boy never did know how to back down."

Benji let out a rough chuckle. "No, sir. He didn't."

Mrs. Wells stepped forward, pressing something into Benji's hands.

A photo.

Sam and Benji, both in there baseball uniforms, standing outside this very house, grinning like fools.

"We kept waiting for you to come back," she whispered. "Figured you'd want this."

Benji's fingers curled around the photo, his chest tightening.

"Thank you," he murmured.

And for the first time since Sam died, he let himself grieve.

Benji stood in front of his family's house as the cicadas hummed in the evening air.

The screen door creaked open.

Then—

"Benji?"

His mother's voice broke through the silence.

And suddenly, he was home.

She ran to him, tears falling freely, pulling him into her arms.

Naomi's laughter rang out as she rushed onto the porch, colliding into him with the force of a hurricane.

His father stood in the doorway, his face unreadable—until it wasn't.

Until he let out a choked breath and pulled Benji into a tight embrace.

Benji's chest ached.

This was what he had fought for.

For them.

For this moment.

And yet, somewhere deep inside—he still felt the loss.

Still felt Sam's absence.

Still felt the weight of everything he had seen, everything he had done.

But for now, he let himself be home.

Even if he didn't quite know where he belonged anymore.

Benji sat at the dinner table, surrounded by his family.

It had been years since they had all been in the same room together.

But now?

Now his mother was watching him like he might disappear again. Naomi had practically attached herself to his arm, refusing to let go. His father sat at the head of the table, silently watching, absorbing everything.

And his brother, Marcus, had just walked through the door.

Marcus froze the moment he saw Benji sitting at the table.

For a moment, he didn't say anything.

Then, finally—he let out a sharp breath, shaking his head.

"Well, I'll be damned," Marcus muttered, stepping forward. "They said you were gone."

Benji smirked, standing up to meet him. "Guess I'm harder to kill than they thought."

Marcus let out a rough chuckle, then pulled him into a tight, bone-crushing hug.

Benji clenched his jaw, returning it just as hard.

For all their differences, for all the times Marcus had doubted the war was worth it—he had still grieved.

Still thought he'd lost his little brother.

And now?

Now he knew Benji had made it back.

When Marcus pulled away, his eyes dropped to Benji's wrist. His brow lifted.

"You still wear that old thing?"

Benji followed his gaze.

The bracelet.

Naomi's bracelet.

The one she had given him before he left.

The one that had been on his wrist through every battle, every near-death moment, every last damn thing the war had thrown at him.

Benji turned to his sister, his voice softer.

"Guess it worked, huh?"

Naomi grinned, eyes glassy. "I told you it was lucky."

Benji chuckled, rubbing his thumb over the worn leather. "Yeah. You did."

The night stretched on, filled with voices, laughter, and warm food.

His mother had made a feast—fried chicken, cornbread, collard greens, mashed potatoes. It was the kind of meal that reminded him of being a boy again.

Of home.

But home wasn't the same.

Because he wasn't the same.

They asked him everything.

About the war. About flying. About what it was like in Italy, in Germany, in places they had only ever read about in the papers.

Benji told them what he could.

Told them about the missions, the dogfights, the long nights where sleep felt impossible.

He told them about the men he had fought beside. The ones who made it, the ones who didn't.

He told them about Tex, about Captain Desmond.

And then—he told them about Sam.

Naomi's smile faltered. "I kept waiting for a letter from him," she whispered. "I thought maybe he'd come home with you."

Benji swallowed hard.

Marcus ran a hand over his face, shaking his head. "Damn."

Their mother bowed her head. "Samson was a good boy."

"The best," Benji murmured.

A long silence settled over the room.

Then his father, quiet as ever, cleared his throat. "And now?" he asked. "Where do you go from here, son?"

Benji let out a slow breath.

This was it.

The moment he had been thinking about since the war ended.

Benji sat back in his chair, running a hand over his jaw.

"I got an offer," he said finally.

His mother's brow lifted. "Offer?"

Benji nodded. "Captain Wright is starting up a flight program in Chicago. A place where kids—especially Black kids—can learn how to fly. No war, no battle. Just flying."

Naomi's eyes lit up. "Like you when you were little?"

Benji chuckled. "Yeah. Like me when I was little."

Marcus whistled, leaning back. "So you're gonna be a teacher now?"

Benji grinned. "Something like that."

Their father nodded slowly, a quiet pride in his eyes. "That's good work, son. That's a legacy."

His mother smiled softly. "I always knew you'd find your way back to the sky."

Benji's chest tightened.

Because she was right.

He belonged in the air.

And now? Now he could make sure others got there, too.

Naomi tilted her head, a mischievous glint in her eye. "And what about Jessica?"

Benji stiffened.

Marcus smirked. "Yeah, what about Jessica?"

Benji sighed, rubbing his temple. "Ain't none of your business."

Naomi gasped, scandalized. "You wrote me letters about her!"

Marcus laughed, shaking his head. "Damn. You really fell for a white girl?"

Benji gave him a warning look, but Marcus just lifted his hands in surrender.

His mother, though, just watched him carefully.

"She wrote you, didn't she?"

Benji hesitated, then nodded.

A soft smile touched his mother's lips. "And what did she say?"

Benji reached into his pocket, fingers brushing over the telegram.

"I don't know yet," he admitted. "But I'm gonna find out."

His mother nodded approvingly. "Then go."

Benji lifted a brow. "Just like that?"

She smiled. "Just like that."

Because she knew.

She knew he'd been fighting wars long before he ever stepped into a plane.

And now?

Now it was time for him to fight for something else.

The Next Night – Montgomery Train Station

The platform was quieter this time.

Benji stood at the edge, duffel bag slung over his shoulder, staring at the train that would take him to Chicago.

His mother hugged him first, whispering, "Be safe, my boy."

Naomi clung to him. "Write me more this time."

Marcus just nodded. "Go make something of yourself."

His father gave him a firm handshake.

Benji grinned.

Then—the whistle blew.

Benji stepped onto the train, turning to take one last look at his family.

Then, as the wheels lurched forward, carrying him away from Montgomery—

He reached into his flight jacket.

Pulled out the telegram.

And reread it.

My heart stopped when I saw your name.

I thought I lost you.

Please write back.

His grip tightened.

Chicago.

His new life.

He leaned back, exhaling slowly as the train carried him forward.

This time—he wasn't running from anything.

This time, he was going home.

CHAPTER 24:

STANDING HER GROUND

July 1945 – Montgomery, Alabama

J essica stepped off the train, the humid Southern air clinging to her skin like a second layer.

It had been years since she last set foot in Montgomery, and yet the city hadn't changed.

The same grand oak trees lined the streets, the same smell of fresh bread drifted from the bakery, the same old men sat outside the barbershop, watching the world pass by.

But she had changed.

She wasn't the same obedient daughter her parents had once controlled.

She had built a life of her own.

And now?

She was back to confront the ghosts she had left behind.

The small café near the courthouse was exactly as she remembered it—quiet, elegant, meant for those who moved in the same social circles as her parents.

Richard was already waiting for her at a corner table, his suit perfectly pressed, his posture as polished as ever.

But when he looked up and saw her, his smile was genuine.

"Jessica," he said, standing to greet her. "I wasn't sure you'd actually come."

Jessica slid into the seat across from him, offering a small smirk. "And miss one of your famous lectures on political strategy? Never."

Richard chuckled, shaking his head. "I take it Chicago is treating you well."

Jessica nodded. "It's where I belong."

"Then why are you back?"

Jessica inhaled, choosing her words carefully.

"I need to close some doors before I can fully move forward."

Richard studied her for a long moment before nodding.

"Well," he said, sipping his coffee, "before you slam them shut, there's something you should consider."

Jessica raised a brow.

Richard leaned forward, lowering his voice. "Your father still has power, Jess. He's still a Senator. And whether you like it or not, that means he's still in the way of progress."

Jessica's stomach tightened.

She knew Richard was right.

Senator Shaw had made a career out of preserving the world exactly as it was.

And that meant fighting against everything Jessica had come to stand for.

Richard tapped the table. "You're working for civil rights now. You know how the system works. You don't need to go to war with your father, but you can use what you know to work around him—to work against him in a way he won't see coming."

Jessica folded her arms. "You really think he can be moved?"

Richard huffed a small laugh. "No. But you don't need him to move. You just need him to get out of the way."

Jessica let the words settle.

Then, finally—she nodded.

She didn't come back to Montgomery for politics.

But if she could strike a blow on her way out?

She would.

Jessica stood at the base of the grand Shaw estate, staring up at the house she had once called home.

It looked smaller now.

Like the power it had once held over her had finally begun to crack.

She had ignored every letter, every phone call, every demand for an explanation from her parents since she left for Chicago.

But now?

Now, she was ready to say her piece.

She climbed the steps, knocked once.

A long pause.

Then—the door opened.

Her mother stood in the doorway, her eyes wide with disbelief.

"Jessica."

Jessica's stomach twisted. It had been so long since she had last seen her mother, but she didn't allow herself to falter.

She straightened her shoulders.

"Is Father home?"

Her mother hesitated, then stepped aside.

Jessica walked in.

The house smelled the same—cigars and expensive perfume, wood polish and lemon tea.

But it didn't feel like home.

It never had.

Her father was in the parlor, a cigar in one hand, a newspaper in the other. When he saw her, he lowered both slowly.

"Well," Senator Shaw mused, leaning back in his chair. "The prodigal daughter returns."

Jessica clenched her jaw, stepping forward.

"I didn't come for pleasantries."

Her father smirked. "No, I imagine not."

Her mother hovered near the doorway, eyes darting between them.

Jessica took a slow breath, forcing herself to stay calm.

"I came to tell you that I'm not afraid of you anymore," she said, her voice even.

Senator Shaw's brow lifted slightly.

"I left because I refused to be a part of this world you built," Jessica continued. "A world where people like you decide who matters and who doesn't."

She swallowed hard. "I came back because I needed to tell you to your face that I love Benjamin Davis. And I don't need your approval."

Her mother sucked in a sharp breath.

Her father, however, just exhaled a slow puff of cigar smoke.

Jessica held his gaze.

"I know you tried to erase him from my life. I know you stole his letters. I know you wanted me to marry Richard to protect your name."

Her father leaned forward. "And yet, here you are. Standing in my house."

Jessica's pulse spiked.

But she didn't let him get to her.

"Not for long," she said. "I'm leaving again. And this time, I'm not coming back."

Her mother's eyes filled with tears.

"Jessica, please—"

Jessica turned to her.

"I don't need your love with conditions," she said, her voice softer. "I need you to accept that I am my own person. And if you can't do that, then I have nothing left to say."

Her mother reached for her.

But Jessica stepped back.

She turned on her heel, walking away for the last time.

Jessica stepped off the porch, her chest tight, her heart hammering.

She had done it.

She had faced them.

And she had walked away.

But as she reached the gate, a familiar voice stopped her.

"Didn't think I'd see you 'round here again."

Jessica turned, and her heart lifted.

Josephine stood by the garden, a warm smile on her weathered face.

Jessica's breath caught. "Josephine."

The older woman wiped her hands on her apron. "You look good, baby."

Jessica let out a shaky laugh. "So do you."

Josephine chuckled. "That's 'cause I don't work here no more. Left last year. Got me a little house of my own now. Spend my days with my grandbabies."

Jessica's throat tightened.

Josephine had been the only mother she had ever truly known.

She stepped forward and wrapped her arms around her, holding tight.

"Thank you," Jessica whispered.

"For what, baby?"

"For everything."

Josephine pulled back, cupping her face. "You were always meant for something greater, Jess. Now go get it."

Jessica nodded, wiping her eyes.

She turned, stepping through the gate—toward a life that was finally hers.

And this time?

She was never looking back.

July 1945 – Montgomery Train Station

The train whistle pierced the night air, sending a rolling wave of steam across the platform.

Jessica clutched her ticket tightly, her pulse steady but fast.

She had done it.

She had faced her parents, spoken her truth, walked away without looking back.

Now, she was heading home.

Home.

Funny how that word had shifted.

Chicago had been her escape, but now—home was no longer a place.

It was a person.

She stepped onto the train, the weight of the last two years lifting with every step forward.

She moved through the narrow aisle, searching for her seat, her fingers brushing the locket around her neck.

The train rumbled beneath her feet, the dim lighting casting a warm glow over the rows of passengers settling in for the journey north.

Then—

Her breath caught.

At first, she thought she was imagining it.

Her mind playing cruel tricks on her, painting a dream she had wished for too many times to count.

But no—

It was real.

There, just a few rows ahead, sitting by the window, his broad frame relaxed yet poised—was him.

Benjamin Davis.

Benji.

Jessica's world tilted.

The sounds around her faded into nothing.

The voices, the rustling of luggage, the clatter of footsteps on the wooden floor—all disappeared.

All she could hear was the rapid pounding of her own heartbeat.

Her legs froze, her breath hitching in her throat as she took him in.

Older.

Stronger.

Sharper.

His uniform, neatly pressed, still bore the weight of war. His posture, though at ease, carried an unspoken exhaustion, the kind that only came from witnessing too much.

And yet—

His face.

His face was the same.

Those deep brown eyes, filled with fire and history and stories she wanted to hear forever.

The lips she had once kissed in secret, whispered promises against in the dark.

His hand rested on his knee, and—

Her gaze caught on something.

Peeking from his pocket.

A telegram.

Her telegram.

A sharp breath escaped her lips.

As if he had heard it—

Benji's head turned.

And then, just like that—

Their eyes met.

The past. The present. The years lost. The love that never left.

It all collided in a single instant.

His shoulders tensed, his breath visibly catching.

For a fraction of a second, he didn't move.

Didn't blink.

Didn't breathe.

Then—

Benji stood.

Slowly.

Deliberately.

The train shifted beneath them, but neither of them moved with it.

It was as if the world had stopped spinning.

Jessica swallowed hard, her fingers tightening around her ticket.

Her lips parted—words forming but never making it out.

Because he was already moving.

Already stepping toward her.

Already closing the space that had kept them apart for too damn long.

Jessica's heart slammed into her ribs.

She tried to say his name, but her voice—her breath—failed her.

But she didn't need to say it.

Because Benji was right there.

In front of her.

So close, she could feel the heat of him, the familiar scent of leather, aviation fuel, and the faintest hint of soap.

His eyes searched hers, desperate, disbelieving.

His throat worked, his jaw tightening.

Then—

A single whisper.

"Jess."

The sound of it broke her.

A choked sob escaped her lips before she could stop it, and before she even had the chance to think—

She threw herself into his arms.

Benji caught her instantly, wrapping her up, holding her tight—like he would never let go.

Her fingers dug into the fabric of his uniform, clutching onto him as if letting go would mean losing him all over again.

His arms were like steel, pulling her flush against him, burying his face into the crook of her neck, breathing her in.

For a moment—neither of them spoke.

They just held on.

Because words weren't enough for this.

Because time had stolen too much from them.

And now, here they were.

Back where they belonged.

Together.

Jessica pulled back just enough to look into his eyes, tears clinging to her lashes.

Benji cupped her face, his thumb brushing over her cheek, his touch reverent, as if he still didn't believe she was real.

"I thought—" Jessica tried, her voice breaking.

Benji's hand tightened at her waist.

"I know," he murmured, his forehead dropping against hers.

A beat.

Then, softer—

"I never stopped."

Jessica let out a shaky laugh, her tears slipping free.

She smiled through them, whispering, "Neither did I."

Benji's breath hitched.

And then—

He kissed her.

God, he kissed her.

And just like that—

The world came rushing back.

The train rumbled beneath them.

The people bustled past.

But none of it mattered.

Because this?

This was everything.

And they weren't letting go.

Not this time.

Not ever again.

July 1945 – Somewhere Between Montgomery and Chicago

The train rocked gently as it pulled away from the station, the low hum of the engine rumbling beneath their feet.

But Jessica barely felt it.

Because all she could feel was him.

Benji's fingers were intertwined with hers, his grip firm—like he was afraid she might vanish if he let go.

Jessica wasn't letting go either.

She had spent too many nights imagining this moment, dreaming of it, wishing for it—only to wake up to an empty space where he should have been.

Not anymore.

Now he was here. Solid. Real. Hers.

But even as their hands remained locked, she could feel it—the weight of the past still hanging between them.

And there was so much to say.

She drew in a slow, shaky breath, still trying to convince herself that this wasn't just another cruel dream.

Then, softly—

"What are you doing on this train?"

Benji exhaled, his free hand resting on his knee, his thumb brushing absentmindedly over his uniform.

"I thought you'd be home," she continued, her voice barely above a whisper.

Benji's grip on her hand tightened slightly.

"I'm not going back to Montgomery," he admitted. "Not for long, anyway."

Jessica's heart stilled.

"Where are you going?"

Benji glanced down at their joined hands, his jaw flexing slightly before looking back at her.

"Chicago."

Jessica's breath caught.

Her fingers twitched against his, but she didn't dare pull away.

She blinked at him, then let out a soft, disbelieving laugh.

Benji raised a brow. "What?"

Jessica shook her head, still smiling. "I live there."

Benji's whole body froze.

His grip on her hand loosened slightly as his brain worked through what she had just said.

"You what?"

Jessica bit her lip, watching the gears turn behind his dark eyes. "I live in Chicago, Benji. I've been there for almost two years."

Benji stared at her like she had just slapped him.

His mouth opened—then shut—then opened again.

"Since when?"

Jessica let out another small laugh, but it was thick with emotion. "Since I left home."

Benji blinked.

The realization hit him all at once—all those lost years, all the nights he spent thinking she was worlds away when she had been in the very same city.

His voice came out low, almost hoarse. "You've been in Chicago all this time?"

Jessica nodded.

Benji's jaw tightened.

He looked away briefly, exhaling sharply, shaking his head like he couldn't believe it.

"I thought—" he started, then stopped, his throat bobbing. "I thought I was gonna have to convince you to come with me. I was gonna bring you with me, Jess. But you were already there?"

Jessica swallowed, her heart hammering. "I was there."

Benji let out a rough chuckle, rubbing a hand over his face, still stunned.

"This whole time," he muttered. "I was planning my life in Chicago, thinking I'd have to find a way to get you there, but you—you were already there, waiting for me."

Jessica's smile faltered slightly.

"I wasn't waiting," she admitted softly. "I didn't think you were coming."

His breath caught.

Jessica looked down at their hands, tightening her grip.

"I thought I lost you." Her voice was barely above a whisper. "I thought you were gone."

Benji inhaled sharply, his chest rising and falling a little deeper now.

"I know," he murmured.

Jessica searched his face, her fingers brushing lightly over his knuckles. "And now?"

Benji exhaled slowly, his dark eyes locking onto hers like he never wanted to look away.

"Now," he murmured, "I'm exactly where I need to be."

Jessica's heart swelled.

She nodded. "Me too."

A hush had settled over the train car.

Jessica could feel it.

The way conversations lowered. The way glances lingered just a second too long.

The way people stared.

Her hand tightened around Benji's.

She turned her head sharply, eyes blazing, daring anyone to speak.

A few passengers looked away quickly, their gazes dropping back to their newspapers, their laps, their coffee cups.

But others—they lingered.

Jessica's pulse spiked with anger.

All her life, she had been told to stay quiet.

To keep her head down.

To obey, to follow, to live within the expectations placed upon her.

And for years, she had.

But not anymore.

She turned toward the closest pair of eyes still watching them—a middle-aged man in a suit, his lips pressed into a hard line.

Jessica held his stare.

And then—she said it.

Loud. Clear. Unshaken.

"Take a good look. Because this? This is the future. And there's not a damn thing you can do to stop it."

Silence crashed over the train car.

Benji's hand squeezed hers gently, a silent reassurance.

Jessica felt his thumb stroke over her knuckles—a reminder that she didn't need to fight every battle.

That he was here. That he saw her.

That nothing—not the stares, not the whispers, not the whole damn world—could change what they were to each other.

Jessica exhaled, turning back to him.

Benji was watching her, a small, knowing smirk tugging at the corner of his lips.

"You always had a fire in you," he murmured.

Jessica tilted her chin. "I learned from the best."

Benji chuckled, shaking his head. "Lord help me."

Jessica just smiled, leaning into him slightly. "You love it."

Benji let out a slow breath, his expression softening.

"Yeah," he murmured. "I do."

The train rocked gently as the night stretched on.

But neither of them moved.

Jessica leaned into him, her head resting against his shoulder.

Benji's arm curled around her, holding her against him like he had been waiting his whole life to do it.

She closed her eyes, breathing him in.

The scent of leather, faint cologne, and something deeply familiar.

Benji pressed a kiss against the top of her head, his voice soft against her skin.

"I don't ever wanna lose you again."

Jessica tightened her grip around his waist.

"You won't," she whispered.

The train thundered forward, carrying them toward the future they had fought so damn hard to reach.

Toward a life they were about to start—together.

CHAPTER 25:

A SPACE OF THEIR OWN

July 1945 – Chicago, Illinois

The train pulled into Union Station late in the evening, the city lights casting golden streaks across the platform.

Chicago was alive. Even at this hour, the streets pulsed with the sounds of car horns, distant laughter, and the faint hum of jazz drifting from a club somewhere down the block.

Jessica stepped off the train first, gripping Benji's hand tightly, as if she needed to tether him to her.

And maybe she did.

Because Benji stood still for a moment, staring at the vast city skyline, exhaling slowly as the weight of everything settled on his shoulders.

No more war.

No more combat missions.

Just... this.

The next chapter.

Jessica turned to him, squeezing his hand. "Come on," she said softly. "You're coming home with me."

Benji raised a brow, a smirk tugging at the corner of his lips. "That an order, counselor?"

Jessica smirked right back. "Damn right."

Benji chuckled, shaking his head as she led him forward.

He didn't argue.

Because for the first time, he didn't have to fight where he was going.

Because he was going exactly where he wanted to be.

Jessica's apartment was small but warm, tucked in a quiet neighborhood just outside the bustling downtown streets.

Benji stepped inside, dropping his bag by the door, exhaling deeply.

Jessica moved through the space with ease, flicking on lamps, kicking off her shoes, shrugging off her coat like she had done this a thousand times before.

Like this was her space.

Her home.

And now?

Now it was his too.

Benji took a slow look around.

There were law books stacked on the small wooden desk by the window, photographs tucked into the mirror frame. A bottle of wine sat on the counter, half-finished from what looked like a long week.

It was lived in.

It was Jessica.

And God, he had never seen anything more beautiful.

Jessica turned to him, watching him carefully. "It's not much, but—"

"It's perfect," Benji cut in.

Jessica's lips parted slightly.

Benji took a step forward, brushing his fingers along the edge of the desk. "This is yours," he murmured. "Your own space. Your own life."

Jessica swallowed. "It is."

Benji turned to her, something soft and unreadable in his gaze. "And you're just… lettin' me step right into it?"

Jessica tilted her head, stepping closer.

"You were never meant to be anywhere else."

Benji let out a slow exhale.

Jessica reached for him then, lifting a hand to cup his face, her thumb brushing along his jaw.

"Stay with me," she whispered.

Benji leaned into her touch.

Like it was the first time he had been allowed to rest.

And maybe, in some ways, it was.

"Yeah," he murmured. "Yeah, I'll stay."

They moved wordlessly into the bedroom, the quiet intimacy of it settling into Benji's bones.

Jessica stepped in front of him, fingers moving to the buttons of his uniform jacket.

He let her, his breath slow, steady, watching her face as she worked each one open.

She pushed it off his shoulders, letting it slide to the floor.

Her hands then went to the fabric of his undershirt, lifting it slowly—until she saw it.

Jessica froze.

A deep, jagged scar stretched across his side, the ugly remnant of battle, of survival, of everything he had endured.

Her breath caught, fingers hovering just above the healed wound.

Benji didn't say anything at first.

He just watched her, his chest rising and falling slowly, as if bracing for her reaction.

Jessica's eyes burned as she lifted her hand, her fingertips barely grazing the raised skin.

"This was from him, wasn't it?" she whispered.

Benji's jaw tensed. He didn't need to ask who she meant.

White Wolf.

The battle that almost killed him.

Jessica swallowed hard, tracing the scar like she was memorizing it.

Benji exhaled, voice quiet. "Through and through. Knocked me clean out of the sky."

Jessica's throat tightened.

She had read about his unit's missions in the paper. She had seen his name listed as MIA, believing she had lost him forever.

And now here he was.

Scarred, but alive.

Jessica cupped his face, her fingers trembling slightly.

"You survived," she whispered.

Benji's lips parted slightly. "I did."

She searched his face, her gaze flickering over every inch of him. "How?"

Benji let out a slow breath, lifting a hand to tuck her hair behind her ear.

"I don't know," he admitted. "But I think… I think I was fightin' to get back to you."

Jessica's breath shook.

She surged forward, pressing her lips to his, not in hunger, not in urgency, but in something deeper.

Something unbreakable.

Benji held her close, their bodies molding together, breathing each other in.

She kissed the scar, her lips soft against the skin that had nearly been his undoing.

Benji's eyes fluttered shut, his hand cupping the back of her head.

She pulled back just enough to look at him, really look at him.

"No more fighting," she whispered.

Benji's fingers curled around her waist. "No more fighting," he echoed.

And for the first time in forever—he meant it.

They moved beneath the covers, the room dimly lit by the glow of the streetlamp outside the window.

Jessica curled into him, resting her head against his chest, her hand sliding over his stomach.

Benji swallowed hard, his arm tightening around her.

For a long moment, neither of them spoke.

Jessica's fingers traced absent patterns against his skin.

Benji let out a slow breath, staring at the ceiling. "I don't know how to stop," he admitted.

Jessica lifted her head slightly. "Stop what?"

Benji swallowed. "The fightin'. The runnin'. The dreamin' about war even when I'm awake."

Jessica shifted, pressing her palm to his chest. "You don't have to stop all at once."

Benji's throat bobbed.

Jessica kissed his shoulder. "You just have to know you're not alone."

Benji let out a slow exhale, his muscles finally starting to relax.

He pressed a kiss to the top of her head, inhaling deeply.

Jessica stirred slightly, the warmth of Benji's body wrapped around her a comfort she hadn't realized she had been missing all these years.

For the first time in what felt like forever, she wasn't alone.

And neither was he.

The soft glow from the streetlamp outside cast gentle shadows across the bedroom, painting Benji's sleeping form in silver and gold. His chest rose and fell steadily, his body pressed against hers, arms instinctively wrapped around her like he was afraid she might disappear if he let go.

Jessica traced slow circles against his bare skin, her fingertips ghosting over his chest, the steady drum of his heartbeat soothing.

For once, he wasn't fighting.

For once, he was still.

But then—

It changed.

Benji's grip on her tightened.

His breathing, once deep and steady, turned sharp, erratic.

Jessica's eyes flickered open, her heart kicking up as she felt his body go rigid.

His jaw clenched, his fingers twitching against her waist.

Then—the first sound.

A low, strangled breath.

Then another.

Jessica sat up instantly.

"Benji?" she whispered.

He didn't wake.

His chest heaved unevenly, his breath coming in short, shallow bursts.

Jessica's stomach twisted.

It was like watching someone fight a war inside themselves.

A war that hadn't ended—even though it was supposed to be over.

Jessica placed her hands on his face, gently but firmly.

"Benji," she said again, stronger this time.

His breath hitched.

Jessica's fingers tightened around his jaw. "Wake up, baby."

Benji gasped.

His eyes flew open, wild, dark, unfocused.

His entire body jerked, his chest rising and falling too fast, like he had just been ripped out of the sky.

Jessica didn't hesitate.

She cupped his face, pressing her forehead to his, her voice soft but steady.

"You're safe."

Benji's breath shuddered.

His hands gripped her waist, like he needed to anchor himself.

Jessica pressed a kiss to his temple.

Again.

And again.

Until his breath started to slow.

Until his fingers weren't trembling anymore.

Until the haze of war started to fade from his eyes.

Benji closed his eyes tightly, his forehead still pressed to hers.

Jessica ran her fingers through his hair, soothing.

"Talk to me," she whispered.

Benji swallowed hard. His throat bobbed once, twice, before he finally spoke.

"It was… Sam." His voice was low, hoarse.

Jessica's chest tightened.

Benji exhaled shakily, his hands still clutching onto her.

"I saw him," he murmured. "We were back in Italy. We were flyin', laughing like we used to… then suddenly, he was just—"

His voice cracked.

Jessica pulled him closer.

She didn't ask what happened next.

She already knew.

Sam was gone.

And Benji was still carrying the weight of it.

Jessica kissed his forehead, her own eyes burning.

"You carry him with you," she whispered.

Benji's arms tightened around her.

Jessica laid back down, pulling him with her, pressing herself into his side.

Benji let out one last, deep exhale.

Jessica ran her fingers soothingly along his arm, whispering against his skin.

"I'm here."

Benji turned his face into her hair, his breathing finally even again.

Jessica held him.

And he let her.

Because for the first time in a long time—

He wasn't fighting alone.

And he never would again.

The first rays of morning light spilled through the curtains, casting soft golden hues across the room.

Jessica woke slowly, feeling the warmth of Benji's body still wrapped around hers.

For a long time, she just laid there, listening.

His breathing was slow, deep. The rhythmic rise and fall of his chest beneath her palm was steady, comforting.

For the first time in years, they weren't running.

They weren't hiding.

They were just... here.

Together.

Jessica turned her head slightly, watching him.

His face was relaxed, his lashes dark against his skin, his features softer than she had ever seen them.

She let her fingertips trace lightly over his jaw, marveling at how different he looked from the boy she once knew.

The war had changed him.

Hardened him.

But right now?

Right now, he wasn't Lieutenant Davis, the fighter pilot.

He was just Benji.

And he was home.

A slow smile curved Jessica's lips.

She leaned in, pressing a soft kiss to his temple.

Then, gently—"Come walk with me."

Benji stretched as they stepped outside, rolling his shoulders and tilting his head back to take in the morning light.

Jessica had seen Chicago wake up hundreds of times before, but watching it through his eyes felt like seeing it for the first time.

The air was crisp, carrying the scent of fresh bread from the bakeries lining the street. The soft hum of the city waking up surrounded them—streetcars rattling along their tracks, the distant sound of a newsboy calling out headlines, the soft chatter of early risers making their way to work.

Benji glanced around, taking it all in.

Jessica grinned, nudging him. "You look like you've never seen a city before."

Benji huffed a small laugh, shaking his head. "I haven't seen this city before."

Jessica looped her arm through his. "Then let me show you."

Benji chuckled but let her lead him down the bustling sidewalk.

Jessica pointed out little things as they walked—the old clock tower down the street, the shop where she bought her first law books, the best place to get fresh fruit in the summer.

And Benji just listened.

Like he wanted to memorize everything about her world.

Finally, she stopped in front of a small café tucked into the corner of the block.

"This is my favorite breakfast spot," she said, tilting her head toward the entrance. "Come on."

Benji opened the door for her, and they stepped inside, the scent of butter and coffee wrapping around them like a warm embrace.

Jessica led them to a small table by the window, where sunlight spilled in golden streaks across the wooden surface.

Benji slid into the chair across from her, already looking at her like she was the most interesting thing in the room.

Jessica smiled, feeling her heart squeeze.

Then—"Let's talk about the future."

Benji raised a brow. "That a command?"

Jessica smirked. "You can take it that way if you want."

Benji let out a soft chuckle, leaning back in his chair, arms folded. "Alright then. What about the future?"

Jessica tilted her head. "You're really gonna do it? The youth aviation program?"

Benji's expression softened. "Yeah. I want to help kids learn how to fly, give them the opportunities I never thought I'd have." He exhaled, running a hand over his jaw. "I didn't think there'd be anything for me after the war, but... I wanna build something. I wanna give back."

Jessica's heart swelled with pride.

"I think that's beautiful, Benji," she murmured.

Benji held her gaze for a long moment, something unspoken passing between them.

Then—

Jessica tilted her head slightly. "What about kids?"

Benji coughed.

Jessica watched, amused, as he choked on his coffee, reaching for a napkin.

His dark eyes went wide. "Kids?"

Jessica fought the grin threatening to break free. "Yeah. You ever think about having them?"

Benji blinked, looking thoroughly caught off guard. "I—uh—"

Jessica leaned forward, chin resting in her hand. "You always wanted to pass on your love of flying, right? Imagine teaching your own son how to fly."

Benji let out a breath, his eyes flickering with something unreadable.

Jessica saw it then.

The flicker of wonder.

Of something he never thought he'd have.

"Damn, Jess," he murmured, rubbing the back of his neck. "You don't start small, do you?"

Jessica laughed softly. "What, does the idea of little Benjis running around scare you?"

Benji smirked, recovering slightly. "A little. But mostly, I'm just tryin' to wrap my head around the fact that we're sitting here talkin' about kids."

Jessica smiled, reaching across the table, taking his hand.

"Well," she murmured, "we have time to figure it out."

Benji squeezed her hand gently.

His gaze softened. "Yeah," he said, voice quieter now. "We do."

Jessica's chest ached.

For years, they had lived moment to moment.

Never thinking beyond the next letter. The next breath.

But now?

Now, they were finally talking about forever.

And for the first time, it didn't feel out of reach.

They spent the rest of breakfast talking about everything—where they would live, what life might look like, how they would build something that lasted.

Benji listened intently as Jessica talked about her work, about the civil rights movement, about all the things she still wanted to change.

And when it was his turn, he spoke about the skies.

About how he wanted to teach young kids what it meant to fly, to dream.

By the time they left the café, the city was fully awake.

The streets bustled with life, the sun climbing higher into the sky.

Benji reached for her hand as they walked.

Jessica glanced at him, smiling. "Getting comfortable, huh?"

Benji smirked, swinging their joined hands slightly. "Damn right."

Jessica let out a soft laugh, leaning into him as they walked.

The world wasn't perfect.

There was still so much left to fight for.

But for the first time in their lives—

They weren't fighting alone.

CHAPTER 26:

LEARNING TO LIVE AGAIN

September 1945 – Chicago, Illinois

It had been a few months since Benji had stepped off that train and into this life.

A life without war.

A life without combat missions.

A life where, for the first time in years, he woke up next to the woman he loved.

It had been an adjustment.

The quiet. The stillness. The way the days stretched ahead of him without a regimented schedule, without orders, without the constant hum of warplanes overhead.

But Jessica made it easier.

Every morning, he woke to the scent of coffee, the soft rustle of newspapers, the steady rhythm of normalcy that he had forgotten existed.

And every night, he fell asleep with her in his arms.

It wasn't perfect—adjusting wasn't easy.

But it was the first time in a long time that he felt like he had a future.

Benji had never been the type of man to sit still.

So when he wasn't working out the logistics for the youth aviation program, he threw himself into helping Jessica.

That meant helping at rallies.

That meant attending meetings.

That meant seeing firsthand what she was fighting for.

And the first time he saw her stand in front of a crowd, her voice strong and unwavering, demanding justice for those who had none—

He felt it.

The same fire he had seen in her when she stood up to people on the train, when she walked away from the life her family tried to trap her in.

She was still fighting.

Just like he was.

And damn if he wasn't proud of her.

But it wasn't just the rallies.

There were smaller things too.

Things he had never thought about before the war.

Like learning how to grocery shop properly without just grabbing rations.

Like learning how to sleep in a bed without waking up expecting an air raid.

Like not feeling on edge every time a car backfired, mistaking it for gunfire.

Jessica noticed.

She always did.

She never pushed, never pried.

But when he had nights where the shadows of war followed him into his dreams, she was there—pulling him back, grounding him.

And when he got restless, uneasy, unsure what to do with his hands after years of always having a mission, she found ways to keep him busy.

One morning, he had been pacing the apartment, and she had tossed a toolbox at him.

"Fix the sink," she said casually.

Benji had blinked at her. "The what?"

Jessica smirked. "The sink. It's been dripping for weeks."

Benji crossed his arms. "You know how to fix a sink."

Jessica raised a brow. "Yeah, but you look like you need something to do."

Benji had just shaken his head, chuckling.

But damn if she wasn't right.

The Apartment That Became Home.

It wasn't a big place.

But it was theirs.

At first, he had felt like a guest.

Now?

Now he knew where everything was.

He knew which cabinet she kept the sugar in, the exact spot she liked to leave her shoes near the door.

He had his own side of the closet.

His uniform was still hanging there, even though he had traded in combat boots for simple shirts and slacks.

The military was still a part of him, always would be.

But now, when he looked in the mirror, he wasn't just Lieutenant Davis, the pilot.

He was Benji.

A man who was learning how to live again.

And every morning when Jessica kissed him before she left for work, when she lingered just a little longer, when she tangled her fingers in his collar before pulling away—

He knew.

He knew that whatever came next—

He wasn't doing it alone.

October 1945 – Chicago, Illinois

Benji hadn't been in a cockpit since the war ended.

Not because he didn't want to—God knew flying was in his blood.

But because, for the first time in his life, it wasn't about survival.

It wasn't about war.

It wasn't about keeping himself or the men around him alive long enough to make it to another mission.

It was about something else entirely.

The first time he walked into the Youth Aviation Program's hangar, he had felt it.

A different kind of adrenaline.

Not the rush of battle, but the quiet hum of something new.

Something worth building.

Something that would outlive him.

And standing at the center of it all—Captain Desmond Wright.

"Thought I'd have to drag you out here," Desmond had said that first day, watching as Benji took in the rows of beat-up training planes, the wide-eyed kids hovering near the hangar doors, too nervous to step inside.

Benji had smirked. "I figured I'd save you the trouble."

Tex had strolled in not long after, grinning as he clapped Benji on the back. "About time you got here, Davis. These kids are ready to learn from a legend."

Benji had laughed, shaking his head. "I ain't a legend, Tex."

Tex had just shrugged. "Try telling them that."

Benji had turned then, really looking at the kids—boys no older than sixteen, maybe seventeen.

Boys who looked at him and saw something larger than life.

And that was when it hit him.

They weren't just here to learn how to fly.

They were here to learn how to dream.

By the second month, Benji had found his rhythm.

The program had started with only a handful of students, most of them Black teenagers who had never even seen the inside of a plane before.

Most of them had walked in hesitant, nervous, unsure if they even belonged here.

But by the time Benji finished with them, they weren't just sitting in cockpits—they were flying.

"Don't fight the wind—feel it," he told them one afternoon as he stood beside a young kid gripping the flight controls a little too tightly. "The plane ain't just metal and bolts—it's got a rhythm. You learn to move with it, and you'll fly like you were born for it."

The kid—**Darius, barely sixteen, all nerves and excitement bundled into one—**nodded quickly, his brow furrowed in concentration.

Tex leaned against the side of the plane, grinning. "Damn, Davis, you sound like a poet."

Benji smirked, adjusting Darius's grip. "Just don't wanna see this boy crash my plane."

Darius laughed, the nerves easing slightly.

And just like that, Benji saw it.

That spark.

That moment where a boy who never thought he could touch the sky realized that maybe, just maybe, he could.

The evenings at the hangar were just as important as the lessons.

After the students were gone, Benji, Desmond, and Tex would sit outside, their legs stretched out, leaning against the hangar wall, watching the last streaks of sunset fade into the horizon.

Tex, always the loudest of them, would light up a cigarette, grin, and say something to break the silence.

"You ever think about what we'd be doing if we weren't flyin'?" he mused one night, exhaling smoke into the cooling autumn air.

Benji huffed a quiet laugh. "Don't think I ever had a plan B."

Desmond smirked. "I did."

Benji and Tex turned to him, surprised.

Desmond leaned back against the wall, stretching out his arms. "I was gonna be a musician."

Tex nearly choked on his cigarette. "You're shittin' me."

Benji just grinned. "No way."

Desmond shook his head, smirking. "My mother taught me how to play piano when I was a kid. Thought maybe I'd end up in some jazz club."

Tex chuckled. "Man, you'd have been too stiff for a jazz club."

Desmond raised a brow. "You sayin' I ain't got rhythm, Tex?"

Tex grinned. "I'm sayin' you got military rhythm."

Benji laughed, shaking his head.

The conversation faded into easy silence.

Then Tex spoke again, his voice quieter this time.

"You think Sam and Ace would've liked this?"

Benji felt his chest tighten.

His smile faded, his fingers tapping idly against his knee.

Desmond exhaled slowly. "They would've," he said, his voice steady.

Tex nodded, staring off into the distance. "Yeah... Yeah, they would've."

Benji swallowed hard, his throat tightening. "Sam would've loved teachin' these kids," he murmured. "And Ace... he would've made damn sure they knew how to pull off some crazy aerial tricks."

Tex chuckled softly. "Man was fearless. Probably would've had 'em upside down their first flight."

Benji smiled, but it was laced with something heavier.

They sat in silence for a long moment.

Then Desmond exhaled, rubbing his hands over his knees. "We make sure they get their wings, then."

Benji swallowed, nodding. "Yeah."

Because Sam and Ace never got the chance to.

But these boys would.

And that was something worth fighting for.

When Benji got back to the apartment that night, Jessica was already home, curled up on the couch with a book, waiting for him.

She looked up when he walked in, a small smile playing at her lips. "How was it?"

Benji leaned against the doorframe, watching her.

Then, without answering, he walked over, leaned down, and kissed her.

Jessica sighed against him, her hands sliding up his chest, her fingers brushing over the scar White Wolf left behind.

Benji pulled back just enough to rest his forehead against hers.

"I think I'm exactly where I'm supposed to be," he murmured.

Jessica smiled against his lips. "Yeah?"

Benji nodded.

She traced her fingers over his jaw, soft, steady.

"Well," she whispered, "then keep going, baby."

Benji exhaled slowly, his arms tightening around her.

Yeah.

He would.

Because this?

This was just the beginning.

November 1945 – Chicago, Illinois

The first real chill of winter had settled over the city, the wind whipping through the streets, rattling windowpanes, and carrying the scent of wood smoke and roasted chestnuts from street vendors.

Benji adjusted the collar of his coat as he stepped out of the aviation program's hangar, his breath fogging in the cold air.

Tex clapped him on the back. "You ready for the long walk home?"

Benji smirked, shoving his hands into his pockets. "You act like I ain't done harder things."

Tex laughed, shaking his head. "Fair enough. I'll see you tomorrow, Davis."

Benji nodded before heading off, taking his usual route through the city—a route that always led him back to her.

By the time he got to the apartment, the lights inside were already on, casting a warm glow against the cold night.

Benji stepped inside, shaking off the cold, breathing in the scent of home.

Jessica was seated at the small dining table, papers and law books spread out around her, a steaming cup of tea sitting untouched beside her.

She didn't notice him at first, too focused on whatever she was reading, her brows furrowed, lips pursed in deep concentration.

Benji just stood there for a moment, watching her.

He had seen her in every light—bathed in moonlight, standing before a crowd with fire in her voice, whispering in the dark after nightmares chased away his sleep.

But this?

This was her element.

Fighting battles not in the sky, but in courtrooms, in offices, in the streets.

Fighting for people who didn't even know she was doing it for them.

Fighting because she couldn't stand not to.

And damn if he didn't love her for it.

Jessica finally glanced up, catching him staring.

She smirked, tilting her head. "You gonna stand there all night, sir?"

Benji huffed a small laugh, shrugging out of his coat. "Maybe. It's a good view."

Jessica rolled her eyes, but there was warmth behind it.

Benji walked over, sliding into the chair across from her, glancing at the papers sprawled across the table.

"Busy day?" he asked.

Jessica sighed, rubbing her temples. "You have no idea. We've been pushing to challenge these housing laws, but it's like running into a brick wall at every turn."

Benji leaned back, studying her. "You ever get tired of fighting?"

Jessica looked at him then, really looked at him.

And he knew what she saw—the same exhaustion that lived in her bones was in his too.

But she just smiled softly, reaching across the table, taking his hand.

"No," she murmured. "Because every fight is worth it."

Benji turned his palm up, threading their fingers together.

He thought about the kids in the aviation program.

The way their eyes lit up when they took to the skies for the first time.

The way their voices carried when they laughed.

The way they looked at him, waiting for guidance, for a chance.

Jessica was right.

Every fight was worth it.

Building Something That Lasts

Later that night, as they lay in bed, the city humming softly beyond their window, Jessica rested her head against Benji's chest, tracing absent circles over his skin.

"You ever think about what's next?" she murmured.

Benji exhaled, rubbing a hand down her back. "What do you mean?"

Jessica tilted her head to look at him. "This." She gestured around them. "Us. The future."

Benji smirked. "Already tryna plan ahead?"

Jessica pinched his side playfully, making him grunt.

"Come on, I'm serious."

Benji chuckled, but there was warmth in his voice.

He thought about it for a moment.

About the program. About the kids. About waking up next to her every morning.

About having something to come home to.

He exhaled, letting his hand trail down her spine. "I think... I think I just wanna keep buildin' something real."

Jessica smiled softly. "Me too."

She rested her chin on his chest, looking up at him.

"What about marriage?" she asked, her voice light, teasing.

Benji raised a brow, but his pulse jumped slightly. "That a proposal?"

Jessica smirked. "Wouldn't you like to know?"

Benji huffed a laugh, shaking his head. "You really don't do anything small, do you?"

Jessica grinned. "Nope."

Benji studied her, his heart settling into something warm, steady.

Then, quietly—"Yeah. One day."

Jessica's smile softened.

She leaned up, pressing a soft kiss to his lips.

"One day," she echoed.

And for the first time, forever didn't feel so far away.

CHAPTER 27:

THE DECISION

December 1945 – Chicago, Illinois

The idea had been lingering in the back of Benji's mind ever since Jessica brought it up that night.

Marriage.

The thought of it had never seemed real to him before.

Before the war, before Jessica, before this life they were building together, he hadn't allowed himself to think about forever.

But now?

Now, it wasn't just some distant dream.

Now, it was right in front of him.

And for the first time in his life, he wasn't afraid to reach for it.

Benji hadn't talked to anyone about it yet.

But he figured if there was one person who could give him solid advice, it was Desmond.

The two of them sat outside the hangar after a long day at the aviation program, the Chicago winter settling in cold and sharp around them.

Tex had left early, muttering something about finding a woman to keep him warm for the night, leaving Benji and Desmond alone in the quiet.

Benji exhaled, rubbing his hands together for warmth. "Can I ask you somethin'?"

Desmond glanced at him, his sharp blue eyes flickering in curiosity. "Depends."

Benji smirked, shaking his head. "It's serious."

Desmond leaned back, stretching his legs out. "Alright. Shoot."

Benji hesitated for a moment, then just said it.

"I'm thinkin' about askin' Jessica to marry me."

Desmond didn't look surprised.

Instead, he just nodded once, like he'd seen this coming all along. "You sure?"

Benji huffed a soft laugh. "More sure than I've ever been about anything."

Desmond studied him for a long moment before speaking.

"You love her?"

Benji didn't even hesitate. "Yeah."

Desmond nodded. "Then don't waste time."

Benji exhaled, his breath fogging in the cold air. "I don't plan to."

Desmond smirked. "Good. Because I'd hate to see what would happen if you let her slip away."

Benji chuckled, shaking his head. "That ain't gonna happen."

Desmond leaned forward, his expression turning serious.

"Listen," he said, his voice steady. "You and I both know marriage ain't just about love. It's about partnership. It's about fightin' together when things get hard. And it will get hard, Benji. Especially for the two of you."

Benji swallowed, knowing exactly what he meant.

An interracial marriage in 1945?

It wouldn't be easy.

They'd have to fight for every inch of space they took up in this world.

But that didn't scare him.

Because nothing had ever felt more worth fighting for.

Benji nodded. "I know."

Desmond studied him, then nodded in approval. "Then you already got what it takes."

Benji let out a slow breath, feeling something solidify inside him.

That was all the confirmation he needed.

The next day, he went to the jewelry store.

It was a small place, tucked away on a quiet street, the kind of place where the glass display cases had been polished so many times they looked like water.

Benji had never bought jewelry before.

But when he walked inside, something in his chest tightened.

This was real.

This was happening.

An older man behind the counter glanced up, adjusting his glasses. "Can I help you, son?"

Benji cleared his throat. "Yeah. I, uh… I'm lookin' for an engagement ring."

The man's face lit up. "Ah. A lucky lady, then."

Benji smiled softly. "Yeah. The luckiest."

The man gestured toward a display case filled with rings, each one glinting under the shop lights.

Benji stared at them, suddenly feeling like he had no idea what he was doing.

The older man chuckled. "First time?"

Benji let out a soft laugh, rubbing the back of his neck. "That obvious?"

The man smiled. "Most fellas look like they're about to disarm a bomb their first time buying a ring."

Benji chuckled, shaking his head. "Feels about the same, to be honest."

The man leaned on the counter. "Tell me about her."

Benji blinked. "What?"

"Your girl," the man said. "Tell me about her."

Benji exhaled slowly.

Where did he even start?

"She's… she's the strongest person I've ever met," he murmured. "Smart as hell, fights harder than anyone I know. But she's got this way of makin' you feel like… like you belong, just by lookin' at you."

The old man smiled. "Sounds like a hell of a woman."

Benji nodded. "She is."

The man tapped the glass. "Then let's find her a ring that fits her."

Benji scanned the display case, his eyes landing on a simple yet elegant ring with a single diamond.

It wasn't the biggest.

It wasn't flashy.

But it was timeless.

And it reminded him of Jessica.

He pointed to it. "That one."

The old man smiled knowingly. "Good choice."

Benji watched as the man carefully placed the ring in a small velvet box, wrapping it up with precision.

Benji held it in his palm, feeling the weight of it.

It was small.

But it carried everything.

As he walked back to the apartment that evening, the cold air biting at his skin, Benji turned the small box over in his hands.

Jessica had given him so much.

Her love.

Her strength.

Her entire damn heart.

And now, he was going to give her his.

For the rest of his life.

Whatever came next—he was ready.

Because Jessica was worth everything.

And he wasn't going to waste another second.

Jessica glanced up from her desk as the front door opened. The cold air rushed in before Benji stepped inside, his cheeks flushed from the wind, a different kind of energy in his stride.

Jessica smiled as she stood, stretching. "You're home early."

Benji just watched her for a moment, his eyes warm, but intent.

"Come with me," he said suddenly.

Jessica blinked. "Where?"

Benji smirked, tilting his head toward the door. "You trust me?"

Jessica raised a brow. "That's a dangerous question."

Benji chuckled, stepping closer, sliding his arms around her waist. "Maybe. But do you?"

Jessica softened, reaching up to run her fingers along the back of his neck. "Always."

Benji kissed her temple, lingering for just a second before pulling back, his eyes full of something unreadable.

"Then come fly with me."

Jessica laughed softly as they approached the airstrip. "So this is what you were up to today?"

Benji led her toward the hangar, a knowing smirk playing at his lips. "You act like you're surprised."

Jessica shook her head, the wind catching her hair as she glanced up at the clear winter sky.

The same sky he had spent years fighting in.

The same sky he had nearly died in.

And yet, he still loved it.

She could see it in the way he moved now, in the way his fingers brushed over the metal of the P-51 Mustang as they reached the plane, reverence in his touch.

Benji turned to her, his voice softer now. "I told you once… that one day, I'd take you flying."

Jessica's heart squeezed.

She remembered.

Back in Montgomery, when the world had felt so much smaller, when their love had been something they had to hide.

She had never thought this moment would come.

And yet, here they were.

Benji held out a hand. "Come on, counselor. Time to see what it's like to really fly."

Jessica hesitated only for a moment before placing her hand in his.

The cockpit was tight, but Jessica barely noticed as Benji helped her into the seat, making sure she was secure.

His fingers brushed her cheek before he pulled away, settling into the pilot's seat, the movements so fluid, so natural, it was clear he had been born to do this.

The engine roared to life, the vibrations thrumming through her bones as they started rolling down the strip.

Jessica felt a flutter of nerves, gripping the edges of her seat, but then Benji glanced back at her, smirking.

"Don't tell me you're scared," he teased.

Jessica huffed. "I'm not scared."

Benji chuckled. "Good. Because this is gonna change your life."

And with that—they lifted off.

The ground fell away beneath them, the city shrinking until it was just a blur of lights and streets and people.

Jessica's breath caught.

For the first time, she understood.

Why he loved this.

Why he needed this.

The weight of the world was gone up here.

There was nothing but endless sky, the hum of the engine, and the man she loved.

Jessica reached out, her fingers brushing over his shoulder. "It's beautiful."

Benji smiled, something soft and knowing in his expression. "Told you."

They soared higher, dipping into the clouds, chasing the wind.

For the first time in so long, she felt free.

And then—

Benji did something unexpected.

He let go of the controls.

Jessica's heart jumped. "Benji—"

"Relax," he murmured, reaching for her hand, guiding it to the controls. "I got you."

Jessica's pulse pounded as she curled her fingers around the stick.

Benji covered her hand with his, his voice low and steady. "Feel the wind. Let it guide you."

Jessica swallowed, following his lead, her body mirroring his movements.

The plane tilted slightly, turning smoothly, the rush of air curling around them like an embrace.

And just like that—she was flying.

Benji grinned at her, his expression full of nothing but pride.

Jessica laughed, breathless, alive. "I can't believe this."

Benji's voice was quieter now. "Believe it."

For a long moment, they just flew.

The world below them didn't exist.

It was just them, the sky, and the wind.

Then—

Benji reached into his pocket.

Jessica barely noticed until he tilted the plane slightly, angling them toward the sun, the light catching on something small and silver in his hand.

Jessica's breath hitched.

Benji turned, his dark eyes locked on hers, steady, unwavering.

"I've loved you since I was too young and too stupid to know what it meant," he murmured. "And after everything—after war, after loss, after all the time we lost—I don't wanna waste another second."

Jessica felt the world slow.

Her pulse thundered in her ears, her chest so full it ached.

Benji lifted the ring, his grip still firm on the controls, like he had planned this perfectly.

Like he had known, all along, this was how it was meant to happen.

"Marry me, Jess." His voice was rough, raw, so full of love it shattered her completely.

Jessica let out a breathless, disbelieving laugh.

She cupped his face, barely able to see through the sting of tears.

"You crazy, reckless, impossible man," she whispered.

Benji smirked. "Is that a yes?"

Jessica nodded, laughter spilling from her lips.

"Yes, you fool. Of course, it's a yes."

Benji exhaled, the tension in his shoulders melting as he slid the ring onto her finger—even as they soared above the world.

Jessica kissed him, deep and desperate and full of everything she had ever felt for him.

The wind rushed around them, the plane tilting slightly, weightless.

And for the first time—

Jessica wasn't just flying.

She was falling.

Hopelessly, completely, forever in love.

The door barely shut behind them before Benji was on her.

Jessica gasped as he grabbed her by the waist, lifting her effortlessly, his strong hands gripping her ass, pulling her flush against him.

His lips crashed onto hers, the kiss hot, demanding, possessive, his body pressed so tightly to hers that she could feel every inch of his desire.

Jessica moaned into his mouth, fisting his shirt, her legs wrapping around his waist as he walked them toward the bedroom, his grip firm and unyielding.

Benji pulled away just enough to growl against her lips, his breath ragged.

"You're mine now," he murmured, his voice thick with need.

Jessica shivered, her nails digging into his shoulders.

"Yes," she whispered. "I'm yours."

Benji's grip tightened.

And then—he threw her onto the bed.

Jessica gasped as she landed on her back, watching as Benji stood at the edge of the bed, his dark eyes burning with hunger.

His chest rose and fell heavily, his fists clenching at his sides as he took her in—flushed, breathless, wanting.

And then—he moved.

He grabbed her ankles, yanked her down to the edge of the bed, and knelt between her thighs.

Jessica barely had time to catch her breath before Benji pushed her dress up, hooked his fingers into her panties, and slid them down her legs in one smooth motion.

A dark smirk played on his lips as he spread her thighs wider, his hands firm, possessive.

"You been thinkin' about this all night, haven't you?" he rasped.

Jessica's breath hitched.

Benji ran his hands slowly up her thighs, his fingers trailing fire across her skin.

She opened her mouth to answer—but then his lips were on her.

Jessica cried out, arching against the bed, her fingers fisting the sheets as his tongue found her, slow and devastating.

Benji groaned against her, his hands gripping her thighs tighter, holding her in place as he devoured her, his tongue swirling, teasing, demanding.

Jessica's hips jerked, seeking more, but Benji held her still, chuckling darkly against her.

"Stay still," he murmured, his voice pure sin.

Jessica whimpered, her head falling back, her body trembling.

Benji slid one hand lower, his fingers teasing her, pushing inside as his mouth continued its slow, torturous assault.

Jessica moaned loudly, her body clenching around him, her fingers diving into his hair, pulling him closer, harder, deeper.

Benji groaned, his grip tightening, his tongue and fingers working in perfect rhythm, pushing her higher and higher until she felt herself teetering on the edge.

"Benji," she gasped, her hips bucking, her entire body shaking.

Benji growled against her, his fingers curling just right, his tongue flicking, sending lightning through her veins.

Jessica cried out, her entire body arching as pleasure crashed over her, consuming her, drowning her in heat and ecstasy.

Benji didn't stop.

He drew out every last tremor, his lips kissing their way up her body, trailing fire over her stomach, between her breasts, along her throat.

By the time he reached her lips, Jessica was still trembling, still breathless, still wanting.

Benji smirked against her mouth.

"Not done with you yet, counselor."

Jessica shuddered, her pulse still racing.

Benji's hands slid over her body, rough and demanding, as he pushed his pants down, freed himself, and pressed the hard length of him against her.

Jessica gasped at the heat of him, the sheer size of him, her body already aching for him again.

Benji tilted her chin up, forcing her to look at him.

"You ready for me?" he murmured, his voice like gravel and silk.

Jessica licked her lips, nodding breathlessly.

Benji grinned darkly.

"Good."

And then—he slammed into her.

Jessica gasped, her nails digging into his back, her legs wrapping tightly around his waist as he filled her, stretched her, consumed her.

Benji groaned, deep and rough, his forehead pressing against hers as he started to move, slow at first, then faster, harder.

Jessica cried out, her body arching beneath him, her nails raking down his back, leaving marks, claiming him just as he claimed her.

Benji gritted his teeth, his thrusts deep, powerful, relentless.

"You feel so damn good," he growled, his grip on her hips bruising, his pace punishing.

Jessica moaned, panting his name, her entire body trembling beneath him.

Benji dipped his head, his mouth claiming hers again, kissing her deep, messy, desperate, like he could devour her whole.

Jessica's body tightened around him, her pleasure building again, hotter, sharper, faster.

Benji groaned, his movements turning more erratic, more desperate.

"Come for me," he murmured against her lips, his voice thick, commanding.

Jessica gasped, her entire body shattering around him, waves of pleasure crashing over her, her nails biting into his skin as she came undone.

Benji followed right after, his body stiffening, a deep, guttural moan ripping from his throat as he found his own release, his arms tightening around her, holding her against him as he buried himself deep.

They stayed like that for a long moment, panting, tangled, spent.

Benji kissed her forehead, then her cheek, then her lips, softer now, slower, lingering.

Jessica sighed, her fingers tracing lazy circles on his back, her heart still racing.

Benji exhaled slowly, pressing his forehead against hers.

"I love you," he murmured.

Jessica smiled sleepily, still breathless.

"I love you more."

Benji chuckled, pulling her closer.

"Impossible."

And with that, they drifted into sleep, tangled in each other, bound by fire, by passion, and by forever.

CHAPTER 28:
PLANNING FOREVER

January 1946 – Chicago, Illinois

The morning after the proposal, Jessica woke up in Benji's arms. Warm. Secure. Loved.

For a long moment, she just lay there, tracing lazy patterns on his chest, listening to the steady rhythm of his heartbeat, feeling the rise and fall of his breath.

She wasn't dreaming.

He had really asked her to marry him.

She had really said yes.

Her lips curled into a soft smile as she tilted her head up to look at him.

Benji was already awake, watching her, his dark eyes filled with something deep and knowing.

"Good morning, fiancé," she teased, voice thick with sleep.

Benji smirked, brushing his fingers through her hair. "Mornin', counselor."

Jessica sighed, stretching against him. "So, should we actually start planning this thing, or do you just wanna keep flying me around until I forget?"

Benji chuckled, his fingers trailing down her spine. "Tempting. But no, I want to do this right."

Jessica bit her lip, watching him. "What do you want?"

Benji exhaled, thinking for a moment. "Something simple. Small. Just people who matter."

Jessica smiled. "I was thinking the same thing."

Benji grinned, rolling on top of her, pinning her hands above her head, pressing a kiss to her lips.

"Then let's get to work, Mrs. Davis-to-be."

Later that afternoon, Benji sat at the kitchen table, the phone pressed to his ear.

The line rang twice before a familiar deep voice answered.

"Hello?"

Benji exhaled, smiling softly. "Hey, Pop."

There was a pause. Then—

"Benji," Elijah Davis said, warmth filling his voice. "What's got you callin' in the middle of the day?"

Benji leaned forward, rubbing his fingers against his temple. "Got some news."

A familiar voice in the background called out, "Who is it?"

His mother.

Benji smiled. "It's me, Ma."

A soft gasp. Then a rushed shuffle, the sound of the phone changing hands.

"Benjamin? Baby, that you?"

Benji chuckled softly. "It's me, Ma."

"Oh, Lord, it's been too long," she scolded. "You know how much I worry."

Benji closed his eyes briefly, letting the warmth of her voice settle over him. "I know, Ma. I'm sorry."

His father cleared his throat in the background. "Boy says he's got news."

His mother gasped dramatically. "Oh, don't tell me! You finally did it, didn't you?"

Benji laughed. "Yeah, Ma. I asked her."

A high-pitched squeal came through the line. "Oh, thank the Lord! About time! When do we meet her?"

Benji chuckled, shaking his head. "Soon. Real soon."

His father's voice came back, steady and warm. "You callin' to ask if I'll marry you two?"

Benji swallowed, gripping the phone a little tighter. "Yeah. I'd be honored if you would."

His mother gasped again. "Elijah, say yes! You ain't gonna make the boy beg, are you?"

His father chuckled. "I wasn't plannin' on it, Clara." Then, after a pause, "Of course, son. It'd be my privilege."

Benji felt something settle in his chest.

His family was with him.

And soon, they'd all be together again.

The next day, Benji walked into the hangar, where Tex and Desmond were arguing over a wrench.

"I told you it was in the damn toolbox," Tex huffed, arms crossed.

Desmond rolled his eyes. "Then why was it under the wing, genius?"

Benji chuckled, shaking his head. "Am I interruptin' a lovers' quarrel?"

Tex grinned. "What's up, Davis?"

Benji rubbed the back of his neck, shifting slightly. "Got a favor to ask."

Tex raised a brow. "Anything. You know that."

Desmond studied him. "This about Jessica?"

Benji nodded. "We're gettin' married."

Tex's grin widened. "Well, hell, about time."

Desmond smirked. "You askin' us to be groomsmen?"

Benji chuckled. "Yeah."

Tex clapped him on the back. "Wouldn't miss it for the world, brother."

Desmond nodded, his voice steady. "You know we got you."

Benji exhaled, relief washing over him.

Because if there were two men he wanted standing beside him that day, it was them.

While Benji was handling his end, Jessica was making her own calls.

Sitting on the couch, she clutched the phone, dialing a number she had memorized by heart.

After two rings, a warm, familiar voice answered.

"Anna speaking."

Jessica smiled. "Hey, Anna, it's me."

"Jessica!" Anna gasped. "Girl, where have you been hiding?"

Jessica laughed softly. "Not hiding. Just… busy."

"Well, you better not be too busy to tell me why you sound so damn happy."

Jessica bit her lip, her chest tightening with excitement. "I'm getting married."

A sharp inhale. Then—

"Oh, my God! Are you serious?"

Jessica grinned. "Dead serious."

A loud squeal rang through the line.

Jessica pulled the phone away, laughing.

"Please say you're calling to ask me to be a bridesmaid," Anna said dramatically.

Jessica chuckled. "Of course. You and Ruby."

Anna gasped again. "I'll call Ruby right now—this is happening. Oh, my God, Jessica, this is happening!"

Jessica laughed, feeling warmth spread through her.

It was happening.

That evening, Jessica sat at the small dining table, writing out two letters.

One to Josephine.

One to Richard.

Josephine had been like a second mother to her, and though she had left working for her family, Jessica still wanted her there.

Richard…

They had a complicated history, but he had been there when she needed him.

And now, she wanted him to see that she was exactly where she was meant to be.

By the time she sealed the envelopes, Benji sat down beside her, watching her thoughtfully.

"You sure about Richard?" he asked.

Jessica nodded. "He deserves to see me happy. And I want him there."

Benji exhaled, then reached over, threading his fingers through hers.

"Then he'll be there."

Jessica smiled, squeezing his hand.

They were really doing this.

They were building something real.

And soon—they'd make it forever.

The days leading up to the wedding passed in a blur of preparation, anticipation, and nerves.

Jessica and Benji had agreed on a small, intimate ceremony, just family and the friends who had become family.

There were no grand ballrooms, no expensive frills. Just love, commitment, and the people who mattered most.

March 1946 – Chicago, Illinois

Jessica stood in front of the full-length mirror, smoothing her hands over the fabric of the dress.

It wasn't extravagant—just a simple white gown with a soft, flowing skirt and delicate lace sleeves.

But the moment she put it on, she knew.

It was perfect.

Anna and Ruby stood behind her, their eyes shining.

"Oh, Jess," Anna breathed. "You look like a dream."

Jessica exhaled, pressing her hands against her stomach. "I feel like I'm gonna throw up."

Ruby laughed, stepping forward to adjust the fabric at Jessica's waist. "That's normal. Weddings do that to people."

Jessica let out a shaky laugh. "I don't know why I'm nervous. It's Benji. I love him. I know this is what I want."

Anna smiled knowingly. "It's not about doubts. It's about knowing this is forever."

Jessica met her gaze in the mirror, her chest tightening.

Forever.

With Benji.

God, she wanted it.

She smoothed her hands over the dress again, inhaling deeply. "Alright. Let's do this."

Anna grinned. "Now that's the bride I know."

Benji stood in front of the mirror, adjusting the collar of his crisp white shirt, smoothing his hands over the navy suit jacket.

Tex leaned against the doorway, arms crossed, smirking.

"Nervous yet?"

Benji huffed. "No."

Tex arched a brow.

Benji sighed, rubbing a hand over the back of his neck. "Okay. Maybe a little."

Tex chuckled. "Thought so."

A knock sounded at the door.

Benji turned as Marcus stepped inside.

His older brother took one look at him, smirked, and shook his head.

"Well, I'll be damned."

Benji narrowed his eyes. "What?"

Marcus crossed his arms. "Never thought I'd see you in a suit, little brother."

Benji chuckled, shaking his head. "Neither did I."

Marcus studied him for a moment, then clapped a hand on his shoulder.

"You happy?"

Benji exhaled, nodding. "Yeah. Happier than I ever thought I could be."

Marcus nodded approvingly. "Then that's all that matters."

Tex smirked. "I give it six months before they got little Benjis runnin' around."

Benji choked on his breath. "Damn, Tex, let me get through the wedding first."

Marcus laughed, shaking his head. "Nah, I agree with him. It's gonna happen."

Benji sighed, adjusting his tie. "You two are a pain in my ass."

Tex grinned. "Yeah, but you love us."

Benji smirked. "Unfortunately."

Benji barely had a moment to catch his breath before another soft knock sounded at the door.

His heart stilled as his mother stepped inside.

Clara Davis looked elegant yet simple, her warm brown eyes gleaming with emotion, her hands folded neatly in front of her.

"Benji," she whispered, taking him in.

Benji swallowed, his throat suddenly tight. "Ma."

Her lips wobbled into a smile as she stepped forward, reaching up to smooth his jacket, like she had when he was a boy.

"My handsome boy," she murmured, her voice thick with pride. "I always knew this day would come."

Benji let out a breathy chuckle. "You sure? I feel like I gave you plenty of reasons to doubt it."

Clara shook her head. "Never."

She hesitated, then pulled something from the small purse at her side.

A folded letter.

Benji frowned as she pressed it into his palm.

"What's this?"

Clara cupped his cheek, her thumb grazing his jawline. "Just something I wrote in case I couldn't get through this without crying."

Benji exhaled, his fingers tightening around the letter.

"Ma—"

She hushed him with a soft pat to his chest.

"Read it later," she said gently. "For now, just know how proud I am of you. How much I love you."

Benji nodded, his throat too tight for words.

Clara pressed a kiss to his forehead.

"Now," she said, stepping back, dabbing at her eyes. "Let's get you married."

Benji swallowed hard, his heart full.

"Yeah," he said. "Let's do this."

Jessica stood in front of the mirror one last time, heart pounding.

Anna and Ruby were behind her, making last-minute adjustments.

Her hands trembled slightly, but not from fear.

From anticipation.

From the weight of this moment.

The door cracked open, and Josephine peeked inside.

"Oh, baby," she whispered, her eyes glistening with emotion. "You are the most beautiful bride I've ever seen."

Jessica smiled, her throat tightening. "Thank you, Josephine."

Josephine stepped inside, smoothing a hand down Jessica's arm.

"I always knew you had a fire in you, child," she said softly. "And I always knew it would lead you right where you belong."

Jessica swallowed past the lump in her throat, gripping Josephine's hand.

"I am exactly where I belong," she whispered.

Josephine nodded. "Then go to him."

Jessica exhaled one last deep breath and turned toward the door.

The soft hum of conversation filled the air as friends and family gathered in the small chapel.

Benji stood at the altar, hands clasped in front of him, his heart pounding louder than any battlefield he'd ever stood on.

Then—

The doors opened.

And there she was.

Jessica.

His Jessica.

She stood at the entrance, a vision in white, her dark hair cascading down her back, her eyes locked on his, shining like the stars.

Benji felt his breath leave him.

Everything else faded.

Every sound, every thought—gone.

All he saw was her.

Tex nudged him, whispering, "Damn, Davis, breathe."

Benji let out a slow breath, his chest tightening with something he had never felt before.

Something bigger than war, bigger than any battle.

This was his forever.

Jessica stepped forward, walking toward him, toward their future, toward a love that had survived everything.

The small chapel had fallen silent.

Only the soft flickering of candlelight and the sound of breathless anticipation filled the space.

Jessica stood before Benji, her hands trembling in his.

This was it.

The moment they became husband and wife.

Benji's fingers tightened around hers, grounding her.

He smiled softly, that familiar warmth in his eyes—the same warmth she had fallen in love with all those years ago.

The reverend, Elijah Davis, cleared his throat, his voice steady yet filled with emotion.

"We are gathered here today to witness the union of Benjamin Davis and Jessica Shaw," he began. "Marriage is a covenant, a promise to stand beside one another in love, in struggle, in joy, and in sorrow."

Jessica swallowed, blinking back tears that threatened to spill over.

Elijah's gaze softened as he looked at his son.

"Benjamin, my boy," he said, his voice rich with pride. "You may now say your vows."

Benji's Vows

Benji exhaled shakily, his grip tightening on Jessica's hands as he met her gaze.

For a long moment, he just looked at her, like he was memorizing every detail of her face—her bright, tear-filled eyes, the way her lips trembled, the way she stood tall despite everything.

Then, in a voice thick with emotion, he spoke.

"Jess," he murmured. "You have been my light in the darkest nights, my reason to keep fighting when I wanted to give up. I've seen the world at its worst, but you… you have always been its best."

Jessica let out a soft, broken sound, her fingers curling around his.

Benji swallowed hard, his thumb brushing against her skin.

"I don't have fancy words or poetry," he admitted, his voice rough, raw. "But I have this—I promise to love you with everything I have, for as long as I have breath in my lungs. I promise to stand beside you, to lift you up when you stumble, to fight for you like I have fought for everything in my life."

A tear slipped down Jessica's cheek.

Benji's voice wavered.

"I promise that no matter what life throws at us—war, loss, hardship, whatever comes—I will always choose you."

Jessica let out a soft sob, gripping his hands tighter.

Benji smiled through the emotion tightening his throat.

"You once told me that love is not about what's easy, but about what's worth it," he murmured. "Jess… You are worth it. Every battle, every struggle, every moment. And I will spend the rest of my life proving it to you."

Jessica couldn't stop the tears from falling now.

Benji reached up, brushing them away gently.

"I love you," he whispered. "I will always love you."

The room was utterly silent, but Jessica could feel the weight of every heart watching, every tearful smile, every soul bearing witness to this moment.

The reverend cleared his throat, voice thick. "Jessica, my dear... your vows?"

Jessica's Vows

Jessica let out a shaky breath, trying to steady herself.

Then, she looked up at Benji, her eyes shining.

"Benji," she whispered. "I once thought that love was meant to be simple. That it came easy, without pain, without sacrifice. But then... I met you."

Benji let out a soft breath of laughter, his lips quirking slightly.

Jessica's fingers tightened around his.

"You taught me that love is not about ease," she continued. "It is about strength. About standing in the storm and choosing each other, over and over, no matter how hard the wind tries to tear us apart."

Benji nodded slightly, his throat bobbing.

Jessica swallowed, her heart hammering.

"I have loved you in the quiet moments, in the impossible moments. In stolen glances and whispered words. And now... I get to love you out loud."

Benji's breath hitched.

Jessica smiled through the tears.

"I promise to stand beside you, to challenge you, to hold you when you need me. I promise that no matter what this world tries to take from us, it will never take this—never take what we are, what we've built, what we've fought for."

Benji's jaw clenched, his eyes wet.

Jessica lifted a trembling hand, placing it over his heart.

"I have never been more sure of anything in my life than I am of this—of you."

Benji's hand came up, covering hers.

Jessica smiled through the tears.

"I love you, Benji," she whispered. "Now and always."

Benji let out a shaky exhale, his forehead pressing against hers for the briefest of moments.

The room was filled with warmth, with love, with something bigger than words.

Elijah cleared his throat again, his voice deep with emotion.

"By the power vested in me…" he paused, smiling softly. "Benjamin, you may now kiss your wife."

Benji did not hesitate.

His hands slid into her hair, pulling her in, sealing the vow with a kiss that spoke of years of longing, of heartbreak, of love that had survived even when the world tried to tear it apart.

Jessica melted against him, her arms winding around his neck, her fingers threading into his hair.

The room erupted into cheers, into claps, into laughter.

Tex whistled loudly. "Damn, Davis, save some for later!"

Benji chuckled against Jessica's lips but didn't let her go right away.

When they finally pulled apart, Jessica was breathless, her heart soaring.

Benji pressed his forehead against hers, grinning.

"Mrs. Davis," he murmured.

Jessica beamed. "Mr. Davis."

And just like that—they were husband and wife.

The small reception that followed was filled with warmth, laughter, and love.

Clara Davis held Benji's face in her hands, kissing his cheeks, her eyes full of happy tears. "You made me so proud today, baby."

Benji hugged her tight. "Love you, Ma."

Naomi wrapped her arms around him, squeezing tight. "You better take care of her, big brother."

Benji chuckled, ruffling her hair. "I will, lil' sis."

Desmond clapped Benji's shoulder. "I expect to see you and the missus on a flight soon. Got a whole world to see now."

Benji grinned. "Wouldn't have it any other way."

Jessica stood beside him, watching the people they loved.

She leaned into Benji, pressing a hand to his chest. "Are you happy?"

Benji smiled down at her, warmth radiating through him.

"More than I ever thought possible," he murmured.

Jessica rested her head against his shoulder, closing her eyes.

Because this was it.

This was forever.

Chapter 29:

New Beginning

March 1946 – Chicago, Illinois

T he morning air carried the last bite of winter, crisp and unforgiving. Jessica Davis wrapped her coat tighter around herself as she walked down the bustling street, her mind racing.

She hadn't told Benji where she was going. She hadn't even told him she'd been feeling sick.

She hadn't wanted to worry him.

But the truth was, she had known.

Deep down, she had known for weeks.

The exhaustion, the nausea, the sudden dizziness when she stood up too fast—it had all been there, gnawing at her like a quiet whisper she had tried to ignore.

At first, she had joked about it. She had laughed with Benji as they lay tangled together in bed, her fingers tracing the lines of his chest.

"What if we had a little one someday?" she had mused, teasing, testing.

"You trying to put ideas in my head, Mrs. Davis?" he had smirked, kissing her shoulder.

"Just wondering if you'd make a good father."

Benji had paused, his breath warm against her skin.

"I'd try my best," he had murmured, voice softer, more serious than she expected.

And now, standing in front of the doctor's office, the teasing didn't feel like teasing anymore.

It felt like reality.

She drew in a breath and stepped inside.

The waiting room smelled like antiseptic and old paper. Women sat scattered in chairs, flipping through magazines or staring absently at the clock on the wall.

Jessica sat near the window, watching the city outside, her hands clasped together tightly in her lap.

The nurse called her name.

"Mrs. Davis?"

She swallowed, standing quickly, smoothing out the skirt of her dress.

She followed the nurse down a narrow hallway lined with closed doors, her heartbeat pounding louder with every step.

Inside the small examination room, she perched on the edge of the table, wrapping her arms around herself.

The door opened, and Dr. Lee stepped inside—a woman in her mid-40s with kind eyes and a steady voice.

"Mrs. Davis," she greeted, setting a file down on the desk. "How are you feeling today?"

Jessica hesitated, then forced herself to speak. "I… I've been exhausted. Nauseous. I thought it was stress, but it's not going away."

Dr. Lee nodded. "And your cycle?"

Jessica swallowed. "Late."

The doctor's expression didn't change, but there was something knowing in her gaze. "I see. Well, let's run a test to be sure."

Jessica nodded stiffly, her chest tight.

A urine sample. A blood draw. Then the waiting.

The longest, most excruciatingly silent minutes of her life.

And then, finally, Dr. Lee returned, a clipboard in hand.

She smiled. "Congratulations, Mrs. Davis. You're pregnant."

Jessica's breath caught in her throat.

Even though she had expected it—felt it in her bones before she ever stepped into this office—hearing the words spoken aloud sent a shiver through her.

Pregnant.

Her hand drifted to her stomach, pressing lightly over the fabric of her coat.

She was carrying Benji's child.

Dr. Lee gave her a moment before continuing.

"We'll monitor you closely, but everything looks good so far," she reassured. "Your body is adjusting, which explains the fatigue. Try to rest when you can."

Jessica barely nodded.

Her mind was spinning.

"Benji doesn't know."

How was she going to tell him?

She had teased him about children, testing the waters, never really expecting to get an answer.

But now?

Now, there was no joking, no teasing.

This was real.

Dr. Lee handed her some papers, going over the next steps—but Jessica barely heard a word.

She left the office in a daze.

While Jessica was grappling with her new reality, Benji was finishing up a lesson at the Youth Aviation Academy.

The sun was high in the sky, warming the tarmac where a group of young cadets stood in a semi-circle, listening as Captain Desmond Wright spoke.

Benji stood beside Tex, arms crossed, watching the boys work through a pre-flight checklist.

"They're getting' better," Tex muttered. "Still a little slow, but they'll get there."

Benji smirked. "You sure about that? The kid on the left forgot the fuel check twice."

Tex chuckled. "Reminds me of you when you first started."

Benji rolled his eyes. "I was never that bad."

Tex snorted. "Yeah, alright, hotshot."

Desmond clapped a hand on Benji's shoulder. "You're doing good work here, Davis," he said. "These kids look up to you."

Benji exhaled, nodding. "Yeah."

But something felt off.

Jessica had been quiet lately. And this morning, she had been distant when he left.

Something was on her mind.

And for some reason, as he stood there watching the cadets, a feeling of unease settled deep in his chest.

By the time Jessica made it back to their apartment, the daylight had begun to fade.

She walked inside slowly, carefully, setting her purse down on the counter.

She stood in the quiet, taking a breath, letting her fingers drift to her stomach once more.

She had wanted to talk to Benji about this someday—about children, about what their future would look like.

But never had she imagined it would come so soon.

She wasn't ready to say the words just yet.

Not tonight.

Tonight, she just needed to hold this moment to herself.

So she stepped into the bedroom, pressing a hand to her stomach, and allowed herself the first, real smile since hearing the news.

Because despite the fear, despite the uncertainty, something warm and hopeful bloomed inside her.

This was Benji's child.

And she was ready.

She just had to find the right way to tell him.

Benji stepped into the apartment, shaking off the chill of the late March air. The scent of the city still clung to him—oil, metal, the crisp bite of wind that rushed off the lake.

He set his hat on the table by the door and glanced toward the living room.

Jessica sat curled up on the couch, a book open in her lap, her face calm but far away.

He had noticed it for weeks now—the way she would drift into thought, the way she would linger in silence just a little too long.

She wasn't unhappy, he could tell that much. But she was somewhere else, and for the life of him, he couldn't figure out where.

Benji rubbed the back of his neck, exhaling softly.

"Hey, baby."

Jessica blinked, looking up as if she had just realized he was there.

She smiled, soft and warm, but there was something about it that didn't reach her eyes. "Hey, baby."

Benji leaned against the doorway, watching her for a beat.

The weight of the day eased just looking at her, but the unease in his chest didn't go away.

"You alright?" he asked.

Jessica hesitated—just for a second. Then she nodded, closing her book. "Yeah. Just tired."

Benji studied her, his jaw ticking slightly. She was holding something back.

Maybe it was work, maybe it was stress—or maybe it was something bigger.

He thought about pushing, about asking again.

But instead, he gave a small nod and pushed off the wall.

"Alright, then," he said, rolling up his sleeves. "I'm cooking tonight."

Jessica's eyebrows shot up. "You?"

Benji smirked, walking toward the kitchen. "That a problem?"

Jessica grinned, setting her book aside as she pulled her legs up onto the couch. "Not at all. I'm just wondering how bad I should be preparing myself."

Benji huffed a laugh. "I ain't that bad."

Jessica raised an eyebrow. "Baby, the last time you tried to cook, you nearly burned the eggs."

Benji pointed at her as he opened the icebox. "That was one time. And in my defense, I was distracted."

Jessica smirked. "By what?"

Benji shot her a look. "You walked in wearing that red slip."

Jessica laughed, tucking a curl behind her ear. "Fair enough."

Benji shook his head, biting back a smile as he pulled out a few ingredients.

Benji wasn't a great cook. Hell, he was barely a decent one.

But tonight, he wanted to do something for her.

She had been so quiet, so distant, and he hated feeling like he wasn't doing enough.

So he moved through the kitchen, focused, determined, ignoring the way Jessica watched him with amusement from the couch.

He grabbed a pan, cracked an egg—too hard, shell pieces fell in.

Jessica snickered.

Benji sighed, scooping them out with his fingers.

He tried again, this time with less force.

Better.

Kind of.

Next, he grabbed some vegetables, chopping them with a little too much confidence.

Jessica stood up, walking over, watching as he narrowly missed his fingertips.

"Baby," she said slowly, biting her lip. "You wanna maybe slow down before you take a finger off?"

Benji shot her a look. "I got this."

Jessica held up her hands. "Alright, Chef Davis. Just don't bleed into the food."

Benji huffed a laugh, shaking his head. "You just sit down and relax. Let me handle this."

Jessica leaned against the counter, arms crossed, watching as he moved around the small kitchen.

She hadn't realized how much she missed this—this easy, effortless part of them.

Where they could laugh, where they could just be Benji and Jessica, without the world outside pressing in on them.

And for the first time that day, the weight of what she was carrying didn't feel quite so heavy.

Benji plated the food—scrambled eggs, toast, and slightly overcooked vegetables.

He set the plates down on the small kitchen table with too much pride.

Jessica looked at her plate, eyes twinkling. "Well, it's… edible."

Benji sat across from her, shaking his head. "You ain't even tried it yet."

Jessica smirked, picking up her fork, taking a small bite.

It was… not bad.

A little burnt, maybe. A little too much salt.

But not bad.

Benji watched her closely, waiting for her reaction.

Jessica pressed her lips together, pretending to consider.

Then, she looked at him dead in the eye and said, "I mean… I don't hate it."

Benji snorted. "Damn, that bad?"

Jessica laughed, shaking her head. "No, no, I swear! It's just—" She grinned. "You might need a little more practice."

Benji sighed dramatically. "Well, there goes my dream of being a chef."

Jessica smiled, shaking her head as she reached for his hand across the table.

"You did good, hotshot," she murmured.

Benji squeezed her fingers, his eyes softening.

For a long moment, they just sat there, holding hands, feeling the warmth between them.

And for the first time in weeks, Jessica felt like she could breathe.

The morning light spilled through the curtains, casting a warm glow over the quiet apartment. The only sound was the steady stream of water from the bathroom, filling the air with steam.

Jessica stood in the doorway, watching Benji's silhouette through the fogged glass of the shower.

She had woken before him, curled against his chest, her thoughts restless.

For weeks, she had carried this secret, letting it settle inside her, growing alongside the new life within her.

But now, there was no more waiting.

With a slow breath, she shed her nightgown, stepping into the bathroom.

The heat enveloped her instantly as she pushed open the glass door, slipping in behind him.

Benji let out a soft breath when her arms wrapped around his waist, her skin warm against his.

"Mm," he murmured, turning his head slightly, a small smile tugging at his lips. "What's this about?"

Jessica pressed her cheek against his back, letting the water drip over both of them. "Just missed you."

Benji chuckled lowly, his hands covering hers where they rested on his stomach.

"You had me all night, Mrs. Davis," he teased, but his voice was soft, teasing.

Jessica smiled, her fingers tracing over his scarred skin, the stories of war etched into his body.

Benji turned in her arms, his hands sliding over her damp skin, his gaze searching hers.

She knew he could sense it—the weight behind her touch, the shift in her energy.

"Jessica," he murmured, brushing his fingers along her cheek. "You sure you're alright?"

Jessica hesitated, then nodded. "I am now."

Benji's brows furrowed slightly, but before he could say anything, she kissed him.

It was slow, deep, lingering, a kiss that held every unspoken word.

Benji responded instantly, his arms tightening around her, pulling her in until there wasn't a space between them.

For a while, there was only the sound of water, the heat of skin, the quiet exchange of love between them.

By the time they stepped out, toweling off, Jessica felt lighter, but the weight of what she was about to tell him still sat in her chest.

Benji sat at the kitchen table, his arms folded, watching Jessica move effortlessly around the kitchen.

Unlike him, she could cook.

Really cook.

She never let him live down the time he'd nearly burned eggs and toast, and he had no shame in admitting that she was miles ahead of him when it came to the kitchen.

Now, he sat back, watching as she moved with ease, scrambling eggs, frying bacon, and flipping pancakes in a way that seemed effortless.

Even though he loved watching her, something in him tightened.

She had been too quiet, too distant lately.

And this morning, she was too focused.

Jessica wasn't just cooking—she was stalling.

Benji exhaled, drumming his fingers against the table.

"You sure you're okay?" he asked again.

Jessica's hand froze for a fraction of a second before she resumed plating the food.

"I'm fine," she said, placing a plate in front of him before sitting across from him.

Benji raised an eyebrow.

She was lying.

And Jessica knew that he knew.

She stared at her plate, shifting the food around with her fork, before finally exhaling.

"Benji," she started softly.

He leaned forward, setting his fork down, his full attention on her.

Jessica's heart pounded.

For all the battles Benji had faced, for all the moments he had come back from near death, this moment felt heavier than anything.

Her voice was barely above a whisper.

"I'm pregnant."

The world stopped.

Benji's fork froze mid-air.

His expression didn't change at first—his eyes widening just slightly, his lips parting like he was about to speak but couldn't.

Jessica felt her stomach twist as the seconds stretched on.

Then—his fork clattered against the plate.

"Oh, shit."

Jessica's breath caught.

His face was unreadable—his eyes darting, his hands gripping the edge of the table like he was trying to steady himself.

Panic flared in her chest.

"I—" She started, suddenly feeling vulnerable. "I know it's a lot—"

But before she could finish, Benji moved.

Fast.

One second he was across the table—the next, he was lifting her into his arms.

Jessica let out a soft gasp, her hands flying to his shoulders.

Benji's grip was gentle, yet unshakable. He held her like she was the most precious thing in the world, like he was afraid she might slip through his fingers if he didn't hold on tight enough.

His lips crashed into hers, deep, breathless, full of something Jessica couldn't quite name.

When he pulled back, his forehead pressed against hers, his breath shaky, his fingers trembling where they held her.

"Jessica…" His voice cracked, his eyes damp. "Thank you."

Jessica let out a breathless laugh, blinking away tears. "For what?"

Benji laughed softly, shaking his head.

"For this. For everything."

He cupped her face, pressing another kiss to her lips, then her forehead, then the tip of her nose.

Jessica smiled, pressing a hand to his chest, feeling the steady beat of his heart.

This was their new beginning.

And they were ready.

Together.

CHAPTER 30:

BUILDING THEIR FUTURE

May 1946 – Chicago, Illinois

The city hummed around him, the rhythmic clatter of streetcars and distant voices blending into the steady pulse of Chicago. Benji stepped off the curb, adjusting the brim of his hat as he made his way down a quiet block on the South Side, where rows of brick houses stood under the warmth of the midday sun.

It had been two months since Jessica told him she was pregnant. Two months of excitement, planning, and quiet moments of awe when he woke in the middle of the night and caught her resting a hand on her growing belly.

He had told his family, and their reactions had been everything he expected—his mother had cried, Naomi had screamed in excitement, and even Marcus, the ever-serious one, had cracked a proud smile. His father had simply clapped a hand on his shoulder, squeezing tight.

"You're gonna be a good father, son."

The words stayed with him, warming him on days like this when he felt the weight of responsibility settling on his shoulders.

It wasn't just about him and Jessica anymore.

He had a family to protect now.

And that meant they needed a home—a real one.

Not the small apartment they lived in, where walls were thin, and the neighbors were loud. Not some cramped space where their child would have to share a bedroom with boxes of old books and Jessica's law school papers.

No.

He needed to find a house.

But this wasn't as simple as walking into any realtor's office and asking for what he wanted.

Because in Chicago—in most places—a Black man looking to buy a home was a problem.

Benji had learned early on that money alone wouldn't open doors for him.

Even now, wearing his best suit, clean-cut, a respected pilot, a man who had fought for his country—none of it mattered if he walked into the wrong office.

So he had asked around quietly.

He started with Tex, who had been in Chicago longer, settling there with his wife after the war.

"Man, you think I could just waltz into one of them fancy real estate offices?" Tex had said with a shake of his head. "No, sir. You need a brother who knows how this game works."

That was how Benji found himself standing outside a small, nondescript office in Bronzeville, a neighborhood where Black families had built their own businesses, their own churches, their own safe spaces.

The sign above the door read:

"William Carter & Sons – Real Estate and Property Management"

Benji took a breath and stepped inside.

Meeting the Right Man

The office was modest, but tidy, lined with maps and photographs of houses pinned to the walls.

Behind the desk sat a man in his late forties, sharp suit, keen eyes, and a careful sort of confidence.

He glanced up when Benji walked in, taking him in with a practiced look.

"You looking to rent or buy?" he asked, his voice calm, measured.

"Buy," Benji said, adjusting his tie. "For my wife and our child on the way."

That got a reaction. A slow nod, a slight smile.

"Congratulations," the man said, standing to shake his hand. "I'm William Carter. Have a seat."

Benji sat, feeling the weight of the moment settle over him.

"I'll be honest with you, Mr. Davis," Carter said, leaning back in his chair. "Buying a house in this city ain't easy for a colored man. They'll tell you a place is sold when it's not. Jack up the price just so you can't afford it. And even if you do get the papers signed, some folks'll make sure you know you're not welcome."

Benji exhaled slowly. None of this was news.

"I figured," he said.

Carter studied him, then nodded. "Good. Now let's talk about what you need."

Benji thought for a moment, then leaned forward.

"I need a safe area," he said. "Somewhere our child can grow up without worrying about trouble every time we walk outside."

Carter nodded, pulling out a map of the South Side.

"And I need it to be close to the academy—the Youth Aviation Program I work at. And near the university, where my wife's finishing law school."

At that, Carter's expression shifted. "Your wife's in law school?"

Benji smiled, a quiet sort of pride settling in his chest. "Yes, sir. And she's going to be damn good at it, too."

Carter smirked. "I like that. We need more of us in those courtrooms."

Benji nodded. "That's what she says, too."

Carter tapped his pen against the desk, thinking.

"You got a budget?"

Benji pulled out a folded envelope—the money he had saved, the money he had earned.

Carter took it, gave a low whistle, then nodded in approval.

"You did good for yourself," he said. "Military treating you right?"

Benji smirked. "Not at all. This is just what I've been saving."

Carter chuckled. "Smart man."

He grabbed a binder, flipping through a few pages before sliding one across the desk.

"This one," he said. "Three bedrooms, quiet street. Good neighbors, mostly working folks. The schools are decent, and it's not far from the academy or the university."

Benji picked up the paper, studying the details.

It wasn't big, but it was enough. A place to build their future.

He could see it already—Jessica standing by the window, sunlight catching in her hair. Their child playing in the yard. The sound of laughter filling the space.

His chest tightened.

"I want to see it," he said.

Carter smiled. "Then let's go."

The drive through the South Side was slow, the city moving around them in a steady hum of life—children playing on sidewalks, women hanging clothes to dry on balconies, men gathered near corner stores talking over newspapers and cigarettes.

Benji sat in the passenger seat of William Carter's old Chevrolet, his fingers tapping restlessly against his knee. The paper with the house's details sat folded in his pocket, but he didn't need to look at it again.

He wasn't just looking for a house.

He was looking for the place where their child would take their first steps, where Jessica would study late into the night, where they would build something that was truly theirs.

Carter took a right turn onto a quiet street lined with brick bungalows and two-story greystones. The neighborhood felt steady, lived in, the kind of place where people knew each other, where kids ran barefoot in the summers, where folks sat on porches in the evenings, watching the world settle.

Benji felt something shift in his chest—a quiet, unspoken hope.

"Here we are," Carter said, pulling up in front of a modest red-brick house with a pitched roof and a small front yard.

It wasn't grand. It wasn't a mansion.

But it looked like home.

Benji stepped out of the car, his shoes crunching on the gravel as he took it in. The white-trimmed windows, the narrow walkway lined with patches of grass, the front porch just big enough for a couple of chairs and a swing.

For a long moment, he just stood there.

His chest felt tight.

"You alright?" Carter asked, watching him carefully.

Benji swallowed, nodding. "Yeah."

It wasn't just a house.

It was a future.

The inside of the house smelled like fresh paint and old wood, the faint scent of polish lingering in the air.

Carter walked ahead, flipping on lights as they stepped inside.

The living room was simple—a fireplace against one wall, a wide front window that let in the afternoon sun, and enough space to fit a couch and maybe a small bookshelf.

Jessica would like that.

She always loved reading by the window, her legs curled under her, the light spilling over her skin.

Benji exhaled slowly, running a hand over the back of his neck as he walked further in.

The kitchen had white cabinets and a deep farmhouse sink, with just enough room for a small table.

He imagined Jessica standing by the stove, humming softly as she cooked, the smell of something warm And familiar with filling the house.

He could picture himself there too—wrapping his arms around her from behind, kissing the side of her neck while she playfully swatted at him to let her work.

He smiled to himself, shaking his head.

"This ain't bad," he murmured.

Carter chuckled. "Told you."

Benji moved through the house, feeling his chest tighten with every step.

The first bedroom was small—perfect for an office, or a guest room, if they ever had company

The second bedroom was slightly bigger. This would be their bedroom.

Then, finally—

The third bedroom.

It wasn't large, but it was cozy, with a big window overlooking the backyard and walls that had been freshly painted a soft, neutral color.

Benji stood in the doorway, gripping the frame, his throat working as he took it all in.

This would be their child's room.

He could almost hear it—the sound of laughter, tiny feet padding across the floor, Jessica's voice soft and warm as she rocked a baby to sleep.

A slow, steady breath left him.

This was it.

This was home.

Carter led him out the back door, where a small fenced yard stretched behind the house.

It wasn't big, but it was enough—enough for a child to run, to play, to grow.

Benji stood at the edge of the porch, hands on his hips, looking out over the patch of grass.

"This house is gonna go fast," Carter said, crossing his arms. "It's a fair price. The owners are selling because they're moving out west, and they'd rather sell to a good family than let some shady investor take it."

Benji nodded slowly.

But he already knew.

This was the one.

He turned to Carter, his decision solidified in his chest.

"I'll take it."

Carter's lips twitched into a smile. "You sure?"

Benji exhaled sharply, looking back at the house—their house.

"I'm sure."

Later that evening, Benji sat on the edge of the bed, the house papers tucked inside his coat pocket.

Jessica was brushing her hair at the vanity, her reflection calm, unaware.

Benji watched her for a moment, taking in the sight of her—the soft curve of her growing belly, the gentle way she moved, the way she belonged here, with him.

He reached into his pocket, pulling out the folded paper.

"Jess," he murmured.

She glanced at him in the mirror. "Mm?"

He swallowed, then smiled. "I bought us a house."

Jessica froze.

She turned slowly, eyes wide, mouth parting slightly as she took in his words.

"You… what?"

Benji smirked, unfolding the paper and holding it out to her.

"I bought us a house," he repeated. "A real home. For us. For the baby."

Jessica stared at him, then at the paper in his hands.

Her fingers trembled as she took it, scanning the details, her breath hitching as she took it all in.

Benji watched as her eyes welled up, a slow smile breaking across her face.

"You—" She let out a breathless laugh, pressing a hand to her stomach. "You really did this?"

Benji chuckled. "You think I'd joke about something like that?"

Jessica let out a soft, disbelieving laugh, shaking her head. "Benji…"

He reached for her, pulling her gently into his lap, his hands settling over the curve of her belly.

"I wanted to give you a home," he murmured against her hair. "Somewhere safe. Somewhere ours."

Jessica leaned into him, burying her face in his neck, her shoulders trembling.

"I love you," she whispered.

Benji pressed a slow, lingering kiss to her temple.

"I love you more."

And as they sat there, wrapped up in each other, Benji knew—

This was the beginning of the life they had fought for.

And he wouldn't trade it for anything.

June 1946 – Chicago, Illinois

The sun sat high in the sky, casting a golden glow over the quiet street as a small moving truck pulled up in front of the red-brick house.

Jessica stood on the sidewalk, one hand on her growing belly, the other shielding her eyes as she took in the sight of their new home.

It still felt surreal.

Even after Benji handed her the keys, after she signed the papers, after she walked through every room imagining their future inside its walls—it still didn't feel quite real.

But today, as they unloaded the truck, as laughter filled the warm June air, as their friends and family helped carry boxes through the front door, it finally hit her.

This was home.

Their home.

Tex was the first to jump out of the truck, rolling up his sleeves.

"Alright, people," he called out, grinning. "Let's get this show on the road."

His wife, Pearl, stood beside Jessica, her hands on her hips, watching the men struggle with the larger pieces of furniture. "Lord help 'em," she muttered. "Men will break their backs before they admit they need a woman's help."

Jessica smirked, glancing at Benji, who was hoisting a heavy oak dresser with Desmond.

Desmond's two boys, Nathaniel (8) and Jacob (6), ran up the front steps carrying pillows and small boxes, eager to be part of the action.

"Where you want these, Mrs. Davis?" Nathaniel called out.

Jessica smiled at how easily the name rolled off his tongue—Mrs. Davis.

She still wasn't used to it, but she loved the sound of it.

"Upstairs, sweetheart," she said warmly. "Second door on the right."

The boys nodded eagerly before rushing inside.

Meanwhile, Desmond's wife, Irene, helped Pearl organize the kitchen, unpacking dishes and stacking them in cabinets while trading playful gossip about their husbands.

"Desmond swears he knows how to fix things," Irene murmured to Jessica as she unwrapped a stack of plates. "But the last time he tried to fix the sink, we had to call a plumber before he flooded the whole kitchen."

Jessica laughed, shaking her head. "Sounds like something Benji would do."

Irene smirked. "Men love to act like they know everything."

Pearl snorted, handing Jessica a bundle of silverware. "And we love 'em anyway."

Jessica glanced toward the living room, where Benji was wiping sweat from his brow, grinning as he and Tex maneuvered the couch into place.

Her heart swelled.

"Yes," she said softly, more to herself than anyone else. "We do."

A few hours later, the sun hung low, casting long shadows across the freshly unpacked living room.

The work was done.

Furniture was in place. Boxes were unpacked. Their home was no longer just walls and floors—it was filled with life, laughter, and the warmth of the people who loved them.

Tex, Pearl, Desmond, Irene, and the kids had stayed for dinner, gathered around the small wooden dining table, plates full of home-cooked food Jessica had somehow managed to pull together despite the chaos of the day.

After everyone had eaten, Tex leaned back, patting his stomach.

"Well, I'll be damned," he said, shaking his head. "I knew Benji married up, but I didn't know you could cook like this, Jess."

Jessica smiled smugly, sipping her tea. "Don't let him fool you—he still burns toast."

The room erupted into laughter, Benji groaning dramatically. "I make one mistake, and y'all never let me live it down."

Desmond chuckled, clapping him on the back. "Welcome to marriage, Davis."

Benji shook his head, but his smile never faded.

He had everything he ever wanted.

As the night stretched on, their guests gradually trickled out, leaving just the two of them.

Benji stood in the middle of the empty living room, looking around.

Jessica stepped up beside him, her head resting against his shoulder.

"You okay?" she murmured.

Benji exhaled slowly. "Yeah. Just... taking it all in."

Jessica slid her arms around his waist, holding him close.

"You did this," she whispered. "You gave us a home."

Benji turned toward her, cupping her face gently, his thumb tracing her cheek.

"We did this," he corrected softly.

Jessica smiled, tilting her chin up to kiss him—slow, deep, full of quiet gratitude.

For everything they had built.

For everything that was still to come.

That night, as they lay in bed for the first time in their new home, the weight of the day settled over them.

Jessica curled against Benji's chest, his heartbeat a steady rhythm beneath her ear.

For the first time in a long time, they felt at peace.

No war. No distance. No uncertainty.

Just them.

And the future they were building together.

As Benji pressed a soft kiss to her forehead, whispering a quiet "I love you," Jessica smiled, her hand resting over the swell of her belly.

"I love you too, hotshot."

And with that, they drifted into sleep—two souls finally at rest, in a home filled with love, in a future that was wholly, beautifully theirs.

CHAPTER 31:

THE MOMENT THEIR WORLD
CHANGED

December 1946 – University of Chicago
Hospital

The winter wind howled against the hospital windows, rattling the
panes as the city outside settled into another frigid December night.
But inside, Jessica was burning up.

The room felt too bright, the overhead lights casting sharp beams over
white walls and metal instruments, the scent of antiseptic thick in the air.

She gritted her teeth, gripping the sheets as another contraction tore
through her.

Benji was beside her, his hand wrapped tightly around hers, his skin warm
and steady. Too steady.

He had been silent for the past ten minutes, watching her with that same focused intensity he had when he was in the cockpit—calculating, waiting, steady under pressure.

Jessica let out a breath, her brow damp, her body aching.

"You don't have to look so damn serious," she muttered.

Benji blinked, his jaw working. "I ain't serious," he said. "I'm terrified."

Jessica let out a breathless laugh, though it quickly turned into a winced groan as another contraction hit.

Benji tensed, squeezing her hand. "Alright, alright, you got this, baby. Just breathe."

Jessica shot him a look. "You breathe!"

Benji exhaled sharply, shaking his head. "Yes, ma'am."

Dr. Lee, standing at the foot of the bed, smiled knowingly as she adjusted her gloves. "Jessica, you're doing beautifully. You're almost there."

Jessica let out a shaky breath, nodding.

She had trusted Dr. Lee from the moment she met her. She was one of the few doctors in the city who didn't flinch when she and Benji walked into a room together—one of the few who spoke to her with kindness, not judgment.

It was why they had chosen this hospital.

Other places would have sent Benji to the waiting room, forced him to pace the halls, alone and powerless.

But not here.

Here, he was by her side, right where he belonged.

Jessica let out a shaky breath, gripping Benji's hand like a lifeline.

She was tired. The contractions had been coming for hours, pulling her under like waves, over and over.

Her body ached, her arms trembled, but she wasn't giving up.

Not when she could already feel him.

Not when she knew that in just a few more minutes, she would be holding their son in her arms.

Benji leaned closer, his voice low, steady. "You're doing so good, baby. Almost there."

Jessica let out a half-laugh, half-sob, resting her forehead against his.

"You—you did this to me," she gasped.

Benji chuckled, pressing a kiss to her damp forehead. "I'll take the blame, sweetheart."

Dr. Lee cleared her throat, smiling. "Alright, Jessica. One more big push, and your baby will be here."

Jessica's chest tightened.

This was it.

She clenched Benji's hand, summoning every ounce of strength she had left, and pushed.

Pain ripped through her—but then, suddenly—

The pressure was gone.

A sharp, piercing cry filled the room.

Jessica gasped, her breath catching in her throat, her entire body going still.

Benji's hand tightened around hers, his grip shaking.

Dr. Lee lifted the tiny, squirming bundle, her voice gentle as she smiled.

"You have a son."

Jessica let out a sob, her eyes blurring with tears as Dr. Lee placed the baby against her chest.

He was so small.

So warm.

His cries were strong, his tiny fingers curling against her skin, searching for comfort.

Her hands trembled as she touched his soft, dark curls, her lips quivering.

"Hey, baby," she whispered.

The moment the words left her lips, his cries softened, his little body settling against her, recognizing her.

Her heart cracked open.

Tears slid down her cheeks as she pressed a kiss to his forehead, her chest so full of love it ached.

Benji was silent.

Jessica turned, and when she saw his face, her heart clenched.

He was staring at their son like he couldn't quite believe he was real.

His fingers hovered near the baby's tiny hand, hesitant, almost afraid.

"Benji," Jessica whispered.

Benji blinked, his throat working.

Then, slowly, he reached out.

The baby's tiny fingers wrapped around his father's pinky, holding tight.

Benji let out a shaky breath, his shoulders dropping as something in his chest cracked wide open.

"Hey, little man," he murmured, his voice rough with emotion.

Jessica watched him, her heart swelling.

She had seen Benji fight. She had seen him bleed. She had seen him in moments of pain, joy, heartbreak.

But she had never seen him like this.

Soft. Overcome.

In love.

Benji exhaled sharply, blinking rapidly before he leaned in, pressing a slow, reverent kiss to her forehead.

"Thank you," he whispered, voice trembling. "Thank you for him."

Jessica closed her eyes, smiling through her tears.

This was their moment.

The moment their world changed forever.

The room was quiet now, save for the soft sound of Jessica humming and the gentle coos of their newborn son.

Benji hadn't moved in the last ten minutes.

He just sat there, his forearm resting on the side of Jessica's bed, his other hand resting lightly on his son's small back as he slept against Jessica's chest.

It was still hard to believe.

The war, the loss, the distance, the fight to get back to her—all of it had led to this.

To him.

Benji traced a finger gently over the baby's tiny hand, marveling at how small he was.

A perfect blend of both of them—Jessica's nose, his own strong cheekbones, soft curls atop his little head.

Benji cleared his throat, his voice rough with emotion.

"We should give him a name."

Jessica smiled sleepily, running her fingers through their son's hair.

"I've been thinking about that," she murmured.

Benji glanced up, his brow lifting. "Oh yeah?"

Jessica met his gaze, and in that moment, he knew.

She didn't even have to say it.

Benji swallowed hard.

"Samson," Jessica whispered. "After Sam."

His chest tightened.

His best friend. The brother who fought beside him, the man who flew at his wing, who had given everything—just like Benji had once sworn they would.

Jessica reached for his hand, squeezing gently.

"You don't have to—"

Benji shook his head quickly.

"No. It's perfect."

Jessica's smile softened.

Benji looked down at their son again, his throat working.

"Samson Elijah Davis," he murmured.

Jessica let out a soft laugh, running her fingers through the baby's soft curls. "Strong name."

Benji smiled, pressing his lips to her damp forehead. "Strong boy."

And just like that, Samson Elijah Davis was officially theirs.

Jessica sighed softly as Samson shifted against her, stirring.

"I should get a nurse," Benji said. "Make sure you're comfortable."

Jessica nodded, still tired but content.

Benji leaned in, pressing one more kiss to her forehead, before standing and stretching.

As he stepped out into the dimly lit hallway, the quiet murmur of two nurses talking near the station caught his ear.

Normally, he wouldn't pay any mind to it—he had more important things to focus on.

But then—

"I feel bad for those mixed babies," one of them said softly, shaking her head. "No one's ever going to accept them."

The other sighed, nodding. "She should put that baby up for adoption. It would be better for him in the long run."

Benji froze.

His entire body went rigid, his fists curling at his sides.

His heart hammered in his chest.

A slow, steady breath left him as he forced himself to stay in place.

It took everything in him not to turn around, not to make a scene, not to tell them exactly what he thought about their words.

Because what good would it do?

They weren't the first people to think this.

And they wouldn't be the last.

But that didn't mean it didn't burn.

It didn't mean he didn't want to set the whole damn hospital on fire with the rage boiling inside him.

Instead, he straightened, rolled his shoulders back, and stepped past them like he hadn't heard a damn thing.

But he had.

And it would never leave him.

Benji stepped back into the room just as a nurse walked in, clipboard in hand, a tight, unreadable expression on her face.

"Mr. and Mrs. Davis," she said briskly, "we need to fill out the birth certificate."

Jessica shifted slightly, adjusting Samson against her chest.

Benji moved to sit beside her, resting a hand on her thigh.

The nurse held up her pen, ready to write.

"Race?" she asked, glancing at Jessica.

Jessica frowned. "Excuse me?"

"Your child's race," the nurse said, her voice clipped. "We can't list two races. It has to be one or the other."

Benji felt his jaw clench.

Jessica's eyes narrowed.

"Why?" she asked, her voice dangerously calm.

The nurse shifted uncomfortably. "Because that's hospital policy."

Jessica sat up straighter, her exhaustion momentarily forgotten.

"And what does the law say?" she asked.

The nurse blinked. "Excuse me?"

Jessica lifted her chin. "What does the law say? Because I know for a fact there's no statute that states a child of mixed-race parents has to be listed as only one. So if this is hospital policy, then I'd like to speak to someone with the authority to change it."

The nurse frowned, clearly irritated. "Mrs. Davis—"

"I'm a lawyer," Jessica cut in smoothly. "And I'd be very interested in hearing your justification for this."

Benji bit the inside of his cheek, trying to hide his smirk.

God, he loved this woman.

The nurse huffed, looking between the two of them.

Before she could respond, Dr. Lee entered the room, her expression sharp.

"What's going on?" she asked, glancing at the tension in the room.

Jessica turned her gaze to the doctor. "We were just discussing whether or not the hospital has the legal right to deny us the ability to accurately list our son's heritage on his birth certificate."

Dr. Lee's expression darkened immediately.

She turned to the nurse, arms crossing over her chest. "Is that what we're doing?"

The nurse shifted uncomfortably. "Doctor, you know the policy—"

"And I know that policy is outdated and discriminatory," Dr. Lee said sharply. "This child will be recorded exactly as he is."

The nurse opened her mouth, then snapped it shut, her face flushing red.

Dr. Lee sighed, rubbing her temple.

"I'll take care of it," she told Jessica, her voice gentler now.

Jessica nodded, still holding Samson protectively against her chest. "Thank you."

Dr. Lee turned to Benji, her expression softer.

"I'm sorry," she said quietly. "I know how hard this will be for him. But I also know he'll have two strong parents to fight for him."

Benji exhaled slowly, nodding.

They had won this battle.

But there would be so many more.

As the nurse left the room, Jessica let out a breath, looking up at Benji.

He could see it in her eyes—the exhaustion, the pain, but also the fire.

They weren't just fighting for their son today.

They would be fighting for him every day.

Benji leaned down, pressing a soft kiss to her lips, then another to his son's forehead.

"Samson Elijah Davis," he murmured against the baby's skin. "A name they'll never forget."

Jessica smiled, tired but unwavering.

"No," she whispered. "They won't."

And together, they sat there, holding the future in their hands—a future they would protect, no matter what.

The world outside the hospital was crisp and cold, the sharp Chicago wind biting against their skin as Benji carefully adjusted the blanket around Samson.

Jessica watched from the hospital entrance, one hand gripping the doorframe, the other pressed gently against her sore abdomen.

She had barely taken her eyes off them since Benji tucked their newborn son into his arms.

He held Samson like he was the most precious thing in the world, his movements careful, his eyes full of something Jessica had never seen before—something deeper than love, heavier than devotion.

Something like awe.

Jessica exhaled softly, stepping beside him.

"Alright, hotshot," she murmured, teasing lightly, her voice still raw from exhaustion. "Let's take our baby home."

Benji looked at her, his lips twitching into a soft smile, before leaning down and pressing a kiss to her temple.

"Let's go home," he murmured.

Tex had insisted on picking them up, arguing that the train was too cold, too crowded for a newborn.

Benji, for once, didn't argue.

So now, as they sat in the back seat of Tex's car, Jessica cradling Samson while Benji hovered like a guardian hawk, Tex kept glancing at them from the front seat, shaking his head with amusement.

"Man, I ain't never seen you look this nervous before," Tex muttered, smirking. "Not even when we were dodging enemy fire."

Benji shot him a glare but didn't look away from his son.

"He's just small," he muttered. "What if the seat ain't safe enough?"

Tex snorted. "He's safer than we ever were flying those Mustangs."

Jessica smiled softly, stroking Samson's tiny fingers.

Benji let out a slow breath, finally leaning back against the seat, resting his arm around Jessica's shoulders.

For the first time in a long time, he wasn't thinking about war.

He wasn't thinking about bullets or planes or dogfights.

For the first time, he was thinking about this moment.

About his family.

The moment they pulled up to their house, Benji was already out of the car, holding his arms out.

Jessica laughed softly, shaking her head before gently transferring Samson into his waiting arms.

Benji held him carefully, adjusting his grip, shielding him from the cold.

Jessica followed him up the walkway, her heart twisting at the sight of him standing on their front porch, cradling their son.

Benji took a deep breath, exhaling through his nose, his jaw tight.

"Benji?" Jessica asked softly.

He looked over at her, his eyes shining.

"I never thought I'd get this," he admitted, his voice low, rough.

Jessica felt a lump form in her throat.

She knew what he meant.

After the war. After Sam, Ace, all the brothers they lost.

After thinking he had lost her.

After believing he would never have this.

And yet—here they were.

Jessica stepped closer, wrapping her arms around his waist, leaning into him.

Benji pressed a kiss to her hair.

"Come on," he whispered. "Let's take him inside."

Jessica sat on the couch, wrapped in a blanket, watching as Benji rocked Samson slowly in his arms.

The house was warm, filled with the soft crackling of the fireplace, the quiet hum of the city outside.

Samson stirred, letting out a tiny sound, but didn't wake.

Benji looked down at him, his features soft in the dim light.

Jessica's heart clenched.

"Benji," she murmured.

He looked up, eyebrows raised.

She smiled.

"You're already a great father."

Benji let out a slow breath, his gaze flickering back to their son.

"I just…" He hesitated, his fingers brushing over the baby's tiny hand. "I want to give him everything. I want to protect him from everything."

Jessica's chest tightened.

She reached for his hand, squeezing gently.

"We will," she promised.

Benji met her gaze, his jaw tightening before he nodded.

A moment of silence passed.

Then, Jessica smirked.

"I think you're going to spoil him."

Benji scoffed. "Damn right, I am."

Jessica laughed softly, resting her head against his shoulder.

Their future was here.

In this house, in these moments, in the tiny heartbeat sleeping between them.

They had fought for this life.

And they would fight every day to protect it.

Benji pressed a kiss to the top of her head, then to Samson's tiny forehead.

"We made it, Jess," he whispered.

Jessica closed her eyes, her fingers curling around his.

"We made it," she echoed.

And in that moment, as their son slept peacefully in his father's arms, they both knew—

This was only the beginning.

CHAPTER 32:

HIS FIRST WORD

February 1947 – Chicago, Illinois

The early morning light crept through the curtains, casting a soft glow across the apartment. Outside, the winter wind howled, rattling the windowpanes, but inside, warmth radiated from the small furnace in the corner of the living room.

Jessica sat at the dining table, flipping through legal texts and case notes spread before her, one hand idly wrapped around a mug of coffee that had long since gone cold.

Across the room, tiny, determined footsteps echoed against the wooden floor.

Benji stood leaning against the doorframe, arms crossed, his dark eyes crinkled with amusement as he watched their son, Samson, wobble his way across the living room.

"He's getting faster," Benji murmured.

Jessica smirked, glancing up. "I think you mean more reckless."

Benji chuckled. "Same thing at that age."

Samson, now a little over a year old, had refused to be still from the moment he first found his footing. He was fearless, his little body in constant motion, his bright eyes always searching for something new to explore.

Jessica watched as he stumbled slightly before catching himself, his chubby fists clenching in excitement.

She shook her head. "I swear, he gets into more trouble every day."

Benji pushed off the doorframe, stepping toward his son. "Just means he's smart. He's figuring things out."

Jessica rolled her eyes, fighting back a smile. "He's going to figure out how to give me a heart attack before he turns two."

Just as she said it, Samson suddenly stopped in the middle of the room, his wide brown eyes locking onto hers.

Jessica's brows furrowed. "What is it, sweetheart?"

For a second, he just stared at her. Then—

"Mama."

Jessica's breath caught.

Benji, halfway across the room, froze in place.

Jessica blinked, her heart slamming against her ribs.

Had she just imagined that?

But then—

Samson let out a small, delighted laugh, clapping his hands before repeating, "Mama!"

Jessica let out a shaky breath, her hand covering her mouth.

Benji exhaled sharply, a slow grin spreading across his face. "Well, damn," he muttered. "Looks like you won this round."

Jessica barely heard him. She was already scooping Samson up into her arms, pressing kisses against his soft curls.

"Oh, baby," she whispered, her voice thick with emotion. "You said Mama."

Samson giggled, gripping onto her sweater with tiny fingers.

Benji stepped beside her, one large hand settling gently on his son's back. His grin wasn't cocky now—just full of something deep, something raw.

Jessica turned to him, her blue eyes shining. "Did you hear him?"

Benji chuckled, leaning in to press a soft kiss to her temple. "I heard him, darlin'."

Jessica cradled Samson closer, pressing her cheek against his tiny head. In that moment, everything else faded away.

They had spent years fighting—against war, against distance, against the world itself.

But now?

Now, they had this.

A home. A future.

And the sweetest sound she had ever heard.

Two months later, the auditorium at the University of Chicago buzzed with excitement as graduates lined up, their black gowns flowing, caps pinned in place.

Jessica stood among them, straight-backed and steady, though her heart raced with something close to disbelief.

She had done it.

She had fought through years of discrimination, the whispered words behind her back, the professors who looked at her like she didn't belong.

And now, she was about to walk across that stage.

Benji sat in the front row, bouncing a restless Samson on his knee, Tex and Desmond beside him, all beaming with pride.

When her name was called—

"Jessica Davis, Juris Doctor."

Benji let out a sharp, piercing whistle, making the crowd chuckle.

Jessica bit back a laugh as she walked across the stage, shaking hands with the dean, her diploma firm in her grip.

As she stepped down, her eyes found Benji's.

He was watching her with that quiet, unwavering pride, the same way he had the first time she ever stood up for something she believed in.

And she knew—this was only the beginning.

Two weeks after graduation, Jessica sat at her new desk in a small law firm on the South Side of Chicago, staring at the first case file placed in front of her.

A housing discrimination case.

She already knew the outcome before she even read the details.

A Black family denied a lease in a predominantly white neighborhood. Threats from the landlord. Police siding against them.

Jessica exhaled sharply, gripping the file.

This was exactly why she had fought to be here.

Still, she wasn't prepared for the backlash that followed.

When she showed up to court, the judge barely acknowledged her presence.

Some of the white lawyers refused to shake her hand.

One client, an elderly Black woman, had walked into the office wide-eyed, whispering, "I never thought I'd see a white woman fightin' for folks like us."

Jessica had just smiled and said, "You're looking at one now."

But it wasn't just in court—the threats came in letters, in phone calls.

She was making waves.

And people weren't ready for it.

One evening, after a long day of fighting an uphill battle, Jessica came home exhausted.

She barely made it through the door before Benji was there, pulling her into his arms, pressing a lingering kiss to her temple.

"How bad?" he murmured.

Jessica let out a slow breath, resting her forehead against his chest.

"Bad," she admitted.

Benji sighed, his arms tightening around her. "They're scared of you."

Jessica let out a humorless chuckle. "I'm just one woman."

Benji pulled back, lifting her chin so she had to look at him.

"You're you," he said, voice steady. "That's more than enough to make 'em shake."

Jessica closed her eyes for a moment, letting herself believe it.

Because if anyone believed in her, it was Benji.

Spring 1947 – Chicago, Illinois

Jessica sat at her desk in the small, dimly lit South Side law office, tapping her pen against a thick case file, her mind racing.

She had spent months fighting to be taken seriously in court, but now, sitting here, staring at another stack of cases where landlords had refused to rent to Black families, she realized—this fight was bigger than she had imagined.

And she wasn't fighting it alone.

Across from her, Ana and Ruby sat reviewing their own files, both deeply engrossed in their work.

Ana Morales was a white woman, sharp as a blade, raised in the working-class neighborhoods of Chicago. She was blunt, brilliant, and fearless. She had been one of the first people to accept Jessica as an equal, making it clear that she didn't give a damn about where Jessica came from—only whether she could hold her own in the courtroom.

And Ruby Johnson—she was a force of nature. A Black woman with a mind sharper than most men in the field, born and raised in Chicago, fighting against the same system that had tried to hold her people down. Ruby had been in this battle long before Jessica ever arrived.

And now?

Now, they were in it together.

Jessica flipped through the file, her brows furrowing as she scanned the notes.

A Black family—a husband, wife, and two children—had applied for a lease in a predominantly white neighborhood. The landlord had initially approved their application over the phone, but when he met them in person, suddenly the unit was "no longer available."

It was the same story, over and over again.

Jessica exhaled sharply, shaking her head. "This is blatant discrimination. And they know it."

Ruby scoffed, leaning back in her chair, arms crossed. "Of course they know it. The question is, can we prove it to a jury full of white folks who don't wanna admit it?"

Ana clicked her tongue, flipping her pencil between her fingers. "We can prove it," she said confidently. "We just need something concrete. A paper trail. Letters rejecting them after confirming availability. Something they can't ignore."

Jessica's mind was already racing.

"If we can get the landlord to contradict himself, we have him," she said, tapping the table. "I'll take lead on this one in court."

Ruby raised a brow, smirking slightly. "You sure, Shaw?"

Jessica met her gaze head-on. "I'm sure."

Ana let out a low whistle. "Alright, hotshot. Let's make it happen."

Courtrooms weren't new to Jessica.

But this one felt different.

She stood at the plaintiff's table, adjusting the sleeves of her navy-blue suit, her heart steady as she glanced across the room at the landlord—a smug, balding man in his fifties, sitting with his own lawyer, both of them looking far too comfortable.

The judge, an older white man with a permanent scowl, barely glanced at her as he motioned for her to begin.

Jessica squared her shoulders, stepped forward, and began.

She walked the judge through every document, every phone record, every statement proving the landlord had lied.

She spoke clearly, concisely, and with unwavering confidence.

And then, she pulled out the final blow.

A signed affidavit from another white tenant, confirming that the apartment had still been available weeks after the Black family had been denied.

The landlord's face went pale.

Ana, sitting beside Jessica, grinned.

Ruby leaned forward slightly, whispering, "That's checkmate."

Jessica turned back to the judge, her voice unwavering. "Your Honor, the evidence is clear. My clients were denied based solely on the color of their skin. I trust this court will not allow such discrimination to continue."

The judge exhaled sharply, rubbing his forehead.

A moment later, he ruled in favor of Jessica's clients.

They had won.

The moment they stepped back into the office, Ana threw her arms up in victory.

"That," she declared, "was a goddamn masterpiece."

Jessica grinned, hanging up her coat. "It was solid work from all of us."

Ruby plopped down at her desk, shaking her head. "Girl, I swear, if I didn't already know you were married, I'd say you were in love with the law."

Jessica snorted, rolling her eyes. "It's about making things right."

Ruby smirked. "Right. And I bet Benji loves hearin' about these cases every damn night."

Jessica let out a small laugh, shaking her head.

But the truth was—he did.

Every night, when she came home exhausted, frustrated, sometimes even scared, Benji was always right there, waiting.

And when she collapsed into bed beside him, he would listen to every word.

And he would never stop believing in her.

Jessica stepped into the apartment, kicking off her heels with a sigh.

She barely made it past the doorway before Benji's arms wrapped around her from behind.

"You look tired," he murmured against her hair.

Jessica melted into his embrace, closing her eyes. "Long day."

Benji hummed. "You win?"

Jessica smirked. "Of course we won."

Benji chuckled, turning her around so he could look at her properly.

His gaze was warm, deep, steady—the kind of look that still made her knees weak.

Jessica reached up, trailing her fingers along his jaw.

"You always knew, didn't you?" she murmured.

Benji's brow quirked slightly. "Knew what?"

"That I could do this," she whispered. "That I belonged in this fight."

Benji smiled, slow and sure, pressing his forehead against hers.

"I knew from the start, Jess."

Jessica swallowed against the lump in her throat, pulling him closer.

Because in a world that had tried to push her into silence, into submission—

Benji had never doubted her.

Not once.

And as she curled into his warmth that night, she knew she had won more than just a case.

She had won the right to fight.

And she would never stop.

1952 – Chicago, Illinois

Jessica gripped Benji's hand tightly, her breaths coming out in short, sharp bursts as she lay in the hospital bed. The dim glow of the overhead lights cast a soft sheen over her face, sweat clinging to her brow.

Benji sat right beside her, unwavering, his strong hand wrapped around hers, anchoring her through every wave of pain.

"You're doing good, Jess," he murmured, voice steady and full of warmth. "Almost there."

Jessica let out a frustrated breath, glaring at him. "Easy for you to say."

Benji chuckled, his fingers brushing over her knuckles. "I mean, I was shot out of the sky, darlin'. But I guess this is a little harder."

Jessica managed a weak laugh, shaking her head before another contraction hit, stealing the breath from her lungs.

A moment later, the doctor's voice cut through the haze.

"One more push, Jessica. You've got this."

Benji pressed a kiss to her temple, whispering encouragements, and with one final push, Jessica felt the tension in her body break.

A sharp, piercing cry filled the room.

Jessica let out a shaky breath, her head falling back against the pillow, tears pricking her eyes.

Benji squeezed her hand, his own eyes shining as he stared at their newborn child.

"It's a girl," the doctor announced, holding up a tiny, wriggling form.

Jessica let out a soft, broken laugh, her chest tightening as she reached for her daughter.

Benji watched, completely entranced, as the nurse placed their baby in Jessica's arms.

The little girl's skin was a shade lighter than her brother's, her dark curls already forming soft ringlets, her tiny fingers curling instinctively around Jessica's thumb.

Benji swallowed thickly, reaching out to gently stroke his daughter's cheek.

"She's beautiful," he whispered.

Jessica, tears slipping down her cheeks, looked up at him.

"What should we call her?" she asked, her voice barely above a breath.

Benji hesitated for only a moment before his lips curved into a soft smile.

"Christine," he murmured. "Christine Davis."

Jessica's heart swelled.

"Christine," she echoed, pressing a soft kiss to her daughter's forehead. "Welcome to the world, baby girl."

Benji leaned down, pressing his lips against Jessica's damp forehead, then to his daughter's tiny fingers.

Their family was growing.

And the world—as broken as it was—just felt a little more whole.

1955 – The Montgomery Bus Boycott

The television flickered in the corner of their small but warm living room, casting shadows along the walls as Jessica sat on the couch, Christine in her arms, Samson curled up beside her.

Benji stood near the doorway, arms crossed, his jaw tight as he watched the black-and-white screen.

The news anchor's voice was calm, too calm for what they were witnessing.

"Rosa Parks, a seamstress in Montgomery, Alabama, was arrested for refusing to give up her bus seat to a white passenger. This act of defiance has sparked outrage among the city's Black community, leading to what is now being called the Montgomery Bus Boycott."

Jessica gripped the edge of Christine's blanket a little tighter.

Samson, now eight years old, glanced between the television and his parents. "Mama, what does boycott mean?"

Jessica exchanged a brief look with Benji, then smoothed a hand over Samson's curls.

"It means people are refusing to ride the buses," she explained gently. "They're standing up to unfair rules."

Samson frowned, his little brow furrowing. "Like how Daddy couldn't go in certain places when he was in the war?"

Jessica's chest ached, but before she could answer, Benji stepped forward.

"Yeah, son," Benji said quietly, crouching down so they were eye level. "Just like that."

Samson blinked, looking back at the screen. "So they're fighting without fighting?"

Jessica smiled softly. "That's right."

Samson nodded slowly, considering it. "That's smart."

Benji let out a soft chuckle, ruffling his son's hair. "Sure is."

Jessica turned back to the TV, her grip tightening on Christine, who was fast asleep in her arms.

"This is the beginning of something bigger," she murmured.

Benji nodded, his eyes dark with understanding.

They had known change was coming.

And now—it was here.

The kids were asleep.

Jessica sat at the edge of the bed, running her fingers through her hair, her mind still spinning from the day's news.

Benji stepped into the room, leaning against the doorframe.

"You okay?" he asked softly.

Jessica sighed, shaking her head. "It just… it never stops, does it?"

Benji let out a slow breath, walking over and sitting beside her.

"Nah," he murmured. "But neither do we."

Jessica looked over at him, her blue eyes filled with something deep, something unshaken.

Benji reached out, tucking a loose strand of hair behind her ear.

"You've been fightin' since the day I met you," he murmured. "Ain't nobody gonna stop you now."

Jessica exhaled, leaning into his touch.

"I don't want our kids growing up in a world like this," she admitted.

Benji pressed a kiss to her temple. "Then we keep fightin.'"

Jessica looked up at him, searching his face. "You think we'll see the world change?"

Benji thought about it for a moment, then nodded.

"Maybe not all of it," he admitted. "But enough to know we made a difference."

Jessica let his words sink in.

Then she reached for his hand, lacing her fingers through his.

"We're in this together," she whispered.

Benji squeezed her hand gently. "Always."

And as they sat there, in the quiet glow of their bedroom, they knew the fight wasn't over.

But neither were they.

CHAPTER 33:

A CHANGING OF THE GUARD

June 1956 – Chicago, Illinois

The sun hung low in the sky, casting a golden glow over the quiet streets of their neighborhood. The house—their home for years now—stood sturdy and warm, the laughter of children drifting from the backyard where Samson and Christine played.

Inside, Jessica sat at the dining table, surrounded by stacks of legal papers, her mind racing through tomorrow's case.

Her career had taken off faster than she could have ever imagined. Employment discrimination. Housing segregation. Police brutality. The cases kept coming, and she couldn't turn them away.

Not when she knew how much it mattered.

Jessica ran a hand through her hair, exhaling slowly.

Ten years ago, she had dreamed of fighting for justice.

Now, she was living it.

The case file in front of her was one of the biggest she had ever taken on.

It was a lawsuit against a major Chicago transit company, which had been accused of refusing to hire Black conductors and drivers, despite a growing demand for jobs.

It was a landmark case, one that could set a precedent for other employment discrimination lawsuits across the country.

Jessica tapped her pen against the table, scanning the details again.

A hardworking father of three, denied a job purely because of the color of his skin.

Her fingers curled into a fist.

They were still fighting the same damn war.

But tomorrow, she would stand before the court and make them listen.

She closed the file, rubbing her temples.

The sound of the front door opening and closing pulled her from her thoughts.

Benji's voice followed.

"Jess?"

She turned toward the hallway, smiling as she stood. "In here."

Benji appeared in the doorway, his sleeves rolled up, his face lit with something excited, something victorious.

Jessica narrowed her eyes playfully. "Why do you look like you just won the lottery?"

Benji grinned. "Because I did."

Jessica raised a brow, stepping closer. "Oh?"

Benji reached for her hands, lacing their fingers together.

"I got the job."

Jessica blinked. "The job?"

Benji's grin widened. "Head instructor. The Youth Aviation Academy."

Jessica's jaw dropped. "Wait—Desmond's job?"

Benji nodded, his eyes shining. "He's retiring. Moving back to New York with his family. And he recommended me to take his place."

Jessica let out a soft, disbelieving laugh. "Benji, that's—"

"I know," he murmured, stepping closer, wrapping his arms around her waist. "I know, Jess."

Jessica looked up at him, her blue eyes full of pride. "You deserve this."

Benji pressed a soft kiss to her forehead.

"So do you," he whispered.

The next morning, Benji walked into the academy, the familiar scent of engine oil and fresh-cut grass filling the air.

He found Desmond in his office, packing up his things, his uniform still crisp, even in retirement.

Desmond looked up, smiling when he saw Benji.

"About time you got here," he teased.

Benji grinned, shaking his head. "Didn't think you'd actually leave, old man."

Desmond chuckled. "Figured it was time."

Benji leaned against the doorframe, watching as his mentor carefully folded his flight jacket, placing it in a box.

"You ever think we'd end up here?" Benji asked.

Desmond paused, his expression thoughtful.

"No," he admitted. "But I always knew you'd go far."

Benji's chest tightened.

Desmond had been the first person—outside of Sam—to truly believe in him.

The man had pulled him out of the wreckage of war, guided him when the world told him he wasn't meant to fly.

And now?

Now, Desmond was passing the torch to him.

Benji swallowed. "I never said it before, but—thank you."

Desmond looked at him, his sharp, blue eyes softening.

"You don't have to thank me, Davis," he said. "You earned this."

Benji exhaled, nodding once.

Desmond clapped a hand on his shoulder. "Now, don't screw it up."

Benji laughed. "Wouldn't dream of it."

That evening, Benji and Jessica sat on the back porch of their home, the cool summer breeze rustling the leaves overhead.

Christine was curled up in Jessica's lap, sucking her thumb as she drifted off to sleep.

Samson sat beside Benji on the steps, his legs stretched out, kicking idly at the wood.

Fireflies flickered in the distance, casting tiny golden lights against the night.

Jessica ran a gentle hand through Christine's soft curls, exhaling deeply.

"You think we've done enough?" she asked softly.

Benji frowned, looking over at her. "Enough?"

Jessica exhaled. "For the fight. For the kids. For—everything."

Benji was quiet for a moment.

Then, he wrapped an arm around her, pulling her closer.

"We're not done yet, Jess," he murmured.

Jessica tilted her head up, her blue eyes searching his. "You think we ever will be?"

Benji let out a slow breath, his gaze dark with understanding.

"Not in this lifetime," he admitted.

Jessica smiled softly, resting her head against his shoulder.

And as they sat there, surrounded by the quiet hum of summer, they knew—

This was only the beginning.

August 28, 1963 – Chicago, Illinois

The house was quiet—but not for long.

Jessica moved through the living room, balancing a tray of sandwiches as the muffled voices from the television hummed in the background.

Benji sat on the couch, Christine curled up beside him, her small fingers absently playing with the fabric of his shirt.

Seventeen-year-old Samson sat on the floor, legs stretched out in front of him, his elbows resting on his knees, eyes locked onto the screen.

Today wasn't just another day.

Today, history was happening.

The March on Washington for Jobs and Freedom had drawn more than 250,000 people—Black, white, young, old—all standing together, demanding change.

Jessica set the tray down, brushing her hands on her skirt before settling beside Benji.

She could feel it in the air. Something monumental.

Something that would change everything.

The screen flickered, and there he was.

Dr. Martin Luther King Jr. stood on the steps of the Lincoln Memorial, a sea of people stretching out before him, their voices lifted in unity.

Jessica reached for Benji's hand.

Christine, now seven, whispered, "Mama, who is that?"

Jessica glanced down at her daughter, brushing a strand of soft curls from her face.

"That's Dr. King, baby."

Christine frowned slightly. "Is he like you? A lawyer?"

Jessica smiled. "Not exactly. He's a preacher. But he fights the same way I do. With words, with truth."

Christine nodded slowly, turning her gaze back to the screen.

The speech had already begun, Dr. King's voice steady, powerful, full of conviction.

"I have a dream that one day, this nation will rise up and live out the true meaning of its creed—'We hold these truths to be self-evident, that all men are created equal.'"

Jessica felt her breath catch.

Benji sat unmoving, his hand tightening around hers.

"I have a dream that one day, on the red hills of Georgia, the sons of former slaves and the sons of former slave owners will be able to sit down together at the table of brotherhood."

Jessica swallowed, her throat thick with emotion.

She thought about her own life. About her father, a man who had tried to control her, to mold her into something she wasn't.

She thought about her mother, who had loved her but never quite understood.

She thought about Benji, about their children—about how far they had come, and how much further they still had to go.

"I have a dream that my four little children will one day live in a nation where they will not be judged by the color of their skin but by the content of their character."

Christine turned to Jessica, her blue eyes filled with something deep, something unspoken.

Samson, silent as ever, sat straighter, his jaw clenched.

Benji exhaled slowly, shaking his head. "Damn."

Jessica nodded. There were no other words.

They were watching the world change before their eyes.

That night, after the kids had gone to bed, Benji sat on the back porch, staring up at the sky.

Samson stepped out, hands shoved into his pockets.

Benji glanced over, then patted the seat beside him. "Couldn't sleep?"

Samson hesitated before sitting down, stretching out his long legs.

For a while, they sat in silence.

Then, Samson spoke.

"Do you think Dr. King is right?" he asked, his voice careful, unsure.

Benji frowned slightly. "What do you mean?"

Samson shrugged. "About things changing. About people… seeing us differently."

Benji let out a slow breath, rubbing his palms together.

"Son, change don't come easy," he said. "It don't come without a fight."

Samson looked down, kicking at a loose rock.

Benji watched him carefully.

"You worried about somethin'?" he asked.

Samson sighed. "There's this guy at school," he admitted. "We were arguing about the march, and he—he said I shouldn't be so proud to be a 'mixed boy,' like it's a bad thing."

Benji went still.

Samson's voice was tight, strained. "Said I should pick a side. That I'll never belong to either."

Benji let out a slow, measured breath.

He reached out, gripping the back of his son's neck gently, firmly.

"You listen to me, alright?" he murmured. "You don't gotta pick nothin'."

Samson swallowed hard.

Benji's grip tightened just a little. "You hear me? You are not less than anybody. Not ever."

Samson looked up, his eyes burning.

Benji gave him a small, steady nod.

"You ain't got to explain who you are to nobody," he continued. "You just be you. And anybody got a problem with that? That's their problem, not yours."

Samson exhaled slowly, nodding. "Yeah."

Benji let his hand drop, exhaling. "Good."

They sat there a little longer, staring at the stars.

And for the first time in a long time, Samson didn't feel alone.

Jessica stepped out of the kitchen, a newspaper folded in her hand.

She found Benji in the front yard, fixing the chain on Christine's bike.

She held up the paper, shaking her head. "They're already tearing him apart."

Benji glanced at the headline. 'King's Dream: Idealistic, but Unrealistic.'

He snorted. "Ain't that always the way?"

Jessica sighed, folding her arms. "Doesn't matter what he says. People like my father—they'll never accept it."

Benji stood, wiping his hands on a rag.

He walked over, took the newspaper from her hands, and tossed it onto the porch.

Then, he took her hands in his, holding them tight.

"They don't have to," he murmured. "We do."

Jessica exhaled.

She thought about their kids. About the fight that wasn't over.

Then she nodded, lifting her chin.

"We will," she whispered.

Benji kissed her forehead.

And as they stood there, the world still shifting around them, they knew—

They would never stop fighting for what was right.

Not for themselves.

Not for their children.

Not for the world Dr. King had dreamed of.

October 1963 – Chicago, Illinois

The house was quiet.

Too quiet.

Jessica stood in the doorway of the living room, watching Benji stare out the window, his broad shoulders tense, his hands shoved deep into his pockets.

The telegram had arrived that morning.

Elijah Davis was gone.

Jessica didn't need to ask what Benji was thinking—she already knew.

This was the moment he had been dreading for years, the moment he had always hoped would be farther down the road.

The moment when his father—**the man who had given him his first taste of the sky, who had shaped him into the man he was—**was no longer there.

She walked up behind him, sliding her arms around his waist, pressing her cheek against his back.

He didn't move for a long time.

Then, he exhaled.

"I should've gone back more," he murmured.

Jessica closed her eyes. "You did what you could."

Benji shook his head. "Not enough."

Jessica swallowed hard, tightening her grip on him.

"You were a good son, Benji," she whispered. "Your father knew that. He was always proud of you."

Benji let out a shaky breath, his body finally relaxing just enough for her to feel it.

But there was still one more thing they had to face.

And it was waiting just outside the door.

Seventeen-year-old Samson stood in the hallway, his fists clenched at his sides, his jaw set.

Jessica had seen that look before—in Benji.

That unshakable determination.

That fire.

When Benji turned, Samson lifted his chin.

"I want to go with you," he said.

Benji stilled.

Jessica's chest tightened.

"Son…" Benji sighed, rubbing a hand over his face.

"I know what you're gonna say," Samson cut in. "That it's dangerous. That it's different down there."

Benji's eyes darkened. "It ain't just different, Samson. It's a whole other world."

Samson's fists clenched harder. "I don't care."

Jessica stepped forward, placing a gentle hand on her son's arm.

"Sam," she murmured, "your father is right. Montgomery is dangerous—especially now, with the movement growing."

Samson's jaw ticked. "I don't care about that."

Benji exhaled sharply, stepping closer.

"You don't get it, son," he said, voice firm. "You think they see me as a threat? You? They'll see you as something worse."

Samson's brow furrowed. "Why?"

Benji's throat worked as he searched for the words.

"Because you're proof that the world is changin'," he finally said. "And there are men out there who hate that more than anything."

Jessica swallowed. That was the truth of it.

Samson set his jaw. "I just don't want you to go alone."

Benji's expression softened, just a little.

Jessica felt her heart ache.

Their son wasn't just stubborn—he was afraid.

Not for himself.

For his father.

Benji sighed, stepping forward. He placed both hands on Samson's shoulders, his grip strong, grounding.

"You don't have to look out for me," he said quietly. "That's my job. Always has been."

Samson's face tightened.

For a moment, Jessica thought he was going to argue.

But then, he dropped his head.

Benji pulled him into a hug.

"I know you wanna be there," Benji murmured, his voice low, rough. "I know."

Samson swallowed hard, nodding against his father's shoulder.

Jessica felt her chest tighten as she watched them.

This wasn't just about a funeral.

This was about a boy growing into a man—one who was realizing, maybe for the first time, how dangerous the world could be.

And no matter how much they wanted to protect him—he would have to face it someday.

Two days later, Benji stepped off the train in Montgomery alone.

The weight of it hit him all at once.

The air was thick, heavy with humidity, and the town felt the same and yet completely different.

He passed men in suits with narrowed eyes, women who quickly turned away, the ghosts of a place that never welcomed him.

But he wasn't here for them.

He was here for his father.

When he arrived at the small, white church, he saw the faces he had been longing for—his mother, his brother Marcus, his sister Naomi.

His mother—frail now, but still strong in spirit—reached for him the moment she saw him.

"Baby," Clara whispered, clutching his hands. "You made it."

Benji swallowed hard, nodding. "Course I did."

Naomi stepped forward, her eyes wet with unshed tears.

"You look good, Benji," she whispered.

Benji pulled her into a hug, squeezing her tightly. "So do you."

Marcus stood back, his expression unreadable.

But when their eyes met, Marcus nodded once.

A silent truce.

Benji turned, taking in the sight of his father's casket.

He took a slow breath, then stepped forward.

He laid a hand against the smooth wood, his fingers shaking just slightly.

He thought of the old crop-duster plane, the warm Alabama air, the way his father had once said, 'The sky don't care about color, boy. Up there, we're all just men.'

His throat tightened.

"I'll keep flyin', Pop," he whispered. "I'll make you proud."

And for the first time in a long time, Benji let himself cry.

A week later, back in Chicago, Jessica stood beside Samson and Christine as they lit a candle in their living room.

Benji watched as his wife and children honored his father in their own way.

Christine, innocent and full of wonder, whispered a soft goodbye.

Samson, strong but quieter now, kept his eyes on the flame.

Jessica reached for Benji's hand, squeezing it gently.

"We're with you," she whispered.

Benji nodded.

And as they stood there, together, he realized—

His father wasn't gone.

He was here.

In Samson, who wanted to protect his family.

In Christine, who carried the same warmth and kindness.

And in Jessica, who had been his anchor through it all.

The fight wasn't over.

But neither was he.

And neither was Elijah Davis.

CHAPTER 34:

A SON'S NEXT CHAPTER

August 1964 – Chicago, Illinois

The suitcase sat in the hallway, neatly packed, waiting to be carried out the front door.

Jessica stood by the kitchen counter, folding her arms, watching Samson like she was memorizing him.

Eighteen years.

Eighteen years of raising him, guiding him, watching him grow into the man standing before her now.

He had been born into a world that tried to tell him he wasn't enough.

And now, he was proving the world wrong.

He was going to Howard University.

He was going to be a lawyer.

Jessica swallowed, her chest tight with emotion.

This was what she had always wanted for him—for him to have choices, freedom, power.

But now that the moment was here?

She wasn't sure how to let him go.

Benji leaned against the doorway, arms crossed, a slow smile on his lips.

"You nervous?" he asked.

Samson glanced up from tying his shoes. "Should I be?"

Benji chuckled. "Probably."

Samson grinned, shaking his head.

Jessica exhaled, stepping forward, cupping her son's face in her hands.

"I am so proud of you," she whispered.

Samson's throat worked as he swallowed. "I know, Mama."

Jessica pulled him into a tight hug.

Benji watched, his own chest swelling with pride.

Samson wasn't just smart—he was fearless.

It wasn't easy being a mixed boy in America, not in 1964.

But Samson had never let it break him.

If anything, it had made him stronger.

Benji stepped forward, clapping a hand on his son's shoulder. "You're gonna do good things, son."

Samson nodded. "That's the plan."

Benji grinned. "Just don't let all them girls distract you."

Jessica shot him a look. "Benji."

Samson chuckled. "I'll try, Dad."

Benji smirked. "That's all I ask."

The ride to the train station was quieter than usual.

Christine, now eight years old, held Samson's hand in the backseat, her tiny fingers curled around his.

"You'll write me, right?" she asked.

Samson squeezed her hand gently. "Every week, squirt."

Christine pouted. "Promise?"

"Promise."

Jessica watched them through the rearview mirror, her heart aching in the best way.

When they arrived, they all stepped onto the platform, the train waiting, the steam rising into the air.

Jessica fixed the collar of Samson's shirt, unable to stop fussing.

"Don't forget to eat," she said.

Samson grinned. "I won't."

Benji shook his head. "Don't forget to study."

Samson laughed. "I definitely won't."

Benji pulled him into a hug, patting his back firmly.

"No matter what happens," Benji murmured, "you always got a home here."

Samson's voice was tight when he answered.

"I know, Dad."

Jessica swallowed past the lump in her throat, placing a kiss on his forehead.

And then—it was time.

Samson grabbed his suitcase, gave them one last smile, and boarded the train.

Christine waved until she couldn't see him anymore.

Benji wrapped an arm around Jessica, holding her close.

And together, they watched their son disappear into the future.

October 1964 – Chicago, Illinois

Jessica sat in her law office, staring at the thick case file spread out before her. The edges were worn from weeks of handling, notes scribbled in the margins, pages flagged with red tabs.

She had fought dozens of civil rights cases over the years—housing discrimination, employment inequality, police brutality.

But this one?

This one was different.

This was the biggest case of her career.

A young Black man, Elijah Carter, had been beaten nearly to death by two white police officers in broad daylight.

There had been witnesses.

There had been photos.

And yet—no arrests had been made.

Because in Chicago, in 1964, the system still protected the men in blue over the men they brutalized.

Jessica gritted her teeth, flipping through the statements.

The officers claimed Elijah had "resisted."

But the bruises on his body? The broken ribs, the fractured skull, the missing teeth?

That wasn't resisting.

That was attempted murder.

And Jessica was going to prove it.

She wasn't in this fight alone.

Jessica leaned back, rubbing her temples as Ana Morales and Ruby Johnson sat across from her, both deep in thought.

Ana, always blunt, flipped through the evidence, shaking her head.

"This case is airtight," she muttered. "But you know damn well that doesn't mean we'll win."

Ruby scoffed, crossing her arms. "We've seen men walk free for less."

Jessica exhaled. "I know. But we have something they don't."

Ana raised a brow. "What's that?"

Jessica's blue eyes burned with determination.

"The truth."

Ruby let out a slow, approving hum. "Alright, Jess. Let's make them listen."

The courtroom was packed.

Jessica stood at the plaintiff's table, adjusting the sleeves of her navy-blue suit, her heart steady despite the tension thickening the air.

She could feel the eyes on her.

Some hostile.

Some expectant.

Some hopeful.

Across the room, the two white officers sat calm, untouched, untouchable—smirking like they had already won.

Jessica tightened her grip on the table.

Not this time.

She stepped forward, her voice strong, unwavering.

"The evidence will show that my client, Elijah Carter, was not only beaten without cause but left for dead. We will prove that these officers acted with clear malice, abusing their power in a way that this city—this country—can no longer ignore."

One of the officers scoffed, shaking his head.

Jessica turned her sharp gaze on him.

"For too long, men like you have gotten away with crimes like this. But today, that changes."

She let the weight of her words settle over the room.

Then, she turned back to the judge.

"The prosecution is ready to present its case."

That night, Jessica sat at the kitchen table, her hands wrapped around a cup of tea, her mind still in the courtroom.

Benji leaned against the counter, arms crossed.

"How bad was it?" he asked.

Jessica let out a dry laugh. "They laughed at me, Benji."

Benji frowned, his jaw tightening.

"They laughed at me when I said we would hold them accountable," she whispered.

Benji walked over, placing a hand on her shoulder. "Let 'em laugh."

Jessica swallowed, looking up at him.

Benji crouched so they were eye level, his gaze steady.

"You ain't fighting for them, Jess. You're fighting for Elijah. For every man before him that never got justice."

Jessica felt her throat tighten.

He was right.

Benji leaned in, pressing a kiss to her forehead.

"You're gonna win this."

Jessica closed her eyes for a moment, letting his words sink in.

Then, she nodded.

"Damn right I will."

The courtroom was silent as Jessica stood, adjusting the cuffs of her navy-blue suit.

Her heart pounded—not with fear, but with determination.

This was it.

Everything she had fought for, every long night, every ounce of research, every sleepless hour had led to this moment.

She took a slow breath, steeling herself.

Then, she looked at the jury—twelve men and women who held Elijah Carter's fate in their hands.

"Ladies and gentlemen of the jury," Jessica began, her voice steady, commanding.

"You have heard the evidence. You have seen the photographs, read the medical reports, and listened to the testimonies of people who witnessed the horror of that day. A young Black man, beaten nearly to death in broad daylight by the very people sworn to protect him."

Her blue eyes swept across the room, lingering on the two white officers sitting smugly at the defense table.

"They want you to believe this was justified," she continued, her voice laced with fire. "They want you to believe that a man, unarmed and walking home from work, somehow deserved to be brutalized to the point of near death."

Jessica turned back to the jury.

"But I ask you—how many times have we heard this before? How many more men must be left broken, discarded in alleyways and hospital beds, before we say 'Enough'?"

The courtroom was breathless.

Jessica stepped forward, closer to the jury.

"These officers expected to walk away from this unscathed. They expected this case to disappear like so many before it. They expected that their word, as white men in uniform, would be enough to erase the truth."

She leaned in.

"But I know you see through that."

A few jurors shifted, their gazes locked onto hers.

"I believe that each of you understands the weight of this moment," Jessica said, her voice dropping to a near whisper, pulling them in.

"Elijah Carter could have been your brother. Your son. Your father. Your friend. If we allow this injustice to continue—if we let this courtroom become just another place where the truth is buried—then we are all guilty."

She took a step back, letting the silence stretch.

Then, with one final breath, she delivered the words that would linger in their minds long after they left this room.

"Today, you have the power to say no more."

Jessica turned, locking eyes with the judge.

"The prosecution rests."

And then—she sat.

The weight of her words hung thick in the air, unmoving, unshakable.

The judge's gavel came down.

And all they could do now was wait.

Jessica sat at the plaintiff's table, her fingers laced together, knuckles white.

The jury had been deliberating for eight hours.

Eight hours of waiting. Eight hours of second-guessing every word she had spoken, every piece of evidence she had laid before them.

She wasn't naïve.

She had fought too many battles to believe justice was ever a certainty, especially when it came to holding white police officers accountable for brutality against Black men.

But still—she had hoped.

Hoped that the truth would be enough.

Hoped that Elijah Carter would finally get the justice he deserved.

The courtroom was packed, tension suffocating the air as the judge finally called the jury back in.

Jessica's heartbeat pounded in her ears.

Elijah's family sat just behind her, clutching hands, bracing for the worst.

She glanced across the room, locking eyes with the two white officers who had nearly beaten Elijah to death.

They sat there calm, unbothered, smug.

Because they, too, had seen this play out before.

They had walked away before.

They expected to do so again.

Jessica inhaled deeply, then stood tall as the jury foreman rose to deliver the verdict.

"In the case of Carter v. Officers Reynolds and McKay, we, the jury, find the defendants—"

Jessica held her breath.

The entire courtroom leaned forward.

"—guilty of assault and battery."

A collective gasp rippled through the room.

Jessica's chest tightened.

She could feel the weight of the moment sinking in, the enormity of what had just happened.

For the first time—a courtroom had held two white officers accountable for the beating of a Black man.

The judge's voice cut through the commotion, calling for order. "Sentencing will be scheduled in thirty days."

Jessica turned to Elijah's family, who sat in stunned silence, tears spilling down his mother's cheeks.

Elijah himself—still battered, still healing—clutched his mother's hand, eyes wide with disbelief.

Jessica finally allowed herself to breathe.

Then—the courtroom erupted.

The officers' attorney shot to his feet, already spewing about appeals and legal loopholes.

One of the convicted men slammed a fist against the table, his face turning red with fury.

But Jessica?

She just stood still, watching it all unfold.

Because this—**this moment—**was proof.

Proof that the world was changing.

Proof that justice could happen.

Proof that all the fights, all the long nights, all the sacrifices—

They had been worth it.

Jessica barely made it down the courthouse steps before the press descended on her.

"Mrs. Davis! What does this verdict mean for future cases of police misconduct?"

"Do you believe this will set a precedent?"

"Are you worried about retaliation?"

Jessica squared her shoulders, her voice clear, unwavering.

"This verdict proves what we've always known—that the law applies to everyone, no matter the uniform they wear. But this is just one battle. The war isn't over."

A flurry of flashes followed her words.

Someone else called out, "Do you think Chicago is ready for this kind of change?"

Jessica paused.

She thought of the housing cases, the countless clients she had represented who were denied homes simply because of the color of their skin.

She thought of the women forced out of jobs because they spoke too loudly, fought too hard.

She thought of Elijah Carter, whose scars would never fully fade.

Then, she met the reporter's gaze.

"I don't know if Chicago is ready," she admitted. "But that doesn't matter. We're making it happen anyway."

And with that, she turned and walked away.

By the time Jessica made it home, the weight of the day had settled deep into her bones.

She barely made it through the front door before Benji wrapped his arms around her.

"You did it," he murmured.

Jessica exhaled against his chest, her fingers gripping the back of his shirt.

"I did."

Benji pulled back just enough to look her in the eyes.

"You won, Jess."

She nodded, but something in her felt… heavy.

"This case was never just about Elijah," she whispered. "It's about all the men who didn't get a trial. All the families who never got a verdict."

Benji cupped her face, his thumbs brushing against her cheekbones.

"And you fought for them too," he said.

Jessica let out a shaky breath.

"Do you think it'll last?" she asked. "Do you think this will actually change things?"

Benji considered her for a long moment.

Then, he kissed her forehead.

"One case won't change the world," he admitted. "But, Jess? You just made history."

Jessica felt her throat tighten.

She leaned into him, holding on, knowing that the fight was far from over.

But tonight?

Tonight, she allowed herself to breathe.

A few months later Jessica stood outside the grand but fading Shaw estate, her fingers curled into the wool of her coat. The house looked smaller than she remembered, less imposing, as if time had chipped away at it the way it had at the man inside.

She hadn't seen her father in years. Hadn't spoken to him since the day she left for Chicago, since the day she chose her life with Benji over the expectations of being a Shaw.

And yet, here she was.

She wasn't sure why she came. It wasn't for forgiveness. It wasn't for reconciliation. It wasn't even for him.

It was for her.

She stepped inside, the air thick with dust and memories. Josephine was long gone—no warmth remained in the house. The butler led her through the halls and into the bedroom where Senator Shaw lay, frail and sunken, but still with that fire in his eyes.

A fire fueled by bitterness instead of love.

"Jessica," he rasped, his voice dry, cracked, but unmistakably sharp. The same voice that once told her she was a disgrace. The same voice that demanded her to forget the love of her life.

Jessica didn't flinch.

She sat in the chair beside his bed, crossing her legs, unrushed, unshaken.

"You look just like your mother," he muttered, staring at her as if seeing someone else.

"She would have been proud of me," Jessica said, watching him carefully. "Even if you weren't."

A dry chuckle escaped him, but it turned into a cough. He wiped his mouth with a shaky hand, his gaze narrowing. "I always knew you stole from me."

Jessica blinked, caught off guard for the first time.

"When you left," he continued, "I checked my accounts. Saw the withdrawal. "Charity". That's what you wrote in the memo pad. Damn fitting."

Jessica exhaled slowly. "You wouldn't have given it to me if I had asked."

His thin lips curled into something resembling a smirk. "Damn right, I wouldn't have."

She tilted her head. "And yet, I used it for exactly what you would have wanted—for my education, for my future. I just made sure that I chose that future, not you."

His throat bobbed. Silence stretched between them, filled only by the slow tick of the grandfather clock down the hall.

"I read about your case," he said at last. His voice was hoarse, distant, but something deep, something raw, lay underneath.

Jessica waited.

He scoffed, shaking his head against the pillow. "You're relentless. Always have been. You really fought for them, huh?"

Jessica folded her hands in her lap. "Yes, I did."

A long pause. Then—his blue eyes, her blue eyes, locked onto hers.

"…You were right about a lot of things."

It wasn't much.

It wasn't an apology.

But it was more than she had ever expected from him.

He let out a long, tired breath. "I wasted a lot of time being angry, Jessica."

"I know," she said softly.

His fingers twitched against the blanket. "I was hard on you."

"You were cruel."

His throat bobbed again, but he didn't deny it.

"I—" His voice cracked, and for the first time in her life, Senator Shaw looked uncertain. Regret flickered across his face, like a man who suddenly realized he had spent his whole life fighting the wrong war.

"I'm sorry." The words barely made it past his lips.

Jessica studied him for a long moment. Then she shook her head.

"I don't need that," she said simply.

He swallowed hard, his gaze flicking away. His fingers clenched in frustration.

She stood, smoothing down her coat.

"I didn't come here for you, Daddy. I came here for me. To close this chapter of my life." She paused, then added, "You made sure I would never need you. And you were right."

His expression twisted, his jaw tightening, but he didn't say anything.

Jessica took a slow breath, then turned for the door.

She had already reached the threshold when his voice—weak, but still laced with that same authority—called after her.

"…I hope you're happy."

Jessica stopped.

For a moment, she let the weight of those words settle.

Then, without turning back, she lifted her chin and said, "I am he makes me very happy."

And with that, she walked out of his life forever.

June 12, 1967 – A Different Kind of Victory

Jessica sat at the kitchen table, coffee in one hand, the morning paper in the other.

Benji stood at the counter, flipping through the pages of his own newspaper, sipping on his coffee.

Christine, now eleven, sat on the floor, doodling in her notebook.

Jessica was halfway through an article about housing discrimination when something caught her eye.

Her breath hitched.

'Loving v. Virginia Ruling: Supreme Court Strikes Down Interracial Marriage Bans.'

Her heart pounded.

She read it again.

And again.

Then, she shot up from her chair.

"Benji," she breathed.

He glanced up, raising an eyebrow. "What?"

Jessica turned the paper around, her hands trembling.

Benji's eyes scanned the headline.

And then—he let out a low whistle.

"Well, I'll be damned."

Jessica's hands pressed over her mouth, emotion swelling in her chest.

"They did it," she whispered. "They actually did it."

Benji set down his coffee, a slow, wide grin spreading across his face.

"They sure as hell did."

Jessica let out a soft laugh, a tear slipping down her cheek.

Benji reached for her, pulling her in, pressing a gentle kiss to her forehead.

"This is big, Jess," he murmured.

Jessica swallowed. "Bigger than big."

Benji chuckled. "Guess we're not criminals anymore, huh?"

Jessica snorted, shaking her head. "About damn time."

Christine looked up from her notebook. "Mama? Daddy? What happened?"

Jessica turned, crouching in front of her daughter.

"A wonderful thing happened today, sweetheart," she said softly. "The Supreme Court ruled that people like your father and me—people of different races—have the right to marry in any state, without the government saying no."

Christine's eyes widened. "But you and Daddy are already married."

Jessica smiled gently. "We are, baby. But there were people just like us—families just like ours—who weren't allowed to be together in other states. Now, they can be."

Christine tilted her head. "That's silly. People should be with who they love."

Benji let out a deep laugh. "Ain't that the truth?"

Jessica cupped her daughter's cheek, pressing a soft kiss to her forehead.

"Yes, baby. It is."

That evening, Benji and Jessica sat in the living room, watching the news coverage of the ruling.

The screen flickered, and then—Mildred Loving's voice filled the room.

"We have thought about other people, but we are not doing it just because somebody had to do it and we wanted to be the ones. We are doing it for us—

because we want to live here in Virginia, with our families, and because we have the right to do that. We believe love is for everyone."

Jessica pressed a hand over her heart.

Benji sat back, his gaze thoughtful.

"She reminds me of you," he said quietly.

Jessica turned to him. "How so?"

Benji smirked. "She don't take no for an answer."

Jessica laughed softly.

Then, she leaned against him, his warmth, his presence, everything she had fought for and would keep fighting for.

"You think the world's finally changing?" she murmured.

Benji exhaled. "Slowly," he admitted. "But yeah. I think it is."

Jessica smiled, gripping his hand.

And as they sat there—watching history unfold, witnessing the world shifting beneath their feet—they knew.

This was only the beginning.

CHAPTER 35:

A WORLD SHAKEN, A LEGACY TAKES FLIGHT

April 4, 1968 – Chicago, Illinois

The house was quiet. Too quiet.

Jessica sat in the living room, the newspaper from that morning still folded on the coffee table, untouched.

She had been reviewing case files, marking notes in the margins, preparing for the next fight in court.

But then the phone rang.

And the world stopped.

Benji had answered.

She had heard it in his voice before she even knew what was wrong. That deep, gut-wrenching kind of disbelief—the kind she had heard when Sam died. When his father passed. When Kennedy was shot.

Jessica had rushed to his side, searching his face, gripping his wrist.

"What is it?" she had asked.

Benji just stared at the receiver, his hand still gripping it like it was the only thing keeping him upright.

Then, he met her eyes.

"It's Dr. King," he whispered. "They killed him."

Jessica's breath left her.

No.

Not him.

Not again.

The evening news played on the small television set in the corner of the living room, grainy black-and-white images flickering like ghosts.

The reporter's voice was somber, heavy, final.

"Dr. Martin Luther King Jr. was shot and killed today in Memphis, Tennessee—"

Jessica squeezed her eyes shut, her fingers curling into fists.

Benji sat on the couch, elbows on his knees, staring at the screen without blinking.

Beside him, Christine—now twelve years old—watched in confusion.

"Daddy?" she whispered.

Benji didn't respond.

Then, a single tear slipped down his face.

Christine's eyes widened.

She had never seen her father cry before.

She crawled onto the couch, wrapping her small arms around him.

Benji exhaled shakily, pulling her in, pressing a hand to the back of her head.

Jessica sat beside them, resting a hand on Benji's back, anchoring them all.

Christine's voice was small, hesitant.

"Why would someone kill him?"

Benji's throat worked as he swallowed.

"Because he was changing the world," he murmured.

Christine was silent for a long time.

Then, her grip tightened.

"Then I'll change it too."

Jessica and Benji both turned to look at her.

And in their daughter's eyes, they saw fire.

Two weeks later, the weight of the world still pressed down on them.

But life didn't stop.

And Christine?

Christine wouldn't let it.

Benji stood outside, watching as she ran circles around the P-51 Mustang that had been converted into a two-seat trainer.

She had begged him for weeks to teach her how to fly.

At first, he had brushed it off.

She was twelve.

She needed to focus on school.

It was too dangerous.

But the truth was—he was scared.

He had lost too many people to the sky.

First Sam. Then Ace.

Even his own father, in a way.

The idea of Christine up there, alone, in the vastness of it all…

He wasn't sure his heart could take it.

But then she had said it.

"I have a dream too, Daddy."

And Benji?

Benji had looked into her eyes and seen himself.

He had seen the same fire, the same hunger, the same longing.

And he had known.

She wasn't just asking.

She was meant to fly.

Jessica stood near the hangar, arms crossed, watching as Benji and Christine strapped into the P-51 Mustang.

It had taken a lot of convincing to let her fly this plane, but the two-seater conversion made it possible for Benji to sit right behind her, controls in front of him just in case.

She had worked hard to get to this moment, studying the mechanics, shadowing Benji during lessons with other students.

Now, it was her turn.

"Alright," Benji said through the headset as he adjusted his harness. "You remember what I told you?"

Christine bounced slightly in her seat, her hands gripping the controls. "Throttle smooth. Keep an eye on the horizon. Feel the plane, don't fight it."

Benji smirked. "Good girl."

Jessica could hear the pride in his voice.

Christine took a deep breath.

"Alright," Benji said. "Let's take her up."

Jessica watched as the Mustang began rolling forward, Christine guiding it down the runway just as she had practiced in taxi drills.

Then, with a steady pull on the yoke, the nose lifted.

Jessica exhaled as the plane climbed into the sky.

She had always known this day would come.

She just hadn't realized how much it would feel like watching Benji all over again.

Benji watched Christine's grip on the controls, her focus unshaken.

"Easy," he coached. "There you go."

Christine let out a breathless laugh.

"Holy shit, I'm flying."

Benji chuckled. "Language."

She grinned, eyes wide with exhilaration.

"I'm really flying, Daddy."

Benji felt his chest tighten.

She was.

His baby girl was flying.

And damn it, she was good.

He leaned forward slightly. "Alright, let's test your turns."

Christine nodded, adjusting smoothly, banking left, then right.

No hesitation.

No panic.

Benji smiled.

She was a natural.

Jessica was waiting for them as they taxied back, hands on her hips, trying to look stern but failing.

Christine hopped out of the cockpit, pulling off her helmet, face flushed with excitement.

"That was amazing!" she gasped.

Benji climbed out after her, shaking his head. "I think I just created a monster."

Christine grinned up at him.

"You gonna tell me I can't do it now?" she teased.

Benji sighed dramatically. "No, baby girl. Looks like you're stuck with the sky now."

Christine beamed, throwing her arms around his waist.

Jessica walked up, ruffling Christine's curls. "How does it feel?"

Christine pulled back, her eyes still shining.

"It feels like home."

Benji's chest swelled with pride.

He had felt that once too.

And now, so did she.

June 1968 – Chicago, Illinois

The house buzzed with energy.

Jessica stood at the kitchen counter, slicing fresh strawberries while Christine paced in front of the window, peering out every few seconds.

"Christine, sweetheart," Jessica teased, "you're going to wear a hole in the floor."

Christine turned, grinning but restless.

"I haven't seen Sam in forever," she said. "What if he's different? What if he—"

Jessica smirked. "He's been at Howard for one year, not in outer space."

Christine huffed but kept pacing.

Then—a car pulled into the driveway.

Christine bolted for the door, flinging it open before the car had even stopped.

Benji stepped onto the porch, arms crossed, watching with amusement.

The second Samson stepped out, Christine launched herself at him.

"Sam!"

Samson barely had time to drop his bag before she collided with him, arms tight around his waist.

He laughed, staggering slightly. "Damn, Chrissy! You tryin' to knock me over?"

Christine pulled back, grinning. "I thought maybe you forgot about me."

Samson rolled his eyes, ruffling her curls. "Like I could ever forget you, squirt."

Jessica stepped forward, smiling as she took in her son.

He looked older, more refined, but there was still that same spark in his eyes.

"Hi, sweetheart," she said, pulling him in for a hug.

Samson sighed against her shoulder. "Hey, Mama."

Then, Benji stepped up, clapping a hand on his son's back.

"You been stayin' outta trouble?"

Samson smirked. "Wouldn't you like to know?"

Benji raised an eyebrow. "Boy—"

Samson grinned. "I'm just messing with you, Dad."

Benji chuckled, shaking his head. "Get inside. Your mama made your favorite."

Samson didn't need to be told twice.

Christine grabbed his bag, practically dragging him into the house.

Jessica leaned into Benji, watching them go.

"He looks happy," she murmured.

Benji nodded, watching his son. "Yeah. He does."

And for the first time in a long time, Benji felt like everything was exactly as it should be.

A week later, Benji sat in the backseat of the P-51 Mustang, watching as Christine adjusted the controls with ease.

She had only been training for a few months, but damn if she wasn't a natural.

"Alright," he said through the radio. "Give me a slow climb, steady hands."

Christine nodded, pulling back gently on the yoke.

The nose lifted smoothly, the horizon dipping behind them.

Benji exhaled, watching her movements.

Her grip was firm, but not rigid.

Her confidence was growing.

"Good," he praised.

Christine grinned.

She didn't just love flying—she craved it.

And Benji?

He was starting to accept that she was built for the sky.

Later that summer, Jessica surprised Benji with something he never saw coming.

She waited until dinner, sliding a set of tickets across the table.

Benji raised an eyebrow. "What's this?"

Jessica smiled softly.

"Italy."

Silence.

Christine's eyes went wide. Samson looked between them.

Benji just stared.

Jessica reached for his hand. "You've never gone back."

Benji exhaled slowly.

"Jess—"

"I know it won't be easy," she murmured. "But you've carried the war with you for so long. Maybe it's time to let some of it go."

Benji swallowed.

Then, he nodded.

"Alright," he whispered.

Christine bounced in her seat. "Are we all going?"

Jessica grinned. "Of course."

Benji laughed softly.

Maybe this was what he needed.

To go back.

To finally say goodbye.

August 1968 – Italy

The air smelled the same.

That was the first thing Benji noticed when they stepped off the plane onto Italian soil.

The warm breeze carried the scent of sunbaked earth, olive trees, and something unmistakably familiar.

It had been more than twenty years since he had last been here.

And yet, as his boots touched the ground, it was as if no time had passed at all.

Jessica watched him carefully, her fingers intertwined with his.

Christine and Samson were a few steps ahead, taking in the foreign country with wide, eager eyes.

Benji's grip on Jessica's hand tightened.

She squeezed back, steady, grounding.

"You alright?" she murmured.

Benji exhaled slowly.

"Not yet," he admitted. "But I will be."

For the first few days, they did what any tourists would do.

They explored Rome, wandering through the ancient ruins, taking in the Colosseum, the Pantheon, the Vatican.

Christine and Samson were in awe, snapping photos, eating too much pasta, soaking it all in.

But Benji?

Benji's mind was somewhere else.

It wasn't Rome that haunted him.

It was further north.

Where the airfields had once been.

Where the war had really been fought.

And so, on the fourth day, they took a train to Tuscany.

To the place where Benji had nearly died.

To the place where, for the first time in his life, he had truly believed he was never coming home.

The small town hadn't changed much.

It was quiet, the kind of place that had seen too much war and chose to forget.

But Benji?

He could never forget.

Jessica, Christine, and Samson walked beside him, sensing the shift in his demeanor.

The closer they got, the heavier the air felt.

And then—there it was.

Or at least, what was left of it.

The old airfield was nothing but an abandoned stretch of land now, weeds breaking through the cracks in the tarmac, rusted-out remains of old buildings barely standing.

Christine exhaled. "This is it?"

Benji nodded.

Jessica glanced up at him. "Where did it happen?"

Benji swallowed hard.

Then, he pointed.

"There."

A spot just beyond the runway, near a break in the trees.

"That's where I crashed."

Samson's eyes widened.

Christine's gaze flickered between the broken airstrip and her father's face.

"You almost died here," she murmured.

Benji let out a short, humorless laugh. "I did die here."

They were silent.

Jessica's hand found his again.

Benji exhaled, closing his eyes.

And suddenly—he was back.

Smoke filled the cockpit.

The Mustang was spinning, alarms screaming in his ears.

Blood slicked his hands—his own.

White Wolf's voice echoed in his head.

"Little Black Bird, you won't fly again."

Benji had gritted his teeth, his hand white-knuckling the controls.

He thought of Sam.

Of Jessica.

Of home.

"Come on, baby, stay with me."

But the plane wasn't listening.

And then—the world had gone dark.

Benji opened his eyes.

The ghosts were still here.

But they didn't scare him anymore.

He let out a slow breath, stepping forward.

Jessica, Samson, and Christine watched quietly as he knelt, pressing a hand to the earth.

And softly, barely above a whisper, he said the words he had never been able to say.

"I made it."

A gust of wind swept through the airstrip, rustling the grass.

Benji closed his eyes.

Then, after a long, long moment, he stood.

Jessica's eyes were damp.

Samson swallowed hard.

Christine stepped forward, slipping her hand into his.

"You ready to go home, Daddy?" she asked.

Benji exhaled.

For the first time in twenty years, he felt lighter.

He nodded.

"Yeah, baby girl," he murmured.

"I'm ready."

November 1968

The house was quiet. A rare kind of quiet.

Jessica leaned against the kitchen counter, swirling the last sip of wine in her glass, her bare feet cool against the hardwood floor. The soft hum of a record player drifted from the living room—some smooth jazz number Benji had put on. The air smelled like the remnants of dinner, the faintest hint of candle wax lingering in the dim light.

She turned, catching sight of him—standing in the doorway, watching her.

His shirt was unbuttoned at the top, sleeves rolled to his forearms, that familiar smirk tugging at his lips. His eyes, dark and knowing, dragged over her like a touch. That look. The one that always sent a slow, simmering heat through her.

"You keep looking at me like that, Mr. Davis," she teased, taking a slow sip of her wine, "I'm gonna start thinking you have something on your mind."

Benji stepped closer, silent, deliberate. When he reached her, he took the wine glass from her hand and set it aside.

Then, his hands found her hips, pulling her gently but firmly against him.

"Oh, I got a lot on my mind," he murmured, his lips brushing the shell of her ear.

Jessica shivered, her fingers curling into the fabric of his shirt. "Oh yeah?"

He kissed just beneath her ear, slow, lingering. "Mhm."

His hands slid over her waist, down to the small of her back, pulling her even closer until there wasn't an inch of space left between them. She could feel the warmth of him, the strength, the familiarity.

Jessica tilted her head, giving him better access as he kissed along her jaw, the faintest scrape of his stubble sending delicious shivers down her spine.

"You know," she breathed, "the house is completely empty tonight."

Benji smirked against her skin. "Mm. You don't say."

She pulled back just enough to look into his eyes. "We don't get nights like this often."

He exhaled softly, his forehead resting against hers. "No, we don't."

A beat of silence passed between them, which was charged, thick with unspoken need.

Then, without another word, Benji bent slightly and swept her up into his arms.

Jessica let out a breathy laugh, wrapping her arms around his neck as he carried her through the house, moving like a man with one destination in mind.

When he reached their bedroom, he nudged the door open with his foot, the dim light from the hallway spilling in.

Gently, he laid her down on the bed, hovering over her, his fingers tracing slow, lazy patterns up her bare arm.

Jessica looked up at him, her hands sliding over his shoulders. "You know," she whispered, "you could've just told me you wanted me."

Benji smirked, leaning down to brush his lips against hers.

"What's the fun in that?"

And then, he kissed her.

Deep. Slow. Thorough.

Jessica sighed into him, her fingers threading through his hair as she pulled him closer. He kissed her like a man who had waited all day for this moment. Like a man who knew every inch of her, every place she wanted to be touched, every way she liked to be loved.

His hands made quick work of the buttons on her blouse, his lips never leaving hers. The warmth of his hands against her skin made her arch into him, made her breath hitch.

Benji pulled back just enough to take her in—the way her hair fanned across the pillow, the way her lips were slightly swollen from his kisses, the way her chest rose and fell in anticipation.

"You're beautiful," he murmured.

Jessica smiled, tugging him down to kiss her again. "Less talking."

He chuckled, deep and low, before pressing his body against hers.

And then—the world melted away.

Nothing but sheets tangled between them, whispered gasps, and the slow, burning intensity that only years of knowing each other could bring.

Tonight, they weren't parents. They weren't activists or teachers or anything else the world asked them to be.

Tonight, they were just Benji and Jessica.

Just them.

Just love.

CHAPTER 36:

A NEW BATTLE IN THE SKIES

January 1974 – Chicago, Illinois

The morning air was crisp as Christine sat at the kitchen table, papers spread in front of her, chewing the end of her pen.

Her acceptance letter to the United States Naval Academy lay open, bold and undeniable.

It was official.

She was going to be a Navy pilot.

Benji leaned against the counter, arms crossed, watching her with a knowing smirk.

"You keep staring at it like that, baby girl, it's gonna disappear."

Christine huffed, setting the pen down. "It just doesn't feel real yet."

Jessica, sitting across from her, smiled softly. "It's real, honey."

Benji pushed off the counter, walking over. "The question is—are you ready?"

Christine met his gaze, determination flickering in her blue eyes.

"I was born ready."

Benji chuckled, resting a hand on her shoulder. "That's my girl."

Joining the Navy as a female pilot in 1974 wasn't just about flying.

It was about fighting.

Fighting against the men who said she didn't belong.

Fighting against the system that tried to keep her grounded.

Christine had known this the moment she applied.

And now, sitting in the recruiter's office, staring at the uniformed officer across from her, she felt the weight of it.

"You're aware," the man said, glancing over her application, "that female aviators are… a relatively new development."

Christine sat straighter. "I'm aware."

He looked up. "You'll be facing challenges that men in your position don't."

Christine tilted her chin up slightly.

"Good."

The recruiter raised a brow. "Good?"

Christine smiled coolly. "I work better when people underestimate me."

For a moment, the recruiter said nothing.

Then, slowly, he leaned back in his chair, nodding.

"Well, Ms. Davis," he said, "let's see what you've got."

That night, Christine sat on the back porch with Benji, the cold wind biting at their skin.

Benji took a slow sip of whiskey, eyes on the dark Chicago sky.

"You scared?" he asked.

Christine exhaled. "No."

Benji smirked. "Liar."

Christine chuckled. "Fine. Maybe a little."

Benji nodded. "Good. That means you understand what you're walking into."

Christine looked at him. "How'd you do it, Daddy? How'd you get through it?"

Benji was quiet for a moment, staring out into the night.

Then, he said:

"You walk in like you own the room, even when they tell you that you don't belong."

Christine swallowed.

Benji turned to her, his gaze steady, strong.

"They're gonna try to break you, Chrissy. They'll say you're not good enough. That a woman don't belong in a cockpit, let alone in the Navy. You can let 'em win, or you can prove 'em wrong."

Christine nodded, gripping her hands together.

Benji leaned forward, resting his elbows on his knees.

"You got somethin' those boys don't," he said.

Christine smirked. "What's that?"

Benji's eyes twinkled.

"You got me as your teacher."

Christine laughed, shaking her head.

Benji smiled, then his expression softened.

"But more than that? You got heart, baby girl."

Christine felt her throat tighten.

Benji reached over, squeezing her hand.

"You fly for you. Nobody else. You hear me?"

Christine nodded. "I hear you, Daddy."

And in that moment, she knew—no matter what the Navy threw at her, she was ready.

May 1990 – Chicago, Illinois

The hangar smelled of oil, sweat, and memories.

Benji stood at the edge of the airfield, watching as a fresh group of students finished their lesson. The sun hung low in the sky, casting golden light over the planes lined up along the tarmac.

He had spent the last four decades in this place—training, teaching, building something that would last long after he was gone.

And now?

Now, it was his time to step away.

But the academy wouldn't be left without a Davis in the cockpit.

Christine was taking his place.

The cadets stood in neat formation, their uniforms pressed, their eyes filled with admiration as Captain Benjamin Davis took the stage.

The banner behind him read:

"Honoring a Legacy of Excellence – Lieutenant Davis Retires After 45 Years of Service."

Benji looked out at the crowd—his students, his family, his life's work.

Jessica sat in the front row, still as breathtaking as the day he met her.

His son, Congressman Samson Davis, had flown in from Washington, D.C., sitting beside his wife and their two young children.

Christine stood tall in her flight suit, her sharp blue eyes locked onto him, pride shining in her gaze.

Benji exhaled, gripping the podium.

"It's funny," he started, his voice strong despite the lump in his throat. "I spent my whole life up there, in the sky. And somehow, I never thought I'd come down."

A soft chuckle rippled through the crowd.

Benji smirked.

"But if you're lucky, real lucky, you find something worth landing for."

His eyes met Jessica's.

The love of his life.

The woman who had been there through it all.

He turned back to the cadets, nodding toward Christine.

"And if you're real, real lucky? You pass the torch to someone even better."

Christine grinned, shaking her head. "Don't start crying, old man."

The crowd laughed.

Benji smirked. "You wish."

A hush fell over the audience as Christine stepped forward.

She took a small box from her pocket, opening it to reveal a pair of gold wings.

"For everything you've done," she said, her voice steady, filled with emotion. "For me. For the academy. For every single one of us standing here today."

Benji felt his chest tighten.

He never needed medals. Never needed awards.

But this?

This meant everything.

Christine pinned the wings onto his lapel, stepping back with a crisp salute.

Benji held her gaze for a long moment.

Then—he returned the salute.

And just like that, his watch had ended.

Later that evening, after the celebration had ended, Benji and Jessica sat on the back porch, wrapped in each other's warmth.

The world was quiet.

Jessica sipped her tea, her fingers laced with his.

"You really did it," she murmured.

Benji exhaled. "Yeah."

Jessica smiled. "How does it feel?"

Benji turned his head, watching the woman he had loved for nearly half a century.

"It feels like I finally landed."

Jessica leaned in, pressing a soft kiss to his lips.

"You'll never land," she whispered against his mouth. "You're still flying, Benji Davis. You always will be."

Benji smirked, shaking his head.

"I love you, Jess."

Jessica smiled. "I know."

And under the soft glow of the porch light, they simply existed—still in love, still together, still flying in their own way.

November 3, 2006 – Chicago, Illinois

The ballroom was filled to capacity, the sound of murmured conversations and clinking glasses echoing off the grand chandeliers.

At the front of the room, a stage stood illuminated, a banner hanging above it in bold, elegant lettering:

"Honoring Jessica Davis – A Lifetime of Legal Excellence & Civil Rights Advocacy."

Jessica sat at the head table, her hands folded in her lap, blue eyes scanning the room, taking it all in.

She had never sought recognition.

The work was always about the people, never about her.

But tonight?

Tonight, the world had come to recognize her fight, her sacrifices, her victories.

And sitting beside her, his hand resting gently over hers, was Benji.

He leaned in, murmuring, "They finally figured out you're a big deal, huh?"

Jessica smirked. "Took them long enough."

Benji chuckled, squeezing her fingers.

A tall, poised woman stepped up to the podium.

It was Ana Morales, her former law partner and lifelong friend.

"Ladies and gentlemen," Ana began, her voice steady but filled with warmth, "tonight, we celebrate a woman whose name has been etched into the history of civil rights law. A woman who refused to stand down, who challenged the law until it bent toward justice. A woman who, against every odd, built a legacy that will outlive us all."

The crowd burst into applause.

Benji turned, smirking. "You're gonna make me jealous."

Jessica rolled her eyes, nudging him gently.

Ana continued.

"Jessica Davis began her legal career fighting cases most attorneys wouldn't touch—cases involving police brutality, segregation, and systemic discrimination. She was in the courtroom before the Loving v. Virginia case, long before the Fair Housing Act, long before the world was ready to accept what she had to say."

The audience listened in rapt attention.

Ana took a slow breath.

"She defended Black families facing eviction from white neighborhoods. She took on wrongful imprisonment cases. She fought for Black veterans who were denied their benefits. She was relentless. And she won."

Another wave of applause erupted.

Jessica swallowed, her throat tight.

Benji leaned in, whispering, "She forgot to mention you had to deal with me all these years."

Jessica smirked. "That's my greatest accomplishment."

Benji chuckled, shaking his head.

Ana turned to Jessica, her expression softening.

"Jessica, I don't think any of us can truly put into words what your work has meant. So instead, let us show you."

She stepped aside as an assistant rolled out a plaque—large, golden, engraved with Jessica's name.

At the top, it read:

"The Jessica Shaw Davis Legal Advocacy Award – Established 2006."

Jessica froze.

She had expected an honor. A medal. Maybe even a speech.

But this?

This was forever.

A law scholarship in her name.

A legacy for the next generation of civil rights attorneys.

The crowd rose to their feet, clapping, cheering.

Tears burned Jessica's eyes as she stood, Benji helping her up gently.

She turned to face him, emotion thick in her throat.

Benji grinned proudly.

"You earned it, Jess."

Jessica exhaled, holding his face for a brief moment, memorizing him in this moment.

Then, she walked toward the podium.

The applause thundered as she took her place.

Jessica set her hands on the podium, steadying herself.

For the first time in her life, she didn't know what to say.

She glanced at the plaque, then back at the audience.

Then—she smiled.

"I didn't do this alone," she began, her voice clear, unwavering.

"I had people who fought alongside me. People who refused to accept injustice as the way things were. People who believed in something bigger than themselves."

Her eyes flickered to Ana. To Ruby. To the lawyers who had stood with her when it was dangerous to do so.

"To the people who are still fighting," Jessica continued, "to the young lawyers sitting in classrooms right now, learning about justice, about resistance, about change—this is for you."

The crowd murmured in approval.

Jessica exhaled.

"I have spent my life arguing cases, trying to prove that the law should serve everyone, not just the privileged few." She shook her head slightly. "I never fought for awards. I never fought for recognition. I fought because I had to."

She turned, looking at her family.

"My husband taught me that."

Benji's expression softened, his chest rising and falling with slow breaths.

"My husband fought in a war for a country that didn't respect him. He came home a hero, but the world refused to see him as one. He fought anyway. And he taught me how to fight too."

Jessica smiled, her throat tight, emotion catching her breath.

"Benji, I never told you this, but… I fought my cases the way you fought in the sky."

Benji blinked, his lips parting slightly, like he didn't know how to respond.

Jessica's voice softened.

"With precision. With strategy. With all the damn fire I had in me."

A small chuckle rippled through the audience.

Benji swallowed, his fingers twitching slightly as if resisting the urge to pull her into his arms.

Jessica looked back at the audience.

"I am honored by this award," she said. "But the fight is far from over. There are still injustices that need to be challenged. There are still laws that need to be rewritten. And so, to every lawyer, every activist, every person who refuses to back down in the face of inequality—I challenge you."

She leaned forward slightly.

"Be relentless."

A wave of applause erupted.

Jessica stepped back, her heart pounding, her hands gripping the sides of the podium as the crowd rose to their feet.

Benji stood first.

Then, Christine.

Then, Samson.

And before she knew it, the entire room was on their feet, clapping for her, for her life, for everything she had built.

Jessica closed her eyes for just a moment, letting it sink in.

She had won battles.

She had lost some, too.

But tonight?

Tonight, she had changed history.

And in the front row, Benji watched her with the same expression he always had.

Like she had hung the moon.

March 29, 2007 – Washington, D.C.

The grand rotunda of the United States Capitol was packed.

Rows of seats filled with dignitaries, politicians, military officers, and—most importantly—the men who had defied history and changed the world.

Benji stood among them, his back straight, his uniform pressed, his medals gleaming under the bright lights.

At 83 years old, he had lived a life longer than he ever imagined, carrying the weight of every friend who didn't make it home.

And today?

Today, the world was finally giving them the honor they had deserved for decades.

The President of the United States stood at the podium, looking out over the crowd.

"Today," he said, his voice steady, reverent, "we recognize the extraordinary service and sacrifice of the Tuskegee Airmen—the first African American military aviators who fought not just for victory in World War II, but for the very right to fight."

A standing ovation erupted.

Benji exhaled, his gaze drifting to the front row.

Jessica sat there, her blue eyes shimmering with pride.

Beside her was Samson, now a congressman, standing tall with his wife and children.

Christine sat beside them, dressed in her own Navy uniform, her hands folded tightly in her lap.

His grandchildren were there too—Jaden, who had followed in his footsteps and become a fighter pilot, and Ava, who was studying law, just like her grand mother.

This was his legacy.

This was his family.

And God, he had never felt prouder.

One by one, the surviving Tuskegee Airmen were called forward.

Benji stepped onto the stage, his heart pounding as the medal was placed around his neck.

Applause thundered through the chamber.

He looked down at the medal—heavy, golden, a symbol of everything they had fought for.

A symbol of Sam. Of Ace. Of Tex. Of Desmond. Of every man who should have been here but wasn't.

He closed his eyes for a moment, whispering to them in his heart.

"We made it, boys."

And then—he saluted.

The moment was etched into history.

That night, after the celebration, Benji stood on the balcony of his hotel room, staring out over Washington, D.C.

Jessica came up behind him, slipping her arms around his waist.

"You did it," she murmured.

Benji sighed. "We did."

Jessica rested her chin on his shoulder. "Thinking about them?"

Benji nodded. "Desmond, Tex… all of them."

Jessica squeezed his hand. "They were here today. I know they were."

Benji closed his eyes. "I hope so."

Jessica smiled softly. "I know so."

And in the quiet, with the city stretching before them, they held each other—two old souls who had lived, loved, and fought for everything they had.

Back at the hotel, Christine poured a glass of whiskey, sliding it to her father.

Benji raised a brow. "Trying to get me drunk?"

Christine smirked. "Maybe."

Samson chuckled, lifting his own glass. "To Dad," he said. "To a legend."

Benji shook his head, smiling. "To all of them," he corrected. "To every man who wore these wings."

Jessica lifted her glass too. "To a life well-lived."

Benji exhaled, staring at his family—his children, his grandchildren, his wife.

He raised his glass.

"To love," he said.

And they drank to that.

CHAPTER 37:

WITNESSING HISTORY

January 20, 2009 – Washington, D.C.

The air was crisp and electric, charged with something Benji had never felt before.

Hope.

He stood tall, his cane in one hand, Jessica's fingers wrapped tightly around the other, surrounded by his family—his children, grandchildren, and great-grandchildren.

Millions filled the National Mall, bundled in thick coats, scarves, and hats, waiting for the moment that would cement itself in history.

At 85 years old, Benji never thought he'd see this.

Jessica, now 87, squeezed his hand gently, watching him more than the stage ahead.

"You alright, hotshot?" she murmured.

Benji let out a slow exhale, his breath visible in the cold air.

"Not yet," he admitted. "But I will be."

The massive screens displayed Barack Obama, his face steady, determined, as he stepped forward to take the oath.

The crowd hushed in anticipation, millions holding their breath as Chief Justice John Roberts raised his hand.

Benji felt Christine shift beside him, her gloved hands clenched in anticipation.

Samson stood still, his posture rigid with emotion, his grandchildren standing beside him.

Benji's great-grandson, Jaden Davis, now 14, leaned in, whispering, "Great-Grandpa, you didn't see this coming?"

Benji let out a soft chuckle, shaking his head.

"Boy," he murmured, "I didn't even think I'd live long enough to dream it."

Jaden fell quiet, processing that.

Benji had seen a world where a Black man could serve his country, could fly higher than the sky itself—but still come home to be treated as less.

Now, a Black man was about to take the highest office in the land.

His great-granddaughter, Elena, only six years old, clung to her father's hand, watching the screen with wide, innocent eyes.

Benji felt a lump form in his throat.

"This world is going to be different for them."

And then—the words came.

"I, Barack Hussein Obama, do solemnly swear…"

Jessica inhaled sharply, her grip on Benji tightening.

"...that I will faithfully execute the Office of President of the United States..."

Christine blinked back tears.

"...and will, to the best of my ability..."

Samson exhaled a shaky breath.

"...preserve, protect, and defend the Constitution of the United States."

A beat of silence.

Then—Obama smiled.

"So help me God."

The roar that followed shook the very earth.

People cheered, sobbed, embraced—history had changed in an instant.

Benji felt it deep in his chest, like something he had carried for decades had finally lifted.

Jessica turned to him, her blue eyes bright with tears.

"You okay?" she whispered.

Benji swallowed, his voice thick with emotion.

"We won, Jess."

Jessica lifted his weathered hand to her lips, pressing a kiss to his fingers.

"Yes," she murmured, "we did."

They stayed rooted in place, watching as Obama addressed the nation, speaking of hope, unity, and the road ahead.

Samson's oldest son, Jack, now in his 40s, stood beside him, shaking his head in disbelief.

"I never thought I'd see this," he admitted.

Benji turned to his grandson, his eyes still misted with emotion.

"I never thought you would either."

Christine smirked, nudging her father's shoulder.

"You're gonna tell me you didn't see this coming?"

Benji raised a brow.

"Chrissy, when I was your age, the only Black men in the White House were workin' in the kitchen."

Christine sobered, her smirk fading into something deeper.

"Yeah," she murmured. "I guess not."

Jessica glanced between them, watching the emotion settle over the family.

And then—Elena, their great-granddaughter, tugged on Benji's sleeve.

"Great-Grandpa?" she asked, her small voice barely rising above the noise.

Benji looked down, his weathered hand resting on her tiny one.

"Yes, baby?"

She pointed at the screen, where Obama stood tall, his family beside him.

"Does this mean I can be president one day?"

Benji's throat tightened.

He crouched slowly, his cane steadying him as he met her wide, hopeful eyes.

"Baby girl," he whispered, "you can be anything you want."

Jessica watched them with a knowing smile.

This was what they had fought for.

For Elena.

For Jaden.

For every child who would grow up never knowing the limitations their ancestors had.

And for the first time in his long life, Benji truly believed the fight had been worth it.

Later that night, after the celebrations had ended and the world had begun to quiet, Benji and Jessica sat together in their hotel suite.

Jessica cradled a cup of tea, watching her husband with knowing eyes.

"You've been quiet," she murmured.

Benji leaned back in his chair, one arm draped lazily over the backrest, his fingers tapping lightly in thought.

He let out a slow breath.

"I told you once that I didn't think we'd ever win," he said.

Jessica set her tea down, her gaze softening.

"I remember."

Benji exhaled.

"I was wrong."

Jessica tilted her head slightly. "What changed?"

Benji lifted his eyes to hers.

"You."

Jessica's breath hitched.

Benji gestured to the city beyond their window, where the White House stood in the distance.

"I thought the war would never end. I thought the fight wouldn't be worth it. But you? You always believed." He smirked. "And damn it, Jess, you were right."

Jessica sighed, shaking her head fondly.

"You think I believed because I was smart?" she teased. "I believed because I had you."

Benji chuckled, reaching for her hand.

They sat there for a long time, just existing together.

Jessica lifted his hand to her cheek, closing her eyes for a moment.

"I love you, Hotshot."

Benji smirked. "I know."

Jessica rolled her eyes.

"Arrogant."

Benji squeezed her hand, his smirk fading into something softer, something deeper.

"Always."

And outside their window, the lights of Washington, D.C. shined like a promise—that they had changed the world, and the world would remember them for it.

February 18, 2025 – Tuskegee, Alabama

The road stretched long and empty, the Alabama sun casting a golden glow over the fields beyond the window.

Benji sat in the backseat of the car, his cane resting against his leg, Jessica's arm looped through his.

Even now, at 101 and 103, they still sat like young lovers—close, hands occasionally brushing, existing in a quiet, familiar rhythm.

Christine drove up front, her husband, Robert, sitting in the passenger seat, occasionally checking the GPS.

Benji exhaled slowly, his old hands folding over each other as he gazed out the window.

It had been a long time since he'd been back.

A lifetime ago.

Jessica watched him from the corner of her eye, noticing the way his fingers tapped lightly against his knee.

She reached over, covering his hand with hers, squeezing gently.

Benji turned to her, a knowing smirk tugging at the corner of his mouth.

"You always know, don't you?" he murmured.

Jessica smiled softly. "You're not that hard to read, Hotshot."

Benji chuckled, leaning his head back against the seat.

They drove in silence for a while, the sounds of the road a gentle hum.

But then—as they passed a familiar stretch of land—Benji's breath hitched.

Jessica noticed immediately, her head turning to follow his gaze.

And then—her heart sank.

It was gone.

The church.

The place that had once held their stolen moments, their whispered promises, their impossible love.

Now, it was an empty lot, overgrown with weeds, a sign for future development planted in the dirt.

Christine, still focused on the road, didn't notice at first.

But Benji did.

And he let out a slow breath, shaking his head.

"Well," he muttered, "that's a damn shame."

Christine glanced in the rearview mirror. "What is?"

Benji exhaled through his nose.

"The church."

Christine frowned, flicking her eyes to the bare stretch of land.

"Oh…" she murmured, understanding now.

Jessica's grip on Benji's hand tightened slightly.

"You always said we'd come back," she whispered.

Benji smirked, but it was a tired smirk—one that carried the weight of time.

"Well, we're back."

Jessica sighed, nodding.

But it wasn't the same.

It would never be the same.

Still, the memories lived.

And that, at least, was something.

The car pulled into the lot, the familiar red-brick buildings standing as proud as ever.

Christine parked, cutting the engine.

"Dad," she said before even turning around. "Take the walker."

Benji grumbled.

"I don't need the damn walker."

Jessica rolled her eyes. "Benji, you're 101. Take the walker."

Benji huffed.

"She's bossier now than she was at 19," he muttered under his breath.

Jessica smirked. "And yet, you still listen."

Christine held back a laugh as she got out, retrieving the walker from the trunk.

By the time she returned, Jessica was already standing outside the car, waiting with an expectant look.

Benji sighed dramatically.

"You enjoy bullying me, don't you?"

Jessica smirked. "Every second."

Benji shook his head, but he took the walker, slowly stepping out of the car.

Jessica looped her arm through his.

Christine and Robert watched them carefully, ensuring they were steady before leading them toward the entrance.

As they stepped inside, a staff member recognized them immediately.

"Oh my god," she whispered, eyes widening in awe.

Christine smiled. "Yeah, that's him."

The woman, no older than 30, covered her mouth in shock, as if she had just met a living legend.

Because she had.

Inside the museum, the air was quiet, reverent.

Benji walked slowly, his steps steady but deliberate, his eyes moving over the photographs, the uniforms, the medals.

Pieces of his life, his past.

But then—they reached the display that made Benji stop.

Jessica felt his body still beside her.

Christine's breath hitched slightly.

Because there, behind glass, stood Benji's flight jacket.

The patches, the worn leather, the faint lettering on the side—his personal mark.

It had been cleaned, preserved, set under soft golden light.

Christine stepped forward, reading the plaque beneath it.

"Major Benjamin Davis – Tuskegee Airman, Fighter Pilot, Instructor. A Man Who Defied the Skies."

Jessica turned to Benji, watching his face.

For a long moment, he didn't say anything.

His hand reached out, almost instinctively, before stopping just shy of the glass.

Christine swallowed hard. "Dad?"

Benji exhaled.

"Well," he murmured, "I guess I finally made it into the history books."

Jessica slid her hand into his.

"You were always there, Benji."

Benji turned to her, his eyes filled with something deep—something unspoken.

And then, finally, he whispered:

"We did it, Jess."

Jessica leaned against him, her cheek resting against his shoulder.

"Yes," she whispered, "we did."

And in that quiet moment, surrounded by their past, their legacy, and their family—they simply stood.

Together.

Still.

Always.

The afternoon sun hung low in the sky, bathing the museum grounds in a soft, golden glow.

Benji and Jessica sat side by side on a weathered wooden bench, their hands resting together on his lap.

Before them, gleaming in the sunlight, stood a Curtiss P-40 Warhawk.

Its shark-mouth nose art was still as fierce as ever, the olive-green fuselage polished to perfection. But what made Benji's breath hitch was the name painted in bold white letters beneath the cockpit:

S. Wells

Benji stared, his fingers twitching against Jessica's palm.

It had been so long.

So many decades since Sam had flown that very plane.

So many decades since Benji had last seen it in the skies—the last time he saw Sam alive.

Jessica followed his gaze, and though her eyesight had softened with time, she didn't need to read the letters to know what had stilled Benji so completely.

"Sam," she whispered.

Benji swallowed hard.

"I never thought I'd see it again," he murmured.

For a long moment, they simply sat in silence, the memories unfolding in the quiet.

Benji could almost hear Sam's voice again—his laughter, his relentless optimism, his unwavering belief that they'd both make it home.

Jessica's fingers curled gently around his.

"He's here, Benji," she said softly.

Benji exhaled, his old chest rising and falling with steady resolve.

"Yeah," he whispered. "He is."

Behind them, the sound of approaching footsteps and soft chatter pulled Benji from his thoughts.

Christine's voice carried through the crisp air. "There they are."

Benji turned just as his family arrived—his children, grandchildren, and great-grandchildren.

Jessica smiled as they all gathered around, the warmth of their love settling into the moment.

Christine approached with an all-too-familiar look, one of mischief and quiet determination.

"Dad, I set something up for you," she said casually.

Benji arched a brow. "Christine…"

She raised her hands innocently. "Nothing big, I promise. Just a little Q&A inside the museum."

Benji huffed. "And you didn't ask me first because…?"

Christine smirked. "Because you would've said no."

Jessica chuckled, patting his hand.

"She's not wrong, Hotshot."

Benji sighed, shaking his head. "Guess I better make it worth their time."

Jaden, his great-grandson, leaned in eagerly. "Great-Grandpa, are you gonna tell them about the time you took down five German fighters?"

Benji smirked. "That's the one you wanna hear again?"

Jaden grinned. "It's the best one."

Benji chuckled, reaching up to ruffle the boy's hair.

Jessica watched him, her heart full.

After everything, after a lifetime of love, loss, war, and peace—this was how he would be remembered.

Not just in museums.

Not just in history books.

But in the hearts of his family.

Before they stood, Benji looked at the P-40 one last time.

He inhaled deeply, as if committing it to memory, as if seeing Sam standing beside it, flashing that reckless grin of his.

"Fly high, brother," he whispered under his breath.

And as Jessica helped him to his feet, as their family moved toward the museum doors, he felt lighter.

As if, after all these years, he had finally landed.

And he was home.

CHAPTER 38:

THE FINAL Q&A

February 18, 2025 – Tuskegee Airmen
National Museum

The small crowd inside the museum hushed as Benji settled into his chair, Jessica beside him, her hand resting lightly on his knee.

Christine had set up a low-key Q&A session, just enough to honor her father without overwhelming him.

Benji exhaled slowly, adjusting his posture as a young woman in her early 30s, a museum historian, stepped up with a warm smile.

"Major Davis," she began, her tone reverent but welcoming, "it's an honor to have you here. We have a few questions from visitors today—if that's alright with you?"

Benji smirked, his old charm still present even at 101.

"Well, I suppose if you dragged me all the way down here, I might as well answer."

The audience chuckled lightly, the tension easing.

The historian smiled. "Alright, first question—what was it like, flying for the first time?"

Benji's eyes softened, his mind slipping back for a moment.

"The first time I was in the sky," he murmured, "I felt free."

A brief pause.

"When you're up there, the world gets real small, and all the things people fight over? The lines, the colors, the borders? They all disappear."

Jessica squeezed his knee gently.

A young man in the back, no older than 20, raised his hand.

"What was the hardest part about the war?"

Benji sighed, rubbing his hands together.

"Losing people," he said simply. "Good men. Friends. My best friend."

He glanced at Jessica briefly.

"And being away from the people you love."

Jessica offered him a small, knowing smile.

Another voice—this time from a young woman seated near the front.

"What do you think was your greatest accomplishment?"

Benji thought for a moment.

"Surviving," he said honestly. "Not just the war. But everything that came after it."

A brief pause.

"Coming home wasn't easy," he admitted. "The world didn't suddenly decide to treat us right just because we proved ourselves. We still had to fight."

The young woman nodded, understanding.

But then, just as Benji glanced over the audience, his gaze caught on something.

A young couple—a Black man and a white woman, sitting together in the back.

They were holding hands, their fingers intertwined, whispering to each other between questions.

Benji's heart clenched.

They reminded him of another young couple, decades ago, who had once sat in the back of a room just like this, holding hands in secret.

His grip on Jessica's knee tightened slightly.

She followed his gaze, and when she saw the couple, she let out a small, soft breath.

Jessica turned to him, a quiet smile playing at her lips.

"You see it, don't you?" she whispered.

Benji swallowed, his throat tightening.

"Yeah," he murmured.

Jessica smiled, leaning in just slightly.

"We won, Benji."

Benji exhaled, nodding.

"Yeah, baby," he whispered. "We did."

The Q&A ended a few minutes later, and Christine helped them outside, back to their bench.

Jessica settled beside him, linking her arm through his as the museum remained alive behind them.

Benji let out a slow, tired breath, staring out at the old airfield.

The wind whistled softly, carrying the echoes of a past that had long since faded.

"I don't think we'll be back here again," Benji murmured.

Jessica sighed, resting her head lightly against his shoulder.

"No," she agreed softly. "I don't think we will."

Benji closed his eyes briefly.

Jessica's fingers brushed over his hand, memorizing the feel of it.

The world had changed.

They had helped change it.

The afternoon sun was soft now, dipping lower in the sky, casting long golden streaks across the quiet airfield.

Benji and Jessica sat close together, still side by side on the weathered bench, their hands clasped gently.

It was a perfect day.

The museum was alive with visitors—families, students, history lovers— all moving through the exhibits, learning the stories of those who had paved the way.

Their family had stayed near them at first, but eventually, Christine and Robert walked over, flanked by their grandchildren and great-grandchildren.

"Y'all need anything?" Christine asked, her voice gentle, but full of concern.

Jessica smiled up at her daughter, shaking her head.

"We're just fine, sweetheart," she murmured.

Benji nodded, his old hands resting atop his cane.

"You all go enjoy the museum," he said. "We've seen it enough."

Christine hesitated, glancing at Robert, but Benji gave her a look, one that made her huff softly before relenting.

"Alright," she said, still studying them carefully. "But if you need anything—"

"We'll call," Jessica promised.

The younger generations hesitated for a moment, as if sensing something unspoken in the air.

Then, with a few final glances, they finally gave in, heading inside, letting them have their moment.

And just like that, it was quiet again.

Jessica sighed, leaning her head gently against Benji's shoulder.

"You know," she murmured, "we really did all of it, didn't we?"

Benji exhaled, his chest rising and falling slowly.

"Yeah, baby," he whispered. "We really did."

Jessica smiled softly.

"Do you remember the first time we danced?" she asked.

Benji chuckled.

"You mean the night that changed everything?" he mused. "Hard to forget."

Jessica smirked, closing her eyes.

"Everyone was staring at us. I could feel my father's rage before he even walked over."

Benji grinned. "Still didn't stop you from saying yes when I asked."

Jessica sighed, her fingers squeezing his.

"I knew then," she murmured. "I knew it was you."

Benji turned his head slightly, his lips brushing her temple.

"I did too."

They sat in comfortable silence, the years folding back in on themselves, the memories stretching across time.

The war.

The love letters.

The heartbreak.

The reunion.

The passion.

The life they built together.

Jessica sighed softly.

"I hope we did enough," she whispered.

Benji frowned slightly, tilting his head toward her.

"Enough?"

Jessica swallowed, her voice thick.

"For our children. Our grandchildren. This world."

Benji exhaled, his grip tightening on hers.

"We did more than enough," he whispered.

Jessica smiled, leaning against him.

They sat in the golden light, the museum still buzzing in the background, but it felt far away.

Right now, in this moment, it was just them.

And it was perfect.

The museum had started to quiet as the evening sun filtered through the large windows, casting golden light across the polished floors.

Benji and Jessica sat on a sturdy wooden bench inside the museum, nestled between exhibits showcasing the history they had lived.

Old photographs of the Red Tails lined the walls, and just across from them, a model of a P-51 Mustang stood proudly—restored, polished, waiting.

Benji leaned back, his hands folded atop his cane, his breathing slow, steady. Jessica sat beside him, her arm tucked around his, their fingers lightly intertwined.

For a long time, neither of them spoke.

They just existed—together.

The museum hummed quietly around them, distant footsteps of visitors moving through, but in this moment, it was just Benji and Jessica, the weight of a hundred years resting softly between them.

Jessica sighed, her head tilting toward him.

"You remember what we used to say?" she murmured.

Benji's lips curved slightly, even as his eyes stayed closed.

"Which one?" he teased, voice low and warm.

Jessica smirked, giving his hand a gentle squeeze.

"You know the one," she whispered.

Benji breathed out slowly.

He knew.

And so, in that familiar deep voice, he murmured it softly, just for her.

"Until I see you in the skies."

Jessica closed her eyes, a soft smile touching her lips.

"Until I see you in the skies," she echoed, voice barely above a whisper.

Her fingers gently curled around his.

Benji let out one last deep, steady breath.

And then, finally, he stilled.

Jessica felt it immediately.

She opened her eyes, looking up at him.

Benji's face was peaceful, his features relaxed in a way that made him look just like the boy she had fallen in love with all those years ago.

Jessica felt no fear.

No sorrow.

Only love.

Her lips quirked up in a soft, knowing smile.

"You stubborn old man," she murmured.

She sighed, leaning into him, resting her head against his shoulder.

Her body felt light, warm, whole.

She let her eyes drift closed, and in the quiet of the museum, Jessica whispered their last words again, just for him.

"Until I see you in the skies."

And then, she, too, stilled.

Christine had stepped out earlier, giving them space, letting them enjoy this moment alone.

But when she came back to check on them, her steps slowed.

They were still sitting together, just as she had left them.

But this time—she knew.

Her breath hitched, her vision blurring with tears.

"Mom? Dad?" she whispered, stepping closer.

No response.

Christine swallowed, her chest tightening.

She knelt down slowly, her trembling hands reaching for her mother's wrist.

Nothing.

Her eyes flickered to her father.

Still. Peaceful.

Christine exhaled shakily, her lips pressing together as the tears came.

But she smiled.

Because somehow—this was exactly how it was supposed to be.

No pain.

No hospital beds.

Just Benji and Jessica, together, their hands still intertwined, in a place that held their history.

Jaden, their great-grandson, appeared in the doorway behind Christine, his voice hesitant.

"Are they...?"

Christine nodded, her voice thick with emotion but steady.

"They're gone," she whispered.

Jaden hesitated, then stepped closer, his gaze settling on them.

He let out a slow, quiet breath.

"They look happy," he murmured.

Christine wiped her cheeks, nodding.

"They were."

She reached forward, gently lacing their fingers together once more, just as they had always been.

Jessica's locket, the one Benji had given her decades ago, rested against her chest, gleaming softly under the museum lights.

Jaden swallowed hard. "What do we do now?"

Christine exhaled, composing herself.

"We take them home," she said softly.

She looked at them one last time, memorizing them in this perfect moment.

Then, with a voice full of love, full of gratitude, she whispered—

"Thank you."

For the love.

For the sacrifices.

For everything.

The museum lights dimmed as the sun set outside.

The world would remember them as Major Benjamin Davis, the legendary Tuskegee Airman, and Jessica Shaw Davis, the groundbreaking civil rights lawyer.

But to the people who knew them, they were just Benji and Jessica.

Two souls who had defied war, hate, and time—all for love.

And as the last of the evening light filtered through the museum, it felt as if they were still there.

Sitting on that bench.

Hand in hand.

Together.

Still.

Always.

CHAPTER 39:

THE LEGACY LIVES ON

The sky was overcast, the wind crisp as it rolled through the city streets. Inside a historic church, every pew was filled—family, friends, and admirers of Benjamin and Jessica Davis gathered to honor them one last time.

It wasn't a funeral.

It was a celebration.

A life well-lived.

A legacy that would never die.

Christine stood at the podium, her voice steady despite the weight of loss pressing against her heart.

"My parents," she began, pausing to gather herself, "lived a life many thought impossible."

The room was silent, reverent.

"They met in a world that told them they shouldn't love each other." Christine smiled, shaking her head. "But if you knew my mother, you knew she never listened to anyone telling her what she couldn't do."

A gentle chuckle rippled through the crowd.

Christine exhaled, steadying herself.

"And my father… my father was a warrior," she continued, her voice thick with emotion. "Not just in the skies, but in life. He carried burdens so that the next generation wouldn't have to."

She glanced down at the front pew, where her own children and grandchildren sat, listening intently.

"I am here because of them," Christine whispered. "We are all here because of them."

She let out a slow breath.

"And now," she said, lifting her chin, "we carry them forward."

After Christine stepped away, Jaden, Benji and Jessica's great-grandson, rose from his seat.

He was young, barely in his twenties, but when he took the stage, his voice was strong.

"My great-grandparents were history," he began, his hands gripping the podium.

"But to me, they were just… them."

He smiled softly.

"My Great-Grandpa used to tell me stories about flying," Jaden said, his eyes glinting with the same fire Benji once had. "How the sky didn't care what color you were. Up there, you were just a man."

He looked up, his chest rising with emotion.

"He taught me to dream big," Jaden whispered. "To never let the world tell me my limits."

His hands tightened on the edges of the podium.

"My Great-Grandma—she fought so people like me wouldn't have to," he said. "She taught me to use my voice. To stand up for what's right."

Jaden swallowed hard, his gaze sweeping the room.

"And now it's my turn," he said. "Now it's all of our turn."

He exhaled deeply, stepping back.

"They're gone," Jaden admitted. "But they'll never really leave us."

His voice softened.

"Because their fight isn't over. And neither is their love."

As the ceremony ended, people filed out, whispering stories, sharing memories, promising to carry their legacy forward.

Outside, a young journalist caught up with Christine.

"Mrs. Davis," she said, holding up a recorder. "Your parents had such an incredible impact on history. What do you think they would want their legacy to be?"

Christine smiled softly, looking up at the gray sky.

She thought about her mother—her fire, her unshakable belief in justice.

She thought about her father—his strength, his heart, his love for the skies.

"They would want us to keep fighting," she said simply.

The journalist nodded, lowering the mic.

"And what about their love story?" she asked.

Christine's smile grew, bittersweet but warm.

She glanced at the young woman.

"Some love stories never end."

And as she walked away, her words lingered in the cold February air.

Because even though Benjamin and Jessica Davis were gone—their love, their fight, their story—would live forever.

A soft breeze moved through the museum, gentle but steady, like an unseen presence whispering through time.

The world faded.

The weight of years lifted.

And suddenly—they were young again.

Jessica stood at the edge of a grand dance floor, wearing the same pale blue dress she had worn that first night—the night Benji had asked her to dance when the world said they shouldn't.

Her blonde curls were perfectly styled, her skin glowing, her lips curved in a familiar mischievous smirk.

And she smelled like lavender and vanilla—just like she always had.

Benji inhaled deeply, his chest filling, his body feeling strong again.

The aches, the stiffness, the decades—they were all gone.

He looked down at his hands—steady, smooth, youthful once more.

And then—he saw her.

Jessica stood across from him, her blue eyes full of life, of love, of something timeless.

Benji exhaled slowly, his lips parting in wonder, in awe, in recognition.

"I know this place," he murmured.

Jessica tilted her head.

"Of course, you do," she said softly.

Benji took a step forward.

Jessica matched him.

Just like before.

Just like always.

Benji reached for her, his hand sliding into hers.

Jessica inhaled sharply at the touch, her fingers curling around his.

For a moment, they just stood there—studying each other, memorizing the way they felt, the way they had always fit together.

Jessica's lips trembled slightly.

"Benji?"

Benji lifted their entwined hands, bringing hers to his lips.

"I'm right here, baby," he murmured.

Jessica exhaled, a tear slipping down her cheek.

Benji caught it with his thumb, smiling softly.

"Why are you crying?"

Jessica let out a small, breathy laugh.

"Because it's you," she whispered. "It's really you."

Benji nodded, his throat tight.

"It's me," he promised.

Jessica took a shaky breath, stepping closer.

"Dance with me?" she whispered.

Benji smiled.

"I thought you'd never ask."

And just like before, he pulled her into his arms, their bodies pressing together, the rhythm of their hearts finding each other once more.

Jessica melted against him, her cheek resting against his chest, the scent of his skin filling her senses.

For a moment, they just held each other, swaying softly in the quiet.

No music.

No crowd.

Just them.

Benji exhaled, burying his face in her hair, breathing her in, memorizing the scent of lavender and vanilla one last time.

Jessica pulled back slightly, looking up at him.

Her eyes were bright, full of love, full of everything they had ever been.

Benji reached up, cupping her cheek, his thumb brushing over her soft skin.

"I love you," he whispered.

Jessica's breath hitched, her hands tightening against his back.

"I love you," she whispered back.

Benji exhaled slowly.

And then, hand in hand, they turned together.

Ahead of them, a golden light stretched across the horizon, endless, inviting.

Jessica squeezed his fingers gently.

"Ready, Hotshot?" she whispered.

Benji smirked, his eyes full of the same fire he'd had since the day they met.

"Always."

Jessica smiled, her heart full, her soul at peace.

And then, as they stepped forward—together, side by side, forever—Jessica whispered their final words, the only ones that ever truly mattered.

"Until I see you in the skies."

And with that—they were gone.

Back in the museum, a small gust of wind stirred the air, rustling the exhibits, making the overhead lights flicker for just a second.

Jaden, their great-grandson, paused.

For a moment, he swore he could smell lavender and vanilla.

He smiled softly, shaking his head.

And somewhere, in a place beyond time—Benji and Jessica danced, forever young, forever in love.

Together.

Still.

Always.

The End.

CALL TO ACTION

Enjoyed One More Dance? I'd love to hear from you!

Leave a Review – Your review on Amazon, Goodreads, or Barnes & Noble helps other readers find this book and means the world to me. Even a few words make a huge difference!

Let's Connect! – Come chat about the book with me on social media! I'd love to hear your thoughts, favorite scenes, and what you want to see next.

TikTok: X. Louis-McGhee

Thank you for reading! Your support means everything.

Coming Soon – Sands of Fire

A fake relationship. A prince she doesn't want… and the man she can't resist.

Stay tuned for the release date! Follow me for updates:

ACKNOWLEDGEMENTS

To my family—this book wouldn't exist without your love, support, and unwavering belief in me.

To my Wife thank you for always encouraging me to chase my dreams, for never doubting my passion, and for reminding me that storytelling is part of who I am. Your support means everything, and I hope this book makes you proud.

To my mom, who taught me the power of perseverance and hard work, thank you for shaping me into the person I am today.

To my little sister, thank you for always being one of my first readers, my biggest fan, Your belief in me, even when I doubted myself, has meant more than I can ever put into words.

And to my extended family, who have always cheered me on from the sidelines, thank you for your love, support.

This book is a piece of my heart, and I'm honored to share it with you all.

With all my love and gratitude,

X. Louis-McGhee

AUTHOR BIO

A storyteller at heart, X. Louis-Mcghee believes the best stories are the ones that make you feel—the kind that stay with you long after the last page is turned. Whether writing about love, loss, or resilience, X. Louis-Mcghee crafts emotionally gripping narratives that explore the complexities of the human heart.

Born April 1st 1987 in Wichita, KS, X. Louis-Mcghee is a devoted family person, sharing life's adventures with their wife and three kids. With a deep appreciation for history, romance, and raw human experiences, their writing brings characters to life in ways that feel authentic and immersive. Passionate about exploring love in all its forms, their work blends sweeping emotion, deep character connections, and rich, cinematic storytelling.

When not writing, X. Louis-Mcghee can be found spending time with family, reflecting on history, or simply enjoying quiet moments that inspire the next story. They believe in love that defies odds, characters that feel like real people, and stories that make you laugh, cry, and dream.

Follow X. Louis-Mcghee on TikTok @X. Louis-Mcghee to stay connected.